NOW BEFORE THE DARK

TERRIBLY SERIOUS DARKNESS, BOOK THREE

SAM HOOKER

IBSN print: 978-1-64548-029-7
ISBN ebook: 978-1-64548-030-3

Cover Design and Interior Formatting
by Qamber Designs and Media
Edited by Lindy Ryan

Published by Black Spot Books
An imprint of Vesuvian Media Group

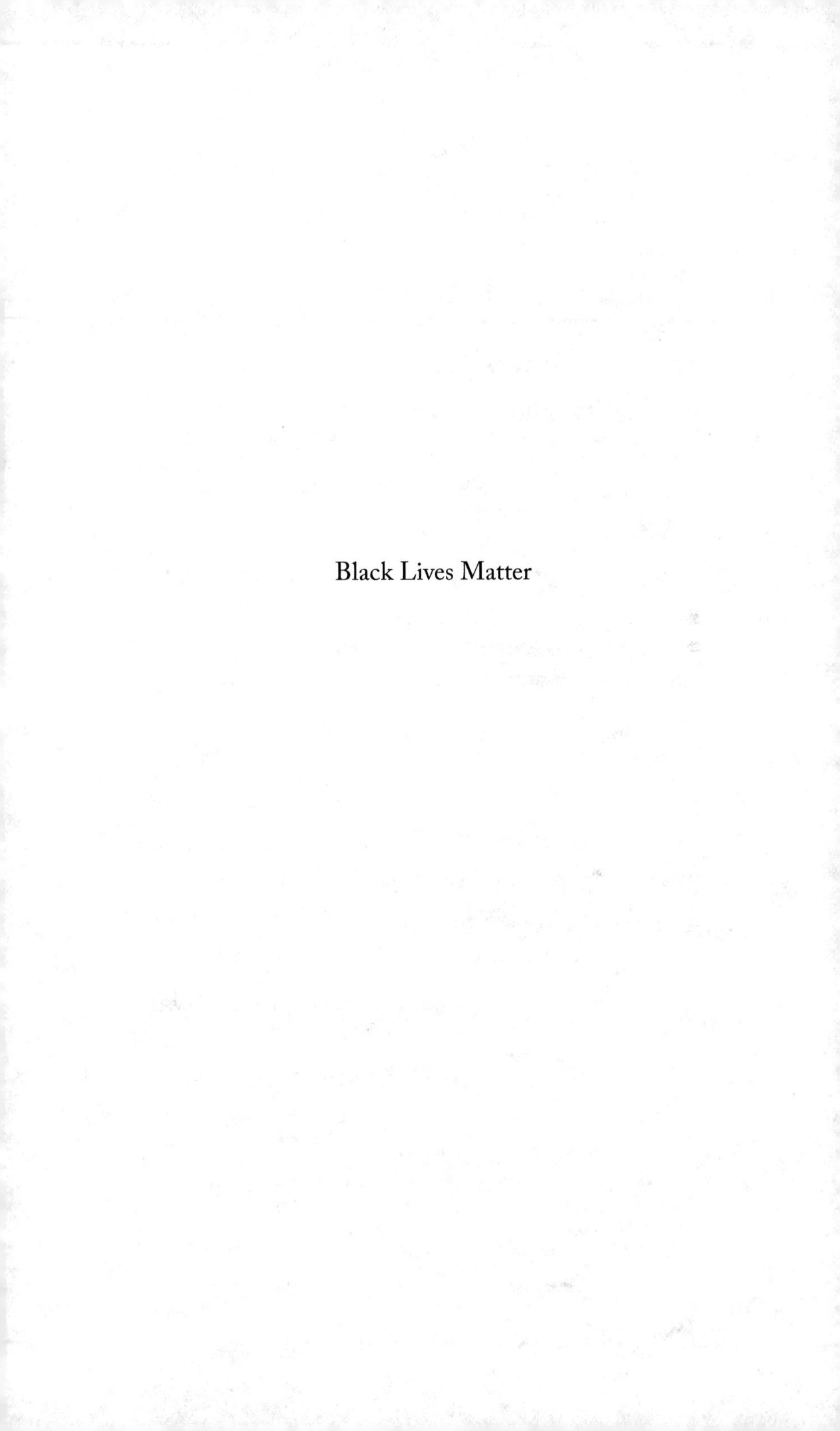

Black Lives Matter

CAST

- *Sloot Peril,* a formerly dead demon with an accounting degree.
- *Dr. Arthur Widdershins,* weapons-grade philosopher.
- *Igor,* a gremlin-cum-bard.
- *Flavia & Walter the Undying,* agents of Uncle.
- *Nicoleta Goremonger,* fabulous wizard.
- *Minerva Meatsacrifice,* Attorney at Chaos.
- *Vlad Defenestratia,* the Invader.
- *Greta Urmacher,* clockmaker. Vlad's paramour.
- *Roman Bloodfrenzy,* an enigma demon with a gambling problem.
- *Constantin Hapsgalt,* former captain of industry.
- *Willie Hapsgalt,* Constantin's son. Half as smart as the silver spoon in his mouth.
- *Nan,* Willie's old nurse.
- *Gwen,* a love demon who's made some bad investments.
- *Agather,* proprietor of the Witchwood.
- *Mrs. Knife,* queen of the goblins and homicidal maniac.
- King Lilacs & General Dandelion of the fairies.
- *Bartleby,* a vampire-obsessed necromancer.
- *The Coolest,* nearly omnipotent demigods with horrible marketing.
- *Franka,* the last remnant of the Skeleton Key Circle.
- *Winking Bob,* the Old Country's most cunning entrepreneur.
- *Myrtle Pastry,* causality demon. Sloot's girlfriend.

- *Baelgoroth the Destroyer,* a demon of indeterminate stature.
- *The Prime Evils,* rulers of the Inferno and last century's dance contest winners.
- *Gregor,* a necromancer in a rotting goblin suit.
- *Domnitor Olaf von Donnerhonig,* Defender of the Old Country and Hero of the People, long may he reign.

FOREWORD BY THE AUTHOR

If you'd like a refresher on the events of the first two books, there are a couple of articles on my blog that should do the trick:

1. Recap: Peril in the Old Country – shkr.us/peril-recap
2. Recap: Soul Remains – shkr.us/soul-recap

ALSO BY SAM HOOKER

Terribly Serious Darkness

Peril in the Old Country

Soul Remains

The Winter Riddle

PESSIMISM AND PREDICTABILITY

It was late, which barely bore mentioning. It was always late these days.

Sloot hadn't slept in months. A wretched benefit of demonhood, not having to sleep, but it wasn't like Sloot had ever been particularly good at it. His nightmares usually weren't as terrible as the waking world, but at least he got to wake in a cold sweat and realize it had all been a dream.

"Unlike that poor sod," said Arthur.

"What?" said Sloot, not looking up from his notes.

"You were being wistful about nightmares again," said the philosopher from his recumbent position on the sofa. "And no, I can't read your mind. You're just predictable."

Sloot sighed. To him, predictability was a virtue. But Arthur's compliment wasn't enough to distract him from the litany of woes piling up around him. The poor sod to whom Arthur referred was a terror-stricken man, clad head-to-toe in black, cowering in the corner and whimpering on occasion. At least Sloot assumed he was a man, and chided himself for it.

This was the modern world, wasn't it? Women could burgle in the modern world. Well, in point of fact, no, it wasn't. Another pseudo-benefit of demonhood was a certain amount of prescience. Just a dollop. Enough insight into the future to know that if everyone was really nice to each other and played their cards just right, they could have a shining utopia. *That's* when the world got modern.

But people weren't going to be nice to each other. That was the sort of pessimism that pessimists called *being realistic*. "Look what we'd have," gloated Sloot's dollop of prescience, "if you weren't so quick to dive for the last seat on public transportation, leaving old ladies to fend for themselves!"

No one did that to the grans of the Old Country, of course. There wasn't an end of their hobnailed boots that wasn't business.

Still, as modern as the world wasn't, Sloot felt a woman was equally capable of dressing up in black and being stricken with infinite terror upon gazing into the eyes of a demon.

"How long is she going to be like that?"

"Switching pronouns back and forth just makes you wrong half the time," said Arthur. "Or more."

If only Sloot could take classes at Infernal University. He just knew there was a class that could teach him how to wipe his or her mind and send them on their way. Alas, Sloot was a demon 100th class, and freshman orientation was for demons 99th class. Or possibly higher. It's left to the discretion of the hazing committee.

Demons nearly always started at 99th level, but Sloot was the opposite of lucky. Not simply unlucky, which would have been a massive improvement. Sloot had the sort of anti-luck that evil wizards wished their curses would cause.

"I really thought I was more scared of him or her, as the case may be."

"He or she is coming up on three days of catatonia," said Arthur. "Given that you can manage complete sentences, I'd say you're wrong."

Sloot couldn't argue with that. Furthermore, he wouldn't. Nothing good comes from arguing with a philosopher, except for masochists who enjoy being harassed by what some other philosopher—who'd been dead for centuries—thought about it.

Being burgled was a natural hazard of living above a jeweler's shop, which hadn't been Sloot's preference, but he'd wanted his old apartment back. The jeweler's shop had been a butcher's shop before, until Mrs. Knife decided she preferred Sloot dead, stabbed him, summoned a bunch of goblins, and gave them matches. Sloot survived thanks to his friends, and the building was only superficially damaged. Had Sloot remained conscious, he'd have heard the groans of disappointment from the fire department as they watched the anti-fire department vanquish the blaze.

The butcher *had* heard the aforementioned groans and sold the property for a pittance when he heard the fire department saying, "I'll bet we could do better." The jeweler who bought it must have been up-to-date on his bribery, as there was not so much as a whiff of kerosene or a stray match to be found within a three-block radius.

An awful twanging offended the air from beneath the table. Sloot sighed.

Sloot he was the second most afraid,
the second most afraid, the second most afraid,
Sloot he was the second most afraid,
but still, he was afraid.

"Would you mind keeping it down?" That was the closest Sloot came to telling Igor, his erstwhile bard, to shut it. Igor wasn't a proper bard but a gremlin bored with sabotage who'd decided to give barding a go.

"Sorry," said Igor, popping his head up to flash Sloot the brownest smile he'd ever seen, "but I've got to work when the muse speaks to me. Obeying the muse, that's basic barding."

"I'll take your word for it," said Sloot. "Any luck finding a proper instrument?"

"What do you mean?" Igor's smile fell, his upper lip returning his wooden teeth to a state of darkness which the termites no doubt preferred.

"Nothing," said Sloot, "it's just … well, the bit of wire was a ruse, wasn't it?"

"A what?"

"You, er, tried to dupe me with a counterfeit agreement."

Igor blinked.

"You tried to hoodwink me."

"Oh, right," Igor chuckled. "We've had some fun times, haven't we, Sloot?"

"I suppose. I just thought you'd eventually take up the lute or something."

"Oh, no sir." Igor's demeanor turned very serious. "A bard doesn't give up on his instrument just because he's no good at playing it! He's just got to practice. That's basic barding."

"No exceptions for instruments that are not, in fact, instruments?"

"I didn't find any in the literature."

Sloot was comforted by the fact that there was literature, but he couldn't help feeling that Igor had misinterpreted it. He couldn't say so without having read the literature himself, but who had the time?

Not sleeping gave Sloot time to get a side job clerking for Winkus, Ordo, and Mirgazhandinuxulluminixighanduminophizio, a large and faceless chaos firm that many Infernal banks employed to handle their most complicated shenanigans. Chaos firms were a lot like law firms, only the other way around. Sloot worked for them as a research clerk and tried not to think about what his research was being used to do.

The pay was horrible, though that was the case for every job in the Inferno. Sloot didn't really care about the money, though every fiber of his being lamented the lack of retirement benefits. He soothed himself by assuming that demons, being immortal, never had to retire and got to keep working for eternity.

The real benefit of the job was provisional access to the Infernal Hall of Records on the 98th circle of the Inferno, which Sloot needed if he was going to sort out the whole "Roman's wager has doomed a large swath of the Narrative" thing. As a demon 100th class, Sloot didn't even have access to the 99th circle, where Myrtle had been banished.

"You're thinking about our girl again," said Arthur. He'd possessed Myrtle for most of her life, from his own beheading until the Fall of Salzstadt, during which both Myrtle and Sloot perished.

"I'd really prefer if you didn't call her 'our girl,'" said Sloot. Myrtle was Sloot's girlfriend, and she'd been Arthur's ... what, victim?

"I've known her longer than you," Arthur sneered.

Sloot didn't retort. Philosophers cared about having arguments, not winning them. That's what people get up to when they've successfully resisted getting jobs. Instead, he threw himself back into the lack of financial records for the brimstone trade over the last three millennia.

Brimstone was everywhere in the Inferno, but that didn't mean it was cheap. Aeons ago, some enterprising middle management demon had developed a scheme to charge outrageous prices for the maintenance and sanitation of brimstone in unincorporated Infernal territory, and his brother-in-law—a legislative demon—had bribed enough Infernal senators to pass a law requiring the maintenance and sanitation of said brimstone.

Shortly thereafter, a group of Infernal mobsters cooked up an even cleverer scheme to undercut the sanctioned maintenance and sanitation company, getting the job done for ten percent less, minus the cost of broken fingers.

Infernal mobsters don't keep records, but a keen accountant like Sloot didn't need them.

"You've got to read between the lines," he'd said. "It's only marginally more difficult when there aren't any lines." There was a lot of eye-crossing involved, and demonic physiology made some severe optical acrobatics possible.

The black-clad figure of indeterminate gender gasped again. Sloot looked over at him or her, as the case may be, his face scrunched in sincerity.

"I'm dreadfully sorry about this," said Sloot. "You must have seen over the past few days that I'm not always dragon-wings-and-flaming-blood. You just startled me, that's all."

The figure shrieked and tried to sink deeper into the corner.

"He tried to rob you," Igor pointed out.

"Not necessarily," Sloot replied. "We are above a jeweler's shop. He or she could have assumed the easiest way in was through the upstairs windows."

"It usually is," Igor conceded. Breaking and entering is mischief, and gremlins know mischief.

"Try shooing it out the door again," said Arthur, rolling over under his blanket to face the back of the sofa. "It's impossible to sleep with all that caterwauling."

"I've tried," said Sloot. "He or she is like a fly. I can't get him or her to flee through the door. He or she just ends up in a different corner."

"Ugh, would you just pick a gender?"

"He or she's already got one."

"It's not like accuracy is important."

"Accuracy is *always* important," chided Sloot. Little gouts of flame flared from his eyes.

"Whatever," said Arthur. "Just keep it down, will you? I don't think I've had a decent night's sleep since I went corporeal again."

That was puzzling to Sloot. The Coolest—a trio of cosmic beings in charge of running the universe, but not their own marketing—placed Sloot in charge of amending the chunk of Narrative that encompassed the Old Country and Carpathia, from back when he'd been a mere accounting clerk until the Dark had spilled over everything. If he could balance everything out, they wouldn't have to erase it from existence.

Then the Coolest did some things that didn't make sense. They made Sloot a demon 100th class, for one. A higher standing would have made his job easier, but they insisted that they couldn't show favoritism. He hadn't argued because he was Sloot Peril.

They'd also brought Arthur back to life, though he'd been a ghost for decades. Why couldn't they have brought Myrtle back from her banishment to the 99th circle of the Inferno instead? She'd have been much more helpful that Arthur, which is to say she'd be any help at all.

Sloot tried to concentrate on his work. Between the intruder's whimpering, Igor's twanging, and Arthur's grousing, it wasn't easy. Then again, if he was going to amend the Narrative, save his girlfriend, and get his life back, "easy" would no doubt play hard-to-get.

THE MORNING CONSTITUTIONAL

A newcomer to Salzstadt would probably say that the city was in shambles. They'd probably say that to a shipmate, a fellow passenger in a coach, or any other person also beating a hasty retreat from the once glorious city. The word "shambles" did it too much justice.

Shambling, though, was appropriate, thanks to the walking dead. To be clear, Salzstadt had never been glorious by the standards of anyone except those whose lives depended on their saying that it was so, namely all of the residents. Not one of them would dare to criticize the Domnitor, long may he reign, lest they be hauled off in the middle of the night by the Ministry of Conversation. That might not sound so bad to a foreigner, who would have no way of knowing that the Ministry of Conversation was formerly the Ministry of Interrogation. The only difference was the name. The Ministry of Propaganda had rebranded a number of government ministries, softening their images if not their truncheons. For further examples, one may refer to the Ministry of Official Inquiry, formerly the Ministry of Etiquette and Guillotines, formerly the

Ministry of Surplus Population Management. No civilized person would want to know what they were called before that. It was a horrible name, and the city had ordinances that criminalized swearing.

"They gonna do away with those, you think?" Igor managed between gasps and wheezes as he tried to keep up with Sloot through the city streets. To be clear, Sloot's pace was leisurely. Igor was in horrid shape.

"I've never seen a law come off the books," Sloot replied. He was overlooking the Great Redaction some twenty years prior. It rescinded the Patisserie Tax, which was not so much a tax as a poorly conceived honorific for the Domnitor's birthday, long may he reign. It had been started by the Ministry of Ministers, formerly not an official ministry at all, but turned into one when it was discovered that the heads of the important ministries spent most of their days in the same pub, and would often make very important decisions following an impressive binge. It was formalized because official ministries have rules regarding the consumption of spirits in the performance of duties. The formalization was deemed a good idea by everyone but the ministers.

The first act of the new ministry exempted bottles of whiskey in the bottom drawers of ministers' desks from consumption rules. The second act was the Patisserie Tax, requiring all families in the city to bake for the Domnitor on his birthday, long may he reign. Being proper government officials, the ministers were entirely out of step with the people of the city, and therefore unaware that there was no such thing as a decent Old Country baker. There were brilliant artists, engineers, and merchants, but not a single baker of note. Perhaps it was a collective evolutionary trait, or an impurity in the drinking water. Perhaps no one had been paying attention and probability boiled over. Whatever the reason, there was nary a risen loaf to be found in all the land.

As a result, when the Domnitor's birthday came around, long

may he reign, the royal courtyard was assaulted with a torrent of grotesque mockeries of pastry. In a fit of questionable inspiration, the Domnitor, long may he reign, decided the easiest way to prevent the offal from turning into a larger problem when the sun started to curdle it was to invite all the people of the city to partake in the bounty. Understanding the penalties for noncompliance, the people did as they were invited.

The result was a severe overcrowding of the city's hospitals and a run on antacids that led to the Great Pharmacy Riots. If the Domnitor, long may he reign, had been the sort of person who required education on any subject, the lesson here would have been that saying "let them eat cake" never ended well.

A dreadful twanging erupted from Igor's bit of wire.

Sloot was doing the same thing again,
the same thing again, the same thing again,
Sloot was doing the same thing again,
which effectively amounted to nothing.

"I always walk to the main gate in the morning."

"And I write epic songs about your exploits," said Igor, a smattering of gasps for breath thrown in for color. "I'm not complaining, mind. My job is really easy when you stick to your routine. I've got thirty songs about your morning constitutionals in the last month, all of them exactly the same."

When Sloot had been properly alive—before being a ghost, before being a demon—he'd soothed his nervous condition every morning by walking to the great gate in Salzstadt's northern wall. He'd placed his hand upon it and taken comfort in its capacity to repel the Carpathian savages who were sure to invade at any moment. He'd been brought up believing that Carpathians were the sorts of people for whom ears and noses served as trophies, currency, or a light snack with spicy sauce.

That was before he found out that he *was* Carpathian. After correcting Vasily Pritygud's report and being promoted to financier to Lord Wilhelm Hapsgalt, Sloot's mother confided in him that she was a Carpathian spy living in Salzstadt, and that the only way she could retire was for Sloot to take her place.

Sloot tried making peace with his seditious heritage. He came to learn that Carpathians weren't all bad. Even Vlad the Invader, their monarch and the most fearsome warrior who ever lived, knew how to use a fork for more than just murder. Still, every morning he placed his hand on the gate and felt comforted. If Sloot were given to introspection, he'd have known it was the routine itself that brought him comfort. It was a connection to his old life, perhaps the last one that remained. But introspection tended to unbottle old feelings, and what was the point of bottling them up if you're just going to confront them later?

Filled once again with comfort in the gate's stability, Sloot turned to walk back home. Igor said the swear word that begins with H and meant "to drag one's backside across the cobbles to distract one's self from the shame of having forgotten one's gran's birthday."

"Language!" Sloot yelped.

"Would you relax?" Igor wheezed. "No goblins anymore, not since the Spilling of the Dark. Give us a minute to rest before we charge back up the hill, will you?"

Igor was right. Ever since the Dark had spilled into the Narrative and the Coolest made Sloot responsible for sorting it out, swearing no longer attracted goblins. Sloot had even witnessed someone saying the E word that ridicules the stripes on one's socks—a particularly offensive slur that foreigners to the Old Country don't seem to understand—to no effect. Sloot reasoned that the Coolest must have temporarily patched the hole that Roman had poked in the Dark. That was how the goblins had been finding their way into the Old Country all this time, following the siren's song of foul language, discourteous behavior, and improvisational comedy.

Roman had been a friend to Sloot in the beginning. Well, not a *friend*, but an ally at least. Well, not an *ally*, rather someone else he was obliged to obey. He'd been nice to Sloot, though. After a fashion. A fashion that the poor wouldn't steal off clotheslines, but he'd had good intentions. The best intentions of a demon determined to win a wager, no matter the cost to anyone else.

Fine, Roman was a real ... the one that begins with P and rhymes with "electorate." But despite the old demon's eternity of deceit and, specifically, the lies he'd told over the last thousand-ish years resulting in the imminent collapse of reality, Sloot thought of Roman as a friend. He had his reasons, which were bottled up and carefully not labelled. Nothing says "leave me alone" like an unlabeled bottle of feelings lurking in the dark.

Sloot and Igor made their way back home. The gremlin swore endlessly along the way, but nobody confronted him. Salts knew a gremlin when they saw one. Involving yourself in gremlins' affairs was an invitation for them to involve themselves in yours.

Bright, sunny days seldom ambled across the Old Country sky. Or rather, they did, but they had to contend with Old Country clouds to get anywhere near the permanently damp cobblestone streets. You didn't mess with Old Country clouds. They were formidable monoliths of the sky. Old, hard, and never short of enough drizzle to make you change your socks when you got home. Sloot had once looked up and thought about the sun. A peal of thunder had answered him. *Just you watch it*, it had rumbled.

Sloot didn't wish for sunny days now. With the recently deceased walking the streets, it was far better for the city's collective sense of smell that the golden sun stay on its own side of the Old Country clouds, and keep its bright blue sky with it.

"Oh, I dunno," Igor mused between gasps, "a lot of good mischief to be done with smells like that. You seen the big hats that grans wear to tea? Lots of places to hide mouldering fingers and such."

"You should save your strength," said Sloot. He'd slowed to a pace that barely counted as walking. It was just above a dead stop, like having a rapid lean against a drifting continent.

"What do you mean?" asked Igor. He hacked and grimaced.

"Well," Sloot began as gently as possible, "you just seem to be having … difficulty."

"Not at all."

"Our progress up the street begs to differ."

Igor stopped, both the little forward progress he'd been making, and his coughing and wheezing. He said a swear word, but it was a mild one implying that one's bad haircut was a genetic shortcoming.

"I'm doing it again," Igor moaned, his eyes shut tight in dismay. He balled his wrinkled little hands into fists at his likewise wrinkled sides.

"Doing what again?"

"Sabotage! It's in my filth, I can't help it!"

Sloot spun himself in a circle trying to get a look at his back.

"No, no signs this time," Igor sighed with a dismissive wave. "It's just … oh, forget it."

Igor started walking up the hill toward the apartment at a standard step with no cardiovascular difficulty.

"Oh," said Sloot He jogged a couple of steps to catch up. He didn't say anything else about it. As averse as he was to having a bard at all, much less a gremlin masquerading as one, Sloot knew Igor was being far harder on himself at that moment than Sloot would have been. He believed Igor when he said he didn't want to do sabotage anymore, that he wanted to dedicate himself to the bardly arts.

They made the rest of the walk in silence, past grans who eyed Igor with suspicion and made a point of showing him they had brooms within easy reach. Sloot hadn't figured out why it was that a gran with a broom was the best defense against the lower Infernal beings, like goblins, gremlins, and imps, but he didn't question it. Grans of the Old Country didn't put up with questions, which they considered the tools of demons. Being a demon himself, Sloot had no means of proving otherwise.

By the time they'd made it back to Sloot's apartment, Igor was smiling again. Sloot assumed gremlins lacked the depth of conscience required for Old Country guilt, which wasn't the mercurial sort that would come and go in the space of an hour.

"So," said Igor brightly as he plopped onto a stool by the apartment's single window, "you going to do any work today?"

"I work every day," said Sloot.

"Oh, right." Igor winked and set himself about tuning his bit of wire. Sloot doubted that Igor understood what the word "tuning" meant. Igor had once assured him that it was a "bard thing," and that he wouldn't expect an accountant to understand. He'd been right about that much, at least.

"I've been doing research day and night," Sloot insisted.

"And that's what passes for work, is it?"

"Of course it does," Sloot began.

"How dare you, sir?" Arthur was suddenly on his feet, startling Sloot. Arthur had seldom left the couch since being brought back to life, and then only to use the facilities.

"All right, all right," said Igor, "no need to get upset."

"I'll be the judge of that!" snarled Arthur. The vein in his forehead jutted and pulsed as though he were deadlifting a pair of horses. "I'm over here having a ponderance about the mysteries of the universe, and you barge in talking about 'work' and 'research'? The gall! The audacity!"

Sloot said nothing. It was a tactic that had served him well during his life and subsequent states of being. People in the throes of a good rant tended to tire themselves out, and any attempt to make them see reason instead of red only prolonged things. This counted double for philosophers, who were unlikely to listen to anything resembling reason from anyone not resembling a philosopher. Sloot had briefly considered growing a beard with no moustache for that very purpose, but abandoned the idea upon realizing demons were only capable of growing pointy goatees and thin moustaches.

"You were napping," said Igor. He gave his bit of wire a final twang and nodded, apparently satisfied that it was in tune, whatever that meant to him.

"I was not!" Arthur's voice cracked, sending the last word cutting shrilly through the air. "Oh, but I wouldn't expect you to recognize the outward appearance of profound thought. It's all subtlety and quiet contemplation! Your unsophisticated minds are overburdened with the lesser affairs of the proletariat to understand."

"Like work, you mean?"

"Precisely!"

Sloot sighed and sat at his little desk. He looked over his notes as Arthur railed about the importance of deep thought, and how it was essential for him to be shielded from the practice of baser matters—manual labor, practical research, hygiene—so that he might come to realizations about the hidden workings of the cosmos.

Unfortunately for Sloot, it was easy for Igor to rile him up by saying, "that doesn't seem very important," or "you can't be serious," or "anybody can just sit around and think." Whether Igor was innocently pondering aloud or mischief was leaking out of him, Sloot couldn't concentrate.

Sloot considered his options, which did not include shushing the freeloading philosopher. Direct confrontation might work for other people, but it would take more than simply becoming a demon to give Sloot Peril that sort of pluck.

He could go for a walk, but Igor would follow him. He claimed bards were required to accompany their heroes on all sojourns with potential for heroics, and walks around the block qualified. He could just ignore Arthur's ranting and Igor's goading thereof, but he knew he'd get drawn in eventually. There was only one place where he knew he could find peace.

"I'm going to the Hall of Records," Sloot declared, standing with an abruptness that left him light-headed.

"I wish you wouldn't," said Igor. "You know I can't follow you there. What if there are heroics?"

"Y-yes," Sloot stammered, equally as uncomfortable with refusing Igor as with the threat of heroics, "but, well, I've got to get on with my research, and—"

"I'm in the middle of deep thought!" Arthur snarled. "Not another word about your blue-collar labors, I mean it!"

"You think research is blue collar work?" asked Igor, possibly innocently.

Sloot slipped away quietly, though for the sheer volume of Arthur's ranting, he'd have been just as inconspicuous if a marching band had played him out.

For all of its convenience, Sloot loathed teleporting. Sure, moving instantly between realms or across infinite spans of space was nice, but it wasn't very *Sloot*. He'd been made a demon for the specific purpose of setting reality straight, and once that was done, he'd find himself back in the blissful humdrum of his boring life.

That was reality. *That* was Sloot. An accountant with a pension and an apartment above a butcher shop. Or a jeweler, that was just as good. As long as he got to pass his golden years in relative anonymity, he'd be happy. Well, content, at any rate.

But Sloot's contentment would have to wait. He teleported into the lobby of the Hall of Records on the 98th level of the Inferno. He waved his badge frantically overhead as a pair of ghostly black shrouds with flaming red eyes descended on him, having sensed his class upon his arrival.

"Provisional access!" Sloot shouted as he cringed. "I'm Roger Bannister, a clerk for Winkus, Ordo, and Mirgazhandinuxullumi-nixighanduminophizio! I have provisional access!"

When he applied for the job, he panicked at the last minute and used an alias. The only one he could think of was Roger Bannister, which he'd once used to infiltrate the inner sanctum of the Serpents of the Earth. It also happened to be the name of a notorious assassin that the cult used from time to time, whom Sloot hoped never to meet.

Sloot's blood ran cold as one of the horrible shades sniffed at him. The other examined his badge. They screeched in disappointment and swept themselves back up into the roiling shadows that loomed at the vaulted ceiling.

If only that were the worst of it, Sloot thought as he queued in the requests line. Even the ludicrously long queue did little to lift his spirits, though trying to figure out the math underlying its patterns was relaxing. He couldn't look at it all at once, of course. That would have driven him mad.

At least Igor isn't here. He thought that as quietly as possible, since optimism was a felony this far down in the Inferno. The Hall of Records was on the 98th level. Sloot's badge gave him provisional access, but Igor was 99th class, so he couldn't get past the shadow monsters.

"Woe betide thee, Mister Bannister," whispered the shambling terror after what seemed like an eternity of waiting. Sloot did his best to avoid its muculent tentacles as he leaned in close enough to hear. "What truth seek ye from the oracle?"

"Hello, Leonard," said Sloot. "I'm still working on the brimstone contracts. I don't suppose there are any records pertaining to the interdimensional transportation of solvents used in the maintenance of unincorporated brimstone deposits?"

A susurrus of whispers flowed in around Leonard like a foreboding tide. They brought their own darkness along with them. Sloot's vision swam as the air went thick with nightmarish smoke. Eventually the tide of whispers ebbed and took their darkness with them.

"Sorry, no," said Leonard. "Anything else?"

"There is one more thing," said Sloot, his voice managing to quaver only slightly. "Do you have anything on partial extractions of corrupted timelines from otherwise salvageable realities?"

Leonard's tentacles oscillated, possibly in thought.

"Is this pertinent to the same matter?"

"Yes." Sloot's guts knotted themselves in the act of lying, no metaphor intended. He'd be half the night sorting that out, but he wasn't making much progress on amending the Narrative. It was assumed that demons would engage in personal business on company time, but you were still expected to be deceitful about it. That was just courtesy.

OUT OF MIND

"What happened?" Sloot gestured to the broken window.

"I told you he'd notice," said Igor.

"You did," Arthur agreed with no discernible inflection. He regarded Sloot's comings and goings with the indifference of a house cat whose bowl was full.

"The burglar," Igor explained. "I guess he—or she—finally found the gumption to make an escape."

"Through the window?"

"Through the window."

Sloot sighed. He was glad to be rid of the uninvited pest, but now he had this to deal with.

"You could just board it up," Igor offered.

"It's the only window," said Sloot. "It would be awfully dreary in here without light."

"Right," said Igor. "*That* would make it dreary in here, 'dreary' being something that this hovel presently is not."

"It's not a hovel," said Sloot.

"Just ignore it," said Arthur.

"We can't just ignore it," said Igor. "That's not going to fix it."

"No," Arthur sighed in agitation, "but it's just as good, isn't it?"

"No, it isn't," said Igor. "Pretending it isn't broken doesn't fix it. I should know, I've broken a lot of things in my day." His expression rode the fence between pride and shame.

"Who said anything about pretending? I said ignore it!"

Sloot and Igor made the mistake of staring blankly at Arthur. In philosophical terms, that was tantamount to pleading ignorance.

Arthur rolled his eyes. "Are the Domnitor's schools not teaching basic ontology?"

"Long may he reign," Sloot reflexively replied.

"Sure," said Arthur, waving the obeisance away in agitation. "Look, it's simple. Objects do not exist absent observation. If no one pays attention to the broken window, it doesn't exist. Understand?"

Sloot found himself in a quandary. On one hand, he knew for a fact that Arthur was wrong. He'd recently read several Infernal texts about reality manipulation which would have turned Arthur's brain into acidic goo had he so much as looked at the covers. Ignoring the broken window would not resolve anything.

On the other hand, neither would asserting the truth. Even if Arthur were capable of admitting that he was wrong, his professional code of conduct would compel him to play devil's advocate and argue the point nonetheless.

"Yes," said Sloot, having done the math. He resolved to have someone fix it later.

"Good," said Arthur with a nod. He then stood and walked over to the apartment's comically small kitchen. Winning arguments always made Arthur hungry.

Sloot's sigh of relief was cut short by the twanging of Igor's bit of wire.

Sloot once more was too afraid,
was too afraid, was too afraid,
Sloot once more was too afraid,
to do his job today.

"I wish you'd stop singing that."

Ashamed and abashed,
Sloot's teeth, they gnashed,
he'd threaten his bard,
who worked so hard—

"You're not my bard! I've been very clear about that."

He said hurtful things,
His words, they sting!

"Igor, please! It's been a very long … however long it's been. It's hard to keep track in the Inferno. Anyway, I did a lot of research today which cost me my last rotted chazrak candle, and now I've got to deal with this window, and—I mean ignore this window, sorry Arthur— and…" he trailed off in a sigh. He wished he could be alone in the apartment, but Arthur had nowhere else to go, and Igor technically outranked him.

"I get it," said Igor, "you've had a hard day. But it's not like you're not going to crack open the ledgers and start amending the Narrative, right? If I'm not barding, what's to stop me getting up to mischief? Idle hands, and that. You understand, right?"

"I understand," Sloot groaned. That was the worst part. He really did. He'd love to have threatened Igor with sinuses full of weevils or something. But even if he did, Igor's nose was so full of termites that the result would probably work out in his favor.

As Igor twanged through a verse about Sloot's resolve being as weak as his handshake, Sloot rolled back the rug covering his magic circle and considered where he should place the new rune he got from the Well of Roiling Bile. He'd just added a series of lunar phases to the fifth segment of the outer ring, so there was no space there. He thought for a while about removing the Gnar Sigil from the third segment of the middle ring, but then what would protect him from the Ire of Golluk? Whatever that was. He'd seen it in a grimoire about temporal undercurrents and didn't want to take any chances.

He practically savored his options, exhausting each one in avoidance of the inevitable truth: at some point, whether he'd accounted for every possible scenario or not, he was going to have to activate the circle, step into the past, and start fixing things.

Never let it be said that Sloot Peril strode boldly into heroics. He summoned Karl instead.

"Sloo-o-o-oot!" brayed the gnarled old goat. He arrived in a puff of sulfur and waved it away with a cloven hoof. "What does my fa-a-avorite customer need today? Ready for that silver upgra-a-ade?"

"Not yet, I'm afraid," said Sloot. "I just need to add this Exigent Septangle, but I seem to be out of room."

Karl stroked his goatee thoughtfully and nodded as he stared at the circle. "Yes, yes. Lo-o-ok, I know it isn't cheap, but upgrading to si-i-ilver would solve a lot of your problems."

"I know, but it's *so* expensive."

Sloot saw his first magic circle in the Hereafter. Willie sat in it to siphon off the excess vitality that the Serpents of the Earth's blood wizards were constantly feeding him. He hadn't known it then, but materials were everything in circles. Sure, you could scrawl one with chalk on cobblestones if you were in a hurry, but the results wouldn't be favorable. Anything you summoned might be really mad at you when it got there, owing to the massive headache your shoddy circle would have caused.

Sloot had redone a six-foot section of his floorboards in a nice mahogany, which had confused the workmen who completed the job. Why not do the other half of the room while he was at it? But Sloot was thrifty, and the money was coming out of his retirement fund.

"I mean," Karl began in a whisper, leaning in close, "you're an accounting demon, right? I know some of your kind. They need money, they just 'mo-o-ove things around,' whatever that means. Why don't you just . . . ?" He finished the sentence by miming a shell game with his front hooves.

"Oh, I couldn't," said Sloot. He shook his head with enough vigor that his little horns sprouted from his forehead. Beyond not wanting to reveal that he wasn't officially an accounting demon, Sloot knew enough about metaphysical economics to predict dire consequences for that sort of thing. You'd have to be some sort of political demon to get away with that level of fraud in the long run.

"Copper on mahogany will have to do for now," said Sloot with a finality that made him severely uncomfortable.

"All ri-i-ight," Karl brayed. "In that case, you've got a Dolorous Appendage in your fourth segment, and it looks like it's tangentially conjuncted with a Malfeasant Crux in the second. Those two cancel each other out!"

"Oh, how silly of me," said Sloot. He tried working up the gumption to point out that it would have been Karl who'd conjuncted them, but that might have led to an argument. "So can you disjunct them and put the Exigent Septangle in place of the Dolorous Appendage?"

He said he could, but it wouldn't be cheap. It never was. They'd yet to do a quick and easy job that cost little enough for Sloot to ask, "oh, is that all?" In fact, Sloot was painfully aware that Karl's time only ever increased in value. He was also painfully aware that few circlesmiths were willing to work for demons 100th class. Karl had explained that Sloot was better off not even asking anyone else, and that it was lucky Sloot talked to him first.

Oh, well. A strong backbone wasn't a requirement for a career in accounting. Sloot wasn't terribly upset about the extra years he'd have to work to replenish his retirement accounts. If all went well, he could still break even when he died the next time around.

"Oooh, that one's pretty," said Igor after Karl left. "What's it do?"

"Well, it works with the rest of them." Sloot pointed to the Exigent Septangle, opened his mouth to elaborate, and then didn't. He gestured to some of the other runes in sequence, then silently finished the thought by waving his hand around the circle a few times.

"And there you have it." Sloot nodded, meekly at first, then with a more forceful meekness that might ask if it was alright to stand up for itself someday.

"Well, at least it's pretty," sighed Igor. He slouched off toward the sofa, twanging at his bit of wire.

He may as well have drawn it in chalk,

Or not at all, as his plan was just talk—

"Hey," said Sloot.

Igor stopped mid-twang and fixed Sloot with an annoyed look. "Yes?"

"It's not just talk," said Sloot. "It's not ready yet, that's all."

Arthur joined Igor in sardonic expression like they'd rehearsed it. Were they doing choreography when Sloot wasn't looking?

"I'm sure it'll be ready any day now," said Igor with an oily smirk.

"It will," said Sloot, turning it up at the end nearly high enough to make a question of it. "It will." A bit firmer that time.

He waited until the time was right,

It couldn't be day, it couldn't be night,

"It just needs a bit more ... something."

Not during his meals, or for several hours after,

"I can't just rush into things, you know."

His baths were on Tuesdays, the weekends were out—

"Enough!" Sloot's razor-sharp teeth very nearly severed his forked tongue as it snaked out a warning in Igor's direction.

"There we go," Igor beamed, "that's more like it!"

Sloot drew in a deep breath and forced his demonic visage down.

"Look," Sloot pleaded, "if it were as easy as opening the ledger and activating the circle—"

"It *is*," said Igor. "I've seen it done a thousand times! Sure, half of those failed because I'd redrawn some lines when no one was looking, but that was my job, wasn't it? I don't think I've ever seen such a well-prepared circle. One look at that would make all the other heroes' bards jealous. 'That's a bard that gets to see some real heroics,' they'd say. 'I wish I could play the bit-o-wire that handsomely.' Yeah, they'd be proper jealous."

"I keep telling you this job has nothing to do with heroics," said Sloot.

"Quest," Igor corrected him. "It's a *quest*, and quests have everything to do with heroics. I can't be a bard if my hero doesn't get up to heroics! They won't let you! It's probably in the manual."

"So there *is* a manual for bards?"

"Probably."

"Look, I'm sorry," said Sloot, who truly was, "but it's just not ready. Soon, though, all right? It's coming along nicely, and before long—"

"Yeah, all right," said Igor with a dismissive wave.

"I don't see what you're getting all worked up about," said Arthur. "It's not like any of this is real."

Sloot blinked. He hardly knew where to begin.

"Magic," Arthur clarified. "It's all just tricks that drifters use to baffle children. Sure, it'll earn them enough spare change to fill their bellies with questionable stew, but there's no such thing as magic."

"You were *dead*," said Sloot.

"Allegedly," Arthur retorted.

"You lived—or, well, *resided*—with wizards in the Hereafter. You have to remember that."

It's widely accepted that the worst thing anyone can say to a philosopher is that they have to do something. You might as well tell them to get a job.

Arthur must have been tired. Or perhaps he didn't consider Sloot a threat. He didn't shout, he didn't spit, and the gesture that he made to dismiss Sloot's assertion didn't even have any of the vulgar fingers sticking out.

"I see no evidence of that." Arthur yawned and set himself about the business of a nap. The sun had nearly set, and if he was quick about it, he could roll a nap straight into a good night's sleep. That was what passed for philosophical efficiency.

"Don't listen to him," said Igor with a sympathetic smirk. "I know you can do it. I wouldn't be your bard otherwise, would I?"

"You're not my bard."

"Ha! At least we can still laugh together," Igor sighed. "It doesn't look like we'll be doing much else."

He turned his attention back to his bit of wire, plucking it experimentally and searching aloud for something that rhymed with "timid."

Sloot sighed.

"Predictable." Arthur didn't turn over to hurl the accusation at Sloot.

"What," asked Sloot, "what did I say this time?"

Arthur grumbled as he turned over. It was the grumble of a man who'd gotten half-nestled and was being roused by a twit who needed chiding.

"That sigh," Arthur carped. "It said, 'oh, I do so dearly *want* to get on with it, I really do! By the Domnitor's breath, may it ever suck and blow through his sainted lungs, I desperately wish that I'd been born less cowardly, so that I might stop whinging and get on with it!' I'm right, aren't I? I know I am."

"Long may he reign," said Sloot.

Arthur had already started renegotiating his merger with the sofa when Sloot sighed an altogether different sigh, one that said, "as much as I hate to admit it, the intolerable know-it-all has hit it on the nose." Arthur harrumphed in self-satisfaction, having mistaken only two things: he'd substituted "elder statesman" for "intolerable know-it-all," and Sloot would never have spoken an oath involving the Domnitor's well-being, long may he reign.

Still, he'd gotten the broad strokes. Sloot really did want to get on with it, but what would happen if he made the wrong changes? He could send more cracks spidering through an already brittle chunk of the Narrative. It could shatter at his slightest touch.

"Permitted!" Igor blurted.

Sloot jumped and clutched his heart. Demons' hearts have nothing to do with their physiology, but old habits die hard.

"What?"

"Rhymes with *insipid*," said Igor with a grin. Then he shrugged. "Close enough to finish this verse. Oh, this will be a big hit on your birthday!"

"All right," Sloot snarled, his eyes flashing red under brows that weren't angry, *per se*, but tired of being messed about. He took his Infernal ledger down from its shelf and stalked over to the circle in a huff that said, "oh, yeah?" with eyes darting apologies around the room for his brashness.

"Hang on," said Igor, "are you finally getting down to business?"

The incantation sounded like a bizarre arrangement of consonants that were members of rival gangs. Sloot had practiced it in sections so he'd be ready to use it when the time came, but he'd never recited it all at once. He did his best to maintain the pacing as he did the gestures toward different points on the circle. He waggled his fingers at the Exigent Septangle with proper vigor, having read the instructions just that morning. When he got to the invectives for the Transpiral Triskadekastar, he was only pretty sure he'd spat them with sufficient disdain. He stumbled his way through the rest, terrified that he'd rip a new hole in the universe if he got so much as a syllable out of place.

He needn't have worried. These incantations were largely ceremonial. The circle itself did all of the real work. But Sloot Peril was a paragon of uneasiness. He'd give a snowball 50/50 odds of surviving the North Pole. Regardless, the only trouble Sloot encountered with the invocation was that it worked.

RUNIC SIDE EFFECTS

"Salzstadt Before" was the title on Sloot's ledger. It represented the Narrative as it was before the Dark spilled into it. It currently balanced to "Salzstadt Now," the crumbling chaos that Sloot was trying to avert. The nightmarish future in which he was a demon and the dead walked the streets of the Domnitor's beloved city, long may he reign.

Salzstadt Before was just as he'd remembered it. Cobblestone streets so clean you could eat off of them, patrolled by city guards eager to make someone do so. Other loyal salts strolled the cobbles as well, every one of them alive in the traditional sense. The salts of Salzstadt Now, by comparison, were thrifty types who wouldn't let something as trivial as complete organ failure put the whole apparatus in the ground.

It was a relief, not being surrounded by the walking dead for a change, but it was hard for Sloot to enjoy with his perception of time turned up. He could see the past and future pouring off of everyone and everything around him. It was like timelines had become a visible dimension. He could see that the silversmith's shop across the street had been an apothecary once, a tailor before that, a haberdashery before that, and so on. It had been many different shops since the city's foundations were stoned in by a crew of hairy-knuckled workers in grubby tunics who did community theater in their time off and didn't talk about it while they were doing stonework.

"Nghaaah," Sloot gurgled. He tried to keep his eyes from crossing, which isn't easy with the complete story of every cobble in the street playing out before his eyes. He fell to his knees.

"You all right, boss?" It was Igor. Sloot's eyes were shut tight. It was helping a bit, but only because it was blocking out the three spatial dimensions. The hyper-perception of time, as it turned out, was not a solely visual experience.

"Er, yes," Sloot lied. "Wait, what are you doing here?"

"Coming with you," Igor replied incredulously. "That's what bards do. It's sure to be in the manual."

Sloot wondered whether there actually was a manual. It didn't help with his present conundrum, though the distraction was strangely soothing.

"You're looking pale," said Igor, who was standing over him. Sloot partially opened one eye and tried focusing on the gremlin, a feat he'd previously avoided at all costs. Gremlins are disgusting creatures who come in all shapes and sizes, though every one of them strongly resembles a wretched pile of filth festooned with wretched filth. Gremlins are not pleasant to behold, and Igor was no exception.

Then again, Igor was the only thing in Salzstadt Before that didn't have time cascading off him in two directions.

"You're normal," Sloot mused. Then he threw up.

"Watch it," said an old gran, upon whose hobnail boots Sloot's lunch now resided. "Oh, that's perfect! I'll have to go around through the back when I get home now. As though I weren't late enough already!"

In addition to the run-of-the-mill abashment that followed the chastisement, Sloot was intrigued. He could see the old gran's past stretching behind her, but there was nothing coming out the other side. As the seconds ticked on he watched them fall in line behind her, but he couldn't see what she'd be getting up to next.

"S-sorry," he managed, but she'd already stomped off in a huff. Sloot climbed unsteadily to his feet.

"Did you mean it?" asked Igor. His bits of filth that passed for eyelashes fluttered.

"Of course," said Sloot. "Good boots are expensive. I'm just glad I don't have some sort of demonic bile that might have eaten through her feet."

"I meant about me being normal." Igor's foot twisted nervously on the ground, and his filthy hands fidgeted with an intense lack of grace. Sloot wasn't sure, but he thought Igor was blushing.

"I just meant that I can't see your timeline."

"What?" Igor's expression descended into dismay. "You mean my unmentionables?"

"No," retorted Sloot, one side of his upper lip curling nostril-ward in revulsion. "I can literally see the past and future of everything but you."

"Oh," said Igor. He turned a confused glance up toward the clouds. Then he shrugged. "At least you weren't making fun of my bathing suit area."

Sloot sincerely hoped that line of inquiry would die of natural causes on the spot.

"The woman," he blurted, "the old gran."

"You ruined her shoes."

"Yeah, sorry. But I couldn't see her future!"

"Well," said Igor, "she was getting on in years, wasn't she? Maybe she was close to what we in the business call *the end of the line*."

"What 'business?' Never mind. Wait, everyone calls it that."

"Everyone? Really? That's a shame. Wish I'd gotten a copyright or something. Could've made a fortune."

"Hang on," said Sloot. He summoned an aethereal representation of his magic circle on the cobbled beneath his feet. It was difficult focusing on it, what with time cascading off of everything and everyone else.

"Oxbugger's Crescent!" he exclaimed.

"Oooh," said Igor, rubbing his hands together, "nice profanity! What's it mean?"

"It's not a swear word," said Sloot. "It's this shape on the inner ring of the second quadrant. It's supposed to improve my causational perception, and it looks like it's turned up too high."

Sloot performed a series of gestures that were entirely unnecessary, but he didn't know who might have been looking. While clerking for Winkus, Ordo, and Mirgazhandinuxulluminixighanduminophizio, he'd learned that demons could get into a lot of trouble for telling people how easy it was to use magic circles. He pinched his fingers together, gave them a twist, and Oxbugger's Crescent dimmed and shrank.

"There," said Sloot, "that's better."

"Am I still normal?" Igor asked hopefully, brazenly fishing for compliments.

"In a manner of speaking."

"I'll take it!"

"I mean I still can't see your timeline. Probably because you followed me here from Salzstadt Now."

Sloot could now only see about ten minutes of anything's timeline in either direction. That was a huge relief. Cobblestones only accomplished as much in ten minutes as a typical bureaucrat might in his entire career.

Sloot dismissed the circle with a wave of his hand and took a stroll through Salzstadt Before. He thought the nostalgia might do him some good. It was the sort of rookie mistake that would have the other demons back at the precinct in stitches, were demons more inclined toward police tropes.

"It's a butcher shop," said Igor, because the obvious wasn't going to state itself.

"It's my apartment," Sloot replied.

"Our apartment is above a jeweler," said Igor, in the patient way that people explain things to their doddering elders.

"It used to be a butcher."

Igor drew in a breath.

"The *jeweler* used to be a butcher, not the apartment," Sloot hastened to add.

Igor drew in another breath.

"The jeweler's *shop* used to be a butcher's *shop*. Honestly, is context entirely lost on gremlins?"

"I dunno," Igor shrugged, "I'm a bard. A gremlin would probably say that they understood quite well, but that wasting your time with inane questions was an effective means of sabotage."

Sloot demonstrated his talent for exasperated sighs just as he walked out of the building. That is to say that Sloot's former mortal self walked out of the building, turned around, and started fumbling with his keys to lock the door behind him.

Sloot panicked. The past slipping off of Sloot Before showed that he'd just forgotten his mother's pocket watch. His future was only a few seconds long, during which he would turn around, see his demonic future self, and have a proper panic.

It was suddenly cold, wet, and nearly impossible to see. Sloot felt like he was falling, and it wasn't until he was below the clouds that he realized he *was* falling rapidly toward a cobblestone street whose immediate future included a forceful impact and several law enforcement officials walking around, asking "what's all this, then?"

Or, quite possibly, it didn't. Sloot had nearly come close enough to find out when he found himself in the cold, wet clouds again. And he was falling again.

Panic returned for a repeat performance about two stories above the cobbles, and Sloot was in the clouds a third time. And a fourth. It was the better part of an hour before Sloot remembered Graznak's Consternation, a rune on his circle's inner ring that—in case of panic—would teleport him a mile straight up. It was popular among nascent demons who had trouble remembering which muscles would unfurl their wings. He'd lost count of how many trips he'd taken to the clouds before he had the leathery black things flapping behind him.

Sloot hated flying because he was terrible at it. That was why he never practiced. He also wasn't very good at identifying flaws in circular logic. Nonetheless, he managed to avoid serious injury with his sloppy landing on the roof of his building.

"Took you long enough," said Igor. He was clinging to the weather vane, attempting to wrench the head from the rooster at its top.

"Sorry," said Sloot. "What happened? Did Sloot Before see me?"

"No, he locked the door and wandered off to put his hand on the wall."

"You followed him, then?"

"No, Arthur was right. You're predictable."

Sloot failed to suppress a grin. "He's already come back for the watch, then?"

"He's standing in the butcher shop line as we speak."

Sloot looked down over the edge to see four elderly salts queued in front of Sloot. He remembered that day. He'd gone back home to get his mother's watch, but had been forced to wait in line for the butcher to pass through the building's only door. Cutting in queues was forbidden in the Old Country, a ghastly breach of etiquette guaranteed to summon goblins. Reliving the memory was stressful, but the next ten minutes of his future spilled off his former self just the way he remembered it.

Sloot sat back on the shingles and sighed with relief. "At least I didn't accidentally alter my own past. I need to avoid that at all costs."

"Then what are we doing here?"

That was worrisome. Why *had* Sloot come back? He'd been so worried about getting his circle in order that he hadn't thought very little about what to do next.

"Well," Sloot began, "I've got to amend the Narrative."

"You're not dead anymore, you know."

The Narrative was what the dead called the land of the living. The dead have trouble perceiving the passage of time, so they spend a lot of it watching the stories of the living play out. Many tried to remain a part of it, haunting their old houses or making soothing noises like tortured moans and rattling chains.

"Demons too," said Sloot, "Anyway, it's my job to fix it, right? I mean, that's why the Coolest made me a demon."

"Sure," said Igor, grunting with the effort of wrenching the head off the rooster. He grinned in satisfaction, then realized what he'd done. He hid the head behind his back and refused to meet Sloot's gaze.

"Old habits," he shrugged. "So you can fix it, then? And throw in some heroics for your loyal bard's sake?"

If only it were that easy, thought Sloot. He looked down over the edge of the roof in time to see himself rushing out of the butcher's door. He winced. He'd always known his running form was the athletic approximation of crying, but to see it in its full glory—well, not *glory.* Whatever the opposite of that might have been.

"Oh, dear," Sloot said aloud, as close to swearing as he cared to wander. He felt it was warranted, given the circumstances.

"It's complicated, I'd imagine."

"It would be less so," Sloot ventured, "if I'd rein in the flailing arms a bit."

"That too," said Igor, suppressing a chuckle as he watched Sloot Before hurtling down the street like a flock of geese fighting over half a sandwich. "I meant fixing reality."

"Oh, yes. Right. This was just a test run, trying out the old circle. Seeing how it handles."

"Right," Igor replied, sounding disappointed. "Well, I suppose there's a song in there somewhere."

LONG MAY HE REIGN

Aside from befouling a pair of boots and getting dropped from the clouds several dozen times, Sloot accomplished astonishingly little on his first foray into Salzstadt Before. He hadn't gone in with a plan, but he was an accomplished accountant. He'd been handed a ledger to sort out. His natural instincts for accounting should have taken over, and … what? He never really had to think back in those halcyon days in the Three Bells counting house. He'd simply waded into an unsorted stack of receipts and bent them to his will. It was effortless.

His ineffectiveness in Salzstadt Before and his longing for his old life tried leading him to his regular pub. The one where patrons bought drinks in pairs to give one to the goblins. But they had a strict "no gremlins" policy, and Igor insisted on tagging along. What if Sloot got up to spontaneous heroics?

This was how Sloot ended up in Dark Corners, a pub he'd never noticed before, even though it was around the corner from his apartment. It was clean, quiet, and true to its name, there were dark corners everywhere. Not just the four one would expect. It was like a box of corners had fallen off a cart, and whoever found them used the savings to convince the building inspector to look the other way. A large part of civil servants' official compensation is the satisfaction of knowing they're doing the Domnitor's work, long may he reign. Bribery helps working salts make ends meet.

People were sitting around a few of the tables, each in a dark corner of its own. All of them were looking at him.

The tide rose in Sloot's throat, apprehension and panic cresting atop a churn of social anxiety. That was normal for Sloot, though he also felt strangely ill at ease. The stares of the other patrons all seemed to ask, "what are you doing here?" in a way that "I live around the corner and thought I'd have a drink" didn't seem equipped to answer.

"Er, hello." Even though his voice trembled, that counted as bold for Sloot. Perhaps knowing that demons were infinitely more powerful than humans had emboldened him. Perhaps he'd been frozen to the spot in fear, like a deer who'd seen anything at all. In either case, the other patrons returned their attentions to their own affairs without further ado.

Sloot found an empty table in a dark corner, ordered a pair of drinks out of habit, and set to sulking. Igor sniffed back a tear.

"What's going on?" asked Sloot.

"Nothing," said Igor. He unscrewed the lid of the salt shaker on the table. "It's just that people don't buy drinks for gremlins. You're a good man, Peril."

Sloot said nothing. He didn't want to encourage Igor, but the gremlin refused to leave him alone, so some goodwill might be a good idea. Sloot surprised himself with that one. It was far closer to guile than he usually found himself. With that sort of social cunning, he might one day have enough friends to forget one of their names.

"Peril?" Sloot heard his name whispered from a table in a dark corner not far from one of his own. It didn't sound like he was intended to have heard it, but demonic hearing was more sensitive than Sloot's sense of etiquette.

"It *is* him," said a familiar voice as he turned around. It was Flavia, his old handler from Uncle.

Uncle knew everything about everything, or at least they'd instilled enough fear and rumors that no one would ever assume otherwise. Thus when they'd dragged Sloot in for a *conversation*, he never thought to question how Flavia had known he was a Carpathian spy.

There she was, in the same white dress she always wore, sitting in a dark corner with Walter the Undying. Both of them were staring at him with their mouths hanging open.

That made sense. The last time they'd seen Sloot, he'd been a ghost. Furthermore, Walter the Undying had just made good on a threat to consign Myrtle to the lowest circle of the Inferno. Most people, upon seeing a ghost whom they'd begrudged walking around in a corporeal sort of way, would naturally let the chin wag a bit. Their eyes went wide.

"This can't be good," said Walter the Undying. He was wearing his black robe with the cowl pulled up, which was doubly mysterious in a place like this. Sloot wondered if wizards were required to keep up airs of mystery at all times, or if it was just a perk of the job. Frankly, neither would have surprised him. He gave a wry smirk at that. He'd always wanted to be a person surprised by neither of two things.

"Now hang on a second," said Flavia, her hands going up in a placating manner. "You've got every right to be angry, but hear us out. For old time's sake?" She'd obviously taken Sloot's smirk for a sadistic one. She worked for Uncle, so she'd probably seen more than a few of those.

"What?" Igor blurted as he fished in his bag for his bit of wire.

"I didn't know we were here on business, I thought you were just sulking! I'm not ready for battle! What sort of thing do bards do for battles? Is it odes? Ballads?"

"There's not going to be a battle," said Sloot. Flavia and Walter the Undying relaxed at that. "Probably," he added. He rarely had the upper hand and thought he'd hang onto it awhile.

"Join us, won't you?" Flavia's voice warbled with nerves. "You and your ... *friend.*" What little measure of composure Flavia had regained ran screaming for the door when Igor emerged from the shadows. She obviously knew a gremlin when she saw one.

"I'm his bard," said Igor, correcting her assumption that he was a standard-issue gremlin.

"He's not my bard."

"We're having a trial basis."

"Fine," said Flavia, more forcibly polite than usual. "Sloot, I hardly know where to begin!"

"Why aren't you dead anymore?" asked Walter the Undying, with all the grace and tact of an agent of Uncle handing you a receipt for your gran.

"He's a *demon,*" sneered Igor, implying how terrified they should be. Gremlins appreciate the free chaos you can get out of terrified people.

"Oh," Flavia and Walter the Undying chuckled in unison. Their relief was evident.

"That's how you were able to find this place," said Walter the Undying. "A demon! How'd you manage it?"

"I'm not sure I'm allowed to say," Sloot began, just under Igor practically shouting, "he was promoted by the Coolest for a secret mission!"

Flavia and Walter the Undying looked at each other in delighted surprise.

"We're going to have to file a coincidence report," Flavia said.

"We would," the wizard replied, "if we weren't engaged in the sort of business in which we are, in fact, engaged."

"Oh, dear," Sloot groaned. "Uncle isn't still trying to—"

"Keep the Domnitor's peace by any means necessary, long may he reign?" Flavia interjected.

"Long may he reign," Sloot obeyed aloud.

"Yes," hissed Flavia in a hush, leaning in closer. "And we still believe the best way to do that is to restructure the leadership."

Sloot's last mission for Uncle—which he failed to complete, dooming Myrtle to the lowest circle of the Inferno—had been to kidnap the Domnitor, long may he reign, so Flavia could implement a puppet government. It was a sensible move when one's monarch was eleven years old and came from a long line of mad despots, but sensible moves were rarely made in government. Sloot wasn't eager to set trends.

"Look," Flavia sang sweetly, leaning back with an easy smile, "I know we parted on less than ideal terms, but I'm willing to let bygones be bygones."

"Bygones?" Sloot balked. "You fired me and consigned my girlfriend to the Inferno!"

"Only because of your dereliction of duty," said Flavia, with mild reproach. "Believe me, I didn't want to have Walter deal with Myrtle that way—"

"The Undying," Walter the Undying interjected.

"Right," said Flavia. Her eyes were tightly shut, as was the fist she shook in lukewarm frustration. "Walter *the Undying*. Sorry to have omitted your well-earned honorific." She took a deep breath and reapplied her placid smile. "Anyway, I think it's fair to say that we were both wrong, but you started it. Now, who'd like to move past this like adults and work together toward the common good?"

"I don't like it," said Igor. That was the gremlin talking. Very little went terribly wrong when cool heads got together to solve a problem. Let that sort of thing go too far, and it would take several well-bribed politicians to get things properly malfunctioning again.

"I never wanted to work together in the first place," said Sloot.

"But you're a patriot," said Flavia. "Think of your duty to your country! I don't like to throw accusations around, but you *were* derelict in your duty, and now you're a disgraced former operative. Do you really want that on your resume? Er, conscience?"

Sloot could have picked apart the flaws in her argument. He could have asked if all of Uncle knew about her *coup d'état* or if she'd gone rogue. He could have pointed out that coercion to commit treason wasn't the same as a legitimate order. And if none of that was good enough, he could have simply yelled some swear words and vowed revenge for Myrtle.

Instead, he wondered if she had a point. It was doubtful, but it was far less confrontational than his other options. Furthermore, Sloot Peril had been raised a true salt of the Old Country. There was no more loyal subject of the Domnitor, long may he reign. He had an opportunity to help Uncle—*Uncle*—and his instinct was to refuse! For a good reason, to be sure, but a sense of duty burned hot in the heart of every salt. So did hypertension. They loved processed meats in the Old Country.

Sloot whimpered. This was real think-for-yourself stuff, far beyond the would-you-like-a-second-cup-of-tea choices that he felt qualified to make.

"I don't want to kidnap anyone," Sloot stated flatly in a whisper.

"I'd never ask you to," Flavia reassured him.

"You did!"

"Bygones," said Flavia with a dismissive wave. "No more kidnapping from here on. All right?"

"All right. Thanks."

"Unless you think it would be best."

"I don't!"

"Well, you don't *now*," said Flavia, "but you might change your mind."

"I won't!"

"You don't have to decide right away." Sloot opened his mouth to protest, but Flavia held up a hand and continued. "All I'm saying is that it's completely up to you how you deliver your results. We just want to help you."

"Help me?"

"We were there, remember?" Walter the Undying produced a ball of glass from within his voluminous black robes. That was wizards for you. It wasn't good enough for wizards to simply take something out of their pocket. It had to be *produced* from within billowing garments. Sloot squirmed at the impracticality, having always appreciated the practicality of pockets. Wizards' robes might have been silly with pockets, but Sloot wasn't about to find out.

Faint lights danced within the little sphere it as it sat upon Walter the Undying's fingertips. Sloot looked into it and saw himself, the Coolest, Roman—everyone who'd been there for the battle and the subsequent spilling of the Dark, including Myrtle.

Sloot's breath caught in his throat. He'd thought about her every day since then, wondered what he might do to free her from the Inferno. Seeing her there, wings unfurled in Walter the Undying's glass bauble, sent a deep pang of regret into his … soul, perhaps? Sloot wasn't sure where pangs did their business. He'd leave that for the poets to figure out, and he wouldn't hold his breath. Poets had more holidays per year than anyone, with the exception of philosophers, whose blithe agnosticism demanded that they either follow or ignore *all* holidays. They'd unanimously opted for the latter.

"We had a feeling the Coolest would send someone to clean all of this up," Flavia explained. "We just never thought they'd pick you! No offense."

"None taken," said Sloot. He was offended, but the last thing he wanted to talk about was his feelings.

"Reality is in a kerfuffle at the moment. You're supposed to put everything in order, am I right?"

"That's the gist of it."

"You don't have to answer right away, but does resting the fate of a nation in the hands of a child seem like putting things in order?"

Sloot said nothing, grateful for having been given permission. Flavia made sense, but she was talking about the Domnitor! Long may he reign.

Flavia smiled during Sloot's thoughtful pause. It was a warm, comforting smile designed to win his trust so she could exploit him for her own ends. Sloot didn't need demonic senses to see her obfuscation, but that was the problem with sinister minds. They often made sense.

"All I'm saying," said Flavia, "is while you're deciding the fate of your mother country and everyone you know and love, consider resting that power with the people who've actually been running things for decades. Doesn't it make sense that we'd know more than a child?"

JUST A LITTLE BLOOD

"Are you all right?"

Sloot continued saying nothing as he walked quickly toward his apartment. The second most irritating thing about Flavia's plot to use the Domnitor, long may he reign, as a puppet was that it made sense. The most irritating thing was his inclination to go along with it.

The good salts of Salzstadt liked things the way they were, or at least they had no intention of learning that they didn't. They were not the sort of people who blithely went along with change just because it made sense. Tradition was important in the Old Country. Change regimes and you may as well scrub out the stew pot while you're at it.

Everyone knows that there is no such thing as a recipe for stew. Not a *proper* stew. They usually start as soup, or so historians have hypothesized, which is a fancy way of saying "guessed," which is good enough for salts who lack the patience for proof. Start adding cutoffs and leftovers to the pot, and over time the soup becomes stew. Thriftiness, which is "cheap" with a clean shirt and a haircut, was an Old Country virtue.

Meats, cheeses, other soups that weren't strong enough to resist the gravity of denser ones, and all manner of other ingredients combine over time to invent new flavors. Some of them are abominations bordering on heresy. Those get carried off by imps in the middle of the night and placed in the collections of arch-demons in the upper circles of the Inferno.

Scrubbing out the stew pot—or having to buy a new one as a result of demonic theft—was a sad, painful occasion in the Old Country. Starting over from scratch was scary, and most salts wanted nothing to do with it. That was most of what Sloot was feeling in the moment. Sure, placing the fate of a nation in the hands of adults who knew what they were doing sounded good, at least at face value. But knowing that the Domnitor, long may he reign, wasn't properly reigning? The uncertainty terrified Sloot. Just when his discomfiture was coming to a crescendo, Igor gave his wire an introductory pluck.

"This probably isn't the best time," said Sloot. He started walking a bit faster.

Once again, Sloot ran away,
He did that once or twice a day,
When things started getting scary,
Sloot was never one to tarry...

As Igor's song progressed, so did Sloot's pace. It went from a quick step, past jogging, and end up in a flat-out sprint. It was only a matter of time before Igor's lyrics referenced their conversation with Flavia. Any onlooking demons might have wondered why he didn't take flight, or perhaps employ Gradozian's Swift, a simple rune that make's a demon's movements fluid and graceful. Very effective for seducing mortals with overly romantic ideas about creatures of darkness.

Sloot was gasping for breath by the time he dove into his

apartment and collapsed on the floor. It was a subconscious affectation. Demons had lungs, but they had nothing to do with breathing. They'd simply been jealous of mortals when smoking had been invented and had fought lengthy court battles to have them included in their standard compensation packages.

"Close the door!" he shrieked, as Igor moseyed in behind him.

"You sound upset," Igor mused.

Sloot rose halfway to his feet, turned, and lunged at the door with half the grace one might expect from a hurled sack of potatoes. Igor dodged and the door slammed shut with a sweat-drenched Sloot crumpled against it.

"Heresy," Sloot wheezed for no reason. "We were talking about heresy in the pub! Did you sing about it?"

"You mean you weren't listening?"

"I asked you not to!"

"Oh, well, that's just great," Igor grumbled. He plopped down on the floor with an off-putting squelch. "You could be more supportive, you know."

"That's tantamount to encouragement," said Sloot. "What if you'd sung about overthrowing the Domnitor, long may he reign?"

"Oh, yeah," said Igor, "I was meaning to ask you about that. What's a dominator?"

Sloot's jaw went slack. Igor may as well have asked him to explain the sun.

"The—well, the *Domnitor*, long may he reign, is ... well, he's—"

"A despot!" shouted an explosion of crocheted blankets from the couch, whence cometh Arthur, nostrils flaring. "He is the muck in which we persist, the boot upon our necks, the foul oppressor who—"

"Be quiet!" shouted Sloot, who had never spoken so forcefully in his life, nor in such an Infernally low register. He strained to coax his horns back into his brow and extinguish his flaming eyes.

"How dare you," growled Arthur. "I was just working up to a proper tirade! Doesn't everyone know that you never interfere with a philosophical tirade?"

"Says who?" asked Igor. It sounded innocent, but then, he was a gremlin.

"Gary the Reponderer! He had a whole series of tirades on the subject, not a one of which was interrupted!"

"I'm sorry," hissed Sloot, "but the window's broken! Anyone in the street could hear you slandering the-"

"I could not have been more clear when I told you to ignore the window! It's broken *now*, isn't it? Thanks to your insolence! Well, there can be no more ignoring it now. You'll have to get it fixed."

"Oh, good," said Igor, leaning in toward Sloot. "At least you've made him forget about the Domnitor."

Sloot winced. "Long may he reign."

"Oh, no, I haven't! Let them hear, let them all hear! The despot's jack-booted thugs are powerless against my irrefutable logic. Let them come! Let them come and do their worst!"

"They *did* their worst," said Sloot. "They beheaded you."

"Nonsense," said Arthur. He gestured to his neck. "Explain this."

"You were dead for years!"

"I got better."

Arthur continued to rail against everything from the Domnitor, long may he reign, to the consistency of pudding and the audacity of those who dared to eat it. Sloot did his best to block it out, wishing that Igor would stop encouraging him by providing occasional points of logic. Nothing enraged Arthur like inconvenient logic. At least they were occupying each other.

Sloot used the distraction to open his ledger, perform the gestures and incantations, and slip into Salzstadt Before on his own. He didn't have a specific agenda other than to practice working in the past without Igor looking over his shoulder. He activated a rune in the fourth quadrant called Sarko's Banality, which effectively reduced everything interesting about him to nothing. It was a sort of dimness. A poor demon's invisibility, not that proper invisibility was expensive, but Sloot *was* poor. Dimness would keep people from noticing him or saying, in a threatening tone, "can I help you with something?"

He strolled the streets, watching the way people's timelines moved around them. He saw the old gran upon whose boot he'd been sick. She'd not had a future spilling off her after that, but she did now. She was minutes away from walking through her back door, cleaning off her boots, berating her grandson for being a shiftless layabout, then venting at length about the vagrant who'd befouled her boots. She rolled that into a litany of complaints about how much better the world had been in her day, at which point Sloot did what anyone would do and stopped paying attention.

What had happened to her future? Sloot assumed that his having interfered with the past had altered her timeline, and that her future simply needed to catch up. It hadn't sent the universe careening off into calamity, it had just made a gran late for chiding young people.

That was comforting. Sloot had been so concerned about permanently damaging the past that he'd been loath to touch anything. But it seemed the past had some elasticity! It wouldn't be broken as easily as Sloot's self-confidence.

Sloot's dimness allowed him to move around unnoticed as long as he did nothing to attract attention. He strolled up the high street until he came to the Domnitor's castle, long may he reign. He slipped past the guards and walked the halls until he came to the grand ballroom. While the lesser ballrooms were impressive as well, he'd specifically wanted to see this one again, before its splendor had been ruined.

As a ghost, he'd seen it full of goblins right before they brought the two crystal chandeliers down next to their pile of rotting meat. A congress of goblins in session is a violent and noxious thing to behold.

He stood in awed silence for a long time, watching the candles send rainbows dancing around the room. It was a warm, decadent elegance of a time he was determined to bring back to his mother country.

He roamed the halls awhile, eventually coming out on the parapet of the castle's tallest tower. To his disappointment, the view was less majestic than he'd assumed it would be. Shouldn't Salzstadt, the shining jewel in the crown of the world, stretch out past the horizon in every direction? Shouldn't the sea itself, in all of its natural splendor, pale in comparison to that of mighty Salzstadt?

Well, it didn't. It was nice, but it was less shining jewel and more bustling drudgery. While the greater glory of the Old Country was ever present in the hearts of its people, the day-to-day truth of it had no eagles soaring aloft. Or if it did, it should be noted that eagles left their mark on that over which they soared.

Oh, well, Sloot thought. Salzstadt's reality never stood a chance of living up to his dreams, like the unathletic children of serious boulderchuck fans. There was still a lot to take in. Where mortal eyes merely got a nice view, Sloot saw the patterns of people's daily lives mingling together, forming patterns, swirling and eddying in pools of the present before washing into the tide of the past.

The patterns had patterns within themselves, forming up with others to make clusters with intricate cliques and social norms. There were the impenetrable circles of hereditary wealth, the institutions of poverty that propped them up, the seedy undercurrent of crime that also propped up the wealthy, and all of that seemed insignificant when compared with the laundry. Sloot could hear his pupils dilating with the strain of trying to take in the vast, incalculable scope of dirty laundry being washed, dried, folded, put away, worn again, and the cycle repeating. He was chagrined to see how much more he could have made as a washer than as an accountant.

And then, just has he thought that the infinite swirling of patterns might coalesce into something useful, an errant thought slipped into his consciousness: it's only laundry while it's unworn and unfolded. Otherwise, it's just clothes.

Sloot heard a snapping sound, and his mind started to drift. Wind whipped around him, and everything sounded as though it were moving through a tunnel. Somewhere in the distance, someone was screaming. The voice sounded remarkably like his own.

Sloot awoke to the sensation of being dragged across sharp rocks. He didn't dislike it as much as he'd have thought. That was demonic physiology for you.

"Wha…" he said groggily.

"Get up," hissed a voice from above him. It belonged to Igor. "We have to get out of here!"

"All right, all *right*," groaned Sloot, flailing at Igor. "Just give me a minute!"

"Quiet!" Igor whispered as loudly as he could. "We don't have a minute! We have to go!"

Sloot blinked. It was dark, though the pre-dawn clouds stung his eyes in a very noon-on-a-summer-day oeuvre.

"We're in the crags," he mused aloud.

"Yes! We're in the sock-chewing crags! Get on your feet and run for it!"

"Relax," said Sloot. He felt a hangover coming on, but not the drinking kind. This one felt inside-out, oily in a way that proper hangovers were miserably dry. "I've been here before. Roman and I swore a blue streak at each other. Didn't draw a single goblin."

"Have you ever bothered to wonder *why* that was?"

Sloot hadn't. He chuckled. Wondering led to questioning, and the questions would likely be answered by the Ministry of Conversation with their most tactful batons. In the Old Country, "I wonder" was as near to a swear word as one could get without summoning a goblin.

Igor squeaked in surprise and pointed to a silhouette a few yards away. It looked like a man in a floppy hat with a leaky bag of sand.

"That's why! Run!"

It must have been the hangover. On most days, the casual insinuation of danger would have thrown Sloot into a flat-out sprint. This time, Igor had to point out a specific threat to get Sloot dashing across the rocky ground. The delay was unfortunate, Sloot would shortly realize, after slamming face-first into an unseen barrier that felt as solid as Salzstadt's main gate.

Sloot heard a mad cackle from the floppy hat behind him, or possibly the man wearing it. He turned in time to see Igor narrowly whiz past the figure before it dropped the leaky bag. It said a swear word, or at least Sloot thought it was a swear word. It wasn't one he recognized, but swearing had a distinct inflection, and people didn't come to the crags to *not* say swear words.

"Nice try, old man!" Igor laughed and shot an obscene gesture toward the floppy-hatted stranger.

"Just a gremlin! What could I want from you, anyway?"

"Watch it," Igor snarled. "Everybody lives somewhere, wouldn't want your home mischiefed, now would you?"

"Good luck finding it," said the stranger. He sounded confident, but his expression was wary. It was lunatic as well, holding onto a private joke that he was happy to keep to himself. He was old and scrawny and dressed in long, flowing robes like a scrap of leather masquerading as a wizard.

"Er, sorry," said Sloot, "but I seem to be stuck in your … what's happening here, exactly?"

"Salt!" shouted the stranger, "mined from beneath Salzstadt herself! That's pure, honest salt there, demon. There's no escaping that until I say so!"

A meandering and imprecise line of salt lay on the ground between the two of them. Sloot followed it with his eyes to find that it was a complete circle, about thirty feet across. He stubbed his toe trying to break the line with his foot. He tried teleporting to no avail. He even tried spreading his wings to see if he could fly over the barrier, but he couldn't make them come out.

"Turn him loose," growled Igor.

"I'd watch my tone, if I were you." The stranger waggled a finger. "I'm calling the shots here! It's lucky for you all I want is a little blood."

"Blood?" Sloot's voice quavered. The sight of blood made him woozy. You never saw blood when things were going well.

"Just a bit," wheedled the stranger. He tossed a little glass vial in Sloot's direction, unaware that the closest thing to athleticism in Sloot's repertoire was a severe aversion to things flying toward him. He cringed with his arms crossed. The vial bounced off his shoulder and shattered on the ground.

"Hey," whined the stranger, "those are expensive!"

"Terribly sorry," said Sloot. "I'd hate to cost you any more money. Perhaps you'd consider leaving my blood where it is?"

"I only need a teeny bit." The stranger smiled in a way that almost made it sound reasonable.

"Don't do it," said Igor.

"Quiet, you!" hissed the stranger.

"Believe me, he can get up to all sorts of mischief with a single drop of demon blood." Igor dodged a half-hearted kick. "You'll never be rid of this one if you give in!"

"Then how do I get out of here?" asked Sloot, who was very good at giving in to requests, reasonable or otherwise.

"You don't," said the stranger, "not in this hallowed place, not imprisoned by salt!"

"There's one way," said Igor, dodging another kick, "but you're not going to like it."

"That's it," snarled the stranger, "I told you to watch it!" He threw another kick, and then another, and then he was chasing Igor around the circle.

"Er, would you mind possibly—" Sloot began as he slowly turned in a circle to follow the chase.

"Hold still!"

Igor suggested a particularly vile place where the stranger might shove "it," whatever "it" was.

"Oh, dear," said Sloot. Whether it was from the spinning around or the swearing, he was feeling a bit woozy. "I think I need to sit down."

"Don't you dare!" shouted Igor. "Keep your eyes on me!"

"I don't take orders from you," Sloot insisted, but kept turning to watch Igor anyway. Taking orders was second nature to Sloot. He was close to vomiting when he completed his third spin and found himself falling through a black void. It only lasted a few seconds, but that's a very long time when one doesn't know what to expect.

The fall ended abruptly upon pavement.

"Ow," said Sloot, predictably. He sat up just in time to see Igor appear beside him in the dim light. It was a cave, and the eerie purple lightning crawling the walls in slow motion left Sloot wishing for a direction in which he might run.

"Relax," said Igor. "The train will be along any moment."

"Where are we?" asked Sloot, louder than he'd intended. Unexpected falls through voids into slow motion lightning had that effect. "And why is that lightning moving so slowly?"

"We're beneath the crags, in the ley lines. Infernal powers go on the fritz close to ley lines, which is why I had to trick you into getting down here."

Sloot had heard of ley lines. They were channels of mystical energy that ran throughout the world, and the "lightning" was harmless to demons. Some demons even claimed that it had regenerative effects, but Sloot had never gone in for homeopathy.

"You tricked me? I thought I just turned around three times, and *poof*."

"Yeah, right," Igor pouted. "No credit where credit is due! I told you, Infernal powers don't work close to ley lines. Not even mine. Trickery's another thing, though. Nothing tells trickery not to work."

"I suppose I should thank you, then." Sloot paused. "Wait a minute, what train?"

"The *train*," said Igor, as if repeating a thing with emphasis would serve as an explanation. "It travels the ley lines."

Sloot tensed again. "The train travels the ley lines."

"Yes."

"And we're standing on the ley lines?"

"Yes."

Igor's apparent calm wasn't confidence, it was resignation. Worriers like Sloot relied on the confidence of others to prevent them sliding into full-on panics, thus Sloot was in a wheezing tizzy when he heard the bell on the front of the train coming toward them.

"Best to get a running start," grumbled Igor. He started jogging down along the ley line away from the train.

"It's going to hit us!" Sloot squawked as he ran along behind the gremlin.

"I told you we should have run from the crags," Igor sang with the inflection exclusively available to I-told-you-sos.

Sloot's shadow came into focus before him as the train's light drew near. A gentle breeze caressed the back of his neck as it rumbled closer, growing steadily until its gale force nearly bowled him over. The rumble became a roar, and Sloot looked over his shoulder just in time to catch the business end of the train fully in the face.

The sensation of being struck in the face by a mystical train didn't directly compare to any other sensation. It reminded him of an ice cream headache, which is a standard headache that's stubbed its toe.

The pain eventually subsided, and Sloot found himself sitting on a bench that he needed to believe had once been clean.

"Where's this train headed?" Igor asked of a spiny, fire-breathing horror with webbed feet.

"Carpathia," it gurgled.

"Wait," said Sloot as he stood slowly, checking to make sure that he was intact. "We're inside the train!"

"Try not to think too hard about it," Igor warned. "Ley lines can only tolerate so much rationality. You'll cause the train to throw an axle."

"But wh—"

The question was cut off by everyone else on the train shouting in incoherent agitation or throwing partially rotten vegetables at him. That was comforting enough to Sloot in the moment. As long as disgruntled mobs could rain down out-of-date produce at will, the world must still be turning.

Sloot kept quiet, avoiding rational thought by forcing himself to wonder whether fish could smell water. He wanted to ponder how he could end up sitting on the train that hit him, or how he'd ended up inside the ley line in the first place, but he figured he'd have plenty of time for that once he'd reached Carpathia.

FIRST OBLITERATION

Sloot should have visited Carpathia before now. It was part of the reality he was supposed to save, after all. They left the train and emerged from a cave whose mouth looked suspiciously like a fanged skull. Not suspiciously—*predictably.* It was Carpathia, after all. Some bats fluttered out from it after them, black wings taking to the blood red evening sky against the silhouette of Castle Ulfhaven in the distance.

"Just like the dioramas from school," Sloot mused.

"Didn't get its reputation for nothing," said Igor. "Not as bad as they say in the Old Country, though. I like Carpathia. They know how to do a rare steak."

Sloot flexed his shoulders. Nothing happened.

"My wings," he said, in both panic and relief.

"Let's walk a bit," said Igor. "Still too close to the ley line. Anything magical, mysterious, or otherwise non-mortal won't work right."

An optimist would have been relieved that his powers would return. A pessimist would have been depressed that he wouldn't soon wake from a horrible dream in which he was a demon ill-suited to save the world. Sloot had tried optimism once. He didn't care for it.

It wasn't long before Sloot felt his powers returning, like blood flowing back into an arm he'd slept on funny. Once he'd gotten past the pins-and-needles bit, he used his handkerchief to grab Igor by the scruff of what he assumed was his neck, and teleported them to the courtyard of Castle Ulfhaven. Or at least he aimed for the courtyard. They ended up just outside of it.

"That's weird," said Sloot. He didn't teleport often, but his arrivals had always been precise.

"I'll say," said Igor. "You get a plus one?"

"Sorry?"

"I thought you had to be at least 90th class to teleport plus one. I guess they're giving them out to everyone now."

Or you don't count as a whole "one," Sloot thought.

"Shall we, then?" Igor made an expansive gesture toward the courtyard.

"I don't want to," said Sloot. It was true, he didn't. He needed to, but there was a lump in his stomach that made him very apprehensive about the prospect.

"Fine by me," Igor shrugged. "I don't want to either."

They stood there in silence, staring at the courtyard.

"But we *do* though, right?"

"They're your friends," said Igor, who had no friends. It was Sloot alone in the uncomfortable position of being simultaneously willing and unwilling to visit the castle. He eventually came to the conclusion that it was the *courtyard* he didn't want to enter, which had to be an enchantment.

Enchantments meant Nicoleta. Reluctantly, awkwardly, Sloot spread his wings and flew into the darkening sky toward the castle's tallest tower.

Nicoleta was in, and she was busy. Vlad's court wizard was famous for her utter lack of subtlety, adding no less than a shower of sparks to every spell she'd ever cast. Based on the seizure-inducing volleys of stars erupting from her tower windows, it was either some sort of wizard holiday or Nicoleta was working on something big. He waited for a lull in the fireworks before moving in a bit closer.

"Er, hello?" was all he managed to call out before his physical form was annihilated. His consciousness remained intact, though that was little comfort as he was pulled, screaming, through a fiery void that stretched infinitely in all directions. Suddenly, the scope of the infinite void condensed itself to the confines of a sphere with Sloot at its center. He was wreathed in violet flames, "he" being a fiery manifestation of his now-non-existent physical form.

Nicoleta was outside the sphere. She was surrounded by a series of magnifying glasses hung from the ceiling on slender brass arms. She appeared to be weaving strands of spider silk into a rune that hurt his feelings.

"Nicoleta?"

She looked up, then over each shoulder, searching for the source of the sound. She huffed in irritation.

"For the last time, I'll read you aloud when it's time to rain fire and blood down on our enemies, and not a moment before!"

"Sorry," said Sloot. "I didn't mean to interrupt."

Nicoleta's head whipped around to stare at Sloot through her array of lenses. One lens lined up with her mouth and another with her right eye, inverting them in Sloot's view and giving her the appearance of something that would hang in a gallery until purchased for far more than it was worth, but only because the artist had been dead for so long.

"Sloot! What are you doing in there?"

"You'd know better than I would," Sloot replied.

Nicoleta mumbled a few educated guesses about what might

have happened while she fashioned a little doll out of snakeskin, a pair of crow's feet, a bundle of sticks, and a length of twine. Sloot assumed he wasn't supposed to understand anything she was saying about magical confluences or inner aura reverberations, but he nodded now and again. It felt like the polite thing to do.

"There," she said at last, grinning at the little doll. "Hop in."

"I'm sorry?"

"For wha— Oh, right." Nicoleta produced a wand from within the folds of her robe and pointed it at him. Sloot's fiery manifestation swirled into a little cyclone of smoke, then shot into the doll. The sticks and the snakeskin rubbed uncomfortably against each other, but the crow's feet were remarkably ergonomic. Nicoleta chucked the doll into a boiling cauldron, and for several minutes Sloot was assaulted by a cacophony of pops and squelches. His lungs grew in, his nostrils sprouted hair, and by the time he'd flopped naked onto the cold stone floor, he was more or less his prior corporeal self.

"Have you always been that red color?"

"I'm not sure," said Sloot. Perhaps blushing had always been a full-body affair, or perhaps it was a demonic power of little utility. Either way, he wished he had more hands to establish some decorum.

Nicoleta giggled. "Don't worry, the clothes come with the spell. There's just a bit of a delay."

"Oh," said Sloot, having realized that trousers were weaving themselves about him as he waited.

"There are easier ways to go about this, you know."

"Easier ways to go about what?"

"Getting into the castle. Why didn't you just draw down the keening rune outside the courtyard?"

"I didn't see any rune." Sloot wiggled his toes. They felt crowy.

"Did you walk here with your eyes closed? How could you have missed it? It's ten feet tall and throwing sparks! Hang on."

Nicoleta peered into a different crystal ball, smaller than the one Sloot had briefly inhabited. "Yep, it's set as low as possible. Demons 99th class should be able to see it."

Sloot sighed. He explained that the Coolest had made him a demon 100th class.

"Wow," said Nicoleta, her brows knitting themselves into amused disbelief. "They really didn't do you any favors, did they?"

Sloot shook his head. "Didn't want it to look like favoritism."

"Mission accomplished," Nicoleta snorted. "I suppose that means the Coolest aren't demons. Demons always lavish favoritism on anyone who can get them what they want. They're practically famous for it."

"I see," said Sloot, for want of anything useful to say instead.

"Sorry, I don't mean to offend, but ... seriously, I didn't even know there *was* a 100th class."

"It's fine," Sloot sighed. "I'll just look harder for the rune next time. Maybe now that I know it's there—"

"I'll just put you on the guest list," said Nicoleta with a wink. "Was that your first time being obliterated?"

Sloot nodded. "And hopefully only."

"Ha! I doubt it. I mean, 100th class? I'm surprised you've lasted this long. Impressed, actually."

Sloot's spirits lifted at that. He didn't often impress outside the counting house.

Nicoleta sighed at the rune she'd been weaving. It was a compound sigh with a little sneer and a full eye roll to round it out. Sloot had seen that exasperation in his coworkers. It said, "I'll get back to you when I'm interested again." He understood the feeling in theory, if not in practice. Sloot had never met a ledger over which he hadn't been pleased to slave.

"Oh, hey," said Nicoleta, perking up slightly, "you're here!"

"Yes, sorry," said Sloot. He'd assumed she'd noticed before, and now assumed he was intruding. He chided himself for not having made an appointment.

"Take a look at something, will you?"

Typically, when people ask Sloot to "take a look at something," the "something" is a tax statement. Sloot's enthusiasm dampened when Nicoleta pulled him to a crystal ball instead. The very one he'd just been inside, in fact. She waved her hand over it dramatically, and a familiar scene coalesced within the globe.

"It's the Fall of Salzstadt," said Sloot.

"I must have been over it a hundred times," said Nicoleta, squinting into the ball as though she were trying to count all of the goblins. Sloot was none too keen to relive the last moments of his life, as seeing one's self trampled to death was a universally unpleasant experience. But he had a hard time looking away.

"Here," said Nicoleta, "let me wind it back a bit." She placed her hand over the ball and moved one finger in a slow, counterclockwise circle. The scene in the ball began moving in reverse. When it started moving forward again, Sloot watched Vlad and her horde of undead smash through the doors of the great cathedral. Gregor made a gesture, then Nicoleta became visible and started floating toward the putrid old necromancer.

"I still don't know how he did it," said Nicoleta. "It shouldn't have been possible!"

She'd been wearing the blood star on a chain around her neck. It snapped off and flew into Gregor's hand. He and Vlad exchanged threats, and then Gregor broke Nicoleta. She screamed as her body twisted and dropped lifeless onto the floor. The scene paused.

"Did you notice anything?"

"I tried not to."

"Oh, come on," Nicoleta huffed. "You're not still coming to grips with your mortal demise, are you? You're a demon! Surely, the philosophical ramifications—oh, stop it! Arthur's not here."

"Sorry," said Sloot, trying his best to relax from a severe wince. "Show me again. I'll watch this time, I promise."

"Really?"

"Of course," said Sloot.

"You promise?"

"Yes, I promise!"

"That's three times," said Nicoleta. She rolled the scene back and it played again. Sloot watched as carefully as he could, but when Nicoleta started screaming under Gregor's torturous grip, he looked away. What happened next was far more unpleasant than Nicoleta's murder.

"Oh, dear," said Nicoleta, though Sloot could barely hear it over the screaming. *His* screaming, to be specific. He'd been overcome by the feeling of having grown a new and vital organ, only to have it slowly torn to pieces. That would have been troubling enough without all of the attorneys who suddenly appeared.

A quick count told Sloot that there were a dozen of them. Most people wouldn't have bothered, but most people weren't neurotic enough about accounting to definitely lose sleep over it later. It hadn't occurred to Sloot in the moment that he didn't sleep anymore, the whole "rending of vital organs" thing was distracting.

The pain—and Sloot's screaming—abated while one of the attorneys read an official-looking document to Nicoleta.

"... further injunctions to be presented in writing, in triplicate, in blood, at the time of incident or analogous point in an alternate timeline, to be specified therein. Please sign here and here to acknowledge the terms as explained. Thank you. And initial here to acknowledge your acknowledgment. Thank you. Just a few more..."

After Nicoleta's wrist had worked up a proper throbbing from the multitude of signatures—one of which absolved the Coolest of any liability for repetitive stress injury as a result of signatory duress—the attorneys turned to Sloot.

"Given the nature of your work for the Coolest," said the principal attorney, who handed Sloot a card, "and their desire to avoid the appearance of favoritism, all invoices related to your defense are your responsibility. We'll send you a bill."

Sloot read the name on the card. "Minerva Meatsacrifice, Managing Partner. Nameless, Redacted, and Meatsacrifice."

"Please sign here," said a messenger imp who appeared next to Sloot, holding a clipboard and an envelope. Sloot signed the former and was given the latter.

"Prompt payment is appreciated," said Ms. Meatsacrifice. "Good day, Mr. Peril. Ms. Goremonger."

"It's *Doctor* Goremonger, thank you." Nicoleta gestured between two shelves where a framed swath of calligraphy proclaimed her a Doctor of Arcane Sciences from the Universitatis Obscurum.

"I see," said Ms. Meatsacrifice with a little bow. Sloot had dealt with enough attorneys to know that was as close as she'd get to an apology. She straightened, nodded and all of the attorneys vanished with a wave reminiscent of a heat mirage.

"What just happened?" asked Sloot in a trembling voice.

"Ahem."

Sloot and Nicoleta turned to see the messenger imp still standing there.

"Sorry," he said, "a bit anticlimactic, I know, but they didn't take me with them when they left. Would you mind?"

Wizards' towers were notoriously difficult to get in and out of. While the Coolest's cadre of attorneys had no difficulty, messenger imps were not so powerful. Nicoleta waved a hand and the imp disappeared. Sloot happened to be standing such that he saw the imp reappear through the window past Nicoleta's shoulder. He yelped and dropped out of sight. Sloot's face took up a concerned glance at Nicoleta.

"They've got wings," she shrugged. "Anyway, to answer your

question, you've got to be more careful about making promises now that you're a demon! Breaking them can have severe consequences."

"Like attorneys?"

"I'd've had leverage against your soul just now, if not for the attorneys."

"Oh."

"Would you relax? I'd only have made you do a little dance or something."

Sloot stuffed the envelope into the breast pocket of his coat, marveled briefly at the fact that his body had been reconstituted with said coat, and went back to the crystal ball with Nicoleta. After reviewing her grisly death several dozen times, Sloot had nothing but increased nausea to show for it.

"I didn't know demons could be nauseated," said Nicoleta. "Well, nausea demons, I'd imagine."

"Either way, I didn't see anything."

Nicoleta sighed. "Thanks for trying, anyway."

"Happy to help," Sloot lied. He was usually terrible at lying, but polite lies fell under the aegis of etiquette. Still, he prepared himself for a penetrating gaze that would force him to reveal the truth—that he'd sooner dig out his own liver with a spoon than watch the Fall of Salzstadt again—but it never came. Nicoleta was still staring at the crystal ball, squinting in irritation at ghosts of past events playing out on an endless loop.

"Is it really that important?" Concern crept into Sloot's voice. "I mean, you're alive now, right? All's well that ends well?"

"For now," Nicoleta bristled. "I'm alive again *for now*. Tell me, Sloot, once you've finished playing god with all of our fates, will I still be breathing? Or is this just a temporary reprieve?"

Sloot's mouth opened to respond before his brain had a chance to prepare any remarks. That might not have dissuaded Sloot's former employer, Lord Wilhelm Hapsgalt, from saying anything, but he'd been wealthy enough to avoid the consequences of his words. Sloot's budget didn't allow for that.

"I don't know," he said at last. It was the truth, and he felt properly guilty about it. After all, when entrusted with the literal fates of nations, who wouldn't use just a little bit of that power to make sure his friends made out all right?

Nicoleta must have felt the guilt radiating from him, or perhaps she just didn't like being gawked at while she was trying to work. In either case, she stopped the replay and looked over at him.

"Look, you have a job to do. As for me, I don't know why I'm alive again, and you can't tell me for how long. All I have are questions, and there's nothing worse for wizards than unanswered questions. I've got to spend every minute I have searching for answers, because time might run out at any moment."

"And how Gregor defeated you is the most important question?"

Nicoleta's eyes narrowed into an expression that could have sliced through a stack of bricks. "If I want revenge, it is."

MOURNING THE LIVING

Getting Igor into Castle Ulfhaven hadn't been easy, which was only partly accurate. It was true that Sloot wasn't able to convince Nicoleta to let a gremlin past the wards, but only because he hadn't tried. Frankly, it wasn't important to Sloot that his erstwhile bard dog his heels through the castle. Thus it had come as something of a shock to see Igor sitting atop a chandelier, worrying the chain that held it up with a file.

Sloot, being a traditionalist, went through the motions of asking Igor how he'd gotten in, interrupting his explanation—never mind, it's not important—and insisting that he stop doing that at once.

"Gremlins don't get invitations," said Igor, after shimmying down the wall. "We take it neither personally nor lying down. And don't worry about the chain, I'd only just got started. Still, maybe don't stand directly underneath it, if you catch my drift." He gave Sloot an exaggerated wink.

"Your meaning was obvious, not clever." Sloot silently congratulated himself on resisting the urge to use sarcasm just then. He considered it the lowest form of wit, which most people agreed was *such* an astute observation.

Castle Ulfhaven hadn't changed a bit since Sloot had seen it last. Everything was stone and steel with spikes coming out of it, or flaming braziers arranged in threatening formations, or piles of skulls beneath stained glass windows depicting scenes of brutal warfare. Sloot kept close watch on Igor as they walked to the throne room.

"Sloot!" Greta shouted, sounding desperately pleased to see him. "Please, come in! How are you? What's happening in … the south?"

Vlad growled. She was fully armored as usual, perched atop her throne and glaring at nothing in particular. It was a good thing, too, because anything on the business end of that glare might have spontaneously combusted.

Igor stopped in his tracks, said a swear word, and pointed at Vlad.

"That's Vlad the Invader!"

Vlad said nothing. Her glare rolled into a glower.

"Naturally," said Sloot. "Who'd you think would be sitting on the Carpathian throne?"

"Well, her, naturally. It's just that it's *her*! In the flesh! Right there!"

Vlad growled again.

"Yes, well…" Sloot trailed off. He'd never thought of Vlad as a celebrity, having been taught his entire life to think of her as a sort of bogeyman. Er, bogeywoman.

"Silence!" Vlad yelled. The command echoed through the room, which seemed specially designed to make that sort of thing happen.

"Don't listen to her," said Greta. "Please, tell me everything. *Anything*. General Grumpy Trousers here has been moping for weeks, and it's driving everyone scurrying for cover. Even Nicoleta is holed up in her tower. What's new in the southern place we don't mention around you know who?" She nodded sideways at Vlad.

Vlad roared, her face red with rage. She leapt to her feet and started hacking at her throne with her massive broadsword, sending lacquered chunks of carved wood flying.

Greta sighed, then shouted, "you'll have to speak up!"

Sloot would have done, but abject fear kept his voice behind his teeth. The sheer brutality of Vlad's tantrum left him unable to think of any words in any language. He even had trouble managing a whimper in the universal language of fear.

Greta rolled her eyes and waited for Vlad to stop. She did, eventually, once she'd reduced her throne to a stump. She turned and sat upon it, settling back into the nothingward glare she'd been about when they'd arrived.

"She's been like this for weeks," said Greta. "She doesn't sleep. You'd think she'd be happy that I'm alive again, but you'd be wrong."

"I *am* happy you're alive!" shouted Vlad, kicking the remnant of her throne as she stood, sending it flying against the wall where it shattered. She glared at Greta, causing Sloot to fear for her safety. Greta seemed unperturbed. It struck Sloot that destroying one's throne was a strange way to convey happiness, but to be fair, he'd never tried it.

"She won't talk to me about it," Greta continued as if Vlad wasn't there. "Maybe she'll talk to you. You're not one of her subjects, right?"

"Well, er—"

"Good." Greta stood and strode from the dais, leaving her fully intact throne precariously close to a very upset Vlad, who looked as though she'd only just gotten started at the day's furniture annihilation and was keen to hit her quota.

Vlad gnashed her teeth. Sloot heard the vein pulsing in her forehead.

Vlad drew in a breath, gripped her sword, and made a classic "I'm about to scream with bloodlust" face. Sloot cringed.

"Don't you dare!" Vlad and Sloot both turned to see Greta leaning back in through the door with one threatening finger held aloft.

"You need to talk to someone," said Greta, "and not someone whom you can cow into a sniveling 'yes, your Dominance' toady. Don't you dare lay a hand on Sloot!"

Sloot considered reintroducing himself to Greta. He'd shown outstanding aptitude for sniveling toadyism in school.

"No murder, no retribution, not so much as a 'how dare you.' Am I clear?"

She was. Greta didn't have any children that Sloot was aware of, but she spoke with the firm, severe countenance of a mother who would not put up with having to count to two, let alone three. Sloot hazarded a sidelong glance at Vlad, and despite his every expectation, her scowl fell. She nodded almost imperceptibly and shuffled her feet.

Greta left. Sloot was alone with Vlad, prompting him to realize that Igor had disappeared. That didn't bode well. Castle Ulfhaven was dangerous enough without gremlin mischief thrown in.

The hall was silent. Sloot remembered being a ghost in the Hereafter, where time had no meaning. Or rather the passage of time seemed to just … not. Sloot was content to wait, thinking perhaps Vlad would drift off to sleep if they were still for long enough. He'd just started to wonder whether he should teleport away and save them both the awkward silence when a distant sound of falling chandelier gave him an idea where Igor had gotten off to.

"How long?" asked Vlad. She didn't appear to have noticed the chandelier. That was elsewhere in the castle, and by the looks of her, Vlad the Invader was entirely in her own misery.

"Until?"

"Until Greta's dead again." Vlad seemed on the verge of having a non-anger emotion. Sloot was unnerved.

"Er, well, what is she, thirty?"

"Do not play games with me, demon." Vlad should have furrowed her brow and snarled threats at Sloot, or given threats a miss and gone straight into disembowelment. That was the Vlad that Sloot knew and feared. But her eyes were soft, pleading. A wall of sadness. It undoubtedly shared space with murderous rage, but the sadness had the run of the place at present.

"Nicoleta says those who were dead shall die again at the end of all this."

"That's probably true," Sloot admitted.

"I can't bear to watch her die again. Name your price."

"My … price?"

"You're a demon now, aren't you?"

"Well, yes, but—"

"Isn't that what demons do? Bargain with me to spare Greta's life."

"I don't know if I can—"

"The Coolest put you in charge, didn't they?"

"They did, but I don't think that—"

"Then make me an offer! What shall I pledge to you? Gold? Blood? My sword? Take them! Take all of them, just spare Greta!"

Sloot felt an itch. It wasn't a physical one, or he'd have been scratching like mad. It was inside of him somewhere, and it was growing. Like a spleen full of mosquitos. He desperately wanted to deal with Vlad, and not out of charity or friendship.

Greed. That was it. Pure, naked, put-it-on-my-account greed. His demonic instincts urged him to strike a bargain with this mortal, but he had no idea where to begin. He imagined it was like asking a girl to dance. The only people who could manage it must have read some sort of manual, and he hadn't.

"I, uh," Sloot began, but couldn't quite finish. "I want to help, but I don't know how!"

"Find out," Vlad barked. Then she cleared her throat. "Please," she added, her mouth twisting around the unfamiliar word. “I will pay any price.”

“*Any* price?” asked Sloot, his tone going creepy and excited, like that of an ice cream man who lives with his mother. Sloot chalked it up to demonic instinct.

“Any price,” Vlad repeated. “Promise me you’ll find a way.”

“I pr…” Sloot trailed off, thinking of his recent legal expenses. “I’ll find a way.”

UP THE RIVER

Sloot's memory of the day the Dark spilled into the Narrative was fuzzy. He remembered most of the events, but the order in which they happened failed him. For example, he couldn't recall whether he'd promised to visit Roman in prison before or after becoming a demon. The distinction was meaningful. If it was before, he could simply carry on with not having gotten around to it. But if it was after, he didn't dare break his promise. He was already in far too much legal debt.

The outer wall of the Infernal prison complex was nearly as foreboding as the deliveries entrance to Castle Ulfhaven. Sloot got the feeling that it was incidental, which made it all the more impressive. The designers at Castle Ulfhaven had worked very hard to get the foreboding just right.

Sloot sighed as he stared at the great steel door, trying to work up his nerve to knock. The door slot slid open with a bang.

"Crime?" demanded the glowing red eyes from the other side of the door.

"I beg your pardon?"

"Load of good that'll do you. Should've tried it on the judge."

"I haven't seen any judge."

"That's the Infernal justice system for you. Crime?"

"Sorry," said Sloot, "I haven't got any."

"What are you in for?"

"Just visiting."

The glowing red eyes seemed to ponder this for a moment of awkward silence.

"Name?"

"Peril. Sloot Peril."

The slot slammed shut. Sloot waited, unable to think of anything more polite to do. A moment later, it slammed open again.

"You're not on the list."

"I didn't know there was a list," said Sloot.

"You've got to have a list. I mean, what sort of a place would this be otherwise?"

Sloot had heard rumors about prisons in Salzstadt, and then duly reported the people who'd repeated them. Rumors had long been outlawed by the Domnitor, long may he reign, and the official truth was firm on the fact that there were no prisons in Salzstadt. Sure, people were abducted from their homes by men in black in the middle of the night, never to return. But as far as the Ministry of Propaganda was willing to speak on the matter, said abductees weren't being tortured in gulags or anything. Sloot had been given the impression they'd been sent to farms outside Salzstadt to run around in the fresh air.

Nevertheless, Sloot *had* heard the rumors. He imagined that such places, were they to exist, would not be likely to prioritize the maintenance of orderly lists. He then promptly stopped imagining, as it did nothing to soothe his nerves about walking into an Infernal prison.

"Right," said Sloot, "so how does one go about getting on the list?"

The glowing red eyes behind the slot blinked a few times.

"Hang on." The slot slammed shut. Sloot heard indistinct murmuring behind the door, then footsteps leading away. The footsteps returned. There was considerably more murmuring. The slot slammed open.

"We don't suppose you'd be amenable to performing a quest, would you?"

"What sort of quest?"

The slot slammed shut. There was more murmuring, then a shout, then more footsteps approaching the other side of the door. That pattern continued for several minutes until the murmuring became a din. The din split into groups, giving Sloot the impression of subcommittees who each had a great deal of murmuring to get done, and would kindly request that any new topics queue up for the next available subcommittee to take it up for further murmuring, possibly during next quarter's new business.

The murmuring abruptly ceased. There was a loud thunk, and the door creaked slowly open into the darkness beyond. There were several pairs of glowing red eyes within, all looking at Sloot. They stared in silence, which was preferable to bellowing with rage and charging at him with axes, though at least then he'd know where he stood.

The darkness grumbled in frustration. Sloot whimpered in reply.

"Ugh, look, would you just…" The tone of the words left unsaid were clearly agitated. They wanted Sloot to do something, but he wasn't the sort of person to *just*. Sloot Peril was a planner.

An extended pause, an exasperated sigh, and the sound of footsteps. A scaly purple hand reached just out of the darkness and beckoned Sloot with one sharp talon.

Oh, dear, thought Sloot. He was there to visit, but that didn't mean he was prepared go in. He rooted himself and racked his brain for what to do next.

A second scaly purple hand joined the first, and they went palms-together in a classic pleading motion. That only made things worse. Resisting a demonic summons was probably good sense, but refusing a "please" without good cause wasn't in Sloot's wheelhouse. He whimpered and shuffled forward.

Following a demon into darkness was terrifying, but terror gave way to mere confusion once he'd crossed the threshold. The foyer rivalled Gildedhearth—Lord Constantin Hapsgalt's ostentatious estate—for its sheer amount of gold-leafed cherubs employed in fountains, frescoes, and other decor. It was decadent in ways that foyers couldn't manage without a string quartet, thanks in part to the string quartet. A dozen demons staring at him with cannibalistic curiosity took the edge off the splendor, but it was impressive nonetheless.

"Finally," huffed the demon who'd done the beckoning. "Now, what's the big idea, visiting?"

Sloot hadn't been prepared for that. He'd thought "visiting" was self-explanatory. Had he knows it wasn't, he'd have brought charts or something.

"Well," Sloot improvised, "when two people who know each other do not occupy the same place—"

"Uh oh," said a much larger demon, whose recurved tusks tickled the tips of his ears when he talked, "he's clever. Be careful!"

It was an interesting feeling, being the cause of a warning. He was more accustomed to "never mind, it's just Sloot," and aspired no higher than "oh, good, Sloot's here," without sarcasm.

"I wasn't trying to be," Sloot said with all the sincerity he could muster.

"He's going to tell," said a scaly red demon with eight arms, all of which were engaged in cracking knuckles as though Sloot required further intimidation.

No, I won't. That would have been the obvious thing to say.

However, having been raised in the Old Country, Sloot loved telling.

"I wouldn't even know who to tell," he said, basking in the relief of a convenient truth. "Nor would I know what to tell them! You have a lovely foyer, by the way."

"You're either very clever," said the purple demon who'd beckoned him in, "or this is some sort of test. Who sent you? Was it Burbleguts?"

"Sorry, I don't know Burbleguts."

"I told you," said the one with the tusks. "Clever."

"Well, that simply won't do," said a very small and slender demon with a moustache that might have been drawn on with a pencil. He looked like a villain posing as a waiter to poison a politician on a train.

"I assure you I'm not," pleaded Sloot. He was briefly dismayed with the veracity he was able to put behind that, but there was plenty of room in his metaphorical bottle for one more feeling. "Look, I just want to have a conversation with … well, I knew him as Roman Bloodfrenzy, but I'm not sure—"

"You're here for Roman?" the purple demon balked. "You know him from the outside?"

"Er, yes?" Sloot couldn't tell from the demon's expression whether that would be a good or bad thing, but he'd already said as much.

"I love that guy," said a brown puddle of a demon that Sloot had previously thought to be a standard puddle. "He's a legend, Roman."

"He is?"

"Oh, yeah," said eight arms with a huge grin. "Real stand-up guy. Tells it like it is. Sticks it to the man."

"Huh." Sloot was flummoxed. "But isn't that you?"

"What?" Purple was scowling at him now. "What would make you think that we're the man?"

"I mean, you're running the prison, right?"

"Technically."

The conversation that unfolded left Sloot feeling that simple answers were things that happened to other people. He didn't know much about souls, but he reckoned if they'd all been assigned fates on the same day, his karmic alarm clock must have wound down on a very crucial morning. By the time he'd shown up, all of the "carefree strolls through charmed lives" were gone. Even the "quick deaths" shelf had been bare.

Few things in the demonic realm were quite as complicated as the Infernal prison system. The Inferno was home to the absolute worst beings in the universe. Putting a prison in it was the sensible thing to do, with naughtiness lying around in toxic concentrations. The central flaw was staffing.

No one wanted to be the warden. The Inferno was run by bureaucracy, so everyone with a rubber stamp had someone in mind for a cushy job like that. Cushy though it might have been, the only desirable job in Infernal prison was "inmate."

There was status in being branded a threat to the Inferno itself. Do a millennium or two in a place like that, and when you got out you could write your own ticket.

Wardens and guards were goody-two-shoes jobs. You'd be universally reviled, but not in a good way. With "law dog" on your resume, you'd get passed over for an internship as a shovel in the sewage pits.

In proper bureaucratic fashion, the matter was tabled dozens of times. The cells filled up, and there was no one to look after things. Boredom had settled in among the inmates, so they just started doing it themselves.

"Not that we go around admitting to it," stressed Purple. "That's a good way to get your evil credit downgraded, volunteering for things."

"Wait," said Sloot, "I'm confused. So I *don't* have to be on a list?"

"Well, no," said the puddle, "but it makes sense that you would, see?"

"I suppose."

"Hence not being on the list is a problem."

"Big problem," said Tusks with a nod. "It's keeping up appearances."

"For whom?"

"Dunno, but we're not about to find out."

"I'm dreadfully sorry about that," said Sloot. "I don't want to get anyone in trouble."

"Trouble would be fine," said Purple. "It's getting caught in the voluntary performance of law and order that would be a problem."

There was a general murmur of assent among the assembled "guardian inmates," as it were.

"Well, it wouldn't be too much trouble to make a list."

The room burst into laughter.

"Look," said Purple, wiping a tear away from his red eye, "we could get into enough good graces just for letting new inmates in. You know what would happen if we did anything that left a paper trail?"

"No, what?"

Purple shrugged. "Commendations, maybe? I don't want to end up employee of the month, and neither do the lads here. We just started barely lifting a finger around here because it was good for a laugh. *Look at me, I'm the sort of rube who brushes his teeth and pays taxes!* That sort of thing. Make a list? Not on my watch."

"All right," said Sloot. "I'll just go and visit Roman then, shall I?"

"Can't let you do that," said Tusks. "You're not on the list."

"But—"

"We can't just stop doing warden stuff," splashed the Puddle. "We've got to be mad with our modicum of power, right?"

"That makes … well, there's some sense…" Sloot waved his

fingers around as though counting butterflies of logic, all of which refused to light upon whatever was happening here. It didn't make any sense, but he was trying to be polite.

"You could break in," said Pencil Moustache.

"Oh, yeah," Purple nodded. "Why didn't I think of that?"

"Break in," said Sloot. "*Into* prison."

"Happens all the time," said Tusks. "Like we said before, people are really keen to get in."

"I wouldn't know where to begin," said Sloot. "Plus, I'm already in."

"You could be casing the joint!"

"I'm not, though."

"Not with that attitude."

They all stood in silence for a few minutes. Sloot wasn't the breaking-and-entering type, he was the list-making type. He was afraid he was out of options.

"How are you at bribery?" asked Pencil Moustache.

"Oh, that's good," said Purple. "I haven't taken a good bribe in ages."

In the end, it had only cost Sloot a deeply obscure fact that he'd come across in his work for the chaos firm. It had seemed entirely uninteresting at the time, but Tusks had laughed himself breathless to learn that Baelgoroth the Destroyer wore lifts in his shoes.

"Does that make him less than twelve inches?"

"Eleven and a half," said Sloot.

"He can't join the Razing of the Dead if he's less than twelve! There's a cartoon mascot on a sign and everything. 'You must be this tall to raze,' it says. Ha! Follow me."

Sloot hadn't seen Roman since the overflowing of the Dark. As he followed Purple down the long hallway toward the maximum security wing, it occurred to him that he'd probably need something to say when he got there.

How's it going seemed too casual, and *hey, remember when you made a horrible mess of reality in order to win a bet, I ought to punch you in the nose for that* was too direct for Sloot Peril. He got sidetracked into worrying about his tendency to overthink things, so he'd come up with nothing by the time Roman's cell came into view. Roman was smiling at him. It was a predatory smile, one that wondered what wine would pair best with nervous accountants.

"Don't step over the line," said Purple, indicating a line of salt on the floor in front of Roman's cell.

"I don't think I can," Sloot replied.

"There's a good lad." Purple nodded to Roman and left.

"Sloot." His name oozed out of Roman's smile, an unlikely confection of spun sugar and vitriol. "How long has it been?"

"I'd have come to visit sooner," Sloot sniveled, "only I've had a lot of..."

"Yes?"

"Wait a minute." Sloot shook his head. "Why am I afraid of you?"

"Ha!" Roman punched the air. "Good lad! Do you have any idea how long I've been waiting for you to ask me that?"

Sloot didn't like any of the possible answers to that question, until he found one that he did. "You haven't," he said. It would have been very suave of him too, had he not turned it up at the end like a question.

"Wrong," said Roman, "though I could be lying. I'll bet they've told you that I'm quite the liar, haven't they?"

"No, they didn't. There was a puddle that said you were a legend."

"Marvin? Good guy. Drowned loads of people in his day, but if you can look past that, he's a real decent sort."

Sloot worried that his moral compass was demagnetizing. There was a time he'd have been aghast at that, but now he was mildly surprised at best. Becoming a demon changes you, he supposed.

"Nice cell," said Sloot, "looks sturdy. Why'd they do the salt around it?"

"That was my idea," said Roman with a conspiratorial wink. "Marketing. If I'm going to be locked away for the next thousand years, I need to foster an image. Dangerous, yeah? I'm one of the few demons who didn't bribe his way in."

"You're either a mad optimist," said Sloot, having a bit of trouble pronouncing the word, "or you're even cleverer than I thought."

"That makes two of us! Worked it out, have you?"

He had. Sloot was looking at the only guilty demon in the prison. The most malevolent evil, the darkest force of chaos in the Inferno. Even if he wasn't released for another *ten* thousand years, what did it matter? Roman was immortal. He'd while away the millennia in his nicely furnished cell. When he got out, the book deal alone would set him up for aeons to follow.

"The bet with Gwen," said Sloot, nearly in a whisper. "That was never the point, was it? This was!"

"Not *never*, but you're not far off. A lot of work went into making this look easy."

Sloot was shocked at the revelation, but only briefly. He'd not been a demon for long, but Roman was an unknowable enigma. He was ancient in a way that Sloot could barely comprehend, like jokes that somehow become funny when one becomes a father.

"How are things in the Old Country?"

"Oh, they're fine," said Sloot.

Roman winced. "That bad, eh?"

"Well, the dead still walk the streets. The Domnitor, long may he reign, has strategically relocated to Stagralla, the Serpents of the Earth hold sway in his absence, and our place in the Narrative is threatened with annihilation. But swearing doesn't call up goblins anymore, so that's nice."

"Sloot! You just did optimism!"

"What? No, I don't think I did."

"You found a silver lining." Roman grinned with paternal pride. "Demonhood looks good on you. Give it five thousand years, you'll see."

"I doubt it."

"You'll see," Roman reiterated. "I used to be a pessimist too, you know. Went through a phase. But look at me now! It just takes time, is all. Trust me, Roman wasn't built in a day. Now, why don't you tell me what's bothering you?"

Sloot reluctantly told Roman about Vlad and Greta. That dredged up a bit of proper remorse from the old enigma.

"It's too bad," said Roman. "Unfortunate side effect of doing significant works of evil. Sometimes the mortals you like get hurt in the process."

"She wanted to bargain with me," said Sloot, "and I *really* wanted to as well, I just didn't know how."

"Didn't know how? What, did you skip orientation?"

"Orientation was held on the 99th level," said Sloot. "I'm 100th class."

"Ah," said Roman with a nod. "The Coolest really didn't do you any favors, did they?"

Sloot shook his head.

"And Myrtle," said Roman. "Still stuck in the Inferno?"

Sloot nodded.

"Shame. You'll have a whale of a time getting her out through the top."

"Through the top?"

"It's the only way," said Roman, nodding solemnly like a cartwright who'd just quoted his best price. "I'll put someone in touch who can help with Vlad and Greta. And while I'm doing you favors for which you'll be eternally grateful, how much do you know about the Three Bells counting house?"

“Quite a lot, actually,” said Sloot, straightening up in the very grateful manner of one who doesn’t often get to put on airs. “I worked there for most of my life, after all.”

“No, not that one. The other one.”

PERIL-PROOF

In happier days, when Sloot had been a lowly clerk in the Three Bells counting house, he'd never noticed the other counting house directly across the street. It was easily the tallest building in all of Salzstadt and he'd somehow spent years overlooking it. Magical concealment, he surmised. Still, Sloot was baffled that he'd never noticed it.

He thought back to those sixteen-hour glory days he'd spent hunched over ledgers in low light that strained his eyes. When he eventually had to leave, he'd tidy up his desk, walk out the front door, and what did he see? Try as he might, he couldn't recall. It was as if he'd simply convinced himself to look elsewhere.

The sign over the door read *Three Bells Accounting Annex*, clear as day. There were no guards, which made sense. Why guard a door no one could see?

"You should go in," said Igor.

"What?" Sloot jumped. "When did you get here?"

"A proper bard knows when his hero is back in town. Strange, I hadn't noticed this building before I saw you looking at it. Probably a lot of things that could go wrong with the plumbing in a building that size. It would be a shame if we were to go in there and…" Igor trailed off.

"Are you threatening the building?"

"What? No! I'm a bard, not a gremlin. I'll thank you to remember that, Mr. Peril."

"But you just … oh, never mind."

"Go on, then."

"What?"

"Go inside! Have a look around. That's why you're here, isn't it?"

"I don't know," said Sloot. That was true. Roman told him the building was here, but he'd not said what Sloot should do about it. Being somewhere was most of what a building did on any given day. It was the people within that were up to something.

"They're up to no good in there," said Igor. His eyes narrowed in disapproval, or possibly envy.

"You don't know that," Sloot replied.

"Don't I? Look, I don't like to talk about it, but I was an accomplished gremlin before I started doing bardistry. I know mischief when I smell it, and this whole place stinks like it came out a skullduggger's backside."

Sloot conceded that legitimate enterprises didn't go to the trouble of magically obscuring their premises.

"It's probably dangerous, then." Sloot gave the front door the sidelong glance traditionally applied to relatives turning up unannounced, inquiring about the quantity of sofas in one's residence, and offering a suspicious number of assurances that it's "for a few days, tops."

"Says the demon," said Igor, plucking his bit of wire experimentally. "Come on, man, you're immortal! And you should really get on with some heroics soon, if you plan on keeping me around."

"I never—"

"Quick, before you lose your nerve! Don't think, just walk up and open the door!" Seconds later, Sloot was picking himself up off the cobbles and regretting having listened to Igor. Sloot Peril did not take risks, a policy he shouldn't have ignored.

"Hoo hoo HOO!" Igor slapped his knee. In a mildly interesting twist, his knee and hand both managed to become filthier as a result.

"I'm glad someone enjoyed that," Sloot grimaced. He used his tongue to count his teeth, all of which were still there, though a few were wigglier than he remembered.

"You should have seen your face!" Igor gasped between fits of laughter. He stopped for a second to mimic Sloot's expression, which combined the shock of everyone yelling "surprise" at a birthday party with the heart attack brought on by the same. He was only able to hold it for a second before he was in stitches again.

"It must be demon-proof or something," said Sloot with a wince.

"It's you-proof, at any rate."

"Why don't you try it?"

"What, traipse into a strange building without a plan? Only a fool would do that."

Sloot's left hip was numb, which made the walk back to his apartment interesting. Other pedestrians avoided eye contact with him, aside from the walking dead, who sneered and debated whether he was making fun of them. Igor attracted plenty of attention though, as he plucked his wire and worked out a shanty about a hero-trouncing door handle.

It was quiet in the apartment. Too quiet.

"Where's Arthur?" asked Igor.

"No idea," said Sloot with a little grin. The philosopher's mound of blankets had been neatly folded and stacked on the couch. Like most of the pleasant moments that had wandered into Sloot's life over the years, this one showed itself out upon realizing it had wandered into the wrong room. There was a note atop the blankets.

"Off to restart the revolution," Sloot read aloud. "I'll be back when I am. Ha ha, that's a little philosophy joke. I will explain it at length when I return. Your intellectual superior, Dr. Arthur Widdershins, PhD."

Sloot sighed.

"Well, that's good news," said Igor.

"How can you possibly think that?"

"Arthur's off the couch. Hasn't he seemed depressed to you?"

"He's off to start a *rebellion*!" cried Sloot, the last word in a whisper.

"*Revolution*, not rebellion. The note's particular about that." Igor shrugged. "As long as it makes him happy, right?"

"No! I can't have the instigator of a—of *one of those* living in my apartment! It's my duty as a true and loyal subject of the Domnitor, long may he reign, to blow my whistle loud and clear for Uncle to hear!"

"Where's the fun in that?"

Fun. That was just the sort of nonsense for which Sloot had no time. There'd be time for fun after reality had been saved. Possibly. The Coolest had warned Sloot they'd be upset if he did a utopia where the Old Country used to be. When he was done, everybody will have to have gotten back to work. Sloot couldn't see how that differed from a utopia, but accepted that other people—people with less hyperactive work ethics—might disagree.

"I'll deal with Arthur when he returns," said Sloot. "Just make sure he doesn't fill the place up with revolutionaries, will you?"

"You can count on me," said Igor, who attempted a ramrod posture and smart salute, but failed at both.

Sloot took his ledger down from the shelf, stood in the circle, chanted and gestured, and found himself standing on the sidewalk in Salzstadt Before. He drew in a deep breath, savoring the musty, humid air, wet goblin stench and all. He permitted himself a moment to look up to the cloudy grey sky and reminisce about better times. Well, simpler times, anyway. Actually, if he were being entirely honest, he'd had very little to reminisce about in those days. That was depressing, so he resolved to avoid complete honesty with himself in future reminiscence.

Sloot went dim by activating Sarko's Banality and walked to the counting house, or rather the accounting *annex*, now that he knew about it. There it was, clear as Old Country water wasn't. He leaned on a lamp post across the street, watching passersby suddenly become interested in something else just before they looked toward the towering building.

Sloot was no good with magic, his thought processes being too deeply rooted in the very real concepts of mathematics. That was his theory anyway. It was wrong, but burdening Sloot with the knowledge that he simply wasn't creative enough for magical thinking wouldn't have helped. Regardless, that was why he had the circle. It did the magic bits for him.

His Sigil of the Some-Seeing Eye—Sigils of the All-Seeing Eye being far more expensive—showed him that there was indeed an anti-demon hex on the door handle. Fortunately, his Quadricle of Nullification was able to turn it off long enough for him to slip inside.

The counting house had always bustled with accountants, but it was nothing compared to the annex. Sloot imagined there must have been someone whose only responsibility was maintaining an accurate count of supervisors in the building at any given time. That person's assistant was probably horribly overworked.

It was easy to tell who the supervisors were. They stalked between the endless rows of desks, propelled by their senses of entitlement and modicums of power that they multiplied exponentially.

They hadn't been asked to do that, or even permitted. They'd shown initiative, which Sloot understood to be a particular brand of toadying that came easily to people who were bad at their jobs. Those who can't will make very sure that those who can *do*. That was the gist of it.

"It's not going to work," said one supervisor to another, in the confident tone of the very rarest of supervisors: one promoted due to merit. One who would much rather have had her sleeves rolled up in the toil of an honest day's work but was made to do a terrible job of leading other people instead.

"It'll be fine," said the more traditional supervisor, who had gotten his job the old-fashioned way: being related to a vice president. He was a squat, balding man, and she a very tall woman half his age. Their difference in height placed her bosom at his eye level, which necessitated competition-level eye contact to avoid conversations with Human Resources.

They were gesturing at a stack of papers, each willing the other to pick it up. Sloot had a hard time shaking the feeling that there was something familiar about the papers.

"It won't be fine. I'm telling you, no one is going to believe this."

"I've been here a long time," the man said in a classic deflectory move. "Just walk it across the street, scowl quite a bit, and say, 'rush this through, will you, you-know-who wants it recorded posthaste.' They'll barely look at it."

"Who is you-know-who?"

"Doesn't matter," he said with a wink. "They'll know, and it will light a fire under them."

"Sounds like you've got a handle on it, then," she said with a smirk.

"Well," he wheedled, "I've not been appointed junior sub-executive supervisor *pro tempore* for nothing, right? It's lucky for you that I'm here to show you the path your first time out."

As their game of coward's chess continued, Sloot got a better look at the top page of the papers. He shuddered at the author's name: Vasily Pritygud.

This was the report. *The* report which could have exposed the Hapsgalts' poverty a long time ago! The one that he "corrected," which got him promoted, which got him roped into spying for Carpathia, which got him killed ... there were several more *whiches* queued up, most of them horrible, and all of them stemming from this stack of papers. As the nascent bureaucrats tried to out-maneuver each other, Sloot's mind worked feverishly. He had to act fast.

Wait a minute, Sloot thought, *no, I don't.*

This was Salzstadt Before! All of this had already happened. He could return to the present, fill the tub, and have a long, hot soak while he thought it over. Well, that was mostly true. The "tub" in his apartment was a leaky bucket with a sliver of soap at the bottom, but it had probably collected enough rainwater on the ledge for a frigid wash-up. Regardless, he didn't have to *act fast.*

He went for a walk in Salzstadt Before, taking in the city as it was when he'd been happy. Well, not happy, perhaps, but at least he'd known what to fear in those days, and he wasn't an agent of any of it. Up until the morning he'd forgotten his mother's watch, it had all been black and white. He had proper fears of demons, Carpathians, heretics, and ink wells without regulation bases, which were prone to tipping over. His loyalty to the Domnitor, long may he reign, had been unwavering. He knew that Uncle was protecting him from miscreants lurking in shadows by lurking one shadow deeper, and anyone they dragged off in the night was guilty of something awful.

Now he *was* a demon, and a Carpathian to boot. Moreover, he was seriously considering a coup to overthrow the Domnitor, long may he reign! Whose side was Uncle really on? It was enough to make him want to say a swear word. He didn't, but it would have felt super. He was sure of it.

He thought through the facts. He'd been late to work, corrected a vastly inaccurate report, and … wait a minute. Was the report inaccurate? He'd thought so. He'd been sure of it. He'd been keeping the books for the Three Bells Shipping Company for decades, and the contents of the report had so vastly differed from everything he'd known to be true that he'd never questioned it. What's more, it had been written by Vasily Pritygud. Sloot was constantly correcting Vasily's work in those days. The fact that he'd written it was more indicative of errors than the errors themselves.

He entertained a harrowing thought: what if Vasily had been right all along?

Sloot returned to the annex and slipped inside. With all the bustle in the accounting pool, it was easier for him to cling to the ceiling and read over shoulders. Right away he saw several glaring inconsistencies, like salt imports. In the thousand years since its founding, Salzstadt had never imported a single grain of salt. It didn't have to. It sat atop a salt mine so large it was embarrassing, really. Salt was the literal and financial foundation of the Old Country.

Sloot remained in the annex for several days during which several shifts changed, but the desks were never empty. It required a lot of work, that much deception. By the time Sloot had seen enough to understand the entire picture, he was on the verge of a nervous breakdown. Sloot had spent most of his life on said verge, from when he'd started teething and his mother had given him the "life is pain" speech, which would also serve as his lullaby from that point forward. Teetering just over the verge then, with his toes hanging off in the breeze.

If the legitimate operation in the counting house was a glass of water, the shadow operation in the annex was the ocean, several lakes, and most of the world's rivers. And it had been raining heavily for decades. It had taken a colossal torrent of creative lying to present Sloot and his coworkers with the fabricated version of reality from which they'd worked for so long. It was so utterly false it had gone all the way around and become a sort of alternative truth in its own right.

The silver lining was that Sloot knew where he was with panic attacks. He'd need to hydrate and stretch before this one, because it was going to be a doozy. It was the once-in-a-lifetime, my-entire-life-has-been-a-lie sort of revelation that warm milk and a nap were woefully underqualified to handle.

He'd been working from cooked books for his entire career! He'd spent his life laundering deception! Vasily had been trying to reveal the truth, and Sloot had been obscuring it!

What *was* the truth, then? Sloot imagined the Serpents of the Earth were somehow at the bottom of it, an elaborate ruse to fund their nefarious schemes. What was he to do? There was no unravelling the lie in theory. It had more weight than the truth now. It was more believable. For better or for worse—almost assuredly worse—he had to expose the lie and let the truth unfold.

ECONOMY OF TRUTH

"You should light the counting house on fire," said Igor, with the casual tone of a husband showing favor for one of the two dresses his wife was holding. The difference was that Igor seemed to understand that his words had consequences.

"How would that solve anything?" Sloot instantly regretted asking. Even if Igor had a solid rationale, Sloot could never bring himself to wage malfeasance upon the counting house. It was sanctified ground as far as he was concerned.

"Can't read reports in a counting house that doesn't exist."

"But I want them to read the report. The right one."

"Oh." Igor chewed a fingernail in thought, which would have been significantly less off-putting had it been one of his own.

"It's like the universe was trying to correct itself by making me forget the watch," said Sloot. He'd barely made it to work in time to make his corrections, thanks to having left his mother's watch at home.

"It's like you teetered on the edge of causality," said Igor, his eyes sparkling. No, not sparkling. More like the burbling gas of a corpse decomposing in a bog. Still, he looked interested.

"I suppose," said Sloot. "Perhaps I just need to give my former self a push."

Igor giggled.

"What's got into you?"

"Just picturing a poorly placed teacup on a table," Igor replied. "One good nudge, and *crash!* Sharp, wet bits of porcelain in the carpet. You'll be finding slivers of that in your foot for years."

"And lighting the counting house on fire, that's a nudge?"

Igor shrugged, then cackled.

In the end, Sloot settled for gossip. He returned to Salzstadt Before, waited until his former self was in the butcher shop line to get into his own apartment, got into the line a few heads back, and struck up a conversation.

"Have you heard?" he asked in the high, gravelly voice that came with his old gran disguise, courtesy of Katzlewurm's Mark of Obfuscation orbiting his circle's upper quadrants. "They found a crack in the wall!"

"What? Where?" The old gramp in front of him turned around.

"Dunno," said Granny Sloot, "but isn't it awful? I mean, I'm sure the Domnitor's best are looking into it, long may he reign."

"Long may he reign," came a dutiful chorus from those within earshot, including a positively frazzled Sloot Before.

"I just hope they fix it soon," Granny Sloot continued. "I mean, I have no reason to expect it's big enough for a filthy Carpathian cannibal to slip through, but…"

"But what? Speculate, woman!"

"Well, there's really no way of knowing where it is, or how big. Oh, dear, is that the time? I must be off; I'll have to buy my cutlets tomorrow."

That had done it. Sloot used the eyes in the back of his head—

courtesy of the Some-Seeing Eye—to see his former self fidget momentarily before leaving the line and sprinting toward the wall. He made a complicated gesture that probably would have hailed a dozen coaches and reappeared in the present.

"What was that?" asked Igor, several flies fleeing his gaping mouth.

"I'm sorry?"

"The thing you just did," said Igor. "It's causing a stir."

"What do you…?" Sloot began, then trailed off. The changes were subtle at first. New events shifted the columns of his memory. He remembered the chill that had washed over him that day. Fear had consumed him, gotten into his blood and chilled it, which would have been a hit at vampire bars if it hadn't been a metaphor.

He hadn't gone to work that day. He'd spent it walking the entirety of the wall, scanning for cracks, certain he'd end up face-to-face with a cannibal at any moment, but not in the traditional sense. According to the Ministry of Foreign Speculation, Carpathian cannibals were known to wear the faces of their victims. The ministry offered no evidence to support their claims, not that Sloot needed any.

Changes to the past didn't roll up to the present all at once. A big change was like a distillery explosion. Anything near the center is vaporized before it knew what happened, while anyone at the farthest reach of the blast feels uncomfortably warm for a moment and wonders what that mild rumbling was. They might not know until the price of whiskey goes up. Grans of the Old Country have rioted for less.

The next half hour or so flowed like mud through the rusty drain of Sloot's memory. Occasional glops of revised history burbled up, pooling into a feculent swamp of regret for having done the right thing, which was confusing at best.

"Are you all right?" Igor's voice sounded very far away, so at least there was that. It was a pity he didn't *smell* very far away. Sloot was still in his apartment, but like his mind, it was muddy and dark. When had it gotten so dark? He slogged through the dim and dank, fumbling for his desk, or maybe the couch.

"Hey now," said Willie, "let's keep it platonic, shall we?"

"Sorry, m'lord, I only meant to ... Willie?"

Light slowly returned to the world, causing Sloot to fervently wish it hadn't. His tiny apartment felt cramped when it had only been him, Igor, and Arthur. The addition of Willie Hapsgalt, his father Constantin, and old Nan in a false beard made matters significantly worse.

"Nan, is that you?" asked Sloot.

"What?" barked Constantin. "What did he say?"

"He was talking to me," Nan shouted into the little brass horn Constantin held to his ear. Her voice was lower than it had been before, in a belabored affectation of masculinity which, Sloot had to admit, was more boisterous than his own.

"It sounded like someone said 'Nan,'" Constantin growled.

"He did—" Willie began.

"*Dunt*," Nan finished. "He didn't! He clearly said 'Man,' because he was talking to me." She stared swords at Sloot, which was like daggers, only worse.

"Er, yes," stammered Sloot. "Er, *Man*, would you mind explaining why the Lords Hapsgalt are in hammocks in my living room?"

"I like to think of it as *my* living room," said Willie. "After all, I live in it. Right, Dad?"

"What?" shouted Constantin.

"I don't have time to answer ridiculous questions," grumbled Nan, or Man, as the case may be. She adjusted the hooks that suspended the crocheted beard from her ears, sat in a rocking chair that Sloot didn't remember having dragged from a refuse heap, and turned to glare blankly at the wall.

Sloot was about to press the issue as politely as possible when the mud swirled through his thoughts again. The three of them had come to live with Sloot after the total collapse of the economy.

"After the *what*?" Sloot squeaked in alarm. Then he did the worst thing a nervous accountant could do under the circumstances. He wondered about his retirement savings. Cold blood thundered in his ears. His vision swam and returned to black. Sloot was so overwhelmed with the horror of his financial position that he didn't feel himself collapse.

As it turned out, this was the best thing that could have happened. Updates to reality are severely hindered by conscious thought, which clings to the events of the now-defunct past. As with most things in life, a good night's sleep would work wonders for sorting it out. Unfortunately for Sloot, he'd never had a good night's sleep in his life, or subsequently. He spent several hours moaning and twitching on the floor, like a dog dreaming of rabbits. Only the rabbits decided they'd had enough of the dog, formed a gang, and acquired several lengths of lead pipe with which they intended to stand their ground.

When Sloot awoke, everyone else in the apartment was snoring a dreadful chorus. It was the middle of the night, and Sloot's head was pounding to the tune of several months' worth of history having reconciled in his brain.

When Sloot didn't turn up to work, the Pritygud report had landed on Mrs. Knife's desk in its unaltered state. Sloot hadn't known Mrs. Knife to be careless, but trust in her own ruthlessness had gotten the better of her. She was so certain the accounting drones would do their jobs she hadn't bothered checking the work.

Following the suppression of a panic by the Domnitor's shock troops, long may he reign, a platoon of financial regulators was sent to undertake the unthinkable: count the Hapsgalts' fortune. When they opened the vault, the task proved horrifyingly simple.

There was nothing. Neither glint of copper nor gleam of gold, not even a scrap of paper insinuating that precious metals may have resided there at some point.

The next panic was not so easily suppressed. The only people not panicking for their livelihoods were the ones selling pitchforks and torches. Sloot's mind reeled with the specifics, but the long-and-short of it was that new swear words were invented to describe just how bad things got.

The collapse of the economy manifested in a very literal sense when Keinherumlungern Square, which was directly above the Hapsgalt vaults, collapsed under the weight of the protesters into the vast chasm where the bulk of the world's gold should have been.

"Oh, dear," Sloot whimpered. He looked around in the desperate hope of finding a distraction but came up empty. Nan and the Lords Hapsgalt swayed gently in their hammocks, rumbling with the noisome snores of the ludicrously wealthy. They were distant cousins of the snores of the proletariat, only louder and more aggressive. They insinuated that anyone thinking of nudging them had just better watch it.

Their servants had quit and their estates had been overrun by the mob. The discovery of Willie's closets had given the rioters a sartorial edge, namely those whose proportions resembled lollipops proficient with high-heeled shoes.

But the Hapsgalts' woes didn't end there. The once-powerful family lost control of the Three Bells Shipping Company. That was where Sloot's woes worsened as well, because Mrs. Knife was running the Three Bells now.

Mrs. Knife! How was that possible? He'd seen with his own eyes when the Coolest made the goblins disappear into the Dark. Mrs. Knife was their queen, hadn't she gone with them? His eyes darted back and forth like a conductor's baton, the tarantella of his panic quickening as new memories caught up with him.

Mrs. Knife was not, in fact, locked away in the Dark with her goblins. However she'd ended up as head of the Three Bells, Sloot had to face the ghastly fact that she was running the show, and Constantin was berthed in a hammock in Sloot's living room, the very model of senility.

That was worrisome on its own merit. Sloot had always known Constantin to be a hale and ruddy man, the very picture of health and virility. He'd started to slide into the indignities of old age while they were ghosts in the Hereafter, and now seemed to have gone into free-fall since his return to the mortal coil. Despite all of the old man's cruelty, avarice, and wickedness, Sloot felt a pang of sympathy for him. He assumed that Constantin's former position as Eye of the Serpent afforded him some magical boons that had long since faded.

The Eye of the Serpent was the living leader of the Serpents of the Earth. When an Eye passed away, he or she would become the Soul of the Serpent, the cult's leader on the other side of the veil.

There was another troubling crouton in the salad of Sloot's discontent. Mrs. Knife was probably still the Eye of the Serpent. That was a lot of power in the hands of a raving lunatic. Not to be confused with the Domnitor, long may he reign, who was far too despotic to put up with being called a lunatic.

This is funny, thought Sloot. He'd done what he'd set out to do, destroyed the global economy in the name of repairing reality, and yet it didn't seem very "repaired." If anything, it had gotten worse. The smell of the city wafted into the apartment through the still-broken window, leaving no doubt that the dead were still walking the streets.

Furthermore, Sloot was still a demon! If he'd done his job, shouldn't he have been corrected back into his mortal life? Never promoted to Willie's financier? He should be working for reduced wages in the counting house, living the life of a loyal salt, blissfully unaware of his Carpathian heritage.

This had just been a single step in the right direction, then. Still a lot of work to do.

A horribly familiar twanging roused Sloot from his reverie.

The economy was doing just fine, Igor crooned,

Until young Peril happened by,

"Knock it off!" shouted Nan.

He couldn't leave well enough alone,

Now everyone is totally oof!

"Totally oof?" Sloot puzzled. He turned to see Igor and Nan's boot sliding to a stop along the far wall, which was not far away, given the size of the room.

"I warned you," said Nan. "And I've got another."

"No, you didn't," said Igor. "I'm sure I'd remember someone saying, 'knock it off, *or I'll throw my boot at you.*'"

Nan held her other boot aloft in silent threat. Igor threw up his hands either because he didn't want to get hit again, or because absconding with one shoe was the more efficient means of vexing his mark. It may have been both.

"Come on, Igor," said Sloot. "They could use some sleep, and I could use a drink."

DEALING WITH DEMONS

Sloot was baffled by the concept of Infernal Prohibition, but only until he thought about it. That was the problem with hearing new concepts: you didn't have time to think.

Infernal Prohibition made sense. Drinking was a vice, and permission takes all the fun out of vices. Laws forbidding demons' drinking had been the work of liquor lobbyists. Even Sloot, who'd sooner break his own legs than the law, saw the allure in getting away with something naughty. He could have gone for a drink in a mortal bar, but Igor insisted, and he knew the secret phrase.

"I'm not a copper," Igor recited into the little panel in the door, which slid shut. The door opened and they walked into the dark, smoky establishment which, like everything else of an Infernal nature, smelled just a bit like brimstone.

"You have to tell them if you're a copper," Igor explained as he climbed up onto a stool next to Sloot.

"Some sort of truth compulsion spell?" asked Sloot. He'd heard tales of Uncle saying just about anything to get into the homes of suspected heretics. Most of the time it was "look what you've gone and made me do," as agents swarmed over a freshly kicked-in door. That would be followed by "please stop resisting," and ultimately "look what you've gone and made me do" again.

Still, there were agents of Uncle who were less strong of leg than others, who had to sweet-talk their way in by saying "we've found your dog," or "you've won the lottery," or in one case that actually worked, "this dog who's just won the lottery says he belongs to you."

Igor shook his head. "Demon coppers drink for free."

"So it's not so much a secret phrase as whether you're a copper or not?"

"Pretty much," said Igor. He took a sip of the drink that was set in front of him. "Half the demons in here are coppers."

"What?" Sloot did his impression of a cornered animal and considered making a run for it.

"Would you relax? They're just here for the free drinks. They almost never raid the place."

"Almost never?"

Igor shrugged and sipped his drink. Sloot started hyperventilating but was interrupted by the smell of an upscale brothel dipped in honey.

"If a drink doesn't relax you," came a sultry voice from behind him, "I've got other ideas."

The hairs on Sloot's neck stood up. He spun around on his stool to see Gwen standing inches from him. The love demon looked different from the last time they'd met, but it was definitely her. She was pink all over like candy floss, and judging from her attire, she'd either just returned from the beach, or was on her way there. Her jet-black hair flowed gently in a breeze that Sloot couldn't feel, and her alluring sheen of sweat smelled like cinnamon.

"Gwen," said Sloot. He cleared his throat. "Um, good to er … see you." He was pointedly doing everything in his power to avoid seeing so much of her, and failing miserably. Gwen was either intentionally shifting from one sultry pose to another, or her swimsuit was having trouble staying on.

"Sloot," Gwen cooed, "how long has it been?"

"I have a girlfriend!" Sloot yelped.

"I meant since we last saw each other." Gwen winked, clearly reveling in Sloot's discomfort. They'd met under unusual circumstances, or at least Sloot hoped that they counted as unusual. He assumed the Coolest didn't intervene in the imminent destruction of reality on a regular basis. Roman's wager with Gwen had been the precursor to that occasion.

"W-well," Sloot stammered, "quite a long, er, in fact … well, not *long*, I didn't mean to imply that, er, well, you know how it is."

Sloot had plenty more awkward and non-committal blathering where that came from, but was interrupted by a familiar twanging.

Along came a bosomful maid,
Whose looks made Sloot Peril afraid,

"I'm fairly certain 'bosomful' isn't a word," said Sloot, diving toward the nearest possible distraction.

She could turn his thick head,
If he took her to bed,
It would be his first time, by the way.

Gwen smiled at Sloot in delight. "Would it, really?"

"No!" blurted Sloot.

"Oooh," Gwen cooed, placing her hands on Sloot's scrawny thighs and leaning in closer. "A man who knows how to please his lover. I like that. I need to confess something to you."

Sloot inhaled sharply as Gwen's pouty lips grazed his ear. He caught a whiff of vanilla in her dark tresses.

He wasn't sure how much time had passed when he awoke. Gwen gave a delighted giggle as he climbed back onto his stool.

"We'll try again another time," she said with a wink.

"Good idea," said Igor, "make him faint again. We can have another round on Sloot."

"What?" Sloot glanced around to see several demons smiling and raising their glasses to him. He briefly enjoyed the novel popularity and dared to hope that the drinks were reasonably priced … in an Infernal bar. He groaned and shook his head.

"Besides," Gwen continued, "our inevitable tryst is only my second reason for coming here to find you."

"Inevitable? I don't—wait, how did you know I'd be here? I didn't even know. Igor dragged me here."

"Not literally," said Igor with a pang of regret.

"Let's just say I make it my business to know what demons want." Gwen spoke slowly, in husky velvet tones that were accustomed to getting their way.

"I can't imagine what your first reason might have been," Sloot said truthfully. He didn't have much of an imagination.

"A little bird told me you're trying to spice up a romance. I thought we could do business."

"Really?" Sloot was wary of trusting the libidinous love demon, but his best intentions were left in the cold. His mind turned to Myrtle. "But she's banished to the lowest circle of the Inferno, I hardly see how we can—"

"Oh, not *you*," said Gwen. "You think I'm that eager to drive you into the arms of another woman? We can discuss my price for that another time." She looked Sloot up and down the way ranchers appraise livestock at auction. She licked her lips. Sloot gripped the edge of the bar and managed to remain conscious.

"I was referring to Vlad the Invader."

"Vlad and Greta?" The little bird must have been Roman. Sloot hadn't imagined that he and Gwen would be on speaking terms in the wake of their thousand-year wager. There was an adage about "strange bedfellows" that fit the occasion, much to Sloot's chagrin.

"They make a cute couple, don't they?" Gwen shifted in her seat, causing Sloot to wonder whether someone had turned up the thermostat. "What's the story there?"

Over the course of the next few drinks, Sloot told Gwen the whole tragic story. Vlad had watched Mrs. Knife slit Greta's throat, the first stroke of the battle that resulted in the Dark spilling into the Narrative. The Coolest brought Greta back to life, but it was probably only temporary. By the time Sloot was finished with his work, assuming he was successful in repairing the Narrative, Greta would be dead again and Vlad still alive to mourn her.

"That does check a lot of boxes," said Gwen. She dabbed her eyes with a lace hanky. Sloot turned away with spinal injury force as Gwen seductively tucked the hanky away in one of very few places her scandalous outfit provided. "But I've got to know, are the two of them serious?"

"That's love demons for you," said Igor confidentially, sitting on Sloot's other side. "Insatiable."

"I'm not asking for myself," Gwen retorted. "Look, times are tough, and I need a job that's really going to boost my numbers."

"They're definitely serious," said Sloot. "As much in love as anyone I've ever known."

"You're *sure*?" Gwen leaned in, her eyes searching Sloot's for sincerity. His vision swam. Even if he'd been capable of lying under normal circumstances, he'd certainly not have been this time.

"Absolutely."

PRIVILEGES REVOKED

Gwen promised to drop in on Vlad. Solving the romantic woes of monarchs was very high-profile work for love demons, and she said it was an ideal opportunity to prove Roman wrong and win the wager.

That, of course, was music to Sloot's ears, much like his erstwhile bard's twanging was not. If Gwen could prove Roman wrong she could get their wager declared a draw. Then perhaps Sloot could prevent Roman having to divulge his essential secret, and the paradox could be avoided! He'd still have a lot of work to do on amending the Narrative, but the hard part would be done.

At last, some good news! He only wished he could share it with Myrtle, who was still banished to the 99th circle of the Inferno. He felt a pang of guilt over that. Mending the Narrative may have been his mission from the Coolest, but Myrtle was his girlfriend. Rescuing her was the most important thing to him, and he'd done next to nothing about it thus far.

His work for the chaos firm got him provisional access to the 98th circle only. Perhaps he could sneak down a stairwell or something? It sounded an awful lot like breaking a rule, but he was fairly certain he'd be able to pass for befuddled and lost if he was caught. He figured there was no harm in finding a stairwell and taking it from there.

Unfortunately for Sloot, he never managed to get close enough to find out. The instant he teleported into the lobby of the Hall of Records, he found himself somewhere considerably smaller. It was a bottle a few inches in circumference, which left no space for Sloot to do things like breathe, move, or feel his feet.

Not being able to breathe was the worst part, not that demons needed to. He'd just been doing it for so long it had become a habit. Technically, the same can be said of mortals, but only insofar as continuing to live may also be considered a habit.

An imp delivered the bottle to a shelf next to dozens of similar bottles, in a stack of similar shelves, next to innumerable rows of similar stacks. One of Sloot's eyes was positioned so that he could look out at the general enormity of the place. His other eye was more internally oriented, giving him a much closer look at his tonsils than he'd ever cared to achieve.

At least one of his eyes had a view. That was what passed for good fortune in this place, then. Possibly. Sloot surmised that he was one of hundreds of millions of bottled demons awaiting … what? Something? Perhaps nothing. It might have been better to be bound entirely in darkness and silence. At least then he'd be alone with his thoughts. There wasn't room in the bottle to think about much more than his elbow, which was jammed into his brain.

Infernal time ticked away. Every few months, an imp would flutter by on tiny wings and leave a jar on a shelf or take one away. Decades passed before one of them came for Sloot's bottle and deposited him in a court room.

He could see that people were talking, but he couldn't hear anything. It had been some eighty years since he'd heard anything, his ears being crammed up against something he'd spent a great deal of time hoping was his shoulder.

He recognized Judge Drenched-In-Blood straight away. He was the heavily armored orcish demigod with the huge hammer and the powdered wig. He used said hammer to gesture in Sloot's bottle's direction. Something that looked like a swarm of black flies came toward Sloot, picked up his bottle, and dropped it unceremoniously on the floor.

Nearly a century of cramped muscles cried out in simultaneous relief and agony. The air on his face, the roar of flames in his ears, and the smell of anything other than his own armpits thanks to unfortunate nasal placement assaulted him all at once.

"Thank you, Bailiff," said the judge. "Now, how does the defendant plead?"

Sloot looked around as his body started to untangle itself. He was meant to be standing in a witness box, and hastened to make his crumpled form do just that. A team of attorneys sat at a table behind him to the right, and there was an empty table behind him to the left. The team of attorneys must have been the prosecution. They were glowering at him in a pointedly you-don't-owe-us-any-money sort of way.

The judge roared and brought his hammer down on the corner of his bench in frustration. Chunks flew around the courtroom, one narrowly missing Sloot. That was unlucky. He'd love to have been rendered unconscious just then.

"Plead, Peril! I don't have all day!"

"I beg your pardon, your Dishonor. May I hear the charges?"

The table of attorneys groaned in unison.

"Ugh, fine," said the Judge. "Bailiff?"

"One count of impersonating a demon of a higher class," buzzed the swarm of flies. "One count of practicing chaos without a license, one count of abusing access to the Hall of Records for personal gain, and 375,496 counts of not kicking stray dogs."

"Not kicking?"

"Is that a typo?" demanded the judge. "It can't be right. He'd have had to go his entire life without ever having once kicked a stray dog."

"Er, that's right, your Dishonor."

The attorneys broke into a round of applause.

"He admitted it!" rejoiced the lead prosecutor. "That counts as a guilty plea, we win!"

"No, wait!" Sloot panicked.

"So you *have* kicked a stray dog?"

"Well, no, but—"

"The defendant has plead guilty. How do you plead on the other charges?"

Sloot said nothing. It was a solid strategy that had served him well in the past. He was guilty, of course, but he didn't see why he should be convicted for it.

"Ugh, he's filibustering," said the lead prosecutor.

Judge Drenched-In-Blood howled with fury and sent his hammer spinning toward the back of the courtroom. It collided with an intern from the intern's perspective. According to everyone else it didn't pause in making a gory stain of him as it continued toward the door it smashed. It didn't pause then, either.

"Not in my court!" shouted the judge. He gestured toward the hammer. It returned to him coated in blood, splinters, and interestingly enough, chocolate sprinkles.

"Am I not entitled to an attorney?" asked Sloot.

The hammer lurched slightly in Sloot's direction, as though it were trying to leap from Judge Drenched-In-Blood's hand and bring its own brand of justice—or whatever they were getting on with in the Infernal Courts—down upon Sloot's head. The judge sneered and leaned toward Sloot.

"That's the problem with your generation," the judge growled, "whichever one you're in. You're entitled to things!" He put the back of his hand against his forehead in mockery. "I want to know what I'm being charged with! I'm entitled to an attorney! You burned my village for no good reason! If you didn't hire an attorney, you're on your own."

Sloot's mind raced. He'd done a bit of clerking for a chaos firm, but he was as capable of defending himself in court as he was of throwing a ball such that another person might catch it.

"Witnesses!" blurted Sloot. "Does the prosecution have any witnesses?"

The lights in the room dimmed. Sloot could hear the blood pulsing through the vein in the judge's forehead.

"Fine," growled the judge between grinding teeth, "call your first witness."

"The prosecution calls Roger Bannister."

Sloot's blood ran cold. The doors, had they not just been destroyed, would have swung open dramatically. A slender man in a tasteful suit ambled in, took a seat on the witness stand, and smirked at Sloot. It was a predatory smirk. It took its time sizing Sloot up, considering which bits of him to use in making a sauce to pour over his more slow-roastable bits.

"State your name for the record," buzzed the bailiff.

"Roger Bannister," said the real Roger Bannister in a reedy tenor that could have cut glass.

Sloot wanted to scream, so he did. It was a high-pitched number with several encores, which did nothing for any outdated notions of masculinity that might have been present.

"Bailiff, restrain the accused!"

While Sloot strongly objected to his mouth playing host to a swarm of stinging black flies, he had to admit it was an effective tactic. He writhed on the floor as quietly as possible, thinking through an apology for his outburst and wondering whether an eternity in this condition might be preferable to the outcome of the trial.

"Mr. Bannister," the bailiff continued, "do you promise to tell something approximating a feasible semblance of the truth, so help you, Very Long List of Princes and Major Nobility of the Inferno?"

Said list was on display in the main lobby of the Courts of Chaos. At one time it was recited in full by every witness to take the stand, but the practice was abbreviated when several Infernal princes complained they were getting headaches from the honorifics echoing in the aether.

"As far as you know," said Roger in the obligatory response.

"You may proceed," the judge nodded to the lead prosecutor.

"Thank you, your Dishonor," she replied. "Mr. Bannister, are you a notorious assassin on retainer with the Serpents of the Earth?"

"That's the rumor," said Roger with a wink. A polite chuckle made its way through the crowd.

"And are you a clerk with the chaos firm of Winkus, Ordo, and Mirgazhandinuxulluminixighanduminophizio?"

"No, no," Roger grinned with the easy humor of a hammer man in an abattoir. "I only have the one alleged occupation."

"And do you recognize the accused?"

The stinging flies worked their way deeper into Sloot's throat as Roger produced a pair of spectacles from his jacket. He put them on reverentially, cleared his throat, and craned his neck to look at Sloot.

"I can't say that I do," said Roger after a moment. He removed the spectacles and returned them to his jacket.

"Well, that's confusing," said the prosecutor. She strolled thoughtfully around the courtroom, her cloven hooves clacking against the polished obsidian floor. "Are you sure that you've never met him?"

"To the best of my recollection," said Roger.

"Then it's unlikely that you ever aided or encouraged the accused in using your identity for any sinister or deviant purpose?"

"Alas, no," said Roger. "He must have done something awful with it to land himself here, and I'd truly love to take the credit, but I cannot."

"Thank you, Mr. Bannister. No further questions, your Dishonor."

"Your witness, Mr. Peril."

Had anyone present wondered what sound an esophagus full of stinging black flies would make, Sloot put the question to rest for them.

The judge sighed. "Bailiff?"

Swarms didn't fully synchronize their movements. It was several minutes before Sloot was able to hack up the last of the bailiff.

"In your own time, Mr. Peril." The judge's words may have been patient, but the roar in which they were delivered were not.

Sloot hacked and coughed, buying himself time to think of something. Anything, really. What could he possibly say to the assassin whose identity he'd stolen twice? It had been an accident both times, but he doubted that would count for much.

"Mr. Bannister," Sloot croaked. "Are you a demon?"

"Objection," said Roger.

"On what grounds?"

"I don't want to answer that."

"Sustained," said the judge. He pounded his hammer on top of his bench. "Mr. Peril, you are ordered to stick to questions that Mr. Bannister feels like answering."

"What? That's not fair!"

The court erupted in laughter. Gouts of flame and bile shot into the air from the noses of a fire drake and pestilence lizard respectively, who were seated in the back row of the gallery.

"Thanks for that," said the judge. He wiped away a mirthful tear. He turned suddenly dour again and slammed his hammer down. "Now, no more joking around! Continue the questioning!"

"Er, yes, your Dishonor. Mr. Bannister, er … would you say that you're good at your job?"

"Objection," said Roger, his eyes flashing with murderous intent. "I wouldn't want to speculate."

"Sustained. I'm warning you, Peril!"

Sloot paused just as he was about to protest. A memory was coming back to him. An unpleasant one, but it might be useful. He was clerking for the chaos firm, digging up some dirt on a middle management demon 67th class. He'd come across a precedent clearly stating that non-demonic attendees of a trial could be compelled to serve the first demon who called dibs. Since Mr. Bannister had refused to declare that he was a demon, there was a slim chance that Sloot could invoke that right now. He could compel Bannister to accept responsibility for Sloot's charges! He'd feel bad about it, even though Bannister was a very bad person. He could order his new servant to seek redemption! Everybody wins!

Sloot cleared his throat. "Your Dishonor, the 37,916th Court of Egregious Atrocities ruled in Banshee v. Alien Cancer that—"

"Objection," said the lead prosecutor, "precedents can only be invoked by officers of the court."

"Sustained," the judge growled through a wicked smile. "That's three sustained objections in a row, Peril. Enough of this, we're jumping to conclusions."

"Conclusions?"

"Conclusions! The court jumps to the conclusion that you are guilty of all charges. Furthermore, we hold you in contempt of court, declare that you are a hostile witness, and are now moving on to the mandatory maximum sentence."

"But—"

"You are hereby sentenced to eternal servitude in the Infernal Carnival as a torture exhibit. There are no appeals. Goodbye, Mr. —"

"Objection!"

"Who dares to object to my sentencing in my own court?"

All eyes turned to the cadre of attorneys marching down the aisle toward the bench. Sloot recognized Minerva Meatsacrifice in the lead.

"Not another word, Mr. Peril." Ms. Meatsacrifice didn't look at Sloot. She walked to the judge's bench, made a gesture that started Sloot's eyes stinging and watering, and a deluge of papers appeared on the judge's bench.

"What is this?" roared the judge.

"It's a stay of punitive authority."

"There's no such thing!"

"There is now." Ms. Meatsacrifice pointed to the swirling platinum sigil at the bottom of the cover page.

"The Coolest?"

Ms. Meatsacrifice nodded.

UNQUESTIONED ANSWERS

Sloot was fired from his job, his provisional access to the Hall of Records was revoked, and he lost his teleportation privileges. Moreover, Ms. Meatsacrifice added the intervention to Sloot's bill.

"I'd probably put up with that, if I were you," Arthur sneered. "Good thing I'm not you, isn't it?"

"Er, yes," said Sloot. "I suppose." He was fairly sure Arthur had intended that as an insult, not that it mattered. Sloot thought about standing up for himself, but he wasn't going to waste the effort on Arthur. Perhaps the philosopher would make up for the unintentional slight by introducing Sloot to his friends, who were having an animated conversation on what Arthur no doubt regarded as *the* couch, and not specifically *Sloot's* couch, regardless of who'd paid for it.

"It's a fight for the soul of the nation," one of them was saying, punctuating his point by punching his open palm. "If we accept that the proletariat *is* the nation itself—which we must, if Ohrstein's Anthroposophic Mandate is to be believed—then the risk of an enlightened primate being handed a sharp stick—"

"I think you've chased the rabbit too far into the hole, Karl," said the other one.

"That's no way for a philosopher to talk, Ernst!" Karl sounded offended. Arthur's icy glare indicated that he agreed. "We've barely begun to scratch the surface of the issue. As far as I'm concerned, no chasm is too deep. We will plumb every depth of this issue, you mark my words!"

"So marked," said Ernst, "but we were only trying to pick a name."

"A name for what?" asked Sloot, nearly certain he wouldn't get an answer he liked.

"It's hard to explain," said Arthur. "It doesn't have a name yet."

"It's not that hard to explain," Karl retorted. "We're undertaking a crucial effort to ensure that the incoming regime is guided by the moral turpitude of learned men."

"Or women," said Ernst.

"I suppose," said Karl, "but where would that leave us?"

"I'm sorry?"

"Excuse me," Sloot began, "but could we—"

"We're men," said Ernst.

Ernst blinked a few times while catching up to Karl's blind sexism. "You're not implying that men and women aren't capable of working together, are you?"

Karl laughed. "Implications are far too passive-aggressive. These are desperate times, and they call for decisive language! I declare it without ambiguity!"

"That's ridiculous."

Sloot cleared his throat. "If I might just—"

"Is it? Have you ever tried working with a woman?"

"Heavens, no," Ernst laughed. "I've never worked a day in my life. I'd like to, don't get me wrong, but my father won't hear of it. But to address your point, were I ever to get a job, I'd certainly not mind working alongside women."

"That's nice," said Sloot, "but there's the matter of—"

"You'd … *like* to?" Arthur was offended the way seagulls are with beachgoers who eat the food they brought with them.

"Sorry, Arthur," said Ernst. "I know what philosophers think of the working class."

"The very life blood of the nation," Arthur declared, "dullards that they are!"

" Yes, right," said Ernst. "Look, I know you won't be moved from your stance, but I don't see it that way. I look forward to having a job someday."

There was the briefest pause. Sloot pounced upon it like a kitten whose bit of string had stopped moving.

"Do you think we could just—"

"It's a phase," said Arthur, waving his hand dismissively. "I blame the curriculum's glamorization of the proletariat. Don't worry, you'll grow out of it."

"No, I believe *this* is a phase. Philosophy, I mean."

"What?" shouted Arthur and Karl in unison.

"It's the middle of the night," grumbled Nan from her hammock. "Some of us are trying to sleep!"

The Hapsgalts' snores indicated that where Nan was trying, they were succeeding.

"Philosophers' prerogative," Arthur spat. "Ponderances are better at volume. And as for you, philosophy isn't a phase! It's the distillation of the natural world into pure and potent truth!"

"It is," Ernst agreed, "but I'm having a phase of it. It's due to end anytime now."

"That's preposterous!" Karl was on his feet. "We've been roommates at the university for three years! How can you absorb all of this truth and simply turn away from it?"

"I'm not turning away from it," said Ernst, "not entirely. It's just that without some sort of practical applicability, the tenets of philosophy just aren't very useful. Conversations over drinks being the exception, of course."

"Where did you learn to use that word?" Arthur demanded.

"Which one?"

"Useful!"

Ernst studied Arthur with a calm demeanor that Sloot had never seen on a philosopher. It was like someone had tried to sedate a rabid wolverine by confusing it with higher mathematics.

"You see, this is what I'm talking about," said Ernst. "It's all well and good to discuss philosophy in the abstract, but until it's put toward some pragmatic end—"

Arthur and Karl lapsed into a fit of wailing that would have gone over well at a funeral, if they could have done it without the contempt. Even Sloot knew it was a bad idea to mention pragmatism in the company of philosophers. The argument raged on into the night, unhindered by further attempts on Sloot's part to ask why the three of them couldn't have gotten on with their treason at the pub.

He resolved to distract himself by looking over the papers on his desk. There was an official document sitting atop his meticulous stacks of notes. It had already been opened, as he enjoyed no semblance of privacy that a regular sort of homeowner might.

Sloot's heart sank. It was an unusual feeling. He loved official documents, and the first time that he got a new one was a particular treat. However, an official Declaration of Gloating from Mrs. Knife was more an inducement to panic than bureaucratic euphoria.

She'd done it. Somehow she'd found out what he was doing and reported him to the Courts of Chaos. He'd been so careful! He'd worked far less than he'd wanted to, mimicking the standard demonic appreciation for a good slacking off. Diligence attracted too much attention. Someone must have ratted him out to her, which he begrudgingly respected. Snitching on a rule-breaker was good citizenship.

It didn't matter. What was done was done. He couldn't teleport or visit the Hall of Records, but at least he hadn't been rendered down for black candles. His circle was serviceable, and he still had his ledger. He could get on with his work, which was exactly what he did.

"What's the plan this time?" asked Igor, who'd followed Sloot into Salzstadt Before despite his attempt to slink away unnoticed.

"Nice try," muttered Sloot. He reckoned it would be harder for Igor to surrender to his mischievous impulses if he couldn't plan ahead. He also didn't *have* a plan, but that was academic.

Cloaked in dimness, Sloot strolled the streets of his beloved city. He had a hard time reminiscing because he knew what Salzstadt was doomed to become. What Roman's wager had done to it.

He was livid with Roman by the time he'd arrived at the counting house. He looked across the street at the magically concealed annex. It seemed painfully obvious now that he knew it was there.

It was late, and there was nobody on the street. He stared up at the gargoyles atop the annex and wondered, *why bother putting gargoyles on a building you don't want anyone to see?*

That was the wealthy for you. Those unseen gargoyles were worth more than Sloot would ever have earned in his life. It inspired a resentment in Sloot that he tried to suppress. There were laws against resenting the wealthy in the Old Country. The wealthy had taken great pains in getting them passed. Well, not pains. Bribes.

Sloot clenched his jaw and stalked back toward his apartment. Despite his most polite inclinations, he chafed at the injustice of it. Why had the wealthy been allowed to visit all this ruin upon his beloved city? Someone ought to do something about it!

That's when it hit him. He was a demon, for the Domnitor's sake! Long may he reign. The Coolest had specifically told him to do something about it. Check the balances, that sort of thing. If not him, who?

His head throbbed as he walked the rest of the way to his apartment.

"Took you long enough," said Igor. He was leaning against the door to the butcher shop, idly tossing a doorknob in the air. "You go to the counting house first?"

"How did you know?"

"Predictable."

"Oh. Where'd you get that?"

"Door." Igor shrugged. "Don't worry, it's not one you're likely to need. It's—"

"I know it's not easy," said Sloot, "but you've got to resist these impulses, especially here! Repairing reality is a tricky business, and the slightest—"

"Yeah, I know, all right?" Igor said a swear word.

Pop. Cackle.

"Oh, dear!" Sloot crouched in alarm. "What was that?"

"What, you don't know that one? It means the smell of eggs on a hot day."

"I know what it means," said Sloot, "but it called a goblin!"

"Of course it did. You ever leave eggs out on a hot day?"

"I thought we couldn't call goblins!" Sloot demonstrated his meaning by saying the swear word that means "a level of hygiene so far gone the sewers want nothing to do with your bath water." Silence followed.

"*You* can't call goblins," said Igor. "Goblins and gremlins are cousins. Plus, we've got special swear glands."

Sloot did his best to avoid thinking about gremlins' glands. A squid of denial filled his mind with ink, bathing it the blessed shadowy blackness of *la la la la la, can't hear you, sorry.*

"Look, no more swearing, all right? And no more mischief.

You can't go around mucking up the past like that!"

"Why not? You're doing it."

"It's my job!"

"Fine," Igor sighed and fished his bit of wire out of his bag. "I'll just stick to my job, then."

Sloot opened his mouth to protest but thought better of it, lesser evils and all. He walked into the alley behind the butcher shop and looked up. The window to his apartment was dark, which made sense. It was the middle of the night. The window across the alley was dark as well.

Curiosity, wanton strumpet that she was, got the better of him. Sloot had spent his life resisting her wiles, resolute in his opinion that wondering about things led to incivility and unrest. Questions like "I wonder what's on the other side of this ocean?" usually ended in imperialism, which was never beneficial in the mutual sense.

Sloot climbed the fire escape of the building across the alley, noticing for the first time that his building lacked one. He just wanted to take a little peek. He was a demon now, wasn't he? The unspoken agreement between Sloot Before and his neighbor to avoid looking into each other's apartments couldn't apply to his future demonic self, could it?

His heart fluttered at the thrill of doing something naughty. Then it turned to ice and dropped into the pit of his stomach at what he saw—or rather what he didn't see, which was anything. Nothing but a fine layer of dust on the pristine wood floors. Not so much as a scuff on the baseboards.

That couldn't be right. Sloot had occasionally caught glimpses of someone much like himself through the window, in the corner of his vision. That sort of thing was inevitable, from time to time. On the bright side, Sloot could congratulate himself on an unblemished record of avoiding eye contact. They had to have some semblance of privacy, after all.

With a flick of his wrist, Sloot summoned a reference to his current page in the ledger. Just as he thought, it was the night before that fateful day when he'd corrected the Pritygud report. He was sure he'd seen his neighbor in the window that very morning, just before he'd recited the Loyalist Oath.

Sloot climbed into the empty apartment through the open window. Perhaps his neighbor had been carried off by Uncle? No, the door was intact and there were no claw marks on the floor. It could have been one of the rare occasions upon which someone had gone quietly, but try as he might, Sloot couldn't make himself believe it.

"Nice place," Igor grunted with the effort of climbing through the window. "Nicer than ours. Why don't we live here?"

Sloot couldn't decide how to respond to that, then realized he didn't want to and skipped a few steps. "Why is it empty?"

"You're the one who can see into the past and the future here."

"You're right," said Sloot, astounded by Igor having been helpful for once. He waved his hand and his magic circle appeared beneath his feet. He located Oxbugger's Crescent, increased its size with a motion, and looked around the room.

"Nothing," said Sloot.

"I didn't say anything." Igor looked over his shoulder to see if Sloot was having a conversation with someone else.

"No, I mean there's nothing. I've looked all the way back to the construction of the apartment. The flower shop on the ground floor used to store pots in here, but that's it. No one has ever lived here. How can that be?"

Sloot reduced Oxbugger's Crescent again and started pacing around the room. It didn't help him think, but if he stood still while considering anything ominous, he was more likely to fall over.

The empty apartment put Sloot in a tizzy,
He fidgeted himself dizzy,

What sort of hero is he?

It was the sort of song, or grotesque imitation of one, that denial was designed to block out. Unfortunately for Sloot, even his mighty capacity for denial had limits. The dam burst, and a deluge of woes crashed over the tiny village of his sanity that had unwisely been built on the valley floor. His pace increased until he was practically running laps around the empty apartment, the thrum of reality's tribulations pounding in his head.

Then he noticed something. It was subtle, but it was enough. The sun had come up, a gentle breeze had refused to come anywhere near the fetid air in the apartment, and a very nervous accountant in the apartment across the alley had clearly just noticed Sloot from the corner of his eye.

Sloot froze. He knew his former self wouldn't look directly at him, but he wasn't equipped to deal with this much existentialism. A panic roared up from the depths of his greatest fears. His vision swam. Did panics scream on their own? If so, this one potentially had a talent for berserking that would earn it a place of honor on any Viking ship. Sloot's blood thundered in his ears. He lost his balance. The room went horribly quiet and dark.

HOWLING WINDS

Sloot's feet were on fire. Not literally, though that might have been better.

"Hold still," said a remarkably muscular person with a deep, yet feminine voice. She needn't have said anything, really. Her left hand's grip on Sloot's foot was as unmoving as the damp stone floor of the torchlit room. Her right hand moved a needle and thread deftly through his big toe, which dangled in a way that toes shouldn't. At least the rest of his toes weren't dangling. They were piled in a brass bowl.

Sloot screamed in an automatic way. He'd done it so often he no longer had to think about it. That left his mind free to reach the conclusion that Arthur was right. He was rather predictable.

His screams stopped of their own accord when Gwen walked into the room. Her plunging neckline made Sloot forget how his mouth worked.

"Poor Sloot," Gwen tittered. "You should have let me know you were coming. This could have been avoided."

"Sorry." Sloot winced as the needle continued its work. He

had no idea where he was, much less the etiquette regarding which demons he should call before visiting, or why the penalty for unannounced arrivals was the removal and reattachment of one's toes. It seemed a horribly inefficient punishment, but that was the Inferno for you.

"It's a good thing they started from the bottom," said Gwen. "Demons' eyes are very potent ingredients in their magic."

"Sorry," said Sloot, "whose magic?"

"The Blessed Few. They run the monastery here at Blasigtopp."

Sloot had heard of Blasigtopp in school, during a geography lesson on the barbaric wastes outside the Old Country. He'd been taught it was much like every other heathen waste: a horrible place where the resident savages had yet to be tamed by the wisdom and grace of the Domnitor, long may he reign. It was technically a nation, and the only one bordering Carpathia that hadn't been invaded by one Vlad or another.

"You wouldn't happen to know how I got here, would you?"

Gwen shrugged. "The better question is how you managed to sleep through having your toes cut off."

"Perhaps," said Sloot. He yelped as his surgeon started on another toe. Over the course of his life, Sloot had awoken countless times as a result of nerves, bad dreams, or for no reason at all. He surmised that waking for a very good reason, like amputation, was simply unfamiliar territory.

"So what brings you all the way up here?" asked Gwen. "Did you miss me?"

"Yes," said Sloot. He shook his head. "No! Er, I'm not sure. I was working in my ledger, and then I woke up and my toes were being sewn back on."

"You're lucky I was here," said Gwen.

"I'm not," said a wrinkled old man in a hat that must have been a practical joke.

"Tough luck, your Thoughtfulness," said Gwen in that breathy way that made everyone in earshot squirm in their seats. "But there are rules against cutting up live demons for parts, you know."

"He looked dead to me," said the old man with an agitated wave. "Got all of his toes off before he woke up. What sort of demon lets that happen, eh?"

"The day doesn't have to be a total loss," Gwen purred. "Surely, there's something else you want?" She raised a salacious eyebrow.

The old man snorted. "That might've worked seventy years ago."

"Ugh," said Gwen, "vows of celibacy make it so difficult to deal with monks."

"What? No," said the old man. "You were just prettier back then."

Gwen's brow wrinkled and her mouth dropped open. Sloot chided himself for noticing how buxom she seemed when she was offended. If he was being entirely forthright, even her eyes going pitch black and her claws coming out didn't detract from her allure. Luckily, he had the searing pain of toe reattachment to distract him.

"You think you can resist me, mortal?" Gwen hissed like a barrel full of snakes.

"Probably not if you *really* decided to turn it on," the old man shrugged. "Oh, that's a long tail you've got. I can sell dried demon's tail by the inch! Valuable stuff!"

"Eww!" Gwen recoiled. "That's not the sort of flesh peddling I go in for, Abbot."

The old man giggled. Sloot yelped. The woman sewing his toes back on menaced the air space around Sloot's nose with a finger.

"Sorry," said Sloot. "Hold still. I know."

"She told you to hold still?" asked the Abbot.

Sloot nodded and whimpered as the needle started into another toe.

"Sister Voracious must really like you. The Blessed Few take vows of silence, you know. We're only allowed one word every five years. She just spent a decade on you."

The look that Sister Voracious shot at Sloot was a threat, a warning, and a dare all rolled into one. *Earn it*, the look seemed to say, *or the stitches come back out*.

"Er, if you don't mind me asking," Sloot said to Gwen, "why are *you* here?"

"Entirely on your account, it seems. Before I saved you from dismemberment for parts, I was seeing to that bit of drama with Vlad the Invader. It's too bad she's so devoted to Greta, we could have some fun together. Still, I suppose that's why their love story is so compelling."

Gwen went on to explain that while most people's love stories are simple affairs, the ones produced by discerning love demons are not. They've got to have smoldering looks, yearnings, and one of the lovers needs powerful arms for wrapping the other one up. None of the awkward advances or "he seems nice enough" of your run-of-the-mill relationship. You'll never land a producer if the phrase "I don't know, what do *you* want for dinner" is a prominent fixture in your standard dialog.

"Thanks for helping Vlad and Greta," said Sloot, "but how does that bring you to Blasigtopp?"

"Vlad needed a little bit of help getting settled."

Sister Voracious stood and regarded her work. Sloot's toes were swollen and purple, and he wasn't sure that there was a name for the color that was oozing around his stitches. He gave them an experimental wiggle and instantly regretted it.

"Let's take a walk," said Gwen.

They say that laughter is the best medicine. Sloot would have traded it for a pint of morphine. The snow on the floor of the courtyard was not as soothing to his reattachments as he'd hoped.

"Ow. Ow! Ow."

"You really haven't been a demon for long, have you?"

"Ow. It depends on how you look at it," said Sloot. In the Narrative, which ghosts called the "land of the living" and demons called the "all you can defile buffet," he'd only been a demon for a matter of months. However, Infernal time worked on an entirely independent scale. Infernal aeons could pass in the blink of a mortal's eye. If Sloot had bothered to keep an accurate accounting—he tried, but there were periods of madness—he'd have known he'd been a demon for 66,837 years, four months, two days, thirteen hours, and change.

"You've got wings, you know. Not that hard for a demon to stay off his feet."

"That's cheating," groused the Abbot.

"I'm sorry," said Sloot.

"You should be. The first test is to cross the courtyard without leaving footprints. Do you have any idea how many supplicants have failed the first test?"

"No, how many?"

"It was a rhetorical question." That was when the Abbot learned you've got to be careful around accountants when numbers are involved.

In the silence that followed, Sloot's idle mind started putting things together. That was unfortunate.

"How did I get here?" he wondered aloud.

"Couldn't tell you," said the Abbot. "I'm not one to question good fortune when it falls out of the sky, which you did. Over there." He pointed vaguely to Sloot's left. There was a trench in the snow about twenty feet long, which ended abruptly at a stone wall.

"You looked dead to me," the Abbot continued, "and you gave us no reason to believe otherwise until you started snoring. We already had your toes off by then."

The Abbot knocked on the heavy wooden doors at the far end of the courtyard. They groaned as a pair of attendants pushed them open. A vast hall of torchlit stone lay beyond, and the sounds of combat echoed within the darkness. That worried Sloot, but it didn't surprise him. After all, Gwen had hinted that Vlad was visiting the monastery as well. Combat followed Vlad like a loyal pet that dutifully tried to kill her at every opportunity.

"That's not a good sign," said Gwen.

"Don't worry about it," said Sloot, his tongue tripping over the unfamiliar phrase. He cleared his throat. "Vlad's always in a fight, unless she's eating or sleeping. Then it's only half the time."

"Not anymore, she's not."

"What?"

They emerged from the dark hallway in a reasonably well-lit room full of mostly unconscious monks. That is to say that most of the monks in the room were unconscious, though several were fully alert. So was Vlad. Sloot barely recognized her in the threadbare clothes that must have been white when she put them on, but were now a patina of grime, sweat, and blood. Sloot's demonic sense of smell told him that none of the blood was hers. That was only slightly less unnerving than the heavy manacles that held Vlad's hands behind her back.

"Why are they attacking her?" asked Sloot, surprised at the feeling of his claws and teeth going sharp. He'd been officially released from service to Carpathian Intelligence, so why did he want to jump to Vlad's defense, if not his sense of duty? Sloot had never been in a fight in his life. He'd experienced several beatings that could have become fights, had he but thrown a punch himself.

"It's her tribulations," Gwen explained. "We usually do financial ones for very wealthy people, but she didn't seem to care about that part."

"I didn't know Vlad was rich," Sloot mused. "She never talked about money."

"Of course she was rich," said Gwen. "She was a monarch,

they're always rich."

"That makes sense, but in my experience the wealthy never let you forget it. Willie still talks about his fortune all the time from his hammock in my living room."

Sloot watched as a pair of monks with swords laid into Vlad mercilessly. She dodged and ducked, never lashing out and striking them, though she managed to put them both on the floor nonetheless.

"She never touched them," marveled Sloot. "She just sort of moved in such a way that they landed themselves atop a pile of their friends. Wait, what do you mean *was*?"

"It's the past tense of *is*," said Gwen.

"Right," Sloot replied, "like when you said that Vlad *was* rich, or that she *was* a monarch."

"You're catching on." Gwen winked at Sloot, making him feel excited and uncomfortable at the same time. Like a carnival attraction, though Gwen hadn't been assembled by intoxicated vagrants.

"Like I said," the love demon continued, "She wasn't eligible for a simple riches-to-rags tribulation. She had to do the grand gesture."

"You don't mean—"

"Oh, yes, I do."

Gwen explained that she dealt with Vlad for the thing that she prized the most: her sword, metaphorically speaking. If Vlad swore never to take up arms again, Gwen would sever death's hold on Greta. She'd die eventually, of course. They both would. But old age was a distant threat, like liver damage to a college student proving his invincibility.

Unfortunately for Vlad, there were complications. She wasn't merely thought of as the greatest warrior ever to have lived, she *was* the greatest warrior ever to have lived. Greta realized that so long as there were people in the world spoiling for a brawl, Vlad would never have a moment's peace. So Greta made her own deal with

Gwen: in exchange for the thing that Greta loved most, the world would forget about Vlad.

"There were two parts to that," said Gwen. "Monarchs are never forgotten, so Vlad gave up her crown."

"You can't be serious!" Sloot considered the ramifications of this as he watched Vlad dodge a sword in such a way that its wielder bounced his head off a pillar and went down for a nap. "If Vlad no longer rules Carpathia, that means … what does that mean?"

"The fairies are running things now," said Gwen. "They had to amend their corporate paperwork, which I'm pretty sure they did correctly."

"What was the second part?" Sloot wondered aloud, at the same time wondering quietly which notary service they'd used for the corporate amendments.

Gwen's face pulled into a rictus of embarrassment. Her head did its best to turtle down into her shoulders.

"You can't plan for every eventuality, you know."

Panic sank into Sloot's stomach. Not the ever-present familiar variety that sent his life flashing before his eyes. This was panic for someone else, someone he knew and liked. Someone who wasn't a seasoned worrier like Sloot Peril.

"What happened?" he asked in as close to a demanding tone as he could muster.

Gwen sighed. "Well, it turned out the thing Greta loved most was Vlad. Since Vlad wasn't hers to give—modern conventions of slavery being what they are—the interpretation of the deal was that she gave up her love for Vlad."

"So Greta no longer loves Vlad?"

"Her heart does," said Gwen, "but her head doesn't know it."

"Let me get this straight," said Sloot, his eyes shut tight with the effort. "Vlad's given up her sword to save Greta's life, and her crown so she can be forgotten. And Greta has forgotten that she loves Vlad?"

"That's most of it," said Gwen, "but here's the thing…"

"There's always a thing," said Sloot.

"Vlad and Greta were love at first sight. It's the only thing they've ever known of each other. Now that Greta's not in love with Vlad—"

"She doesn't even recognize her?"

Gwen put on an apologetic smirk, pointed one finger toward her nose, then toward Sloot.

The Abbot laughed. Not much happened atop the windy mountain, and this was far more entertainment than he usually got.

"I didn't mean for this to happen," said Gwen, "honestly! But you know how it is. We make deals! Deals have a price!"

"Yes," said Sloot, "but you're still coming up short. You've taken Vlad's sword, her crown, and her heart. What does Vlad have?"

"She's saved her true love!"

"Whom you've taken away!"

"Not on purpose."

Sloot knew life wasn't fair. Bad things happened to good people all the time. His mother had explained that to him in the context of bedtime. Still, it didn't take a seasoned accountant to see the imbalance in this transaction.

"You haven't produced a love story," said Sloot.

"I know," she said dismissively. "It's not great for my ratings, but my next one—"

"There will be no next one," said Sloot.

"Is that a threat?"

"It's a fact. You're not authorized to make deals ending in tragedy and power grabs. Those are for political demons, and it won't be long before they get wind of what you're up to."

"You wouldn't!"

"I don't have to. Your name will be all over the Infernal copies of the fairies' amended documents. Do you know how many intern demons are forced to read those? Pointing out your involvement to a political demon will score them tons of toadying points. Your days are numbered, unless you add a 'happily ever after' to the end of this."

Gwen stamped her foot and pouted. It had probably gotten her what she wanted numerous times before, but she was up against simple mathematics on this one. She'd never match that for seduction in Sloot Peril's eyes.

Sloot glanced at Vlad, who was sitting atop several dozen monks and glaring at Gwen. She shifted her eyes to meet Sloot's and gave him a little nod. From anyone else, a gesture so subtle might have meant "thanks for passing the salt," or "I'll be with you in a minute," or possibly even "I've got a nervous tick, please don't read anything into that." But coming from Vlad Defenestratia, thirty-seventh ruler of Carpathia and greatest warrior the world had ever seen, it was sincere gratitude to a true friend.

"Oh!" Gwen exclaimed.

Sloot ducked.

"Love stories like this come along once in a thousand years! No, less than that! Sloot, do you know what this means?"

"I can assure you that I do not."

Gwen took a couple of deep breaths and tried to calm herself. She seemed unable to decide whether she was quivering with excitement or desperation, but either way she was quivering. Sloot tried not to stare.

"Careful," warned the Abbot, "I wouldn't do anything to make his toes curl for a few weeks."

"Two lovers," Gwen managed to say after several deep breaths, while choking back tears. "Two bargains, two sacrifices, each for the other. This is the stuff of pure, uncut romance! There could even be heroics! What's more romantic than heroics?"

Joint pension accounts with low-premium life insurance, thought

Sloot. He knew that wasn't what she was thinking, but it didn't matter. He had his own idea of romance, and he only cared what Myrtle thought about it.

"Vlad remembers Greta," said Gwen, "but not the other way around. If Vlad can win Greta's love again now that she's a penniless pacifist, it will be the most heartwarming story ever told! When the board of directors hears that I produced it, they'll make me a partner for sure!"

"Yeah," Sloot nodded, "all right. Then Vlad and Greta get their happily-ever-after." It made sense, even with Vlad putting the "fist" in "pacifist."

Sloot gasped. Another thought had occurred to him. Roman's paradox, the reality-shredding monstrosity that he was tasked with setting right, was based on his proof that love was the greatest evil in the universe. If he won, Gwen would have to reveal the number of Unknowable Secrets to him. That would lead to Roman learning his own core secret—which was Unknowable—causing the universe to unravel. If he lost, he'd have to reveal his core secret to Gwen, causing the universe to unravel.

The wager should never have been possible, yet there they were. There was no outcome that left the universe *raveled.* Until now.

"What is it?" asked Gwen.

"It could nullify the whole thing," said Sloot.

"What whole thing?"

"Vlad and Greta! Their love won Roman his wager against you by demonstrating the havoc and nastiness that love can cause. But if that *very same* love can also prove to be the most heartwarming story ever told, there's a chance the wager would count as a no-decision. All bets are off!"

Gwen's eyes slowly widened with realization. Tears welled in her eyes, threatening to spill over.

"Oh, dear," said Sloot. Then spill they did.

"Oh, Sloot!" Gwen flung her arms around Sloot and pressed her ... *self* against him. She was soft and warm. Parts of her best not mentioned were *heaving*. He'd had these sorts of fantasies before he met Myrtle, and they'd made him flee his own bedroom in discomfort then as well. But now he was firmly planted in the frightful sensuality of Gwen's embrace.

"Sloot, you brilliant little kitten! This could be the best thing that's ever happened to me. Oh, I could just kiss you!"

Sloot felt woozy. Everything went black.

MATTERS OF NO CONSEQUENCE

Consider this a warning: There is no understanding Infernal Bureaucracy. Even the executive bureaucrats on the 8th circle have no idea what's going on beneath them, for the very reason that it *is* beneath them. You don't get to where they are by wasting your time with hard work and expertise. It's mostly schmoozing over cocktails or golf, which was invented on the 44th circle for the specific purpose of ruining large swaths of nature with minimal effort.

The largest Infernal bureaucratic system capable of being understood in the slightest is the delivery network. In a central bullpen on the 50th floor, a team of half-mad demons works as diligently as permitted to maintain the maximum allowed level of efficiency of interdepartmental communication, which is nearly half a percent. They managed the various pneumatic tubes, imp messengers, scheduled prophecies, tea leaf readings, etcetera which worked together—so to speak—in the worst example of symbiosis in the universe to deliver messages from one department to another. Occasionally.

An envelope that had originated in Requests decades ago had recently been fished out of sewage and placed on the desk of Barbarella Sarcophage, a middle management demon in Interments and Exhumations on the 23rd level.

"He says you have to sign for it," said Ms. Sarcophage's assistant, a well-dressed talent demon who was working his way up. As luck would have it, he spoke sewer imp.

"I'm not signing anything, Scabrot. Get that wretched thing out of here!"

The nerve! Asking a middle management demon to give the shape of her name to a piece of paper! Not one of the demons who'd spawned from her clutch had ever signed anything unless threats were involved, and she wasn't about to be the first.

Scabrot adjusted his silk cravat, which he shouldn't have been able to afford on his salary, which he didn't have. Ms. Sarcophage suppressed a smile of approval for the young demon's ingenuity, not that she approved of that sort of thing, but she thought fondly that it must have been embezzlement. All of the most sartorial demons are either cunning embezzlers or the Prime Evils, who embezzle better than any of them.

"It's not that simple, ma'am," said Scabrot.

Good, thought Ms. Sarcophage, considering herself a proud casualty in the righteous war on efficiency. "Why not?"

"You're not going to like it."

"When do I ever?"

Scabrot sighed. "He's got a knife, ma'am."

"What? No, he hasn't!"

The imp cackled and said something that must have been a swear word.

"He insists that he does, ma'am."

"Straight to threats, then?" Ms. Sarcophage threw up her hands in frustration. "I'm entitled to bribery before coercion, it's in my contract!"

The imp burbled something unintelligible, spat on the floor, and cackled again.

"He says he's reviewed your contract," said Scabrot. "He says there was an Exception of Inverse Proportions for Matters of No Consequence."

An Exception of Inverse Proportions for Matters of No Consequence—informally referred to as a "nonsie"—allows document bearers to bypass standard protocols when dealing with middle management demons, but only in cases of trivial matters. The more pointless the document, the more forceful the nonsie.

"I'll let my attorney be the judge of that," growled Ms. Sarcophage. "Void!"

The crystal ball on her desk went inky black and spoke with a voice that would have melted the sanity right off any mortals within earshot.

"You summoned?"

"Would you tell this *thing* that he and his nonsie have no power here?"

"Bring forth the document," said the Void. A sickly yellow eye appeared within the crystal ball's inky blackness, and a monocle materialized in front of it. The imp opened the sewage-flecked envelope and held it up in front of the eye. When it finished reading, a cacophony like the screaming of a million souls tearing their hair echoed from within the crystal ball.

"We dare not object," shuddered the Void.

"What? But you're my attorney!"

"Sign the horrible thing, Barbarella! No charge for this consultation! I was never here!"

The crystal ball went silent and clear. The imp handed the document to Ms. Sarcophage with all the smugness of the kid on the playground who had a force field that protected him from everything. There was always one.

Ms. Sarcophage, having skimmed the document, said a swear word. "This has to be the single most pointless thing I've ever read!" She read it again. "I didn't know they even made demons 100th class. He must have waited in line for a thousand years for this."

The imp babbled something.

"1,700 years," Scabrot translated. "Wait, seriously?"

The imp nodded.

"This isn't even a request of Infernal proportions," moaned Ms. Sarcophage. "In the eternal history of the Inferno, this has to be the single most trivial request ever made! I don't have any choice but to sign this, do I?"

Scabrot took the document, read it, and gasped. "No, ma'am, I don't think you do."

"Ugh, fine," she replied. "But you roll up your sleeve. I'm not about to use my own blood."

And there it was. The last leg of a seemingly impossible journey was complete. All that was left was finding an instructor to make a dancer of Sloot Peril.

HEX BALL CHANGE

The Witchwood was the oldest witchery in Carpathia, and Agather had been running it for never-you-mind-how-many years. Sloot had visited twice before, but this time still counted as a first. It was his first time as a demon, his first time without Myrtle, and his first encounter with Agather's red carpet.

"Sloot Peril," said the old witch from behind a marginally toothy grin. "How long's it been?"

"Hard to say," said Sloot. "Hard to tell time when you're dead."

"I've heard. Well, I suppose ye'll be wanting to get started, then."

"I suppose we should, yes. Er, with what, please?"

"With yer dancing lessons, of course."

"Oh." Sloot's mind drew a blank. His mind didn't stand much chance of catching up, given that it was up to its metaphorical elbows with dread for the horrid black shapes slithering around on the red carpet beneath him.

"They'd have devoured ye by now if they were going to." Agather seemed impatient. "Ye did make an official Infernal request for dancing lessons, didn't ye?"

"Oh, that. What? Yes! I mean, I did, but—"

"Right then," said Agather. "Come away from there and show us what ye've got."

Sloot wasted no time in leaping from the carpet at Agather's invitation. It was more of a prance, really. One that had stopped at the pub along the way and told the publican to leave the bottle. He lost control of his feet altogether and landed on his face.

"That's it then, is it?"

" No," said Sloot with sufficient doubt to have earned a standing ovation from the Royal Skeptics Society of Salzstadt. They hadn't existed for many years, owing to the Domnitor's firm belief that they shouldn't. Long may he reign.

"Hang on," said Sloot, after trying to get to his feet and falling again. "Am I hexed? You hexed Myrtle last time we were here. She couldn't keep her feet either."

Agather chuckled. "Yer a demon 100th class. I'd no sooner feel the need to hex a butterfly."

"Oh."

"Unless it was a Carpathian Bloodwing, of course."

"Of course." Sloot tried getting to his feet more slowly, focusing on the gentle humiliation of inspiring less apprehension than a butterfly, Carpathian or otherwise. Humiliation was familiar territory, a rock-solid handhold on the way up to bad posture. It probably also didn't help that his toes had recently been severed and reattached.

"Okay then," said Agather once Sloot had managed to get his feet under himself, "give it another go."

Sloot gave her a bewildered look and stared at his open hands.

"Yer dance moves," said Agather, the first notes of irritation creeping into her voice. That didn't bode well.

"I, er," Sloot cleared his throat. "Well, that is to say, I thought you were going to … you know."

"Ye thought that I was going to what?"

"Well, the request," Sloot stammered. "I mean, I *did* ask for—"

"Dancing lessons?"

Sloot blushed, which brought out the scales in his cheeks and got his ears smoking. "Well, yes," he managed.

"Yes, yes, that's why yer here. We need to establish a baseline first, see what we're working with. So let's have it then, eh? Strut yer stuff! Give us a twirl, why don't ye?"

Well, here goes nothing, thought Sloot. He was right about that.

"Whenever yer ready," said Agather.

"I think I've finished."

A breath worked itself in and out of Agather in a slow, measured pace reserved for geological epochs. Her expression was placid, unmoving. Not the peaceful serenity of a swan gliding aimlessly across a lake, but the pre-mischief consideration of a toddler pondering whether a tureen of soup would be more comfortable on the sofa.

"This wasn't the agreement," Agather growled at last.

"What agreement?" asked Sloot.

"Ye didn't think a ballet demon was going to give yer lesson, did ye?"

"No," said Sloot. In fact, he'd never thought anyone would address his request at all. "But to be perfectly frank, you don't strike me as the dance instructor type."

"I see," said Agather. "Know many dance instructors, do ye?"

"Well, no, but—"

"Don't talk to me about *buts*," Agather warned. Sloot suppressed a giggle.

Dancing isn't exactly magic, but it's close. That's how witches know about it. They get a lot done with what seems like magic, but isn't quite. Not entirely, anyway. Most witches aren't dancers themselves, aside from the naked-around-the-bonfire sense, which is a lot more prevalent in salacious stories than reality. But they understand the theory better than anyone else, dancers aside.

"Sorry I'm late," said Igor.

"Gremlin!" Agather suddenly had a broom gripped tightly in her hands and was spinning on her heel. The bristles connected with Igor at alarming speed, sending him sprawling like a flightless bird mid-reminder that it was better off on the ground. He collided with a tree and landed roughly among its roots, which started coiling around him.

"A little help," he choked.

"Fat chance!" shouted Agather. "Got to take them out as soon as they turn up. Don't fight it, ye little bugger!"

"Sloot," Igor choked, "tell her you know me!"

Sloot hesitated. Could anybody really *know* anybody? It was a useless sort of rhetoric, but in an unusual turn of events, Sloot wished that Arthur were there. He'd certainly have found a way to stretch even the least significant trivium into a conversation that would have to include a break for lunch.

"How does he know yer name?" Agather leered at Sloot with a probing glare that was all business. He should have been able to lie. He was a demon after all, but he was also Sloot Peril.

"He's my … well, he's auditioning to be my bard."

"Ye poor simple sod." Agather shook her head. "I knew ye were gullible, but look at him! He's a gremlin! They can't be bards. Have ye lost yer head?"

"Once," said Sloot. "Look, I know he's a gremlin, and I know gremlins don't often become bards, but—"

"Never," said Agather. "Gremlins *never* become bards." The roots didn't let up on Igor. He started turning purple, or at least the bits that Sloot could see through his filth did.

"Even if that's true," said Sloot, "do you think it's because none have ever tried, or because no one's ever let them try?"

Agather nearly voiced a retort before an appeal to reason gave her pause. Reason was a real rant killer.

Agather snapped her fingers.

"Ow!" shouted Igor, who bolted toward a little pool of water, a stream of black smoke issuing from his backside.

"Shame on ye," Agather said to Sloot in mock disdain, "tempting an innocent old witch with a riddle like that."

"I didn't mean to, I only—"

"He doesn't come back in here," said Agather, her finger waggling with gravitas. "You hear me, fancy mister bard? Ye try and sneak in here again, and I'll give ye far worse than the old smoky nether truss!"

"Fine!" shouted Igor, his soaked and sputtering form dragging itself onto dry land. "Ugh, what was in that pool?"

"It's a spring," said Agather. "Pure spring water."

"Oh, that's just great," moaned Igor. "It's wreaking havoc with my musk! I'm going to have to start all over again!"

"Work that out on yer own time," Agather snapped. "And as for ye," she said to Sloot, "we've our work cut out for us, ain't we?"

DEVIL'S ADVOCATE

First dance lessons are simple affairs. A few steps in geometric shapes, what to do with one's hands, and if the instructor is supremely lucky, there's neither crying nor swearing. Sloot ended his first lesson with aspirations to that level. Agather assured him they had a long way to go before Sloot simply didn't know how to dance. At present, he seemed to have taken lessons in how to *not* dance. He swore to Agather that he wasn't the *prima non-ballerina* in some grotesque Infernal dance company.

Nevertheless, Agather seemed sure she could teach him. It was just going to take time. For Sloot, this presented a natural quitting opportunity. However, it was the last thing Myrtle had asked of him. She had her hell to endure, and this was his.

Sloot was dead tired. He rode the train back to the crags, dodged the crusty old wizard and his bag of salt, and walked back to his apartment. It was agony on par with listening to lazy people talk about how ripped they'd be after they started exercising next month. Sloot yearned to put his feet up for a few hours and soothe his recently reattached toes.

"On your feet," said Arthur. He hadn't even waited for Sloot to sit down. He just knew the look of a man who desperately wanted to sit.

"Please, no," Sloot groaned. "What?"

"We've got to get to the pub."

It was more demand than invitation, but nobody invited Sloot to do anything these days. Or any days, really. He went along for novelty's sake, hoping perhaps he'd die soon enough to avoid regretting it for long.

"Gentlemen," shouted Arthur, his hands held high. Everyone in the pub turned to look at him. The publican closed and locked the door.

"Ahem," said someone among the crowd. Most of them looked barely old enough to enter a pub at all.

Arthur sighed. "And *ladies*. I suppose I'll have to get used to saying that. *Gentlemen and ladies*. Doesn't exactly roll off the tongue, does it? No matter. I call this meeting of the Coordinated Revolution of Artists and Philosophers to order. Seeing as there is no old business, I'll get straight to new business, shall I?"

"Wait," said Sloot, "what—"

"It was a rhetorical question!" Arthur snapped.

"I have a matter of new business," said a woman who was clearly one of the artists. If the paint splatters on her smock hadn't been a dead giveaway, she'd stood from her chair to speak. Philosophers knew to save their strength.

Arthur grit his teeth. "And your name is?"

"Annabella Forp."

Arthur looked over a piece of paper. "You're not on the agenda."

"What agenda?"

"For the meeting! You really should have put your name down during the previous meeting's business."

"There was no previous meeting!"

"Revolutions have to start somewhere, Miss Forp."

There was a ripple of subdued laughter from the philosophers and some of the more erudite artists, those being the ones whose parents were wealthy enough to be nonplussed over their failure to graduate. Graduation was the worst thing that could happen to the child of an aristocrat. Graduates were expected to find jobs.

"Fine," she said. "Then I'd like to put my name—"

"Not now," snapped Arthur, "you don't have the floor!"

"All I want—"

"Look, if you ask me—which you can't, because you don't have the floor—we've brought you lot in too early. This has to be a thinking man's rebellion!"

"We're tired of talking," growled Annabella, "it's time we did something!"

Several people, all of whom had paint on their smocks, erupted in shouts of "yeah," and "that's right," and "I was told there would be free drinks at this thing!" Other people, most of whom had fresh leather patches sewn onto their elbows, harrumphed and grumbled about the impatience of the unwashed masses and the lack of free drinks.

The bar thrummed with dangerous potential. Philosophers are thinkers who leave the *doing* to everyone else. Only no one does what philosophers say. It's too abstract. Artists get along with abstract, and they're prone to doing things like, well, *doing things*. They're capable of making signs and often willing to walk around with them. No matter which way Sloot looked at it, this didn't end well.

The situation devolved into an argument. Someone broke the end of a bottle on the bar and started waving it around. To make matters worse, that someone was Arthur.

"Right," Arthur shouted, "in your seats, all of you! We're going to have a calm and rational discussion about the proletariat's capacity for peaceful coexistence in civilized society, and the next person to talk out of turn gets a new smile carved into their neck!"

The revolution exchanged glances among themselves. All that prevented them converting to a mob and stomping Arthur into a stain on the floorboards was the lack of someone willing to hit him first. Philosophers are no good at combat, but Arthur had the broken bottle. He was bound to get at least one stab in.

The mob was averted. The revolution took their seats.

"New business," Arthur seethed. He'd calmed down a bit but hadn't dropped the bottle. "What else is there but the Domnitor, long may he reign?"

"Long may he reign," echoed the room.

"His reign of terror is coming to an end!"

The polite applause thundered in Sloot's ears. His breathing came in panicked gulps. This was real heresy! It was his duty to defend the good name of the Domnitor, long may he reign!

"Demon!" shouted someone. Sloot looked up to see several people pointing at him, staring with eyes wide. It was then that he realized his horns had come out.

"Relax," said Arthur, "he's with us."

"What?" Sloot balked. He was sure he'd remember having been invited to join a group. "I'm afraid there's been some sort of mistake."

"No mistake," said Arthur. "Trust me, it makes perfect sense you'd join up with the revolution."

"I beg to differ."

"That makes perfect sense, too. Look, I don't want to waste time with detailed explanations of why I'm right and your wrong."

"You've got better ways to waste their time, have you?" asked Igor with a wink.

"Gremlin!" shouted someone else.

"It's fine," said someone in the crowd. "If Arthur's invited a demon, he'll have good reasons for inviting a gremlin as well."

"I didn't invite him," said Arthur.

"He's joking," said Igor.

"How dare you!" As far as philosophers were concerned, humor was an illusion woven by the simple-minded to escape hard truths. Philosophers had far superior means of denial, not that you could make them admit it.

"I didn't invite him," Arthur repeated firmly, "but it's fine, he's quit mischief. He's trying to be a bard."

"Oh, that's arts!" said Annabella Forp.

"He's doing a redemption?" asked Karl.

"I suppose he is."

"More like a career change," said Igor.

"Huh."

"What do you mean, 'huh?'" Arthur's voice had dimmed subtly, which meant he was gearing up for an argument.

"Nothing," said Karl, "I just took you for a determinist."

"Well, that's just—" Arthur shouted, then paused and deflated. "Well, it's true, actually."

"But you believe that the gremlin can become a bard."

"No!" Arthur's fury flared back up. It was like it had never left. "I said he's *trying* to be a bard! I never said I believed in him."

"I'm still in the room, you know," Igor mumbled.

"For now," said Arthur. "All right, before we vote, we have to hear from the opposition. Sloot?"

"I'm sorry?" asked Sloot.

"You're the Devil's Advocate," said Arthur. "Do your job!"

Arthur motioned for Sloot to step up to the lectern, which was just a slightly taller table than the rest. Sloot did what came naturally and froze while he panicked.

"I'm the what?"

"The Devil's Advocate," said Arthur. "In order for this to be a proper democracy, we have to listen to an opposing viewpoint before we unanimously come to our foregone conclusion. You're a fan of the Domnitor, long may he reign—"

"Long may he reign," echoed everyone else.

"And you're a devil to boot. It's a no-brainer, really."

"I'm not a devil," said Sloot. "I'm a demon."

"And that's different?"

"It is."

"How? And don't use the concept of duality to answer. You're not qualified."

Sloot took Arthur at his word. He certainly didn't feel qualified.

"Look, it's not important," said Sloot. "I just don't understand why—"

"I'll be the judge of what's important," said Arthur, his voice rising half an octave in indignation. "Now, tell us why we should accept the Domnitor's iron boot on our necks, long may he reign!"

"Long may he reign," everyone repeated.

Making Sausage

If Sloot had hoped his speech would turn out differently, he hadn't let on. Not even to himself.

It wasn't that he was unprepared. Far from it. He'd spent his whole life in the fervent belief that the Domnitor, long may he reign, was the best thing to happen to the Old Country since before it had earned that moniker.

Nor was it that he was afraid of public speaking. He was, of course, just like any sensible person would be. It was one of many untested fears rattling around in the empty space where Sloot's courage should have been.

It was the collective will of the artists and philosophers that had turned up for the meeting. Sloot knew fanaticism when he saw it. There was no reasoning with fanatics. He'd know, he was one. All you could do was try and convince them you weren't a threat, and hope they didn't consider you worth tiring out their pitchfork arms.

Nevertheless, Sloot gave it his all. He didn't want to be Devil's Advocate for the Coordinated Revolution of Artists and Philosophers, whose natural acronym couldn't be used in the Old Country for goblin-related reasons, but he did his best. He reminded the revolutionaries that the Domnitor, long may he reign, kept them safe from everything but his government's ministries. He pointed out that the mighty walls of Salzstadt had never been breached by roving hordes of bloodthirsty cannibals, his denial working overtime to squash the fact that he'd been outside the wall and hadn't seen a single cannibal. He even reminded them that throwing in against the Domnitor, long may he reign, was grounds for being stripped of citizenship and set adrift on a block of ice in the Port of Salzstadt. The harbor master had sole discretion over whether you'd be given an oar.

It didn't change their minds, of course. People who turned up to revolutions brought the truth with them.

The only thing—or rather *person*—actually, *thing* was probably more accurate—that surprised Sloot was Igor. He was pleading for them to disperse when Igor twanged his bit of wire. To Sloot's utter bafflement, feet began to tap. Hands began to clap. A voice began humming a melody. Others joined in. Then there was a harmony. Then there were single tears in eyes cast heavenward, or rotting timbers-ward in any case.

"Wait," pleaded Sloot, "what are you doing?"

"We're not doing anything," said Ernst, whose foot was tapping along with the impromptu arrangement.

"Yes, you are," Sloot insisted. "Look at your foot!"

"Oh, that. Yes, well, that's just the spirit of the thing."

"Spirit of what thing? That's just Igor and his bit of wire!"

"It started there, true enough," said Ernst. "But look at what's been made of it! The righteous cause has given wings to Igor's music, and—"

"Come with me," said Arthur. He grabbed Sloot by the shoulder and dragged him out into the street, which was entirely unnecessary. Sloot was never one to question a firm demand.

It was neither foggy nor raining on the lamplit street, but the air was cold and wet nonetheless. Never let it be said that a Salzstadt night would let a mere lack of precipitation rob it of its traditional clammy discomforts.

"What do you think you're doing?" Arthur demanded, closing his coat against the chill.

"I was advocating for the Domnitor, long may he reign," said Sloot with an air of superiority that he didn't get to use very often. "I thought that was what you wanted."

"Yes, but why did you bring Igor?"

"He came on his own."

"Yes," Arthur seethed, "and now he's made that *thing*!"

"What thing?"

"The spirit of the thing," Arthur bristled. "You heard Ernst. Do you have any idea what you've done?"

"What's the matter with the singing? I thought you'd be pleased about that."

Arthur scoffed. "Pleased? Do you know nothing about idealism?"

"Yes," said Sloot. "Or possibly no," he added, the linguistic ambiguity of Arthur's question having caught up to him.

Arthur sighed in aggravation. Sloot knew the philosopher well enough to recognize the hidden glee behind his facade of annoyance. Philosophers love explaining things to people, though they take the view that if everyone knows how much they enjoy it, they'll stop asking. If philosophers were capable of objectivity, they might realize that no one has ever actually asked.

"Reality is a perceptual construct," Arthur explained. "Perception requires a mind, ideals don't. You start setting revolutions to music, and the ideals start doing the thinking! Reality is now being perceived by a non-mind on behalf of sentient beings. You're severing the link between perception and the reality you're supposed to fix!"

Arthur was making philosophical sausage. It was made of cast-off bits of proper philosophy, ground up in the mind of someone who'd barely passed his exams and shoved into a flimsy casing that had fallen off a cart, don't ask any questions. It was a farce at best, but throw it on a plate with enough ketchup, and you'll get someone to swallow it.

"That sounds bad," said Sloot. "How do we fix it?"

"We have to act quickly," said Arthur. "Get back in there and cast some doubt over the whole thing. That's your job, after all, *Devil's Advocate*."

"That's what I was trying to do," Sloot replied. "It isn't working!"

"How could it?" Arthur snapped. "It's a righteous revolution stirring up in there, and none of your precious Domnitor's propaganda can assuage the souls of the people crying out for justice!"

"Long may he reign," said Sloot.

"Long may he reign. Look, I'll go in first and put a stop to the singing. You get your head together and come in after a couple of minutes. Got it?"

Sloot nodded.

"And no wheedling, or saying please," Arthur warned. "You have to be bold! Strong arguments! Convince them!"

"You said it's not possible."

Arthur harrumphed. "Not with that attitude." He turned on his heel and stormed back into the pub.

Sloot was at a loss, but that was nothing new. What could he say? He'd used his best arguments before, and they'd bounced off the revolutionaries' collective sense of righteousness without leaving a dent.

"Pssst," went a shadow in the alley next to the bar.

"I haven't got any money!" shouted Sloot. It was true, not that his natural defenses needed it to be.

"Keep your voice down," hissed the shadow.

"Flavia?" Sloot squinted into the gloom. He walked into the alley.

"What are you doing here?" he asked.

"Nothing to do with you, actually," said Flavia, "or at least I'd never have thought in a million years. How did you get mixed up with a revolution?"

"I didn't! Not on purpose. I thought we were just going to a pub!"

"And yet here you are," said Flavia, "hobnobbing with the primary conspirator!"

"I know what it looks like, but … wait a minute, you're trying to overthrow the Domnitor too, long may he reign!"

"Long may he reign," Flavia repeated. "I am not! I'm just trying to augment the hierarchy a bit"

"Well, I think we're all better off leaving the Domnitor right where he is, long may he reign."

"Long may he reign."

"They're not listening to reason in there," Sloot said. "What am I supposed to say to them?"

The door to the pub swung open. Angry voices raised in angry song. Igor marched into the street with the revolution in tow, twanging his bit of wire for all it was worth.

"Come on, Sloot!" Arthur was near the front of the column, carrying a pitchfork.

"But—" Sloot turned toward Flavia, but she'd disappeared. He was on his own. He ran to catch up to the mob, falling in step beside Arthur.

"What happened?" he hissed.

"What does it look like," Arthur beamed. "The revolution is underway! Get in line or be left behind!"

"We are in line," said Sloot, "but what about severing reality and all that? What happened to casting doubt?"

"Plenty of time for that later," said Arthur. "We're in the middle of a glorious revolution! The dawn will see a new order in Salzstadt!"

Sloot groaned and chided himself for not having seen this coming. Arthur was a philosopher by occupation, but he was a revolutionary at heart. That was his purpose in life, overthrowing things. Philosophy made him good at arguments, but he didn't have to argue when the people were ready to give him what he wanted. At the moment, he was one of those herd-following sheep against whom he'd so often railed. Sloot could only hope that the mob was headed somewhere other than calamity.

CORPORATE SPONSORSHIP

If there was a single worst place in the city for the mob to end up, they found it. Only Sloot could see the accounting annex on the other side of the street. The doors of the counting house were closed and locked, as they should be in the middle of the night.

"This is it, gentlemen!" shouted Arthur.

"And ladies," shouted someone within the crowd.

"Yes, yes," grumbled Arthur, swinging his pitchfork around in agitation, nearly catching someone's ear in the process. "Gentlemen *and ladies*, this is where the glorious revolution begins!"

"I thought that was in the pub," said Karl.

Arthur closed his eyes and sighed from the bottom of his soul. "There are several nascent stages to a revolution. It's not started all at once! Please step outside your literal mind long enough to—"

"Oh, that's rich," shouted a torch-bearing man with only light green paint on his smock. Sloot recognized a minimalist when he saw one. "A philosopher telling an artist to step outside his literal mind? We invented abstract, sir!"

"Actually," said Nerissa Spatzerbrechen, Dean of Humanities

at the University of Salzstadt, "it was Ludmilla the Unhinged who had the first abstract thought on record. She was the first philosopher to be burned for—"

"Oh! Oh! Oh!" mocked the minimalist, "Look at me, I'm a dandy professor! I've got facts from books! Stand back while I use my literal sources as evidence of abstract—"

"Abstract thought is rooted in truth, you lackadaisical half-wit! You wouldn't know a qualified citation if it bit you on the face!"

"That can be arranged!" To the minimalist's horror, a scrawny teenager in a threadbare suit leapt toward him, gleaming white teeth emerging from a patchy forest that may or may not grow up to become a beard someday.

In all the universe, no one ranks higher in terms of self-assurance than a freshman philosopher. Freshman anthropologists have done qualitative studies to determine whether their wispy beards play a role in the inflation of the ego, but have come to no consensus.

The freshman's teeth sank into the minimalist's shoulder. The rest of the mob wasted no time joining the fray. The sounds of sketchbooks and textbooks thwumped in the night amid cries of "there are important sketches in there," and "everyone saw you tear the pages, you're responsible for the library fines!"

"Gentlemen, please!" shouted Arthur. "We mustn't *oof*—"

"And ladies, you hack!" Annabella Forp, her fist still coiled and low from her jab to Arthur's gut.

The scuffle went on until the artists decided the whole thing was derivative and pedestrian, not to mention they were losing. They weren't, actually, but the philosophers managed to convince them the whole thing was pointless, as was life. Ennui was good common ground for artists and philosophers, though it took the wind out of revolutions.

"Do not lose heart," said Arthur, wiping his bloody nose on his tweed sleeve. "This is our moment! We are at the gates! Gentlemen, we—yes, and ladies—we must take up the banner and stride boldly into the fray! Not this fray, but one against a common enemy!"

Igor began to twang. Feet began to tap.

"Oh, dear," moaned Sloot. He'd hoped for a fleeting moment that the in-fighting would result in everyone storming off to different pubs with an *oh yeah? I'll just start my own glorious revolution! And there will be free drinks this time!*

No such luck. The spirit of the thing wasn't having it. Voices rose in harmony, fists pumped in the air, and the rabble of punchy, slightly inebriated intellectuals remembered that they were revolutionaries.

"The heart of the Old Country is her industry," said Arthur. "If we can—"

"Should the glorious revolution persist in the antiquated practice of sexualized personifications?" asked Ernst.

"We'll table that for next meeting's new business," Arthur intoned, now fully enraptured in the revolutionary spirit. "Today we cast off the chains of oppression and overthrow the Domnitor!"

"Long may he reign!" shouted the frenzied revolutionaries in a single voice. They charged the front door of the counting house. Its hinges offered no resistance to their combined weight, leaving the door to be trampled underfoot as the glorious revolution flooded into the building.

It was empty, with the exception of some broken furniture and a revolution. It occurred to Sloot that an invasion not unlike this one must have already happened when the economy collapsed.

That would be why the door gave way so easily, thought Sloot. *Having already been broken down once, it knew the drill.*

"We've searched everywhere," said Karl. "There's nothing here."

"Oh, there's something here," said Arthur. "Places have power, you know."

"You mean like wizards' towers?"

"No, not like wizards' towers!" Arthur chided. "That's the naked, obvious sort of power that anyone could point out!"

Arthur wasn't wrong. The Three Bells counting house had been Salzstadt's financial epicenter for centuries. Money, secrets, and the fates of people the world over moved through it faster than questionable meats through tourists who didn't know which food carts are reputable. The whole place hummed with leftover potency. Sloot couldn't fathom how one might tap into it, but then neither did he understand how the revolution had its own spirit. These were the sorts of mysteries that didn't file nicely into columns, and that was why Sloot's job was so difficult.

"Anyway," Arthur continued, "if it were true in the literal sense that there was *nothing* here, we'd be in a multi-existential paradox. I defy you to maintain a viable definition of self in absence of same!"

"You've got me there." Karl sighed in the specific exasperation of a philosopher questioning whether conversations with other philosophers were entirely futile.

"There's about to be a lot less 'something' here," said a voice that could freeze the sun. "Or a lot fewer 'someones,' anyway."

Sloot turned to see Mrs. Knife standing among the revolutionaries, few of whom appeared to grasp their proximity to calamity. She leered at Sloot with her downcast brow furrowed, her namesake idly twirling between her fingers. She seemed to be trying to guess how much blood Sloot had in him before measuring it out the fun way.

"Who are you?" demanded the freshman philosopher, whose sense of self-worth placed him solidly at the top of any ladder upon which he happened to be standing. He didn't live long enough to reconcile that metaphorical standing with physically lying in a pool of his own blood.

"That's who I am." Mrs. Knife grinned. Her eyes darted around the room, assessing threats and ranking them in order of how much blood she could harvest. Her knife had moved so quickly through the freshman's throat that barely a trickle had clung to the steel.

"So," said Igor with the inflection of a whisper, but at a conversational volume, "that must be Mrs. Knife."

Sloot whimpered and tried to remain still. He didn't dare hope she hadn't seen him, but he wouldn't know until he tried.

"She looks really dangerous," Igor continued at full volume. "Didn't she almost murder you once?"

"Shh," Sloot hissed.

"And she's queen of the goblins. I don't think mortals can stab demons, but—"

"Shh!"

"—she probably could. She could cut you to ribbons."

"Be quiet!"

"You might not even die of it, being a demon and all." Igor shivered. "That would take some adjustment, living as a pile of meat ribbons."

"Not a bad idea," growled Mrs. Knife, "but better than you deserve, Peril. And where do all of you think you're going?"

Most of the revolutionaries had been slinking door- or window-wise. They froze in their tracks.

"Excellent question," Arthur boomed, his utter lack of awareness doing precious little for his personal safety. "You cowards are supposed to be a revolution! There's no running away in revolution! One of your comrades is fallen! Get in there and fight!"

Mrs. Knife wore an expression that really wished they would. Arthur himself didn't seem eager to make the next contribution to the blood pooling on the floor. Even if Sloot loosed his demonic fury—assuming he had some he didn't know about—he doubted that all of them put together stood a chance against Mrs. Knife. That was the sort of careful pragmatism that had kept Sloot safe for most of his life, but not the sort to which idealists are prone.

Sloot needed to defuse the situation the revolution learned the true meaning of the word "bloodbath."

Twang went Igor's bit of wire.

"Oh, dear," groaned Sloot.

They took over the counting house down by the sea,
Sloot and the spineless revolutionaries,

"Hey," said Annabella, "who's he calling spineless?"

They all ran away at the drop of a hat,
When they saw the knife on the crazy old bat.

"I wouldn't call her that," Sloot warned, "if I were you."

A grunt of amusement stirred in Mrs. Knife's throat. It spun a cocoon of dry, papery laughter, which hatched a horrid butterfly of maniacal cackling.

"We didn't run away," Annabella insisted.

"What?"

"At the drop of a hat or otherwise."

"Some of us did," said a philosopher who'd gotten some paint on himself, or possible an artist with a penchant for leather elbow patches. "Terrence the Painter and Gustav Heringstiefel bolted past me before that kid's body hit the floor."

"What did you say?" The point of Mrs. Knife's dagger seemed to focus on him.

"I mean, I think they never came in, or else they'd have seen that dead body who'd been there the whole time."

"Nobody else needs to die," said Mrs. Knife. She sheathed her blade with a deftness that left no doubt she could have it back out in a flash if anyone had aspirations verging on heroics. "Did the gremlin say you were a revolution?"

Everyone looked at Arthur, who in turn looked at Sloot. Ah, yes, that was the sort of day this was turning out to be. The sort where he was ultimately responsible for everyone else's bad ideas when the time came to settle up.

"Please don't involve me in this," said Sloot, who hadn't wanted to be Devil's Advocate in the first place.

The corners of Mrs. Knife's mouth turned up. No one with a passing knowledge of human emotions would have referred to it as a smile, though it might technically have qualified.

"Typical demon," Mrs. Knife spat. "Lures you fine people onto private property in the middle of the night for his own nefarious ends, then pretends he's just a bystander."

"Yeah," said the revolutionaries in unrehearsed non-unison. Sloot could see a solid mob mentality taking shape. The first thing that sounded reasonable was likely to gain traction among them. He had to proceed with caution. Luckily, Sloot knew all about that.

"Fine," said Sloot. "If I'm in charge as soon as things turn ugly, then we're sorry to have bothered you, Mrs. Knife. Everyone out, please send us a bill for the door."

The revolution began silently shuffling toward the door. Sloot dared to hope that was the end of it, which was among the sillier things he'd done that week.

"Not so fast," said Mrs. Knife.

"Yeah," said Arthur, pointing a bony finger at Sloot. "Who do you think you are?"

"Yeah," cascaded the revolution. They stopped shuffling and resumed glaring at Sloot with their arms crossed.

"We can come to an arrangement about the door," said Mrs. Knife, still staring at Sloot. "I know, why don't you let me join your revolution?"

Everyone turned to look at Sloot. Sloot said a swear word. Mrs. Knife cackled.

"Not this again," said Sloot. He forced a smile at the revolution. "All right, fine. If you actually want my advice, it's a terrible idea. It's painfully obvious that she's plotting something."

Everyone turned to look at Arthur, who cleared his throat with enough theatric flair to make Sloot look for the popcorn vendor.

"That's precisely what I thought you'd say." Arthur's chest puffed to its limit, making it appear slightly less concave than usual. "As Devil's Advocate, you're incapable of offering advice that won't lead us to ruin. Welcome to the revolution, Mrs. Knife!"

Sloot heard a sizzling sound that could either have been a polite round of applause or his brain frying in its own juices.

"You can't be serious!" shouted Sloot, though he didn't know why he'd bothered. Neither philosophers nor artists tend to truck with serious. It makes their abstract all murky.

"Oh, can't we?" asked Mrs. Knife. "We take the revolution very seriously, indeed. Tell me, how much blood has been shed in service to the cause?"

The revolution shifted around and declined to make eye contact with anything but boot laces.

"Well," said Arthur after a while, "there was that guy." He motioned vaguely toward the late freshman, whose pool of blood had begun to congeal.

"Revolutions demand blood," said Mrs. Knife, over-pronouncing the word with no small amount of delight. "Have we truly shed none before now?"

The communal lack of eye contact was joined by shrugged shoulders and mumbled excuses about not knowing whose blood the revolution required.

"Plenty of things have changed without bloodshed!" Sloot was incredulous. "Don't you know your history? Lord Horst Forellenschnüffler overruled the Minister of Civil Defense to get a minimum age instituted for military service, and he didn't have to spill any blood to do it."

"What of the soldiers?" asked Mrs. Knife. "So many of them had to retire until their twelfth birthdays and get jobs in the salt mines. Wouldn't it have been worth a bit of blood to see that injustice undone? Won't someone think of the children?"

"Yeah!" shouted the revolution, relieved that Mrs. Knife was paying attention to someone else.

"The revolution has grown soft and complacent," said Mrs. Knife. "It's time for new leadership."

"What?" balked Sloot and Arthur in unison. A sense of dread so familiar it was almost comfortable washed over Sloot. He didn't have to be a causality demon to see where this was going.

"Pipe down, Peril, I'll deal with you in a minute."

Sloot was accustomed to being regarded as the smallest threat in the room. That wasn't an accident. He'd gone to great lengths to avoid offending anyone. You only ended up with enemies when people were offended. Offend enough people and they'll call you a villain. Villains needed elaborate outfits that Sloot's primitive fashion sense could never achieve.

"As for you," Mrs. Knife continued, shifting her glare to Arthur, "how much blood have you shed for the cause?"

"All of it."

What little mirth had been freeloading in Mrs. Knife's expression got off the couch, showered, shaved, and shuffled off to seek gainful employment. Her blade was in her hand again.

"All of it? What do you mean?"

"My head was severed," said Arthur, with no small amount of pride. Then again, Arthur's pride didn't come in small amounts.

"And then what," puzzled Mrs. Knife, "it grew back?"

"Don't be absurd! I came back to life after that goblin wizard blew up Willie and spilled the Dark over everything."

"Why?"

For quite possibly the first time in his life, Arthur had no response. Whether Mrs. Knife was insanely clever, insanely lucky, or simply insane, she'd stumbled onto the philosopher's greatest weakness: the simple existential question in a proper existential context.

Why had Arthur been brought back to life? It defied logic, and philosophers were armed with little else. He stood there, mouth open to deliver a response that would not come forth, moustaches bristling with angst, finger hovering in mid-now-you-listen-here.

"Anybody else have questions about the new leadership?" Mrs. Knife dared her fellow and sister revolutionaries, none of whom lacked a reason to give their bootlaces another inspection.

"Good. And as for you, Peril," said Mrs. Knife, pausing with the tip of her knife menacing Sloot-wise. The pause went on longer that Sloot expected, which threw him even farther off-balance than he was before.

Sloot whimpered. Mrs. Knife grinned and sheathed her namesake.

"Not yet," she said. "Killing you would be a mercy. I'll see to it you suffer endlessly before I put you to my knife."

"I had a theory about that," Igor began. "I'm not sure you can kill a demon with a knife."

"Don't be so sure," Mrs. Knife growled at the gremlin.

"I'm not sure at all," Igor replied. "But I'm fairly certain you can't."

Sloot blurted a noise that was equal parts giggle, cough, wheeze, and sob. There was no point in coming up with a word for it, as it would never come up again in the course of any history.

"Perhaps we could give her the benefit of the doubt," said Sloot in a heavily suggestive tone.

"We could," said Igor, squinting at the ceiling as he considered the idea, "but if I were a betting man—which I am—I'd put my money against it."

"Then it's a good thing you haven't any money!"

"Only because you haven't paid me."

"You're not—"

"Silence!" Mrs. Knife's blade was in her hand again. "You're making it very difficult for me to leave your guts where they are,

Peril! I've already taken your job, your teleportation privileges, and any privacy you may have had in your new hovel. Are you really so eager to lose your guts as well? I'm starting to wonder whether I loathe you as much as *you* do."

Sloot wondered the same as he and Arthur were violently herded toward the door and tossed out into the street. Igor sauntered out after them, having avoided the tossing for want of someone willing to touch a gremlin with their bare hands. It was said that the black plague had staunchly refused to go anywhere near them.

"Oh, well," said Igor. "Easy come, easy go, eh?"

In a single maneuver, Arthur threw himself down on the cobbles and commenced an impressive tantrum. He offended the air with a nasal wail and flailed about in useless rage.

"Easy come? You mutton-headed clown! That was my life's work!"

"Really?" Igor looked to Sloot. "He just got off the couch a couple of days ago."

"True," said Sloot, "but to be fair, he's only been alive for a matter of weeks. This time around, I mean."

"The first one!" Arthur shouted. "The first Philosophers' Rebellion! At least that one got squashed by the Domnitor, long may he reign."

"Long may he reign," Sloot repeated.

"This one didn't even make it that far! Co-opted by a lunatic!"

"A different lunatic," Igor corrected.

Arthur's tantrum raged until it ran out of steam, which didn't take very long. Philosophers' stamina is notoriously fraught. Their physical endurance is comparable to the attention span of squirrels. Once his screaming and thrashing had reduced itself to mild flailing with the occasional moan, Sloot scooped him up and carried him back to the apartment.

THIS IS FINE

Sloot had given up on referring to it as *his* apartment. He simply counted himself fortunate he made so little money that it qualified as a shed, which enabled him to declare everyone and everything in it firewood. There was a potential downside, but only if winter lasted more than six weeks longer than the Ministry of Meteorology predicted.

The only sounds in the apartment were occasional pathetic groans from a grown man, man-child, or alleged man.

"Where is that blasted chamber maid?" Constantin demanded.

"At her new job, if I had to guess," grumbled Nan, still disguised as "Man."

"I know why all of the servants left," said Willie, "but it sounds like you need to explain it to Dad again. And speak loudly enough for me to hear."

"You don't have any money," said Nan in the lowest tones she could manage.

"Oh, Nan," chided Willie, "it's not polite to talk about money!"

"Nan?" Constantin nearly sat up in his hammock. "How did

that coddler get in here? Fetch me my crossbow!"

"He said 'Man,' Lord Hapsgalt. He was talking to me."

"It's all right," Willie continued as though no one else had spoken. "I know the working class aren't as smart as real people. Just try explaining it to him again, but don't talk about money."

"He's right," Arthur moaned. "Money is as meaningless as everything else! Why bother aspiring to high-minded ideals when heavy-handed tactics are futile?"

"I mean, even if that were the case," said Willie, "why would servants care about money? It's not like they have enough to be rich."

Sloot sighed. It wouldn't be long before Arthur's sense of moral outrage had him shouting until his throat was raw, so he'd be his old self soon enough. Constantin was little more than the sedentary human equivalent of classism at full volume. Nan still got to coddle Willie, and she didn't seem to care about anything else.

Sloot worried about Willie, though. The little lordling was the evolutionary result of capitalism having been left in the tender embrace of the aristocracy long enough for nature to take its course. It wasn't his fault. The financial sector was bound to produce him on a long enough timeline.

"So what do you think?" asked Igor.

Panic crept up Sloot's back, into his brain, and displaced the panic that was there already. That was just a resting level of panic, which would hiss and scamper away when anything more potent happened along. Someone had been talking to Sloot and he hadn't been listening! He'd lose a corner off his etiquette card for that.

"Sorry?" Sloot realized it had only been Igor he'd been ignoring. He calmed down considerably.

"My trial period," Igor whined. "You said you'd re-evaluate when the time was right!"

"Yes, and … wait, you think that *this* is the right time to ask me for an evaluation?"

"I figured it couldn't hurt," said Igor. He flashed a smile that reminded Sloot of tree bark after a woodpecker had given it a vigorous once-over.

"Are you joking? After you enticed Mrs. Knife with the prospect of cutting me into a pile of living ribbons?"

"Oh, that," said Igor. "That was just riffing on logic. Bound to happen with that many philosophers around. Besides, that wasn't part of my official duties. I wasn't playing an instrument at the time, was I?"

"Well, no," Sloot admitted.

"I was just reporting the facts. Can't hold that against me."

"Wait, yes I can! You're not a journalist, you're a bard!"

"A ha! You admitted it!"

"What? No, I just meant—"

"No need, I accept the position! No backsies!"

It was just as well that Sloot couldn't come up with a cogent retort. He wouldn't have been able to deliver it while being forcefully ejected from the apartment through the window.

This is fine, Sloot thought as he hurtled through the streets of Salzstadt without any say in the matter. A bit of decorum would have been nice, but whoever was summoning him seemed to have an urgent need to speak to his posterior, and therefore was working to ensure that it arrived first.

He zigged and zagged through the streets, ultimately turning down a narrow alley in the street of fishmongers and crashing into a bin full of refuse relevant to that occupation.

"Ow," said Sloot, and then "ew."

"Sorry," said Walter the Undying.

"What did I tell you about controlling perception?" asked Flavia.

"Oh, right. I meant, you had that coming, and don't test me because there's more where that came from!"

"That's better."

"Seriously, I could mess you up, man!" Walter the Undying lurched toward Sloot with a fist. Sloot flinched.

"All right, that's enough," said Flavia. "So, Sloot, what have you got to say for yourself?"

"Sorry for the smell," said Sloot. He fished a wet glob of guts out of his pocket and returned it to the bin whence it–and he–had come.

"Clever," said Flavia. "What happened in the counting house?"

"Mrs. Knife," he said plainly.

Flavia deflated. She'd obviously had a proper "I'm very disappointed in you" queued up, but like everyone else who moved in Salzstadt's clandestine circles, she knew that very little stood in Mrs. Knife's way, and it tended to get stabbed when it did.

"What happened?" she asked. "I mean, the fact that we no longer have a revolution to deal with is good news, but I didn't even know that Mrs. Knife was … why are you looking at me like that?"

"Well," said Sloot who, despite everything that had happened, found himself loathe to disappoint Flavia, "the revolution is still in the picture."

Flavia and Walter the Undying exchanged a glance, both grasping for the remnant of seconds ago, when they were blissfully unaware of the truth.

"Seriously?" asked Flavia. "How are they still a threat if they're all dead?"

"They're not dead," said Sloot. "Well, there was a freshman. It probably doesn't matter. Everyone else was still alive when Arthur and I were chucked out."

Flavia's mouth moved wordlessly for a bit as her brain moved the pieces around. Her eyes went wide for a second before her training took over, plastering a sweet smile across her face.

"Sloot," she cooed, "you wouldn't happen to know who's leading the revolution now, would you?"

Sloot's brow contorted under the wave of queasiness that came over him. He nodded slowly.

Flavia sighed, but her face remained placid. "It's Mrs. Knife, isn't it?"

Sloot nodded again.

Flavia said a swear word.

"What does that mean?" asked Walter the Undying.

"It means that we're out of options. We have to lean harder on our assets, if you know what I mean."

Sloot sighed. "I'm pretty sure I do."

Flavia really leaned into her sparkling laugh. Sloot had never been good at seeing through facades, but Flavia's was so transparent that even Sloot recognized her desperation.

"Sloot," said Flavia sweetly, "I really hate to ask, what with everything you've got on your plate at the moment, but we really need your help in sorting this out."

"What, the revolution?"

"Well, yes," said Flavia, drawing out the words in preparation to add a very big "and" to them. "And we feel the best way to do that is to deliver the Domnitor to our … stewardship. Long may he reign."

"Long may he reign," said Walter the Undying.

"Long may he reign," said Sloot. "Right, I'm considering that, but I'm not quite sure that—"

"How is Myrtle?" asked Flavia.

Sloot's expression darkened in a way that those of mortals cannot. His eyes went jet black, his horns shot skyward, and a black mist roiled around him. His posture went unusually rigid as he rose to his full height.

"I don't know," Sloot over-enunciated in a pair of octaves. "I haven't seen her since you two banished her to the lowest circle of the Inferno."

"Back, demon!" shouted Walter the Undying. He produced a silver medallion from within his robes, and the sight of it send Sloot scrambling backward up the wall behind him. He hissed at it.

"Oh, Sloot!" Flavia's right hand covered her heart. Her left fanned her face. "I thought the two of you were just dating, I didn't know you felt this strongly for her! Oh, that's nice. Even between demons, love is just so…" she trailed off, doing her best not to cry.

All of this was making Sloot terribly uncomfortable. He didn't like going all scary demon in the face, and Walter the Undying's medallion was freaking him out. He didn't think it would hurt him, but it reminded him of the way the tip of one's nose itched if one thought about it hard enough. It gave him the impression he'd get that on his whole body forever if it touched him.

"What do you want?" he growled.

Flavia cleared her throat. "Well, if you could move things along and deliver the Domnitor to us, long may he reign—"

"Long may he reign," echoed Sloot and Walter the Undying.

"Then we could mop up this silly little revolution and restore order. Wouldn't you like that, Sloot? To restore order?"

"Of course," said Sloot, who was midway through descending the wall and assuming a more human appearance. "But I only get one shot at amending the Narrative, and I have to make sure it's the right decision before I do anything."

"I understand," said Flavia, "I really do. But don't you trust me, after everything we've been through?"

"You kidnapped me," said Sloot, "blackmailed me, banished my girlfriend to—"

"Yes, all right," said Flavia. "Have I ever lied to you?"

"No," Sloot admitted, "not that I'm aware, but that's—"

"Then believe me when I tell you we have the best interests of the Old Country at heart. Honest! As much as we love him, our beloved nation cannot continue under the rule of a child. We're not trying to overthrow the government, just restructure it so it works."

"I understand," said Sloot. "But what's the rush?"

"We weren't worried about the revolution when it was philosophers, but they got artists involved. Artists like to *do* things, not just sit around yelling at each other about how things ought to be done. And now Mrs. Knife is running the show. It's a real threat, Sloot! If things continue to progress at this rate, there will be new flags flying over the city within the week! Is that what you want?"

"Of course not," said Sloot, "but I need more time!"

"The Old Country is nearly out of time," said Flavia. "If you don't deliver soon, I'll have to have Myrtle demoted."

"That's … well, that would be bad, but—"

"Oh, it's really bad," said Walter the Undying. He was still holding the medallion in front of himself. Sloot scratched the tip of his nose and gave them a quizzical look.

"She's already a demon 99th class working on the 99th level," Flavia explained. "There are loads of demons down there, some of them middle management demons who have never gotten to assert their authority over anyone. Ever."

"I've heard about what they've done to demons 100th class who get cast down there," said Walter the Undying. "It isn't pretty."

"You want to see someone go mad with power?" asked Flavia. "Give a middle management demon 99th class a whiff of someone they outrank. I've seen Viking berserkers with more restraint."

Walter the Undying offered to send Sloot back to his apartment, but Sloot said he'd walk. Even if the wizard's technique weren't so brutalizing, he was in no hurry to get home to the constant shouting match that his apartment had become. He needed to think. Even if he wanted to hand rulership of the Old Country over to Flavia, he had no idea where the Domnitor was, long may he reign. Stagralla, maybe? That's where Vlad hauled him back from exile. It seemed foolish to go back there again, but does that mean it's the last place anyone would look?

Everyone was asleep when he returned home. Arthur was sleep-weeping, two words which should combine in a satisfying portmanteau, but do not.

Perhaps Sloot could find the Domnitor, long may he reign. He'd been there when the Coolest had intervened at the end of the battle, hadn't he? He took the ledger down off the shelf and stood in his circle.

"Oh, no you don't," said Igor. His face was as stern as Sloot had ever seen it. "You need to tell me when you're going to charge through the window rear-end first! Where have you been, anyway?"

"I was with—" Sloot looked around. Was everyone really sleeping? It didn't matter.

"I was called away on an urgent matter," he said. "I didn't even know where I was going myself, until I got there."

"That's beside the point," Igor insisted. "Now that I'm your official bard, you can't—"

"Keep it down, would you?" barked Nan in a whisper. "Willie needs fourteen hours or he's a cranky little monster."

"Sorry," whispered Sloot. He motioned for Igor to follow him, performed the series of gestures, and was standing on a rolling hillside in the Old Country Before, not far from the Carpathian border.

"This is near the end, isn't it?" asked Igor.

"Very near. Look, I've got to get some work done. Even if you were my official bard—"

"Which I am!"

"—not, I'd still be in charge. I don't answer to you!"

"But you can't have adventures without me. That's in the rules!"

"What rules?"

"The unwritten rules."

"That's ridiculous," said Sloot, whose life had been spent in staunch reverence for the rules. Rules which had been written down, thank you very much. What fun were rules that you couldn't point to in a book, and say things like, "this subsection clearly states," and so on?

"If it's not written down," Sloot concluded, "it's not rules."

"Be careful," Igor warned. "You can't go around flaunting the unwritten rules like that."

"Oh, can't I? What would happen if I did?"

"Someone would come along and write them down, that's what." There was nothing flippant about Igor's low, grave tone. No winks or nudges, no innuendoes.

"And what would be so bad about that?"

"You must have a bit of bureaucracy demon in you," said Igor. He motioned toward the battle. "You've got work to do, right? I'll explain on the way."

Against every instinct he possessed, Sloot walked toward the battle. Igor explained along the way that in the absence of bureaucracy, people find ways to get along with each other without books full of statutes or the threat of litigation.

"Bad enough they can't get by with unspoken agreements," said Igor. "Speaking them aloud opens them up to arguments. 'You said this,' and 'I don't remember agreeing to that,' and 'oh, yeah? Well, I've changed my mind.' That's how things end up getting written down, and then it's all 'that's not what they meant when they wrote that.' It's not natural, keeping people honest like that."

"Then why did you try to make me sign a contract when we first met?" asked Sloot. "If writing things down is so awful."

"Oh, that?" Igor flashed a smile that could have curdled milk. "That was just a bit of skullduggery, see? I was a recently reformed gremlin at the time. Still finding my seat on the wagon, as it were. Can't hold that against me."

"Against the rules, I suppose?"

"No," said Igor, "it's just mean. Stop dragging rules into everything. Haven't you been listening?"

They stood at the edge of the battlefield, watching Vlad dispatch scores of goblins. Eventually, Bartleby tripped Gregor, who shot Willie, who exploded. The Dark spilled out over everything, the Coolest's cleanup team did their work, and there they all stood. The Domnitor, long may he reign, was nowhere to be seen.

"Perhaps it was a trick of the light," said Sloot. He turned Pfalzgraf's Rune of Reckoning back half an arc and watched the events play out again, resolving to watch more forcefully this time. He realized after he'd missed it again that he didn't know how to do that.

He turned it back again and resolved not to blink. That's when he realized that demons didn't need to blink, and he'd only been doing it as an affectation. He had a mild panic attack while he wondered how many other things he didn't know about himself, then turned it back again.

Nothing. The Domnitor, long may he reign, was there one moment and not the next. It was as if someone had simply magicked him away.

"Maybe that's it," Sloot mumbled to himself.

"Maybe what's what?" asked Igor.

"Someone seems to have magicked the Domnitor away, long may he reign."

"Ah," said Igor with a sagely nod. "The plot thickens."

Having never read fiction, Sloot assumed that was a cooking metaphor and delved no further. He found metaphors disagreeable, culinary or otherwise. He turned Pfalzgraf's Rune of Reckoning back again and watched all of the wizarding types as the events played out. Bartleby was giving Gregor a hard time, so it was neither of them. Nicoleta was floating above the battlefield with Willie and Sloot's former self, though she occasionally made little magical maneuvers that Sloot didn't recognize.

Sloot watched the fairies for a while too, but they were largely occupied with fending off the goblin horde and doing a very good job of it. He knew fairies had magic, but no motive to kidnap the Domnitor, long may he reign. Unless they thought saddling a child with that much power was unfair.

"Could it be?"

"Could what be?"

"I'll tell you on the way," said Sloot. "We're going to Carpathia."

FLEISCHVERKAUFENARM

Sloot hated the train, but that was the point of public transportation. It was invented by business magnates who made their fortunes from horses and carriages. But despite its intentionally crafted discomforts, the train was the fastest way to Carpathia. He needed to hurry for Myrtle's sake, thanks to Flavia's threat. Plus, Sloot didn't want her spending any more time in Infernal Sewage than necessary.

Fortunately, there were no creepy old men in floppy hats dragging bags of salt around the crags. No obstacles between Sloot and a long, sweaty train ride with a bunch of filthy demons except his ardent desire to be anywhere else.

"I miss teleporting," said Sloot.

"Same here," croaked a deeply unsettling corpse who literally had a frog in its throat. The frog seemed to be calling the shots from its perch inside the man's mouth, which gaped with the intensity of a teenager glimpsing the undergarments of his heart's desire, which could literally have been anyone.

"Same here," burbled a slime demon in a bucket on the seat

next to him.

"Same with just about everyone on the train," said the frog in the corpse suit. The milky white eyes above it stared blankly toward an advertisement for Diet Brimstone, not bothering to blink away the flies which tiptoed across them. "Nice suit," it said to Sloot. "Any chance I can buy it off you?"

"What?"

"I'm sure we can work out a price," Igor interjected. "Sloot, how much do your legs weigh?"

"You can't sell my body!"

"Yeah, right, sentimental value," said Igor loudly. Then he whispered to Sloot, "keep it up, we'll get top dollar!"

"It's not a sales tactic," Sloot yelped. "I've only got the one!"

"Shame," said the frog. Its corpse suit shrugged, making the faint sound of creaking leather.

They passed the rest of the ride in *Fleischverkaufenarm*, which means "an awkward silence following the unsuccessful sale of a colleague's carcass." Sloot was unaware that there was a word for it. It was unlikely he'd have been comforted to know it was common enough to require one.

The sun was setting when they emerged from the skull cave. Crimson clouds drifted across the horizon, lazy thunder rolling along with them. Sloot tried to keep himself upwind of Igor as they walked through the forest path toward the castle.

"That's proper foreboding," said Igor. "They've got the best foreboding in Carpathia. There's really good dread in the Old Country, but not foreboding like this."

Sloot couldn't disagree. Though civic statutes demanded he extoll the superiority of the Old Country in all foreign affairs, Igor was right. No one did foreboding like Carpathia. If you so much as squinted at a Carpathian shadow, a wolf would howl in the distance.

"Look, sorry I tried to sell your chassis to a frog demon," said

Igor. "I don't suppose they give you Bard of the Month when you go around doing things like that."

"Don't mention it," said Sloot.

"So Bard of the Month is still on the table, then?"

"I wouldn't count on it."

"Don't decide right away," said Igor. "Let's focus on the matter at hand, right? What is that, anyway?"

"I've got to figure out what happened to the Domnitor, long may he reign. I'm hoping the fairies know something."

"Sorry," said Igor, "but when you said 'fairies,' you don't mean, like, *the* fairies, do you?"

It hadn't occurred to Sloot that there might be more than the ones he knew.

"Little winged folk," said Sloot. "About your height? Always going on about equity?"

Igor said a swear word. "What are you hanging around with them for? They're bad news, Sloot. Can't trust fairies."

"Really? They've always been nice to me."

"Yeah," said Igor. "They really are, aren't they?"

"Yes," said Sloot. "That's what I said. Are you saying they're not?"

"Not exactly. Just a bit *too* nice, if you catch my drift."

"I don't."

"I'd better sit this one out," said Igor. "We go way back, the fairies and me."

"Suit yourself."

"Seriously? Are you trying to be funny?"

"What?"

"You'd really take a meeting without your bard? Your partner?"

Sloot sighed. A light rain chilled the air as the castle loomed nearer. He was able to see Nicoleta's keening rune in front of the courtyard now, and was surprised he'd missed it the first time. It was enormous.

Igor folded his arms in a huff.

"Look, do what you like," said Sloot. "I need to talk to the fairies."

"Hmmph!" Igor closed his eyes and turned his head skyward in the fashion of children confronted with unfamiliar vegetables. Sloot fought his natural urge to pacify anyone who was upset with him for any reason at all and walked in through the courtyard. He was in a hurry.

"Halt, please!" came a small voice from beside the main entrance. An exceptionally well-dressed guard holding a tiny spear cleared her throat. She looked as though she were about to say something, then changed course at the last minute.

"Hang on," she said, "I know you. Aren't you the ghost who came to warn us about the goblins coming north, please?"

"Er, yes," said Sloot. As a rule, he didn't like being recognized. It got you pulled into conversations. But when you're ten times everyone else's height and translucent to boot, anonymity can be hard to come by.

"You're not a ghost anymore."

"No," said Sloot. "I'm a demon now."

"How'd you get past the keening rune, please?"

"I'm on the guest list."

"Oh," said the guard in a tone that had been told they were all sold out of ice cream.

"Is something wrong?"

"Well, since you were gracious enough to ask—thank you—it just doesn't seem fair that we'd have a guest list that everybody isn't on."

Sloot did his best to avoid looking smug, but this was his first taste of exclusivity. From this side of it, anyway. He hadn't had many opportunities to do smug, and he wasn't sure he knew what he should be suppressing.

"Yes, well, I've been a friend to Carpathia for a long time now," said Sloot, his Old Country patriotism threatening to kick him in the shins. "I used to be in Carpathian Intelligence, you know." He was sure he could hear his mother crying somewhere, but then remembered that she was Carpathian Intelligence too. It must have been the wolves he'd heard.

"I wouldn't know," grumbled the guard, "but apparently someone did. Not very fair, if you ask me."

They stood there for a moment in awkward silence.

"Can I just," Sloot nodded toward the door, "go in, then? Please?"

"Sure, why not, please?" said the guard, her voice dripping with the sincerity of a crocodile smiling at a gazelle. "After all, you're on the guest list! That's very special indeed!"

There wasn't a fiber of Sloot's being that was content to walk away from someone who was upset with him, but he was running out of time. He shouted an apology as he rushed through the doors, into the foyer, and down the hallway beyond.

"Sloot!" exclaimed King Lilacs. "How long has it been, please?"

"Too long, your Majesty," said Sloot.

"Yes," said General Dandelion, who was sitting beside Lilacs on what had once been Vlad's throne, "but could you say precisely how long, please?"

Sloot puzzled for a moment. "A few months, I think? Since the unpleasantness with the Dark spilling out and everything."

Lilacs and Dandelion looked over at a fairy wearing a sartorial masterpiece. His tailor had not skimped on the shoulder pads. A tiny book hovered mid-air in front of him, and a tiny quill bothered it with alacrity.

"Is that good enough, please?" asked Dandelion.

"I'm sorry, General," said the stenographer, "but I'm not supposed to accept it if it's vague. I'll just have to enter 'first meeting since *indeterminate*.'"

The three of them sighed in unison. Lilacs and Dandelion swung their feet back and forth. Unlike the other fairies, they wore simple loincloths that left little of their hairy voluptuousness to the imagination. Fairy tailors were second to none in the known world, and the rest of their kind were always clad in exquisite tailoring. It made sense in fairy terms. It wouldn't be fair for Lilacs and Dandelion to hold such exalted positions *and* be fabulously garbed.

"That's a shame," said Lilacs. "Oh, I do enjoy concise record-keeping! But you can't win them all, can you, please?"

"No, your Majesty," said the stenographer.

"Wouldn't be fair," added Dandelion.

"Sorry I couldn't be more help," said Sloot.

"Thank you for saying that," said Lilacs, "but it's not *really* that important, all things considered."

"Not everything can be treated with the utmost importance," said Dandelion.

"No," Lilacs agreed, "wouldn't be fair to the matters of actual utmost importance."

"I suppose not," said Sloot, trying to wrap his head around the fairies' concept of fairness. He'd been brought up to believe that all things involving the Domnitor were of the utmost importance, long may he reign. And given that all things fell under his purview, people in the Old Country tended to treat everything as matters of life and death. On the whole, understanding that made it far easier for foreign devils, or rather, *tourists,* to understand why the Old Country operated the way it did.

"Well, I have a matter of some importance to bring before you," said Sloot. "Please."

"By all means," said Lilacs. "It's been a while since we've had one of those! Ever since Vlad abdicated, it's been mostly humdrum affairs of state."

"That's true," said Dandelion. "Oh, is it an invasion, please? We're ready for an invasion! When Vlad abdicated, the curse was broken and people from all over Carpathia joined up!"

Vlad's grandfather, Vlad the 35th, broke a centuries-old agreement that exempted a nomadic clan called the Virag from reality. Ashkar, their leader, refused to swear fealty to an oath-breaker, so Vlad the 35th burned him and slaughtered the Virag, an act that they condemned as "heavy, man."

As he burned, Ashkar—who would later come back as Gregor—wove a curse that prevented anyone from joining the Carpathian army so long as there was a Defenestratia ruling the land. The fairies found a loophole for their own army by setting up a corporation for joint-but-separate rulership. That was how their army fought the goblins alongside Vlad.

"The curse is lifted!" exclaimed Sloot.

"That's right," said Lilacs. "When Vlad stepped down, we were all that was left. We dissolved the corporation—"

"But kept the corporate picnic schedule," Dandelion interjected.

"Yes, by unanimous consent. I'm now King Lilacs of Carpathia, technically speaking, if you please."

"And I'm General of the Carpathian Army," said Dandelion. "Fairies and big folk alike."

"We've both had to move into the dungeons," said Lilacs.

"The dungeons?" Sloot was shocked. He'd spent a little time in the dungeons of Castle Ulfhaven when he'd first arrived there long ago. It was hardly a place fit for a king.

"The dungeons," Lilacs confirmed. "Vlad's apartments were far too opulent."

"Wouldn't be fair," said Dandelion.

"Besides," Lilacs continued, "Greta is still living there. She's already lost her lady love, even the memory of her. Wouldn't be fair to toss her into the street, would it, please?"

"No," said Dandelion. "It wouldn't."

"So what was this matter of importance that brought you here, please?"

Sloot blinked. It took a moment to shift the gears in his mind.

"Right," he said, "yes, that. Thank you."

"You're welcome."

As a loyal salt of Salzstadt, it pained Sloot to discuss Old Country affairs of state with foreign dignitaries, even when said "affairs of state" amounted to a *coup d'état*. Nevertheless, he managed to tell the king and the general about Uncle's plot to make the Domnitor, long may he reign, their puppet, and their threats to demote Myrtle to demon 100th class if Sloot didn't turn the Domnitor over in three days. Long may he reign.

"Well, that's not fair," said Lilacs.

"Your Majesty," said the stenographer, "would you like to clarify for the record which bits are unfair, please?"

"Gladly, thank you. All of it! Every last wretched detail! A young boy is expected to rule over a kingdom! His ministries are trying to overthrow him! There's blackmail, mistreatment of demons—there's nothing to like about any of this!"

"Thank you, your Majesty."

"You're welcome. Thank you for your thanks."

"You're welcome, please."

"Thank you, please."

There was a flash of amber light and the sound of breaking glass.

"What was that?" asked Sloot.

"We were stuck in a loop. Clever of Nicoleta to put that enchantment on the throne room for us. We could have been here for hours."

"Yes," Dandelion nodded. "Remind me to thank her later."

"So noted," said the stenographer.

"Do you know where the Domnitor is, long may he reign?" asked Sloot. "Please?"

"I'm afraid not," said Lilacs. "I don't, in any case. Honeysuckle, if you please?"

The stenographer flipped quickly through the pages of his book.

"Sorry," he said. "Nothing here."

"Oh well," said Lilacs, "thank you for looking."

"You're welcome."

There was another flash of amber light and the sound of breaking glass.

"Oh, come on, please," said Dandelion. "That was simple courtesies!"

"Remind me to ask Nicoleta to turn down the enchantment's sensitivity, please," said Lilacs.

"So noted," said Honeysuckle.

"Thank you."

"I can't imagine where he'd have gotten to," said Sloot.

"I'll bet Nicoleta could shed some light on that," said Dandelion.

All of the fairies turned their attention toward a very complex rune embossed in the floor to Sloot's left. He didn't recognize it. Looking directly at it made his teeth ache.

"That's odd," said Dandelion. "We've said her name three times in the last minute or so, and that usually—"

The space around the rune in the floor erupted in showers of hot pink sparks, swirling purple screamers, gouts of flame in green and blue, and other bits of pyro-pageantry that sent Sloot diving behind a statue of some Vlad or another. After a moment, the fireworks ceased and there were a pair of silhouettes in the lavender smoke.

"I svear," said one of the figures, "if you don't hold still this vill melt the flesh straight off your—Sloot!"

"Bartleby?"

Bartleby the vampire-obsessed necromancer had a wand in each hand, the tips resting in Nicoleta's ears. Nicoleta was glowing green and her hair was wiggling like snakes who'd gotten into the liquor cabinet.

"Don't distract him!" shouted Nicoleta. Then she waved Bartleby off and shouted a swear word in frustration. It wasn't one that Sloot had heard before, but he recognized the cadence of angry swearing. That was universal.

"Remind me to dispel that 'say my name three times' enchantment," said Nicoleta as her green glow subsided.

"So noted," said Honeysuckle.

"Hi, Sloot," said Nicoleta.

"Sorry if this is a bad time," said Sloot.

"It's fine," said Nicoleta, "we were just dying my hair. What can I do for you?"

Lilacs had Honeysuckle read back the official minutes of the meeting to bring Nicoleta up to speed on Uncle's plot, their threats against Myrtle, and the missing Domnitor, long may he reign.

"It does sound like someone magicked him away," Nicoleta agreed. "Have you checked with Franka?"

Franka! Sloot smacked his forehead with his palm. He'd completely forgotten about her because she hadn't attended the battle at the Carpathian border. He hadn't seen her since she and Vlad had fought their way past a literal mountain of goblins to stop the Serpents of the Earth from controlling an evil constellation of stars.

Franka was all that was left of the Skeleton Key Circle, a secret order that guarded the remains of the former Souls of the Serpents of the Earth.

"It was the only life she'd ever known," said Nicoleta. "It makes sense that she'd want to continue the work. She probably made off with all the Soul remains while Vlad was killing Gregor."

"*Almost* killing Gregor," Bartleby corrected. "He vas able to possess the body of a goblin, so he's probably vith them in the Dark now."

"But why would she have the Domnitor?" asked Sloot. "Long

may he reign." He was subjected to a ruthless smirking by all in attendance. He knew better than to try and defend himself. Historically, that was a mild reaction for praising a foreign dictator in the throne room of Castle Ulfhaven.

"Amassing power?" suggested Nicoleta. "It's what I'd do if I were trying to reconstitute a decimated secret society."

Sloot thought briefly of the Serpents of the Earth. He hadn't heard anything from them in a while. Secret societies are a lot like children in that they're probably up to the most mischief when they're being a little *too* quiet.

"She's pretty good vith magic," said Bartleby, whose magical skills were generally limited to spells that made things look *vicked cool.* "She could have tiptoed in, nabbed the Domnitor, and tiptoed out."

"Long may—" Sloot cut the phrase short in response to a severely perturbed glance from Lilacs. *Long may he reign*, he observed in silence.

"Can you help me find her?" asked Sloot.

Nicoleta and Bartleby exchanged a glance.

"What?"

"We're a little busy at the moment," said Nicoleta. "Important wizard stuff. But you're not going to go along with it, are you?"

"Go along with what?"

"Handing the—*that boy* over to Uncle. It's blackmail! It's also kidnapping and political upheaval, none of which seems like you, Sloot."

She had him there, but Sloot shrugged his shoulders. "It's Myrtle."

"Aww," the room chorused.

"Well, naturally, we can't let Myrtle suffer any more than she already has." Nicoleta fidgeted. "I suppose I can spare Bartleby for a bit, if you promise to have him back here before the Freezing

Moon."

"Are you sure ve have time, Nicoleta? I mean, the thing in the cauldron is—"

"Yes, yes," said Nicoleta. "No need to bother everyone about the *stew we're cooking*."

"Riiight," said Bartleby with an exaggerated nod. "Vell, it sounds like this Uncle just needs a bit of fear put into him. It vould be fun to conjure the old Snakes in Boiling Blood charm for someone who vould be properly horrified."

"Good," said Nicoleta, "that's settled. We should do more, though. What's the plan to get Myrtle out of there?"

"What? Oh," Sloot stammered. "Well, I'm taking dance lessons."

Blank stares at Sloot became furtive glances among everyone else.

"And that's supposed to help somehow, please?" asked Dandelion. His expression was genuinely curious. As a military thinker, he'd naturally be open to out-of-the box thinking on tactics.

"I think so," Sloot shrugged. "It seemed important to Myrtle, and she's a causality demon. Or she was when she made me promise to take her dancing."

"That makes sense," said Nicoleta, revealing to Sloot that she was horrible at bluffing.

Lilacs cleared his throat meaningfully. "I wonder if Greta would like to tag along."

"Yes!" blurted Nicoleta, as though further evidence of her lack of subtlety was needed. "I mean, yeah, sounds like a good idea, probably."

"It vould do her some good to get out of the castle," said Bartleby, oblivious to the surreptitious head-shaking happening all around him.

"Er, yes," said Sloot. "She's more than welcome, but why are you all so eager to get rid of her?"

A peal of nervous laughter erupted in the room and died just as quickly.

"She's not dealing with the transition well," said Nicoleta. "She went from royal consort in love to shut-in without a purpose who can't remember who she's in love *with*."

"It's enough to make anyone irritable," said Dandelion.

"Well," said Sloot, who'd never get anything done if he avoided social awkwardness, "if you think it's best."

Everyone agreed that it was. A bit too vigorously for Sloot's taste, but also too vigorously for him to argue. Bartleby and Greta left for Salzstadt straight away, but Sloot had an errand to run first.

"Yer getting the jump at the end all wrong," shouted Agather. "Yer supposed to be like a feather. *One* feather, not a sack."

At least Igor was enjoying himself. Cackling at Sloot's constant missteps was justice for their argument about the fairies.

"Tell me again why I'm wearing these?" asked Sloot.

"They're leg warmers."

"But my legs aren't cold."

"Of course not, yer wearing leg warmers. Now, from the top again, and if ye forget the big flourish after the spin, there'll be extra spiders in yer shirt."

Sloot was deathly afraid of spiders—among other things—and a handful made him a much more expressive dancer. Of course, Sloot was an accountant. He knew all about diminishing returns. Two might have been more effective than one, but thirty-five and thirty-six were about the same.

"Make him do the hip wiggle again," yelled Igor. "That one's my favorite!"

"Less talky, more twangy," growled Agather. She generally didn't approve of music but conceded that if you weren't naked around a bonfire, dancing tended to require it. Thus Igor had been permitted to attend Sloot's lessons, being his official bard and all.

"Bard *pro tempore*," Sloot insisted.

"Ooo," said Igor, "that sounds like it comes with a hat with feathers in!"

"It means—"

"Focus!" shouted Agather. "Stay on the beat or I'll put the beat on ye."

Sloot's feet were both lefts,
Though one was on the right,
And his steps were a mess,
Something, something, underbite

"I don't have an underbite," said Sloot as he lurched and over-extended his shoulders. He heard a crunch, and the world was searing pain.

"Well, at least yer—I SAID AT LEAST YER GIVING IT YER ALL," Agather shouted over Sloot's screams of agony. She produced a scarf from beneath a number of other scarfs she was wearing, wrapped it tightly around Sloot's head, and started twisting back and forth.

"Should he have attempted the lutz while his feet were crossed like that?" asked Igor.

"Never ye mind about that," said Agather, grunting with the effort of jerking Sloot's neck about. There were a series of pops and crunches that coaxed more muffled screams from Sloot. His eyes bulged and went fiery red, and a corrosive yellow goo frothed from his nose.

"But no," Agather conceded. "He shouldn't've."

Agather eventually gave a satisfied nod at one crunching sound in particular and allowed Sloot to fall on his face. He lay there twitching.

"He's not dead, is he?"

"Of course not," said Agather. "If killing a demon were as easy as some bad dancing and a bit of a throttle, everyone would be doing it. Oh, foo. That was my fourth best scarf!"

Agather wandered over to her cauldron and gave it a stir. It seemed to soothe the bubbling concoction.

"Can't leave these things alone for too long," she said.

"Is he going to be all right?" asked Igor.

"As right as he's ever been," said Agather, not looking up from her cauldron. "Ye can take him home as soon as he can walk. Don't be late for the next lesson."

MEANWHILE IN SALZSTADT

Sloot had been called lots of swear words that he'd never heard. He avoided learning new profanity at all cost, not out of a sense of decency *per se*, but because of the Old Country's goblin problem. There had been a statute on record since long before Sloot was born that criminalized the learning of swear words. For some reason that Sloot will never understand, there wasn't a specific law against *saying* swear words. Perhaps the Ministry of Information Defense felt that the rule against learning them would be sufficient.

It wasn't, of course. So long as one was not caught in the act of learning a swear word, one was free to employ it at will to any given bad day, stubbed toe, fight to the death, or piano recital.

Given his stunted swearing vocabulary, Greta's torrent of profanity was mostly lost on him. He understood her tone, though, and tried to focus on the ulcer that her consternation was enflaming in his guts. It distracted him from any good swear words that he might otherwise have learned.

"You lied to me," she said at last. She didn't have the look of a woman loath to repeat a swear word, so Sloot proceeded as mildly as he could.

"There must be some sort of mistake," said Sloot. "Perhaps we could go up and talk about this inside?"

They were standing outside Sloot's apartment. Greta stood in front of the door like a legion of Carpathian berserkers chewing at their tethers.

"We're not going up there," Greta fumed. "You thought I'd forget, didn't you?" Her face contorted in sadness and rage. She shut her eyes, balled her fists, and shook.

"She looks really mad," said Igor with a manic grin.

"Yes, thank you, Igor," Sloot hissed.

"What did you lie about? I'll work out a melody while you confess."

"I don't know! Would you please keep your voice down?"

"Oh, that's just fine," shouted Greta. "Sloot's embarrassed, is he? Oh, bother! I wouldn't want to irk the Infernal Prince of Lies!"

"Oh, dear," Sloot groaned, please don't—"

"Right," said a deep, gravelly voice behind Sloot. "What's all this then?"

Sloot whirled around and instantly wished that he hadn't. He'd seen scores of imps flying around at Infernal Bureaucracy, but none of them had been nine feet tall and wearing a suit of human skin.

"Vicked," said Bartleby through a toothy grin.

"Yeah," said the giant imp, "I thought as much. You're infringing upon Infernal copyrights, aren't you?"

"What?" balked Sloot. "No! I mean, what?"

"I, Azgarog, Baron of the Noxious Sulfur Pits and Arbiter of Impish Calamity have been summoned to this place in defense of copyrights held by Zelchior, the Thousand-Horned Scion of the Nightmare Realms and Infernal Prince of Lies. Dare you deny that they were infringed upon by you this very night?"

"No!" cried Sloot. "Well, yes. Perhaps? I don't know if—"

"Are you Sloot Peril?" Azgarog demanded, having read Sloot's name from a scroll that smoldered in his grip.

"Y-yes," Sloot admitted.

"Yes?" Azgarog shook his head and squinted one bloodshot eye in confusion. "Wow, just a simple *yes*. What are you playing at, Peril? If that is your real name."

"I-it is," trembled Sloot. "I'm not playing at anything. That's just my name, I'm afraid."

"Huh." Azgarog shrugged. "I'm not used to getting straight answers from demons. Hey, wait a minute," growled Azgarog, his eyes narrowing. "Nice try. Who are you, really?"

Sloot briefly considered giving his name as Roger Bannister, though it hadn't ended well for him the last time he'd "borrowed" that name. He wasn't creative enough to conjure another fake name on the spot, so he decided to play along with the truth and see where it got him.

"Sloot Peril," said Sloot.

Azgarog eyed Sloot with suspicion, then read his smoldering scroll with more scrutiny.

"This says you're on special assignment to the Coolest," he said with no small measure of incredulity. He looked Sloot up and down. "You're so puny! You're only, what, 80th class?"

"100th, actually."

Azgarog sighed. "Look, either you're lying because you're an insanity demon or something, or you're telling the truth because you're really, really bad at this. Either way, I'm letting you off with a warning. I've seen the Coolest's attorneys. I'd be tied up in the courts for the rest of eternity if they decided to make it personal."

Sloot said nothing. It was starting to look like he was going to escape Infernal retribution for once, and he didn't want to jinx it.

"Just keep away from Zelchior's honorifics, would you?"

"Er, yes, sir. Happy to, sir!"

"Fine," said Azgarog after a long glare. "Don't make me come back up here." He snapped his fingers and disappeared in a puff of noxious smoke.

"Did you see that guy?" asked Bartleby, grinning from ear to ear. "He vas enormous! And that exit!"

"It reeked," Greta coughed. She wiped tears from her eyes and tried to regain her composure.

"Still," said Bartleby, "vicked cool."

"You called him cunning," said Greta. She was glaring at Sloot again.

"Who, Azgarog?"

"No, Willie."

"When?"

"When we first met! You and Roman came into my shop. I told you that Willie wasn't my fiancé, though he seemed to think so. You and Roman called him cunning and benevolent. You said he was only pretending to be an imbecile, and that I should play along."

It had been Roman's idea. Sloot had gone along with it, so it was no good using that as an excuse.

"So I played along," Greta spat, "and what did it get me? Murdered!"

"I'm so sorry about that," said Sloot. "I never meant for—"

"There was Carpathia, of course," Greta interjected, reminding Sloot that only one voice had a place in a monologue. "That was nice for a while, until I somehow managed to misplace the love of my life, whose name is…"

She said a swear word.

"I really thought that might work this time," Greta lamented. "Why is this happening to me? Why can't I remember my true love? Did I imagine it?"

Greta stared daggers at Sloot. Sloot moved as little as possible, since his presence in the world seemed to be the thing offending her the most.

"I asked you a question!" Greta roared. "Several, in fact! I know you have answers, Peril! Now, talk!"

Sloot opened his mouth to speak, but he meowed instead.

"That reminds me," said Igor, "I'm famished."

Greta gawked at Igor. "Is he joking? Who is—*what* is he? Never mind. I must have gone completely insane, because I just heard a 'meow' where a series of meaningful answers should have been."

"Sorry," said Sloot. "What I meant to say was *meow*."

The words were there. Right there at the front of Sloot's mind, queued and ready to get on with the business of conveying meaning. But every time he tried, he meowed.

"I'm not a violent person," said Greta, "or at least I haven't been. Feel free to start making sense, or at least sentences."

"I'm trying!" Sloot insisted. "I want very much to explain that *meow*, but every time I try—"

"Bad kitty." Sloot melted at the ridiculously sultry voice.

"*Meow*! What are you doing here?"

"Nothing you can talk about," said Gwen with a wink. "A girl's got to have some secrets, right? Quit trying to spill mine."

"I know you," said Greta. She squinted at Gwen.

"I don't believe we've met," Gwen cooed, "but I'd love to get better acquainted, if you—"

"Don't try that with me, missy. Why can't Sloot tell me what's going on? You've got something to do with it, don't you? What are you—"

"Shhh," Gwen whispered. With the grace of a cat appearing from nowhere at the sound of kibble pouring into a bowl, she closed the distance between Greta and herself and wrapped her in an embrace that only ever happens in certain types of novels. The ones with the covers that make Sloot blush.

Sloot was sure he'd have fainted, had he been in Greta's position. Bartleby *did* faint, so the threat was real. Greta's reaction, on the other hand, would have been more at home in a cage surrounded by wrinkled old men shouting and waving money. Gwen went sailing through the air and collided with a lamp post. She landed on the cobbles in a heap.

"What—"

"How dare you?" Greta was livid. Sloot had seen greater composure on the battlefield, and counted himself truly fortunate that he no longer slept. Greta's expression wasn't the sort of thing that didn't turn up in nightmares.

"That should've … how did you—"

"My one true love is still out there," Greta fumed, "and I won't be distracted by some tart in a flimsy night shirt. Run along, floozy!"

Gwen stared at Greta in a mixture of confusion and awe, her mouth hanging open.

"I'll find you later," she said to Sloot, then disappeared in a puff of lavender smoke.

"Who was that?" Greta shrieked.

"Blood chips!" Bartleby exclaimed as he bolted upright. He shook his head. "Vhat happened? Vhat did I miss?"

"Blood chips?" asked Igor.

Bartleby stared up into the night sky for a moment, then sighed. "Those aren't a thing, are they?"

Igor shook his head.

"Pity," said Bartleby. "They vere delightful in my dream. Who vas that voman?"

"I think we'd all like to know," said Greta. "Sloot? Don't you dare meow at me again."

"*Meow.*" Sloot's hands clamped over his mouth in a panic.

"What did I just say?" Greta's hands rested on her hips, the unmistakable overture to an Old Country dust-up.

"I'm sorry! I can't help it! I was just trying to say that her name is *meow*, and that she's a *meow*—"

"Enough!" Greta shouted. "Ugh!" She leaned against a lamp post and buried her face in her hands.

"It's obviously an enchantment," said Bartleby. "Vhatever she is, she doesn't vant you discussing it."

"Oh, come on," said Igor. "You probably just haven't tried hard enough. Give it another go, eh? Bound to work eventually."

"*Meow.*"

"Sloot!" Greta's shout was muffled by her hands.

"Keep at it," Igor encouraged him. "It ... wait, there I go thinking like a gremlin again. Sorry!"

"Are you not a gremlin?" asked Bartleby.

"Reformed. I'm a bard now."

"Sloot, I didn't know you had a bard! Moving up in the vorld, eh?"

"No," said Sloot, "not really. It's a long story. Look, I really am ... Greta?"

"Don't follow me!" shouted Greta. She was a block away, walking down the middle of the street. "I said *don't* follow me!" She added, though she hadn't turned around to see Sloot's single, tentative step forward.

"Don't listen to her," Igor urged him. "Women always say that when they want you to follow them!"

Sloot shook his head. Whether Igor had slipped into gremlin mischief again, or was acting on pig-headed misconceptions of manliness, Sloot knew better.

"She'll be fine," said Bartleby. "Vlad taught her a few of those kill-a-man-vith-your-pinky-toe moves before she left."

"Vlad," said Sloot. Then his brain caught up. "Gwen. Gwen! Her name is Gwen, and she made a deal with Vlad to save Greta's life in exchange for her sword, her crown, and her heart. There!

Why couldn't I say that before?"

"The enchantment," said Bartleby. "You couldn't say it in front of Greta. That comes standard vith demonic bargains. I'll bet Vlad has to vin Greta's heart again, but vithout her vealth and power."

"That's right," said Sloot. "Very perceptive of you."

Bartleby shrugged. "I've been around avhile. You see one demonic bargain … anyvay, vhat can you tell me about this Uncle?"

Sloot got Bartleby into the apartment as quickly as he could. It wasn't advisable to discuss Uncle in the open air, even for a demon and a necromancer.

"Hey, Villie! Vhat are you doing here?"

"An excellent question," Sloot dared to mutter under his breath.

"Bartleby! You know, I'm not sure. I don't usually go into rooms this small. Hey, wasn't I wearing this an hour ago?"

"It's late," barked Nan. "Willie, you can play with your friends in the morning. Now, go to sleep!"

"Nan, is that you?"

"What? Nan?" Constantin bolted nearly upright and almost stayed that way, but hammocks are not conducive to that orientation. Neither was Constantin, for that matter. "Where is she? You stay away from my Willie, you wretched-"

"He said *Man*," said Nan. "This is … Sergeant Bartleby. We served together during the war, didn't we, Sarge?" Nan's eyes went severely you'll-play-along-if-you-know-what's-good-for-you.

"Er, yes," said Bartleby. His eyes flashed as his brain caught up. "Right! Oh, those were the days, veren't they? Ve vere all really left-right-left, salute you vith our boots on soldiers in this man's army, veren't ve?"

"That's right," said Nan, nodding with her best you-just-watch-it stare.

"Ve sure gave the salties vhat for, didn't ve, Captain Man?"

"What?" exclaimed Constantin. He nearly fell out of his

hammock. "Whose side are you on? Have either of you been bull-whipped by a Hapsgalt, sirs?"

"He said *faulties*, Lord Hapsgalt!" shouted Nan. She glared at Bartleby. "That's what the enlisted men called the foreign hordes, for it was all their fault we had to pummel them in the Domnitor's name."

"Long may he reign," chorused the room.

Bartleby blushed, or would have done if any of his blood was above room temperature.

"I was there, too!" blurted Igor. "Me and Sloot! We were privates, and always getting mixed up in capers. Sloot had to peel potatoes a lot, and I had a really cool eyepatch—"

"Yes, thank you, Private Igor," said Nan with all the exasperation of any officer who's had to deal with upstart enlisted men.

Constantin glared around the room. His eyes weren't what they used to be since he'd died, come back to life, and was no longer receiving the rejuvenative benefits of blood wizards pouring vitality into you around the clock. Ah, the evil old days.

"Carry on," he grumbled at last, then fell into snoring slumber in a single step.

"It's complicated in the Old Country," whispered Bartleby, who couldn't manage to get the taste of his own foot out of his mouth.

"It's not so bad," said Willie. "All you've got to do is pretend it's okay that poor people are allowed to live, because who's going to grow the turnips? And eat the turnips, for that matter. Nan, can I say a swear?"

Sloot cringed.

"Permission granted," said Nan.

"Turnips are *yucky*," said Willie from behind a conspiratorial grin.

"What are you writing there?" Sloot asked Igor, who was scribbling on the outside of his filthy bag with a bit of charcoal. "It looks like *thee ninnee hayts tornaps*."

"In case I decide to take up cooking," said Igor. "So I know what to put—what *not* to put in the food."

Sloot resolved not to worry about it. He couldn't see Nan—or Captain Man, or whoever she was now—letting Willie anywhere near a plate that Igor was involved in making.

Bartleby opened his mouth as though to ask a question, then thought better of it.

"Bartleby?" asked Sloot.

"Vell," said Bartleby, grasping at sentences, "it's just that … no offense intended, but … you have a lovely apartment, Sloot. Or possibly a sizable closet. It's just that, vell, like Villie said, he usually doesn't go into rooms this … cozy."

"Small," said Willie. "I said 'small.' And I didn't say 'depressing' because that would be rude. And 'rude' is just the truth when it's said by poors."

"Yes, well," Sloot began, "that's because … wait, where's Arthur?"

"He went to the pub," said Willie. "He said something about another revolution, but I stopped listening because he was sure there wouldn't be any balloons."

"Oh, dear," said Sloot.

"Vhat, is there danger?"

"Probably not," said Sloot. He hoped all the revolution-minded people in the pub had already been swept up in the last one.

"Ooo," said Bartleby, "is that a magic circle? It is! Hey, that's a nice Hermetic Quantifier in the lower arc."

"Thanks," said Sloot.

Realization dawned on Bartleby with so much force that Sloot swore he heard a cock crow.

"You're vorking on normalizing reality after the spilling of the Dark!"

Sloot nodded.

"That's vhy your Aethereal Recalcitrance is inverted. You've got Ascendant Domain over the locality!"

"Well," said Sloot, "when you look at it like that, I mean … I don't like to brag … er, is that good? Whatever that is?"

Bartleby's fangs glistened in the moonlight streaming from the window. They had ample room to do so, his jaw having hit the floor.

"Ve're going in." Bartleby was as giddy as a kid opening his Snugglewatch gift.

Further cajoling wasn't necessary, though Bartleby would gladly have obliged. The curious bit was that Bartleby had to transform into mist and join Sloot in the circle in order to tag along. Igor had been standing on the other side of the room, but still managed to appear with them in Salzstadt Before a few moments later.

"Hard to keep gremlins out of anything," said Igor. "The buggers."

"Vicked," said Bartleby, after he coalesced from mist. "Ascendant Domain! It's a small locality, but you've got Ascendant Domain! Vell played, Sloot."

"Hang on," said Sloot. He reached for the circle, rubbed the Glyph of Shifting Locus, and the three of them were transported instantly to the then-empty apartment across the alley from Sloot's. "What's this *Ascendant Domain* thing? Is there an ointment I can get for it, or—"

"You really don't know?" Bartleby's askance look was particularly disturbing, owing to the countless hours he'd invested in eyebrow exercises. "Sloot, you're essentially a god here, just vithout the omniscience!"

"Oh, dear," said Sloot. "Isn't that was the worst sort of god that one could be?"

Bartleby shrugged. "It depends on how you feel about mischief."

"Mischief?" Igor folded his pocketknife, his name now crudely carved into the baseboard by the door. He forced his eager expression to dissipate. "I mean, that certainly wouldn't do, would it, Mr. Peril?"

"Of course not," said Sloot. Igor sagged.

"Suit yourself," said Bartleby. "Still, vicked cool to vield that much control."

"I suppose," said Sloot. "Anyway, what do you want to know about Uncle?"

"Yes, Uncle," said Bartleby. His gaze was fixed sullenly on the floor, and he fiddled with the hem of his robe. "You're probably right. No sense marveling at Ascendant Domain vhen ve could be talking about practical matters."

"Er, sorry," said Sloot, who had reached the limits of his knowledge of Ascendant Domain upon having heard the phrase. "It's just that Nicoleta seemed in a hurry to have you back, so I thought—"

"Oh, right! I nearly forgot about that. Vicked cool stuff she's vorking on. I'm … oh, I'm not sure how much I can tell you."

Sloot didn't want to pry, but he couldn't help being just a bit curious.

"You can tell her about my Ascendant Domain," Sloot offered.

"That sounds fair. Ve're all friends, right?"

"More or less," said Sloot, glancing at Igor.

"All right. I'm helping Nicoleta vork through the Rite of Lichery."

Bartleby had clearly paused for a reaction more animated than the blank stare he got.

"She's becoming a lich." He drew his cloak up to his nose and did spooky eyebrows. A lightning bolt flashed in the window behind him.

Sloot blinked but did nothing else.

"A lich is a vizard who has … vell, *they* say they've 'taken death as a lover,' but I don't think it's as literal as that."

Sloot grimaced. "That's quite a thing, isn't it?"

"The vay she sees it, she's living on borrowed time," Bartleby explained. "Lots of vizards become liches vhen they're very old so they can continue doing magic after their bodies give out. Vhy they don't just svitch to necromancy is beyond me. Anyvay, Nicoleta really knows her stuff, but most vizards have a lifetime to vork up to the Rite of Lichery. Nicoleta reckons that she's only got until you've normalized reality, and then she'll be dead again."

"Vlad thought the same of Greta," said Sloot. "Is it true? Will everyone be dead again when I've completed my work?"

Bartleby shrugged. "Hard to say. They shouldn't be alive now, but they are. Ve've vandered off the path, Sloot. All ve've got now is guesses. Okay, my turn. Vhy is Villie living in your apartment?"

Sloot explained the collapse of the Salzstadt economy, and the fact that the Hapsgalts hadn't had any money for a long time. He tried to be as brief as possible, as it was obvious that Bartleby was still dwelling on Sloot's Ascendant Domain.

"I still don't understand," said Bartleby. "*Vhy* vas the vault never counted?"

"No one thought they had to," said Sloot. "The Hapsgalts had so much money on ledger that everyone just trusted the numbers. Counting one's money is a very distasteful thing in their circles."

"How do they buy things?"

"Credit." He told Bartleby about the hidden-in-plain-sight accounting annex across the street from the counting house, and how Vasily Pritygud's uncorrected report had brought their shell game to a devastating end.

"Vicked," said Bartleby, his eyebrows contorted in a bird's nest of horror and admiration. "I've done some real sacrilege in my day, but I've never come up vith anything that diabolical. Vell, there vas one time in a graveyard, but the dead don't usually mind those sorts of things."

"Right," said Sloot. He might have told Bartleby of his horror at having seen his own shrunken head dangling from Roman's belt, had he been more in touch with his own emotions. He relied instead on his capacity for denial, which would lecture you on the dangers of breathing rather than acknowledge a sinking ship.

"Perhaps ve should deal vith the matter at hand," said Bartleby. "Who is this Uncle I'm supposed to harass for you?"

THE MERGING DARKNESS

Sloot had expected Bartleby to be impressed with the inside of Dark Corners. He thought he'd say it was "vicked cool," whatever that meant.

"It's nice," he said, "but darkness isn't mysterious if everybody is doing it."

"I can take care of that," said Igor.

"Please don't light any fires," Sloot pleaded.

"I am a *bard*, sir, not a casual pyromaniac."

"Then you weren't digging in your sack for a flint?"

"I hardly see how that's relevant."

"Sloot!" came an impossibly cheery voice from one of the many dark corners of the pub. Sloot peered around in the gloom until he caught sight of Flavia waving at him.

"You didn't tell me you vere a regular here," said Bartleby.

"I'm not," Sloot replied. "That's Flavia. She's my contact with Uncle."

"I see," said Bartleby. His expression darkened. That was impressive, considering where it had started. "I'll just get to vork then, shall I?"

Thunder rumbled from a distance that didn't exist within the walls of the pub. The few candles which gave the place its dim lighting flickered, the hue of their flames reddening with menace. Sloot's pulse quickened as he turned to see Bartleby melting into a horrific new shape, like a wolf in bat's pajamas, with black smoke pouring from … well, the flap, he supposed.

"Ugh, vampires," said Walter the Undying as he waggled his wand in Bartleby's direction. "I'll deal with this one. I thought we weren't letting them—"

A low reverberation echoed from the Bartleby-wolf-bat. It spread its wings and raised its hackles in an inducement to terror so theatrical that Sloot began to hyperventilate, despite his lack of need to respire.

"Why isn't this working?" A measure of dread eased its way into Walter the Undying's voice. He waggled his wand more forcefully.

"Walter," said Flavia, the same dread in her voice.

The wizard made a series of flicks with his wand, each of which sent a bright white bolt screaming toward Bartleby. They passed through him like remonstrances of disappointment through a moody teenager, not seeming to touch him at all.

"I shall enjoy this," Bartleby snarled. "Make peace vith vhatever *hey!*"

The pub abruptly returned to its usual gloom, and Bartleby was his regular decrepit-in-a-strangely-youthful-way self once again. He was pinned to the ceiling by some unseen force, but otherwise back to his semblance of normal.

"*Tsk, tsk, tsk,*" chided a gleefully monstrous voice from just behind Sloot. "You really should have thought this through, Peril."

Sloot threw himself on the floor and scuttled under a table.

"What is the meaning of this?" demanded Bartleby. "If you like your entrails vhere they are, I suggest…"

It wasn't the first time someone had trailed off mid-threat after making eye contact with Mrs. Knife.

"Glad we're on her side now," said Walter the Undying.

"What?" exclaimed Sloot. He shot a "say it ain't so" look at Flavia, albeit one with better grammar.

"Sorry, Sloot," Flavia wheedled, "but your results have been less than reliable. Joining up with Mrs. Knife seemed more promising."

"Joining up?"

"It was your idea, Peril," sneered Mrs. Knife. She kept her dagger pointed in Bartleby's direction, as though it were a magic wand. Sloot had never seen Mrs. Knife do magic, but then again, he avoided looking directly at her.

"Me? But how—"

"Your little band of revolutionaries. To be *honest*," she grimaced at the word, "I didn't think you had it in you. You've always been a by-the-book type, haven't you, Peril?"

"They weren't my revolutionaries," Sloot whimpered.

"Not anymore. Neither is Uncle, and neither are the Serpents of the Earth! Not that they ever were. They're all working for me now!"

Mrs. Knife's ever-murderous sneer was shone with delight. *Mine,* it gloated, with all the fervor of a toddler hoarding dollies. But there was something about it that didn't make sense.

"Why?" asked Sloot.

Mrs. Knife's head leaned to one side. "Perhaps they can tell a born leader when they see one? Or perhaps it's self-preservation. People understand that I always get my way."

"Er, yes," said Sloot, "but why do you care?"

"This is vhat villains do," Bartleby grunted. "They amass power to keep people avay from their veakness."

"He's right," Igor chimed in. "I'm pretty sure I've read that."

"You're guessing," snapped Mrs. Knife, "and you're wrong. Shall I tell you?"

"Don't do us any favors," Bartleby spat.

"I'd be doing *myself* a favor. That's my favorite kind."

This was proper villainy. A careless villain would tell you their plans just before you escaped inevitable death by means of improbable chance, leaving you at liberty to gird your loins and defeat them with panache. If said careless villain were also sloppy, it might not even take that long. It might end with a "not so fast," half a minute of turning the tables, and then it's "curses, foiled again" as the sunset fills up with plucky hero and love interest.

But Mrs. Knife was neither careless nor lazy. She was the meticulous sort of villain who found the time to practice steely leering, to make sure you knew she was a proper lunatic.

"You're cleverer than you look, Peril," Mrs. Knife seethed.

"Oh, dear," said Sloot. No one ever meant that as a compliment. It ended in a silent *so I'm going to work harder at making your life difficult from now on.*

"So clever, in fact, that you've managed to come back from the dead and seize the very fabric of reality for yourself. I wouldn't have thought it possible, especially after I put my blade between your ribs and left you to burn." She'd started on the edge of praise but ended with her teeth grinding so hard that Sloot could have sworn he'd heard one crack.

"Please," said Sloot, throwing up his hands, "just tell me what you want!"

All of the tension fled Mrs. Knife's demeanor. She smiled and rolled her eyes as if in relief, basking in the feeling of the world making sense again.

"And that," she said, pausing for emphasis, "is why *I'm* clever. Your power is mine, Peril. As long as I'm able to get my hands on you, what's yours is mine. That's why I had your teleportation privileges revoked. Or did you think that was petty revenge?"

"Well, I—" Sloot fell silent under Mrs. Knife's cold gaze,

which made a range of assertions from "it was a rhetorical question" to "I wonder how your liver would taste pan-fried in lard."

"What I *want*, Peril, is what I've always wanted. Revenge."

"Make up your mind, vill you?" shouted Bartleby.

Mrs. Knife hissed at the necromancer and waved her dagger in his direction. He slid across the ceiling and bumped his head on the rough timbers.

"Blow it out your ears," Bartleby mocked. "Vhat kind of villain are you? I've seen grass stains menace children's short pants vith more style. You can't even decide vhere you stand on revenge!"

Mrs. Knife's eyes rolled back and closed. Her non-dagger-wielding hand balled into a fist and shook.

"I don't care about revenge on Peril," said Mrs. Knife through clenched teeth. "I want revenge against the dwarves in Svartalfheim!"

Sloot hadn't seen that coming, but it made perfect sense insofar as deranged maniacs were capable. Hundreds of years ago, the dwarves banished the goblins to the Dark. Mrs. Knife was their queen, standard limitations of human longevity having been summarily ignored. She'd sworn revenge back then, and she wasn't one to walk away from a vendetta over something as insignificant as the passage of centuries, or reality teetering on the brink of annihilation.

"You're insane." No amount of fear could have kept that truth behind Sloot's teeth. It was too big to remain silent.

"Sticks and stones, Peril," she snarled. It was clear to Sloot that it was meant as a threat, not a rebuttal of his words.

"It won't work," said Sloot. "If I fix things so that you get to march on Svartalfheim, the Coolest will—"

"That's not my problem," said Mrs. Knife. "You're going to give me everything you've got. The Old Country, Carpathia, and don't think I've forgotten my stars!"

"The Serpent of the Sky," said Bartleby, "to show the goblins the way to Svartalfheim!"

"Indeed. You will give me revenge, Peril! You can't balance reality when all of it stands against you!"

The worst things about villains was their tendency to be right. Not in deed or intent, but with regard to the letter of the law. Laws are a villain's most fearsome weapon. Without laws, there would be no villains.

"Go," said Mrs. Knife. "Get on with my bidding. I've got work to do." Her gaze turned up to Bartleby like a cat with a mouthful of mouse.

"I'm not leaving without Bartleby." Sloot hated the words for coming out of his mouth, but there they were. Weird necromancer though he may have been, Bartleby was Sloot's friend. He didn't have many of those.

"What about me?" asked Igor.

"I insist that *you* go with him," said Mrs. Knife. "It'll be harder for Peril to work against me with a gremlin at his heels."

"I'm a bard, not—"

"That's no excuse for shoddy work," said Mrs. Knife, affording Sloot a waggle of her dagger, as though the threats presently on file were insufficient. "You'll deliver the Domnitor to Flavia post-haste."

"Long may he reign," said roughly half the people in the pub, Sloot among them.

"Sure." Mrs. Knife chuckled. "Run along, pet. We'll talk about my stars as soon as you've returned."

"But Bartleby," said Sloot, his voice cracking under the weight of what little resolve he had left.

"Don't vorry about me," said the necromancer. He didn't look at Sloot. His gaze fixed on Mrs. Knife, so full of daggers that had you thrown it an apple, it would have lost a toe catching it.

Walking out of the Dark Corners was the second hardest thing Sloot had ever done, following only watching Myrtle insist that Walter the Undying banish her to the lowest circle of the Inferno.

“That was close,” said Igor. “Are you hungry? I could do with a kebab.”

“You must be joking,” said Sloot, the tips of his ears beginning to smolder with the sort of rage that only demons had in them.

“Meat on sticks? What’s not to like?”

All of a sudden, there was a fury in Sloot Peril the likes of which he’d never felt before. His claws came out. His horns followed suit. He threw his head back and unleashed something between a roar and a howl, casting upon the heavens all of the iniquity and anguish that had built up in his soul, or whatever it was demons had in lieu of same. In a very un-Sloot-like fit of morality, he came to a decision. A firm decision. He wasn’t leaving Bartleby to his fate. He was a demon, wasn’t he? Demon 100th class who’d never failed to say “pardon me” much less willingly cause physical harm to anyone, but a demon nonetheless.

Wasn’t he full of molten blood? Didn’t he have the killer instinct? Honestly, he had no idea. But his eyes were a deeper shade of black than usual at the moment, and it *felt* like the truth. He’d unlocked some primal facet of demonology that had been in his craw the whole time—whatever a craw was—and while it was doing the thinking, no wizard or bureaucrat or goblin queen stood a chance against him.

“Don’t do it,” said Igor, his voice edged with fear. Probably fear of not getting kebabs, but fear nonetheless.

Sloot bared his fangs. It took muscles he’d never used before. He broke into a flat-out run that was embarrassing to behold, but he didn’t care. Blind rage tended to have that effect.

The door fell away like wet paper. He barreled not into the pub, but into a void that was, well, *void*. The absence of all things engulfed him, its vastness invading his senses. The world melted away, and there was nowhere for his rage to go but back into himself. He roiled in it for one horrible moment, and then he felt …

fine. Just *fine.* Not good, not bad, just an absence that went with voids, he supposed.

It was like being dead again. Time must have been passing, but he had no reference point other than himself.

"Hello, Sloot. How've you been?"

The rest of the Coolest weren't with him. They were alone in the void, Donovan in his white linen suit, and Sloot festooned with claws, scales, and grotesque new muscles that made it impossible to turn his neck very far. He hoped this wasn't permanent. Accounting required a lot of desk time, and the optimal physique for that was as little as possible.

"It'll wear off." Donovan could read Sloot's thoughts, but he probably didn't have to. Sloot was predictable lately. "That's why you're here, in fact."

"Ghrazulfant!" bellowed Sloot, or something approaching that.

"You can say that again," said Donovan with a sigh. "That'll wear off, too. But until it does, could you try enunciating? The Infernal language is really quite beautiful when you don't mumble."

Sloot had a hundred questions, but said nothing for fear of mumbling in the presence of godlike beings. Sloot Peril wasn't a mumbler.

"Time is passing," said Donovan, apparently plucking questions from Sloot's mind at random, "just not here. This is a pocket void I maintain for occasions like these. Very convenient for when one of my demons needs to sit and regain his wits."

Sloot's jaw dropped farther than he'd intended to let it, thanks to his heavy tusks. It was the first time he'd been put in time out since he was a child.

"Don't think of it like that," said Donovan. "You're not being punished, you've done nothing wrong! It's just that the course of action that started unfolding when you charged that door was ... well, let's just say it would have made your job a lot harder."

Sloot closed his mouth. He stared at Donovan in silence.

"Oh, fine," Donovan griped, "it would have made your job impossible! Believe me, it would be easier all around if I'd just let you shred Mrs. Knife and be done with it. We'd have gone way past any chance of balancing things, though. I'd have to let Marco get on with his razing."

Sloot's head was spinning. Shred Mrs. Knife? Was he capable of such a thing?

"You'd better believe it," said Donovan. "Look at you! She's tough as nails, the queen of the goblins, but you're like one of those … what do you call them? Big deal in a thousand years or so. Some nations have them just for pointing at other nations, but they'd be mad to ever use them. Wait, no, that's not here. Forget I said anything. The point is, yes. You could turn Mrs. Knife into a fine mist with one hand tied behind your back. The real question is how you got this way. We made you 100th class for a reason, remember? No favoritism!"

Sloot shrugged his massive shoulders. It sounded like continental drift.

"It's not your fault. You're the oddity, after all. If anything, it's my fault for thinking the usual rules would apply to you. Allistair?"

Nothing happened.

"The void," said Donovan, tapping his forehead. "I keep forgetting it applies to me, too. I come in here to let off steam every once in a while."

Donovan sighed. He put his hands on his hips and turned to look out over all of the nothing that there wasn't. The torrent of blood rushing in Sloot's ears eventually subsided. He started to relax, his grotesque muscles subsiding into something he felt capable of managing.

"May I ask you a question?"

Donovan smiled, probably congratulating himself for not responding with the obvious joke. "I think you've earned it."

"It's just, well, do we have free will or not?"

"Oof," said Donovan, his eyes rolling. "That's not really a yes-or-no question."

"So, no," said Sloot, whose mind went from bubbling kettle to boiling ocean when he realized what he'd said. He'd rarely used that sort of boldness with anyone, and here he was lambasting gods with it.

"I admire your pluck," said Donovan, with a smile that added, "just watch where you're aiming it."

"But it's not that simple," he continued. "At a basic level, everyone has free will. That's the problem. When people's wills collide, it stands to reason one must triumph over the other."

Sloot nodded.

"I won't get into the math," said Donovan, much to Sloot's disappointment, "but if you expand that concept to include everyone in the universe … basically, you get bureaucracy."

"Bureaucracies don't have free will."

"And neither does anyone living under them. Take your Old Country, for instance."

Sloot stood up a bit straighter. His chest, insofar as it was capable, puffed out.

"What would you say is the state of free will there?"

"Every man, woman, and child is free to exercise their free will within the boundaries of the law for the greater glory of the Domnitor, long may he reign!"

"Oh, this is interesting," said Igor.

"How did you get in here?" Donovan squawked.

"Followed Sloot," the gremlin replied, jerking a thumb over his shoulder. "You could do a lot with a place like this, you know. I've got a cousin—"

"The oddity," Donovan groaned. "Why do I even bother?

Should I have let the Chaos Courts sentence you to being rended for candles? Or allowed that wizard to take possession of your soul? Or let you send your world's tenuous balance spiraling into calamity because you were upset about your friend?"

"Bartleby," said Igor. "Decent chap. Is he all right, then?"

"Mrs. Knife reduced him to a pile of ashes," said Donovan. "Other than that, he's fine."

"Oh, we should get back, then!" Igor rubbed his hands together. "You can get a pretty penny for necromancer ashes."

"Igor!" chided Sloot.

"What?"

"Enough!" snapped Donovan. "Look, I'm sending you back. This will be the last time I intervene. Maybe you're right, maybe I'm hindering you by saving you from certain destruction."

"Let's not be too hasty," said Sloot.

"No, no more interference, and that's that. Even if it looks like you're going to set fire to the whole thing, I've got to let you do it. You're the oddity, right? Nothing you do is bound to make sense to us, but we let this mess happen in the first place, didn't we?"

"That's true," said Igor with a condescending nod.

"Are you *sure* you need an insolent gremlin tagging along with you?"

"Actually, I'm quite sure that I *don't*," Sloot replied.

"Hey!"

"Oh, there I go again!" Donovan wailed. "I can't control the whole universe! Well, I shouldn't. Not this time. Well, *probably* not this time." He paused in thought. "Oh, get out of here before I change my mind."

STILL ALIVE AGAIN

"You'll have to go in there eventually," said Igor.

"I don't see it that way," Sloot replied. He stared at the front door to his apartment with the same suspicion that traveling musicians regard soap.

"It's your apartment."

"Is it?"

"I wouldn't do existentialism," Igor warned in a hush. "Arthur could be anywhere."

"Arthur. There's another friend I've lost to Mrs. Knife."

"Arthur's not dead," said Igor. "Well, not anymore. Or *again*, as far as I know. And did he really count as a friend?"

"Now who's doing existentialism?"

"That's not existentialism," said Igor. "It's just questions."

Saying "existentialism" aloud three times hadn't summoned Arthur, so Igor was probably right about him being still alive again.

"Whatever," said Sloot. "I still don't want to go in there. What if Mrs. Knife is there?"

"What could Mrs. Knife possibly want with a pair of formerly wealthy invalids and a nanny in a fake beard?"

"The same thing she wanted with a bunch of artists and philosophers calling themselves a revolution, I'd imagine."

"Fair enough," Igor conceded. "You could get up to a lot of mischief with that many idiots."

Someone was laughing inside the apartment. Two someones. It sounded to Sloot as if they were taking turns. Curiosity finally got the better of him and he opened the door.

"Mister Peril!" *Man* stormed over and put *his* face uncomfortably close to Sloot's. "If I find out you had anything to do with this, there's going to be a consequence!"

"Anything to do with what?"

"Oh, hi Sloot," said Willie. He was sitting on the sofa, taking turns laughing with a gaunt and strangely alluring woman.

"She says she wants to kill Willie!" shouted Nan, pointing an accusing finger at the stranger. "And the elder Lord Hapsgalt is all for it!"

"I'm sorry," said Sloot, "I don't believe we've been introduced. I'm—"

"Sloot," said the strange woman, "it's me, Bartleby!"

"Bartleby?"

"Nonsense!" shouted Constantin. "I've met Sergeant Bartleby! He's no woman!"

"Er, that's his sister." Nan's jaw clenched beneath her fake beard. She remained as stoic as possible in the face of Constantin's scrutiny.

"Right," said Bartleby. "Ve vork together now that the var is over."

"And you both go by 'Bartleby?'"

"Father vasn't a creative man," said Bartleby.

"Good," said Constantin, who thought of creativity as a withering ailment that doomed youths to sell painted driftwood in open-air markets. He couldn't fathom why they'd work so hard at disappointing their parents, but he couldn't conceive of another goal they might have had in mind.

"You've got to put a stop to this," Nan insisted.

"Lady Bartleby is going to vampire me," said Willie. "I get a new cape!"

"What? I mean, that's great, Willie. Bartleby, may I speak with you in private?"

"Sure," Bartleby replied. She stood and straightened her dress. "Try not to die of natural causes before I return, Villie."

"I can do what I want," Willie insisted, crossing his arms for emphasis. "I'm a big boy. Isn't that right, Daddy?"

"You tell her, boy!"

Sloot sighed. He gestured over the circle and led Bartleby into Salzstadt Before with Igor in tow.

"Nice corpse," said Igor, once they had the privacy of Sloot's apartment in the past. "Someone you knew?"

Bartleby shook her head. "Bit of a vhirlvind necromance, as it vere. I usually get to know my new vessels before I move in, but it vas urgent."

"Mrs. Knife," said Sloot. "She did reduce you to a pile of ashes, then?"

"How did you know?" Bartleby's eyes narrowed with curiosity. "Never mind. Alas, yes. Oh, I vas fond of that vessel! I'd just gotten the blood upgraded to ichor, too. Now I have to start all over again."

"You hopped into a new body!" Sloot had seen Gregor do that right before Vlad smashed him into goo with her hammer.

"There vas no shortage of corrupted souls in that place," Bartleby chuckled. "I just kept qviet after Mrs. Knife incinerated me. Did you know that her dagger is enchanted like a vand? She probably used it to keep Gregor in line, and since he and I apprenticed under the same master, it vorked on me too. Anyvay, she's amassed qvite an army."

"I know," Sloot moaned. "We've got to reduce her strength! I can't fix any of this if I've got that much opposition."

"That brings us to Villie," said Bartleby. She grinned in a way that was weird without fangs.

"What can Willie do? He's not even rich anymore. That was all he had going for him."

"Oh, I don't know," said Bartleby. "He vas alvays a snappy dresser."

"And now he's broke."

"He's still got his lineage."

"And what is that worth without the family fortune?"

"Qvite a lot to the Serpents of the Earth. Mrs. Knife became the Eye by murdering Villie, making him the Soul. Now that Villie is alive again, that seat is empty."

"Empty? Shouldn't it have reverted to … well, not Constantin, since he's alive again too. Who was the Soul while he was the Eye?"

"His mother, Otthilda. She vas a real nightmare, and not in the fun, vake-up-screaming-in-a-cold-sveat vay. But no, it doesn't revert. They just vait for the Eye to die, and poof! New Soul."

"I don't see how they get any business done that way."

"They don't," said Bartleby. "Not really. But vhen you're talking about a society that's nearly a thousand years old, a couple of decades don't matter much."

Sloot couldn't imagine not appointing an interim officer. An unthinkable omission in his mind, but they were evil, after all.

"So how is turning Willie into a vampire supposed to help?"

"I've taken a look at the Book of Black Law," said Bartleby. "There's no precedent for a Soul spontaneously coming back to life. There *vas* a case around three hundred years ago vhen the Eye vas particularly sqveamish, so he faked his own death."

"He faked his own death?" Sloot had seen the ceremony where the new Eye murders the old one. Technically, he'd seen it twice. They'd just happened within the space of the same minute, when

Willie stabbed Constantin and Mrs. Knife stabbed Willie. "How did that work?"

"A fake knife vith a blade on a spring," Bartleby explained. "He vas buried alive as a varning to others. Anyvay, I'm pretty sure that if Villie becomes a vampire, since he'd technically be dead again, he'd automatically be the Soul again."

"Wouldn't it be easier to just murder him?" Sloot squeaked in alarm. He'd just casually suggested murder! In front of a lady, no less! Well, insofar as Bartleby was a lady.

"Oh, sure," said Bartleby. Her tone rivalled Sloot's for nonchalance, which somehow made his chagrin worse. "But if ve make him a vampire, he's technically eligible to be the Eye as vell. A vampire vas Eye of the Serpent for the better part of a century. That vas how I found out about the Serpents, studying the histories of influential vampires."

"Hang on," said Sloot, "how is any of this supposed to help? Even if Willie was the Soul, he can't stand up to Mrs. Knife. If we made him a vampire, wouldn't he have to challenge Mrs. Knife to be the Eye?"

"Not directly. Mrs. Knife vas never chosen to be the Eye, she just ritually committed the right murder at the right time. Villie could petition the Convocation of Shades."

It's a busy occasion for the Serpents of the Earth when the Eye descends into death. He or she becomes the Soul of the Serpent; the old Soul becomes a Shade and joins the Convocation of Shades; and about a dozen people—including the new Soul's financier—have to be assassinated in order to properly staff the transition. That last fact came as a shock to Sloot, who'd been Willie's financier before he'd known anything about the Serpents of the Earth. Had they already scheduled an assassin for Sloot? As cults went, the Serpents tended to be thorough.

"Mrs. Knife could just find a way to die or something," said

Sloot. “Then she’d be the Soul.”

“Not if Villie vas both.”

As a rule, Sloot didn’t count murder among the potential answers to his problems. It tended to create more problems than it solved. Not that he knew from personal experience, but Sloot was an accountant. He could do projections.

Vampirism, on the other hand, wasn’t murder *per se*. Sure, it would briefly be the same to Willie, but he’d already died once, hadn’t he? It couldn’t be that bad the second time around, now that he had the hang of it. Besides, he was definitely going to die again, possibly soon. Was there any real harm in taking a detour into undeath?

A *simple* death would make Willie the Soul of the Serpent again, and Mrs. Knife would control him. However, if he was both the Soul and the Eye…

“Mrs. Knife would have no control over the Serpents of the Earth,” Sloot concluded.

“The only downside,” said Bartleby, “is that there vould be no grand schemes coming out of the Serpents of the Earth for a vhile. As fun as Villie is, he’s not much of a schemer.”

“Ha! Nice one,” said Igor.

“How’s that?”

“This is a prank on Willie, Mrs. Knife, and the Serpents of the Earth at the same time! Kudos to you, I wish I’d thought of it.”

“Do you?” asked Sloot, pointedly.

“No,” Igor sighed, “for I am a bard, and bards do not devise and execute devious pranks for their own glory and amusement.”

“I can’t believe I’m going to say this,” said Sloot, “but how soon can we murder Willie? Does he have to sacrifice something to something else on an altar?”

“If only it vere that simple,” said Bartleby. “There are forms.”

INVOKING THE SHADES

"Is that all the legs ye've got?" demanded Agather.

"Last time I checked," said Sloot. He wasn't being flippant. He was constantly learning new things about being a demon, and he knew the value of double-checking numbers.

"There's things in the Pit that have dozens," Agather warned him.

"Does that make them better dancers?"

"I doubt it," said Agather. "But if ye have to dance with any of them, we should practice some evasive maneuvers."

Sloot groaned. He didn't want to dance with anyone but Myrtle. He'd promised to take *her* dancing. He was sure he'd remember if she'd said "promise you'll go dancing with a colossal centipede" or suchlike.

How many legs must Sloot dance upon,
Before he's trampled to death?

"Your ballads have taken a somber turn of late," said Sloot.

Igor shrugged. "I go where inspiration doesn't say I can't."

There's a common misperception that inspiration is the same

for demons and mortals alike. A spark that sends the fuse of imagination burning toward the powder keg of creativity. For demons, it's more like organized crime. Anyone who gets mixed up with it is bound to end up at the bottom of a river sooner or later.

At least Sloot managed to avoid injuring himself, which made that his most successful dance lesson yet. He still wasn't fond of the leg warmers, but Agather insisted. Some sort of motherly instinct, he supposed. His own mother had made him put on a sweater when she was cold often enough.

The sun was setting over Salzstadt when Sloot returned to his apartment.

"Sloot! Vhere have you been?"

Bartleby had wasted no time in vamping up her wardrobe. Behind her, Sloot saw Nan and Constantin in their hammocks and a simple pine coffin in the middle of the room. Arthur was nowhere to be found.

"You look different," Sloot replied.

Bartleby grinned and turned in a slow circle, giving Sloot more of an eyeful that he was ready to take in.

"Vhat do you think?"

"It's very, er, vampire." Bartleby wasn't a vampire, but she was enamored of their physical aspect. Sloot hadn't expected that to change for having switched bodies. However, while vampire men wore black cloaks over tuxedos and had jet black widow's peaks, vampires of the female persuasion wore revealing black dresses with necklines that could more accurately be referred to as "navel lines." Sloot's inner monologue reminded him he had a girlfriend.

"Thanks! It vas good to get back into character. You should see Villie, he'll be up soon."

"Up?" Sloot looked at the coffin. "You mean he's a vampire already?"

"He is," said Bartleby with a certain amount of pride. "He got through the initiation vithout screaming once! Of course, he fainted on the vay there, but ve take the victories ve get."

"Naturally," said Sloot. He'd assumed it would take longer to transform Willie into a creature of the night, given there was paperwork. What kind of operation were the vampires running? One where the forms were processed quickly and with a minimum of oversight, apparently. Vampire bureaucracy didn't specifically fall under the auspices of his mission, but Sloot made a mental note to see if he could amend things to provide them a bit of red tape. Red tape was good for bureaucracy. It prevented accidents from speeding.

"Anyvay, ve've got to go see the Convocation of Shades as soon as he arises. They're none too pleased vith this dead-no-alive-no-sorry-dead-again business. They don't like it vhen their records have so many corrections and footnotes."

Sloot nodded in solidarity. The Convocation of Shades may have been a malevolent bunch of spirits, but they were a malevolent bunch of spirits who knew the value of a tidy ledger.

Through the window, Sloot saw the last line of amber disappeared over the horizon. In the distance, a wolf howled.

"Sounds like Villie's avake."

Between Carpathian ambiance and vampires waking after sunset, it occurred to Sloot that distant howling must have been a solid career choice for wolves.

A hand emerged from beneath the coffin lid. The lid raised silently, and Willie got up with a minimum of difficulty.

"When do I get to turn into a bat?" he asked.

"Ahem," said Bartleby.

"Sorry. *Vhen* do I get to turn into a bat?"

"You'll have to master rising from your coffin stiff as a board first," said Bartleby. "And ve'll get the lid creaking ominously soon enough. That's the problem vith new coffins and their greased hinges."

At least Willie was good at wearing a tuxedo. The same could be said of store mannequins, but they didn't have Willie's charming wit. Then again, neither did Willie.

Willie was upset about being hurried out of the apartment without any breakfast and was further bewildered that he didn't want his usual sugary breakfast cereal.

"It doesn't matter," said Bartleby. "Ve'll get you a qvick bite later. Right now, ve have to go see the Convocation of Shades."

They couldn't have been more conspicuous. Two vampires, an accountant, and a woman in a false beard pushing an old man in a wheelchair through the streets of Salzstadt. Sloot couldn't imagine what the punchline might have been, had they but walked into a bar.

"You passed it again!" shouted Constantin. "You've got the direction sense of a newborn baby!"

"And you've got its bladder control," Nan retorted.

"No one can control a Hapsgalt man's bladder, sir! You're lucky mine doesn't thrash you within an inch of your life for your insolence! Now turn around and try not to embarrass yourself this time."

"I'm following you!"

"As well you should be!"

Constantin eventually led them to one of the many nondescript black doors in the city. Had it not been pointed out to him, Sloot would have missed it entirely. A shrouded figure opened the door to Constantin's coded knock, which was complicated the way bureaucrats like their requisition forms. Sloot was surprised that the senile old man could remember it, but found it more credible than Willie ever learning it in the first place.

"Who comes before the Black Door?"

"The Soul of the Serpent," said Willie, after Bartleby's second nudge.

"The Soul of the Serpent is dead."

"Obviously," said Bartleby.

"No I'm not," Willie protested. "I'm standing right here! Aren't I? I mean, Arthur was telling me about the perception of reality, and I haven't really been sure about—"

"The Soul of the Serpent has passed through the White Door," the voice clarified. "Death for the dead. The Soul of the Serpent is no more."

"That's preposterous!" shrieked Willie, with all the affectation that he could no longer afford. "I'm not no more, I'm … still more! Daddy, tell them I'm standing right here!"

"What?" shouted Constantin.

"Vait a minute," said Bartleby. She shoved her way in front of Willie. "The Soul of the Serpent has re-emerged through the Red Door, and now stands before you."

"Not possible," the voice behind the door concluded. "There's no return from beyond the White Door. Everybody knows that!"

"Then why don't I know that?" Willie countered. Sloot could tell he was getting agitated from having to wait outside. It was altogether possible that the little Lord Hapsgalt didn't know the meaning of the word "wait."

"Vhat about the prophecy?" asked Bartleby.

"What prophecy?"

"The Soul's Return," said Bartleby.

"I've never heard of any Soul's Return."

"Oh, vell," Bartleby retorted, "I suppose they discuss every prophecy in the Book of Black Law vith the guy who guards the Black Door, do they?"

"I should think so," said the voice from the other side of the door, in a tone it hoped was convincing enough to include itself.

"Right," said Bartleby. "Management is alvays qvick to give you the information you need to do your jobs."

"Usually, but—"

"And vhen things go wrong, they say, 'it's fine, you had no vay of knowing,' and take the blame themselves."

"That's not what happened to Evan," said another voice.

"Be quiet!" hissed the first one. "I'm handling this!"

"So vhen the Convocation of Shades finds out that you turned the Soul avay from the Black Door, they'll all have a good laugh about it, right?"

"Hang on a minute—"

"No, no," said Bartleby, "ve've taken enough of your time already. Do tell your master that ve vere here, von't you?"

The latch moved and the door opened. A hooded figure leaned out from the shadows.

"Which one of you is the Soul?"

"I am, of course!" shouted Constantin.

"For the last time," said Bartleby, pinching the bridge of her nose, "no, you're not!"

"I'm pretty sure I'm the important one here," said Willie. His winning smile stumbled over his new fangs, which glinted just a bit *too* white in the moonlight.

"Constantin is a Shade," said Bartleby. "Ve're here to return him to the Convocation."

"But he's alive," said the hooded figure.

"If you call this living," the old man grumbled.

"A temporary state of affairs," said Sloot. "I assure you, he'll be dead again very soon."

"Is that a threat, sir?" Constantin perked up. "It's been ages since I gave somebody the business for one of those!"

"So he went beyond the White Door and re-emerged from the Red Door as well?"

"Well, I don't know if I'd go that far." Sloot had a feeling that the doors everyone kept talking about were metaphorical. Metaphors weren't Sloot's strong suit, so he avoided going on the record with them.

"Right," said the hooded figure. "I might not have been told if the Soul was coming for a visit, or if a Shade was missing, or if the laws that govern the transitions between realms had been overturned. But 'two vampires, an accountant, an invalid and a bearded lady knock on the Black Door' sounds like the setup to a bad joke."

"That's what I thought, too," said Sloot, who was more than a little bit proud to still be recognizable as an accountant after all this time.

"Ugh, ve don't have time for this. Villie, do that thing I taught you."

Willie cleared his throat, gathered the hem of his cloak in his hand, and burst out laughing.

"Villie, come on! I'd do it myself, but I'm not really a vampire."

"You're not a vampire?" The hooded figure looked Bartleby up and down, lingering a bit longer than was proper.

Willie tried again, but only ended up laughing harder.

"Villie!"

"I'm sorry," said Willie, drying a bloody tear from one eye. "It's just so weird! Sorry. *Vierd.*"

"Look," said the hooded figure, still ogling Bartleby, "this just doesn't—"

"Look into my eyes," said Willie. Everyone did, Sloot included. As a mere demon 100th class, he didn't have the spiritual fortitude to ignore Willie's commanding voice. The fledgling vampire's cloak covered the bottom of his face, and a shaft of moonlight illuminated his cold, dead eyes. They were wide, crazed, peering deeply into the hooded figure guarding the door.

"Invite us in," Willie demanded. "And tell everybody not to be taller than me."

Sloot hunched down a bit. He liked following orders. He'd learned in school it was the surest way to keep forcible handfuls of dirt out of one's diet.

In through the Black Door they went, past a few more hooded

figures who were intent on insisting in the future that at the time, they'd been somewhere else entirely. Predictably, the cold stone hallway was poorly lit.

Honestly, Sloot thought, *will evil not work if you try carrying it out in a cheery room with ample natural light and decent ventilation?*

On they went, following the ominous creaking of Constantin's wheelchair in the gloom. It was a bit much, but that was evil for you. They passed several doors, some going so far as to have cobwebs all over them.

They were ushered into the room at the end of the hall. Through the boons of demonic vision, Sloot saw that it was a round chamber with no other doors. He made eye contact with Bartleby, or at least thought he did. Her eyes had gone completely black, so there was no way to know for sure where she was looking. Were his eyes all black too? That was an off-putting thought, though he supposed it would only matter to those who could see in the dark.

"What's going on?" demanded Nan. "Someone turn on a light!"

All things evil have a penchant for the dramatic, hence black flames erupted from the sconces on the walls at that very moment. Had Nan been more patient, they'd have lingered in the silent darkness awhile longer.

"Cool," said Bartleby and Willie in unison.

"Yeah, cool," said Sloot, who actually felt it was trite and over-the-top. All the same, he liked to fit in.

"What mockery is this?" something unseen whispered aloud. The hairs attempted to flee the back of Sloot's neck.

"Constantin," hissed the horrible voice, "is that you?"

"How dare you?" shouted the old man. "Who gave you leave to call me familiar?"

"It's him," hissed the voice. Others hissed in response. They sounded farther away, more deeply seated in the blackness. Sloot's patience for the constant one-upmanship of evil was thinning.

"Show yourselves!" Constantin bellowed into the darkness. "You can't hide from the Soul of the Serpent!"

"What have you done to him?" hissed the voice.

"Er, well, it's a long story," said Sloot.

"Time is meaningless," hissed the voice. "What have you done to my son?"

"Gran-Gran?" asked Willie, in a rare fit of having picked up context.

"Wilhelm? A vampire!" The voice, which Sloot surmised was Constantin's mother, Otthilda, led the voices behind her in a chorus of hissing.

"That's right, Gran-Gran," said Willie. "I don't mean to brag, but I'm really good at it. I stared at a scary man and made him open a door!"

The hissing stopped abruptly. Sloot thought he heard a snigger.

"That's very nice, Wilhelm." There was a thick and awkward silence that everyone but Willie seemed to hear, broken only by a smatter of otherworldly sniggering.

"You dare disturb the sleepless eternity of the Convocation for this mockery of my bloodline?" demanded Otthilda.

Willie looked at Bartleby. Bartleby looked at Sloot.

"Oh, bother," said Sloot. He racked his brain for a clever way to say *here's your Soul back, he's not terribly bright, but would you consider letting him be the Eye as well?*

"Er, we do humbly beseech the Convocation," Sloot began, reckoning that centuries-old ghosts expected formality, "to welcome the Soul of the Serpent back to his rightful place."

"Who, Wilhelm?" asked Otthilda.

"Er, yes," said Sloot.

"But didn't he pass through the White Door?"

"In these shoes?" Willie scoffed. "Not likely! I mean, maybe if it was the first weekend of the month and there was herringbone carpet-"

"Silence!" shouted Otthilda. She was echoed by the Shades behind her. "Wilhelm has passed through the White Door, whence none return. We await the passing of the Eye, who shall become the Soul in her own time."

"Mrs. Knife?"

A sigh escaped the Convocation. Sloot was impressed. The dead expressed exasperation with gravitas.

"We chafe of that interloper," Otthilda growled. "Constantin would have made a powerful Soul, and she robbed us of that."

It would have sounded like great news to anyone else, but Sloot Peril knew better than to take heart when hope glimmered too brightly. There was always a catch.

"May we be of service in the matter?" asked Sloot.

"You can kill Mrs. Knife," said Otthilda.

"No, you can't," said Constantin. "She's my cousin! I'll not have you running around, murdering Hapsgalts, you—"

"She's only legally your cousin," said Otthilda. "Tricky maneuvering with the aid of a particularly cunning chaos firm."

Sloot couldn't help wondering if the firm happened to be Winkus, Ordo, and Mirgazhandinuxulluminixighanduminophizio, but he knew nothing pleasant would come of asking. He was grasping for something more useful to say when the wailing started.

Sloot knew that wailing. He'd done a bit of it himself when he was dead. It was a depressing sort of lament, the rough equivalent of saying "I'm so bored I could die if I wasn't dead already." But it was more than that. A tortured numbness, like blood flowing back into a hand that's been asleep for an eternity.

"What's the matter?" asked Sloot.

"The bones," wailed Otthilda, "the bones!" The rest of the Convocation echoed the sentiment. "Our spirits are restless and cannot be soothed but through the bones! But where? Where are our bones?"

"The Soul remains," said Bartleby. "Vhat happened to them after that business vith the Serpent of the Sky?"

Sloot couldn't remember. He'd been drained of his vitality and nearly cast into the Well of the Void immediately after the battle. The fates of a bunch of old bones weren't a major concern at the time.

What about Franka? She was the last living keeper from the Skeleton Key Circle, and he hadn't seen her since then. Perhaps she had them.

"Er, pardon me, your ... horrible ... darkness? What if I were able to find your bones?"

"Do you know how to soothe the bones?"

"No, but I know someone who does."

"The Skeleton Key Circle," said Otthilda. "Lost! All lost!"

"Not all of them," said Sloot. "There may still be one."

"What is your price?"

"Remove Mrs. Knife from power," said Sloot. "Make Willie the Eye and the Soul. Vampires are both dead and alive, right?"

The air was still, disturbed only by the susurrus of the Convocation whispering among themselves. Sloot could have listened in if he wanted, but you never knew what sort of madness you might catch that way.

"Very well," said Otthilda. "Restore the Skeleton Key Circle, soothe the bones, and Wilhelm shall rule as Eye and Soul."

LONG FORGOTTEN DEAD

Sloot limped away from another exhausting dance lesson with Agather. His progress was slow, but he was starting to understand some basic technique. Agather insisted that dancing had more to do with feelings. Or rather, feeling. Or rather, *feelin'*. To hear her tell it, until Sloot was able to surrender to the rhythm and let his hips think for themselves, he wasn't going to get it. As far as Sloot was concerned, if logic couldn't be applied to it, he'd rather give it a miss.

At least Igor had gotten something out of it, even if said something was a new ballad about Sloot's general lack of coordination and the way he cried when he was out of breath.

"It's like a frightened pig hiccupping backwards while gargling mud," Igor marveled. "I can't think of a word for it. Oh! I can invent a portmanteau!"

"Isn't that the man who throws you off the train if you haven't paid?"

"No, it's like brunch."

"Oh," said Sloot. Brunch was his least favorite form of torture.

You had to drink bubbly wine in orange juice while a cook who aspired to be a chef tried creativity on eggs. You had to eat it with people you pretended to like, and you had to skip work to do it. Sloot suspected brunch was a level of the Inferno that had transubstantiated.

The train screeched to a halt in Crags Station. Sloot and Igor shuffled along in a column of other low-level demons.

"Lots of demons coming into Salzstadt today," Igor remarked.

Sloot said nothing. He couldn't stop thinking about Myrtle. He hadn't spoken to her in ages, and he felt like he was failing her. Sure, a rescue was likely impossible, but he was her boyfriend! Not the dashing type who didn't turn around when things exploded, but shouldn't he have started on a plan?

He basked in the damp, chilly gloom of Salzstadt as he plodded back toward his apartment. He wasn't eager to face whatever fresh lunacy awaited him there, so he detoured to the city's main gate. Feeling its solidity had always soothed him, and his resting level of anxiety had been obscenely high since, well, birth.

"What's the matter?" asked Igor.

"It's no good," said Sloot. He stood there, palm pressed against the gate, trembling with the exertion of will. "It's always worked before."

"Maybe you're supposed to pull," Igor offered.

"No, you—" Sloot's teeth locked together, biting off the swear word that Igor so richly deserved. He sighed. "It's not just the gate, it's the city! It's always calmed my nerves, but..."

"Were you going to finish that?" asked Igor, as though the sentence were half a croissant.

"How can I? The truth is ... the truth, the *real truth* is..."

They believed in tradition in the Old Country. It was more than just hanging out flags or wearing antiquated hats on holidays. For a salt, tradition was a responsibility. It wasn't enough to simply believe that the Old Country was the pinnacle of civilization, capable of withstanding all foes. They had to know it was true.

That was the problem. Sloot knew the mighty gates of Salzstadt weren't impenetrable. He'd just come from the crags with a dozen other demons who'd ridden the same train! If a train full of demons could come and go as it pleased, what use was the gate? The foreign devils were already in.

Sloot could see the truth, that the Old Country was no different from any other place. The Domnitor, long may he reign, wasn't infallible. That led to all sorts of seditious thoughts. What if he could do better, but didn't want to? What if there was someone else who could do the job better?

Twang, went Igor's bit of wire.

"For pity's sake," Sloot groaned.

Peril cried out for pity,

He was sad about his city,

People turned their heads in Igor's direction.

"Please, not now!" Sloot glanced around nervously. "Stop singing, I beg you!"

He begged his best friend,

To sing the friend song again,

To help him open up the gates of the city.

"What? No!"

"Hey!" shouted a yokel, who'd either lost a shoe or found one. "This guy's trying to open the gates!"

Had Sloot not been in immediate danger, he might have appreciated the speed at which the mob assembled. With staggering efficiency, they made quick work of their requisite suspicious mumbling so they could get on with the angry shouting.

"Are you mad?" spat a gran, fists on her hips and hobnail boots at the ready. "It's nothing but cannibals out there!"

"They're standing on each other's shoulders to look over the wall!" shouted the one-shoed yokel. "What fool don't know that?"

"Please," shouted Sloot, I wasn't—"

"The *foreign* sort of fool," screeched a street urchin with dirt on his face and an over-large cap slightly askew atop an unruly brown mop. He'd have been adorable if he didn't have the same bloodlust in his eyes as the rest of the mob.

Igor backed away, suppressing a grin. What to do? Sloot had to think fast. He didn't have instincts to speak of, but he'd lived in the city his entire life. He wasn't just a resident, he was a denizen. He had a grasp of the hasty generalizations and knee-jerk reactions that beat instincts any day.

"Yeah," he snarled, "who's he think he is, trying to bring the foreign hordes down upon us?"

"Yeah," rumbled the pitchfork section. Someone had a torch, too.

"It was you—"

"Who saw it with my own eyes!" interrupted Sloot. "I sent him running for the crags! If you hurry, you can catch him!"

"Sent him running?" shouted the apoplectic gran. "Why would you do that? Why didn't you blow your whistle so we could wallop him on the spot?"

"Er, because foreign devils don't respect our traditions! He made off with my whistle. Oh, where is my justice? After him, quickly!"

"But why didn't you—"

"For the Domnitor!" shouted Sloot, his fist leaping into the air like a dandelion on the breeze.

"Long may he reign!" the mob shouted in response, and they were off.

Sloot collapsed to the cobbles as soon as they were out of sight. He couldn't hold back his tears.

"Oh, yeah," said Igor, "my portmanteau! What do you think of 'hiccuffle?'"

"What is wrong with you?" Sloot wailed. "You nearly got me killed!"

"Don't be so dramatic." Igor waved a claw in nonchalance. "It was just a mob with pitchforks. Can't kill a demon with pitchforks."

Sloot hiccuffled a couple of times as he calmed down. "How do you think they get them so quickly?"

"Can't have a mob without pitchforks," said Igor. It wasn't a good answer, but it wasn't wrong either. They walked back to the apartment in silence. It was empty.

"Finally," said Igor, "a little peace and quiet around here!" He twanged absently at his bit of wire.

Sloot sighed. Peace and quiet, indeed. Well, it was as close as he'd been in quite a while. He flung himself down on the couch to enjoy the relative stillness for a moment, expecting to land on a rumpled blanket, but getting something more like a sack of kindling instead. He jumped, yelped, and found himself clinging to the ceiling. Demonic instinct rushed past decorum and he hissed at the sofa.

"How dare you, sir?" demanded Arthur.

"I knew it was too good to be true," Igor wailed. "Is it too much to ask that a demon and his bard have a moment alone?"

"My sincerest apologies, Arthur," said Sloot as he crawled down the wall. "We haven't seen you in days, where have you been?"

"Taking it to the streets," growled Arthur in a voice that could have turned a plank into sawdust. "Fighting back against that very sort of policing! Am I not free to come and go as I please?"

"You're free to go anytime you like," said Sloot.

"More like taking it to the pub," Igor interjected.

"I've been taking it to where the people are. Lots of them happen to be in pubs."

"Are you doing another revolution?"

"How else am I going to end tyranny and usher is a new, enlightened era? Everything was going according to plan with the last revolution until you ruined it. Thanks for that, by the way."

"I think that was sarcasm," Igor whispered to Sloot.

"I got that, thanks," he replied. "Look, Arthur, I'm sorry about your revolution, but I hardly think—"

"Oh, that's clear. And now all of the good revolutionaries are taken! Nothing but salt miners in the pubs now. They've got no interest in abstract thinking."

"I suppose not," said Sloot. He wasn't interested in Arthur's lame attempts at revolution, and he needed to find Franka. He opened his ledger and stood in his circle.

"Don't follow me this time," Sloot warned Igor.

"You can't go without me," Igor insisted. "I'm your bard! How am I supposed to write about your epic adventures if you have them without me?"

"Trust me this time," said Sloot. "I'm not doing an adventure, just reviewing the facts."

"That's as much adventure as you usually get up to," grumbled Igor.

Sloot turned the Descending Pentacle to align with the proper lunar phase, faced the Mortifying Octet, and added a couple of counterclockwise wrist flicks to his usual incantation. He spread his wings, finished the complicated gestures, and found himself hovering high above a teetering pile of goblins climbing each other toward Bartleby's portal. He loathed flying, but at this point in time, it was the lesser evil.

Igor, on the other hand, plummeted down into the teetering pile.

"I warned you," Sloot called after him. He thought briefly about going after him, but there might be repercussions if he interfered in the battle. Besides, Igor always seemed to find his way home, much to Sloot's chagrin.

Just as he lost sight of Igor, he caught sight of himself. More specifically, the ghost of himself peeking up from within the pile of goblins. He yelped in surprise and clamped a hand over his mouth, not that he needed to worry. The din of the battle was easily enough to drown him out.

He heard a roar of fury from his right and turned to see Myrtle, wings and claws a blur, fighting the goblins at the top of the pile. He hadn't seen her for so long he'd forgotten how lovely she was, flaming eyes and razor-sharp teeth notwithstanding. He watched for a moment, during which she dispatched more goblins than he'd summoned by swearing in his whole life. As much as he wished that he could reach out to her, tell her he loved her, he knew he couldn't risk interrupting her at this critical moment. What if the goblins climbed past her and got into Nicoleta's tower?

He eventually tore himself away and made a clumsy circle toward the circle of stones where Gregor and his wizards were about their detestable magic. He kept his eyes on Franka as Gregor called forth the Serpent of the Sky, which rose up into the heavens and winked out. Franka went sword-first through the wizards then disrobed a couple of them, causing Sloot to seriously question how much he knew about her.

While Vlad exchanged taunts with Gregor, Franka used the robes of the fallen wizards to make a pair of sacks, gather up the Soul remains, and slink off into the night. Sloot followed at a distance.

Franka walked through the eastern woods with her impromptu sacks for a few hours, though it took Sloot a full week in demonic time to follow her. Franka knew how to cover her tracks. Anyone who wasn't able to use a magic circle to repeatedly turn back time and try again would have found it impossible. Franka employed magical countermeasures to throw off humans, demons, the undead, the dead, time travelers, dwarves, goblins, fairies, and letter carriers bearing junk mail from places where she hadn't lived in years.

She continued into the eastern mountains along the border until she came to an abandoned village. Both the Old Country and Carpathia could have claimed it as their sovereign territory, though he doubted either knew it existed. One swear word could have divined the side of the border upon which it fell, but Sloot was content to let the mystery remain.

Just north of the village was an ancient graveyard. The names on the stones had long since worn away. Whoever lay beneath them, there was no one to remember them now. Except for Franka, perhaps, who seemed to know her way around the place. She approached an ivy-shrouded mausoleum, pulled a rusty iron ring in a gargoyle's mouth, and a stone staircase opened in the floor. She lit a candle and Sloot followed her down into the rough-hewn tunnel.

Several hundred feet below, the stairs opened into massive cavern. The ceiling was lost in the darkness above. On the mossy ground before them lay another graveyard, which looked far older than the one above.

A graveyard built atop a graveyard, though Sloot. He shuddered at the complexity of haunting such a place, and thought Bartleby would consider it heaven.

The mausoleum at the center of the lower graveyard, while ancient and decrepit, was far larger than any Sloot had seen in the Salzstadt Cemetery. He'd have to keep Willie away from it at all costs, for fear he'd spread the word. The city's wealthiest families would raze their least profitable tenements to make room for intensely fashionable mausoleums.

A quick chant and a few gestures from Franka's wand opened a section of the wall. He followed her inside. A few of the rooms, to Sloot's surprise, were well-appointed with modern amenities. He conjectured neither to the sacrilegiosity of the arrangement, nor to whether "sacrilegiosity" was a word.

The walls of the mausoleum were covered with tiny alcoves.

With a wave of Franka's wand, many of the alcoves shone with the light of a single candle. It was a surprisingly warm and inviting place, given its purpose.

Franka walked past the cozy rooms and into the mausoleum proper. She set the bags down and laid the Soul remains reverently around a massive stone table. She walked around the table for an hour or so, whispering incantations, studying the bones, and arranging them into piles. It had been at least two days since she'd slept. She ultimately abandoned the task, went back to the cozy rooms, and collapsed onto a sofa.

Watching someone sleep is boring. It's also creepy if they don't know you're there. Sloot therefore employed his circle to speed things up. He'd expected to go farther ahead, but Franka was on her feet and fully refreshed after an hour. Part of the magic employed by her order, Sloot surmised. He wished he'd had that while he was alive, fantasizing wistfully about a twenty-two-hour workday.

He sped up the passage of time again as she finished sorting out the remains, then had to back up when she suddenly disappeared. He watched as she opened a portal with her wand and stepped through it. It closed too quickly for Sloot to follow, but he knew where she was. Even after death, rebirth as a demon, and the passage of several thousand years of demonic time, Sloot would be hard-pressed to have forgotten his mother's apartment.

OUT OF RETIREMENT

"Shove off."

The voice sounded like the first successful transplant of a bear's voice box into a person. Sloot's natural apologize-and-flee inclination kicked in, but he stopped himself mid-performance. Perhaps demonic hearing was more sensitive than human. Perhaps the depth of the voice was too over-the-top. He knocked again.

"Er, Franka? It's Sloot. Look, I just need—"

The door flew open and Sloot was violently yanked inside. He heard the door slam shut behind him as he landed on the floor with a severe lack of grace. Given his mother's paranoia, it fell short of being his most violent entry into the apartment. Then again, his mother seldom followed with standing on his throat and pointing a wand in his face.

"Nice to see you too," he croaked.

"*Praesto,*" said Franka, giving her wand a swirl. Sloot felt his face go momentarily numb, as if he'd slept on it funny.

"Is it really you, Sloot?"

"It is," Sloot gasped. "Look, I don't need to breathe ... but your boot is making it hard ... to talk."

Franka considered it for a moment before taking a couple of steps back. She didn't put her wand away, though. It remained pointing Sloot-wise.

"What are you?" she asked. "And how did you find me?"

"Demon," Sloot replied as he stood. "I'm tasked with amending the Narrative, fixing all of that business with the Dark spilling out. I can work with the past, so I was able to track you through the graveyard after the Serpent of the Sky business."

"That's not possible," said Franka, eyes frantically scanning the room for a punchline. "I always keep my wards up! You couldn't have scried on me, in the past or otherwise!"

"It's not scrying. Well, I don't think it is. Truth be told, I'm not sure what scrying is."

"You were able to track me in the past and you don't know what scrying is?"

Sloot explained his ledger and, as far as he understood it, his Ascendant Domain that goes along with it.

Franka gasped. "Ascendant Domain? That's incredible! It's also a huge relief. If that was what it took to find me, Zurogravia should still be secure."

"Zurogravia?"

"That place," said Franka, "the graveyards. You can't tell anyone about it, not a soul!"

"Can I ask how you know my mother?"

"She was a friend of Sir Berthold." Franka turned away at the mention of her old mentor, who'd been murdered by Mrs. Knife. Sloot knew it was a sore subject. Franka should have had more time to learn from him before inheriting his duties, but such was life. Or rather, the unscheduled cessation thereof.

"The shadows are a noisy place," she continued. "Everybody

knows everybody else. Spies, the Serpents of the Earth, graffiti artists—all the worst elements of society. Sladia was one of the few who knew about us. I don't know how she found out, but very few secrets … are."

Sloot nodded. Since the day he'd taken his mother's place in Carpathian Intelligence, he'd assumed everything was a secret, and that everyone else already knew. That was how you stayed alive in the game. Of course, he'd died, so maybe not.

"Anyway, I ran into Sladia, we got to talking, and she told me I could use her old apartment if I needed it."

"Nice of her," said Sloot, feeling only slightly overlooked. She'd never offered him use of her apartment. Then again, she'd always been very invested in teaching Sloot self-reliance. She and old Constantin had similar views on coddling.

"You're a fan of boulderchuck, are you?" asked Sloot. His mother had gone back to Carpathia after retirement, to her old hometown of Kadaverstraag. There she'd found employment coaching the Corpse Grinders, the local boulderchuck team.

"I don't really follow sports."

"You're too young to have worked with her in the salt mines," Sloot puzzled aloud. "Wait a minute. She's not retired!"

"'Retirement' is a fuzzy term in the espionage game," said Franka. "Just when you think you're out, they pull you back in for one last job. Good spies have half a dozen 'one last jobs' before they disappear, only to be found in some antiquated village where they've been making shoes for the locals after ten years."

"What happens then?"

"They get pulled back in for one last job."

"Ah."

"Come with me," said Franka. She led Sloot into the next room and began searching the sofa cushions. "Close the door. And the curtains."

Predictably, Sloot did as he was told. Franka finished searching the room, though for what, Sloot refused to guess. Guessing was the same as gambling, and he was far too risk-averse for that sort of nonsense.

"I need your help," she said at last, apparently satisfied that whatever she sought wasn't there. "I need to rebuild the Skeleton Key Circle."

Grey clouds of suspicion threatened freezing rain over the fields of Sloot's good fortune. That was precisely what he'd hoped to talk her into, and there she was offering it up. He'd heard of the concept of "playing it cool" and thought he'd give it a try.

"Oh, that. Yes, well, that would be … *ahem.* Do go on."

"Well, you've got Ascendant Domain over Salzstadt, right? Over the last few months?"

Sloot nodded.

"That means you can find things that are hidden. Zurogravia, for instance."

"You need me to find something?"

"The Steward's journal. It's got all the answers, everything I need to restore the Circle."

"And you can soothe the Soul remains once you have it?"

Franka looked surprised. "How do you know about that?"

"It's a long story," said Sloot. "Willie's a vampire. If you soothe the bones, the Convocation of Shades will make him Eye and Soul of the Serpent, forcing Mrs. Knife out. Actually, not that long a story, I suppose."

"That'll make it easier to get my revenge," said Franka, a murderous twinkle in her eye. She smirked. "You're starting to think like a spy. Find me that journal and we both get what we want."

"Any idea where should I start looking?"

"You're the one with Ascendant Domain," said Franka. "You'd know better than I would."

DOING BUSINESS

Sloot went for a walk. It wasn't his first mistake, and it wouldn't be his last.

He had a lot on his mind and needed to clear out the cobwebs. This was not a metaphor, as any student of demonic physiology would know. The things that Sloot didn't know were happening within him were a rare blessing to him. Ignorant bliss.

"Am I going to have trouble with you?"

That sort of sentence usually came from brutes whose shoulder muscles had overtaken their necks, not little girls who looked to be about eight years old. However, her face lacked none of the subtle hope that Sloot would put up a fight.

"I should hope not," said Sloot, giving her a little bow.

"All right," she replied, with a mixture of suspicion and disappointment. "We'll try it the easy way. Kindly follow me, please."

She turned and started walking down an alley. She turned after a few steps and seemed surprised that Sloot had followed.

"Well, what do you know? She said it would be easy."

"Who said?"

"Never you mind," said the girl, who maintained a surprisingly brisk pace for her stature. "You'll really just wander off behind anyone who asks you politely?"

"That seems to be the case," said Sloot.

"You don't think that's dangerous?"

Sloot pondered that for a while. It did seem unwise, yet there he was, fully invested in the rhythm of one foot placing itself in front of the next.

"Not really," Sloot eventually replied. "Your run-of-the-mill muggers don't ask politely, and people who want to see me badly enough usually go straight to the hard way. I'm just considering inevitability."

"Suit yourself," the girl sneered at his use of a seven-syllable word. That sort of language wouldn't make you any friends on the mean streets of Salzstadt.

Through alleys they zigged, across streets they zagged, and eventually they came to a ladder running up the back of a four-story building. The girl climbed it with alarming speed, leaving Sloot to creep gingerly upward at a pace scarcely faster than grass growing in the winter. He emerged eventually atop the roof on his hands and knees.

"Did you forget you had wings?" The girl was leaning against a chimney, her arms folded.

"It's broad daylight!" Sloot pointed out, glad for a reason that had nothing to do with his fear of flying.

"The dead are walking the streets."

"All the same," said Sloot. It would be just his luck for Old Country denial to accommodate the walking dead, but not flying demons. "This is it, then?"

"Not quite," said the girl. She flashed him a wicked grin and sprinted for the opposite edge of the roof. Sloot screamed as she leapt and plummeted from view.

Sloot crawled quickly toward the opposite edge, stopped about ten feet from it, then sat down and scooted cautiously the rest of the way. Peering over the edge, where human eyes would have seen nothing but blackness in the hole leading deep below the surface, Sloot saw feathers. Thousands, perhaps millions of feathers.

He'd once read the Ministry of Beef, Poultry, and War's regulations regarding the proper handling of chickens from cover to cover. Parts of it had been redacted. Then again, Sloot had yet to read a book that had all its words laying out in the open for anyone to read. Had he found one, he'd have reported it to the Ministry of Information Defense as likely subversive material.

According to the poultry regulations, a massive quantity of chicken feathers was required for a military project which had been entirely redacted, save for the words "the cannibals will never see it coming." Sloot surmised he was looking down upon a government storage facility for a military project that he had no desire to know anything about. Plausible deniability was a constant companion to a loyal salt.

"Come on!" shouted the girl from atop the pile. Sloot doubted he'd have heard her through human ears, and decided against testing the capacity of demonic lungs for yelling.

There was another ladder on this side of the building, too. It was nearly sunset by the time he reached street level. He fidgeted as he looked down into the hole.

"You've got to be joking," said the little girl. "You'll jump from there, right? I'm starving!"

Pretending he hadn't heard her, Sloot scanned the edge of the hole for another ladder. It was at least thirty feet to the bottom, where the feather pile tapered toward the ground.

"Please?" asked the little girl. "I'm so hungry."

Sloot steeled his nerves. There was no ladder in sight. There weren't any people either, which might have convinced him to unfurl his wings in the fading light of day and get on with it, had he but been someone else entirely.

The girl closed her eyes, drew in a deep breath, and let it out slowly. When her eyes opened again, they looked as though they'd grown several inches.

"Pwease?" Her voice crackled on the edge of tears. Her voice echoed in the chasm of her belly, which had never known so much as a crust of bread. It was *kinder* magic, the sort that all children possess, but few are clever enough to harness intentionally.

Sloot toppled into the hole, sobbing from his wretched heart. He shrieked as he hit the feathers.

"Finally," said the girl. "Now keep up! I wasn't kidding about being hungry."

"Sorry," said Sloot, the fog of pity clearing before him. Not the fog of self-pity, of course. He'd never seen past that a day in his life.

He followed the girl through a door and into the sewer tunnels. On they walked at the girl's frenzied pace until things started to look familiar.

"We're in the Black Market," said Sloot.

"Duh," said the girl's irritated glare.

"Why didn't we just go in the regular way?"

"That *was* the regular way," she quipped. If Sloot had known anything at all about children, he'd have understood. Why take the door when you can leap several stories onto a huge pile of government feathers?

"You're taking me to Winking Bob, then?"

"Keep your voice down! And yes."

"It's fine, I know the way from here."

"You think you'll get rid of me that easily after all this, then?"

"What?"

She came abruptly to a halt and whirled on Sloot. He tripped over her and experienced the particular sensation of the sewer floor introducing itself to one's nose. As pungent as it is painful.

"I could have taken any number of jobs today," shouted the girl as Sloot got to his feet. She'd managed to keep hers. "Do you know how many sweet shops I could've been chased out of? Or pennies I could have taken from old men who wanted to seem kindly? Loads. But Bob asked for a favor, and you don't say no to Bob. This shouldn't have taken my whole day, but since it did, I intend to collect my favor. Is that all right with you, spawn of the Inferno, or do I need to start crying?"

"I didn't—"

"The bad man took me from my Gran!" she sobbed.

"All right! I'm sorry!" There were some things you didn't get away with anywhere. Sloot imagined that even the proprietor of the Black Market stall selling loose fingers would have qualms with kidnapping.

They came at last to the huge iron door. The little girl banged on it with the hammer that lay beside it.

"Yes?" came a familiar voice as the little window slid open. "Oh, it's you."

The window slid shut and the door opened. The fearsome pile of muscles named Edmund nodded for Sloot to enter.

"Took you long enough," he said.

"Wasn't my fault," said the girl. She pointed at Sloot. "He's a coward."

Edmund and Sloot both nodded. Edmund tossed a silver coin to the girl.

"Get yourself something to eat," he said. "Not the beef. It isn't beef."

"It hasn't been beef for months," said the girl. "Tell Bob we're even for the fruit cart?"

"That sounds fair."

The girl skipped away. Edmund closed the door, opened the

only other door in the room, and ushered Sloot through. They emerged in what appeared to be the dusty ruin of an old pub.

"Wasn't there a different room on this side of the door before?" asked Sloot.

"The presence or absence of alleged spaces in relation to doors which may or may not exist maintain no inherent relevance to meetings which may or may not take place at this or any future date," Edmund replied.

"Sloot Peril!" His name slithered sickly sweet from the sly tongue of Winking Bob. She was seated at the one clean table in the far corner of the pub, a pair of frosty drinks in front of her.

"How long has it been?" she asked.

"Since the Dark spilled out," said Sloot. "Since Myrtle was banished to the lowest circle of the Inferno, made possible by a drop of her blood. Tell me, where did Walter the Undying get that?"

"That would be telling." Bob's smile didn't falter a hair's breadth as she waggled a playful finger.

"Implied references to information may or may not be available, factual, or relevant, and are not admissible as evidence in future legal matters."

"Thank you, Edmund."

"You asked," said Sloot.

"Allegedly."

"It doesn't matter! You've got enough disclaimers to ensure I can't do anything about anything, in perpetuity, so I'm not going to try. What do you want from me?"

Winking Bob sighed. "You've got the foresight that comes along with the game, I'll grant you. But you've never figured out the *raison d'etre*? Honestly, Sloot, you should have learned to have a little fun by now."

Having fun in dire situations was indeed the sort of thing that successful spies learned to do. Of course, Sloot was accustomed to being the exception to the rule in cases like this.

"Oh, well," said Bob. "Tell me, how are things going with your endeavor?"

"How do you know about that?" asked Sloot.

"Attendees of alleged meetings," said Edmund, "which may or may not be in progress at this or any future juncture, are advised to refrain from inferences to the possession of knowledge by other parties allegedly present at same."

"Thank you, Edmund. Come on, Sloot. Let's not ruin this reunion of friends by insulting each other's intelligence. Edmund?"

As Edmund rattled off another disclaimer about inferences made by words like "reunion" and "friends" and "this," Sloot couldn't help wondering how she'd known. If his endeavor had been to balance the financial records of the Three Bells' shipping fleet, he'd not have thought twice about it. But this was an assignment from the Coolest, who were more akin to gods than captains of industry. Winking Bob had spies everywhere, everyone knew that. But spying on the architects of the Narrative? Surely, even Winking Bob wasn't capable of that.

"It's fine," said Sloot. "Things are coming along, you know? Lining up nicely. I'm sure I'll have it all wrapped up soon."

"You should learn to bluff," said Winking Bob.

"Certainly not." Bluffing, as Sloot understood it, was a clever form of lying. He had the capacity for neither.

"I'm only trying to help," said Bob.

That did it. Sloot couldn't say for sure exactly what *it* was, but it made Winking Bob make sense. She was All Business, and what was business? Money. Sloot knew how to follow the money. Bob wasn't bluffing, she wanted to help. It just wasn't him she was interested in helping.

"No offense," said Sloot, "but even if I needed your help, it's never worth the price."

Bob shrugged. Sloot was impressed. He'd waylaid her with the single worst insult in an accountant's portfolio—economic viability—and she ignored it like a salesman facing polite refusal.

"I'm expensive," Bob admitted. "But I'm worth it."

"Thanks all the same. Out the way I came in, then?"

"I don't understand you, Peril. If you don't want my help, why did you come?"

"Because you asked."

"I *asked*?"

"I was as surprised as you," said Sloot. "First time for everything, I suppose."

"What are you playing at, Peril?"

Sloot suppressed his panic. He'd never had the upper hand in a *tete-a-tete* with Winking Bob, and he wasn't sure he liked the feeling. But it was apparent that Winking Bob knew something he didn't, and he'd come all this way.

"I've come to you before when I needed something," said Sloot, "and you've summoned me when you wanted something. Not asked, *summoned*. Why ask nicely now?"

"Because we're old friends now," said Bob. "I don't summon my friends."

"Declarations of friendship should not be misconstrued as awarding interest in any business arrangements existing, planned, unplanned, or theoretical in this or any other metaphysically analogous context."

"Thank you, Edmund."

"Malarkey," said Sloot. It was as close to swearing as he liked to get.

"I beg your pardon?"

"You're being nice. You're trying to get on my good side. You either want me to do you a favor or you're trying to kill me. And people don't usually do the latter in their own house. Er, pub."

"I'm impressed," said Bob, who perhaps actually was. "I admit it, I do want something from you. But in light of what I have to trade, it doesn't seem like a big request. I'd really be doing you a bigger favor than-"

"Please," Sloot interrupted, "can we skip this part? I've got no stomach for salesmanship."

Bob sighed and rolled her eyes. "Accountants," she said under her breath. "Very well. You're trying to mend the Narrative with your little ledger, yes?"

"In a manner of speaking," said Sloot, who couldn't help taking offense to her commentary on the size of his ledger.

"If I had to guess," Bob continued, "I'd say the hard part would be establishing the patterns. Finding a point in time when everything was more or less in working order, then offsetting the unexpected variables from there. Am I warm?"

"Hardly," Sloot quipped, "but you're surprisingly accurate."

"What if I were to tell you how to find that starting point?"

"How could you possibly know?"

"I don't *know*," said Bob. "I said I could tell you how to find it. Would you be interested?"

"It would depend on the price."

Sloot desperately needed to learn the art of bluffing. He was interested, that was as plain as the nose on his face, which was quite plain indeed. The very continuation of existence hung in the balance! Sloot was right about the cost of Winking Bob's help, but was any cost really too high if everything ceased to be?

"Very little to you, I imagine," said Bob. "A bauble, really."

She was downplaying again. Sloot was tired of that game. He blinked more meaningfully than any verbal response might have conveyed.

"You're no fun," sighed Bob. "Fine. I want the Three Bells Shipping Company."

"What? Why?"

Sloot was baffled. Didn't Bob already have wealth and power beyond what most ever dream to achieve? He supposed that greed for its own sake was a sufficient motivator. He had worked for the Hapsgalts for a very long time, after all.

"It's basically worthless," said Sloot, skipping straight to the facts. "There's not a penny left in the coffers, and its assets are forfeit to the Domnitor, long may he reign, that he might use them to help salvage our crumbling economy. What could you possibly want with it?"

"In a word," said Bob, "legitimacy. I've got money. Enough to keep the Three Bells in business long enough to start turning a profit again. If I call in all of my markers, I can buy back most of the ships, put crews on them, and get them moving back and forth between the ports."

"And what happens when the Domnitor asks you where the money came from? Long may he reign."

"I've met the Domnitor," said Bob. "He's a very—yes, long may he reign, please don't interrupt—he's a very smart boy, very clever when he's told how to be. Clever enough not to pursue amateur dentistry on gift horses."

"It would be the financially responsible to ask—"

"It would be folly!" Bob exclaimed. "The only reason the economy isn't in free-fall anymore is that it's hit rock bottom. The Domnitor, long may he reign, will take the terms he can get because he doesn't want the people to starve. He doesn't care about them specifically, but when his guards' bellies start to rumble, you'd be surprised at how quickly they start seeing themselves as 'the people' too."

Bob had thought this through. That was dangerous, but it wasn't the most dangerous thing. That was Sloot's inability to find a glaring flaw in the idea. He was horrified to find himself seriously considering it.

He couldn't turn the Old Country into a utopia, right? The Coolest had been clear about that. It would look suspicious to the Auditors. Neither could he leave it in utter ruin. It's got to be a place worth saving, after all. Giving Winking Bob a monopoly on the legitimate *and* illegitimate business in Salzstadt would definitely be a problem, but not in the cosmic, existential sense. In the short term, she'd be operating with razor-thin margins. It would be years before she was rich enough to get up to any proper villainy.

"So where's this starting point?" asked Sloot.

Bob grinned with sufficient avarice for Sloot to hear it. She leaned forward in her chair.

"Do we have a deal?"

It was a good thing that Sloot wasn't able to slip into Infernal time at will. If given infinite time to ponder his options, he could easily have spent several millennia getting dressed every morning. Of course, he'd have to wear something in the meantime. If Infernal time was recursive, Sloot could theoretically experience an approximation of the heat death of the universe in the blink of an eye. Of course, he'd have to decide which eye to blink, so there would be some lead-up time.

He thought as quickly as he could, weighing the potential benefits and disasters against each other, and as he did he noticed a strange new feeling coming over him. A sort of eagerness mingled with his trademark indecision. Demons loved making deals. It was in their blood, regardless of whom said blood had come from. Nascent instincts came to bear.

"Provided your information proves useful," said Sloot, "we can make an arrangement."

"I can't make any guarantees," said Bob. "Edmund?"

"The afore stated disclosure regarding guarantees shall be accepted as applying to any future instance of assurances offered by parties present, whose names have been redacted."

"I understand," said Sloot, "hence the clause. Demon or not, I'm not giving anything away for free."

"Neither am I," said Bob.

"Allegedly," said Edmund.

"Correct," said Sloot. "And if your information is worthless, then you'll have gotten nothing for nothing."

Bob stared into Sloot, her eyes searching for some deception, some trick, some double-dealing. Sloot wasn't offended. He was a demon, after all. How much were you supposed to trust Infernal beings who gambled with souls, never slept, and inspired the depressing music that teenagers loved so much? But there was something else in her gaze, tempering the suspicion. It was something like pride, or possibly admiration.

"Very well," said Bob. She extended her hand. "I'll tell you what I know, and if it helps you succeed in your endeavor to amend the Narrative, you'll give me control of the Three Bells Shipping Company."

"In its current state," said Sloot, extending his hand as well, inches from Bob's. "And I define 'helpful' with no interference from you or Edmund."

Bob winced. She pulled her hand back a couple of inches, squinted toward the ceiling, and then pushed her hand into Sloot's. Her grip was surprisingly strong. Sloot was sure his hand would remain shaken for days to come.

"We have a deal," said Bob. "Can I offer you a drink to celebrate?"

"What, no contract?"

"Oh, there's a contract," said an imp who appeared in a puff of black smoke that smelled of brimstone. He extended a parchment and quill toward Sloot. "Sign here, please."

"What is this?"

"Standard Writ of Demonic Pact," said the imp. "All of the standard inclusions and penalties apply. Your own blood is fine."

Sloot stabbed the quill into his palm and scrawled his name at the bottom of the page. The signature was black. That was disconcerting.

"Thank you," said the imp. He turned to Winking Bob. "We have your signature on file." He nodded and disappeared in a puff of smoke.

"Now," said Bob, "about that drink."

Over the drink, Bob told Sloot–amidst a sprinkling of disclaimers by Edmund–about the Infernal Ball, an event hosted once per century by the Prime Evils. All ninety-nine circles are decked out in whatever finery they can afford. Drinks, dancing, and debauchery serve not only to kick-start the rumor mill for the hundred years to come, but to offer one and all a unique opportunity to meet the Prime Evils themselves.

"That sounds festive," said Sloot. Stating the facts was a tried-and-true means of keeping the conversation moving along without stopping at his discomfort. He'd never done well at parties. He had a nervous laugh that emerged around polite conversation and canapes.

"I'm sure," said Bob.

"Use of the word 'sure' shall not be understood as assurance in this context," said Edmund, "nor misconstrued to have any bearing on any other words in its sentence of origin, if said sentence can be considered to have been 'stated,' as defined in the Libris Confundamus, 395th edition."

"Here's the thing," said Bob, leaning forward in a proper conspiratorial way. She glanced quickly left and right to complete the overture. "What do you know about the Axial Ledger?"

"Nothing," Sloot said with an abundance of confidence and a twinge of excitement. Nothing like a mystery ledger to get his blood moving.

"You're in good company," Bob continued. "Nobody really knows much about it, only that it contains all of the answers."

"What, like to life? The universe? Everything?"

"In a manner of speaking, yes. But no. Not really."

"Oh."

"From what I've been told by entirely reliable sources—"

"The reliability of alleged sources has been ascertained by proprietary algorithms not available for public review."

"Yes, thank you, Edmund. The Axial Ledger is a sort of master proof. You compare it to any assertion, hypothesis, or statement of facts, and it tells you how accurate it is."

"That sounds fun," said Sloot.

"I'm sure," said Bob, who held a hand out to Edmund in afterthought. "Same disclaimer as before, no need to repeat it I think."

Edmund's mouth had already opened. He shut it and frowned in disappointment.

"Furthermore," Bob continued, obviously vexed for the lapse in pacing of her exposition, "in revealing any inaccuracies or flaws, it is capable of deriving corrections."

"So you can use it to, what? Fix bad ideas?"

"Possibly," said Bob, "or in your case, find the problematic entries in another ledger."

Sloot's eyes went wide over the course of a protracted moment as the realization dawned on him.

Sloot gasped. "Salzstadt Before!"

Winking Bob winked.

"I can compare it to this Axial Ledger and see all of the deviations from reality!"

"Yes."

"And it will tell me how to fix them!"

"Possibly."

"Where is it?"

"That's where the Infernal Ball comes in," said Bob. "The ledger is kept in a vault on the first circle of the Inferno."

Sloot's heart sank. It made a disquieting *clunk.* He doubted he'd ever get used to demonic physiology.

"The Prime Evils are the only demons who can enter that level," Sloot moaned.

"Usually," said Bob, "except for the dance contest at the ball."

A bell went off in Sloot's head, fortunately entirely metaphorical this time. Dancing! This had to be why Myrtle had pushed him toward it!

"It starts at the bottom," said Bob. "The best dancers on the 99th circle move up to the 98th. The best dancers there move up to the 97th, and so on."

Whatever excitement Sloot had felt at realizing the point of his dance lessons fizzled.

"Myrtle wants me to dance up 99 circles of the Inferno?"

"Competitively."

TRANSVERSE OCTOHEDRON

It would never have occurred to Sloot that having only one problem at a time might be worse than having several. He'd only ever had several, and the concept of having just one was an unprepared tourist on Sloot's shores. Even if it had spoken the language, there was no word for it.

Really big problems are based on the central difficulty of putting clothes on a toddler. They're evasive, never standing still; they never go down without a fight; and it's best to pounce when you catch them not paying attention. It's helpful to have more than one because they let their guard down when they see you chasing another one.

Sloot fretted over his deal with Winking Bob. She offered him one solution for multiple problems, but there would be consequences. He didn't know what they'd be, but you didn't solve all of your problems this easily. Sooner or later, he'd have to deal with Bob in a very severe way, and he wasn't looking forward to it.

Fortunately, finding the Steward was simple. No one knew who or where the Steward was at any given time, except for Sloot

Peril at one particular moment. The same moment when he'd found Franka, right after their meeting at the Cross. He'd go back there, follow a different thread—hopefully not the one that led to Mrs. Knife—then follow the Steward and find out where he hid his journal.

Simple. Yes. Or, in point of fact, no.

"What you need is a Tra-a-ansverse Octohedron," said Karl. "Very pricey, not to mention de-e-elicate."

Sloot sighed. "Well, I've got a lot riding on it. Does it come with a manual?"

Goat demon laughter sounded like that of a regular goat. It also sounded like goatish crying, which also sounded like goatish swearing at farmers with cold hands at milking time, which also sounded like goatish war cries. The difference was subtle, but important if you happened to be standing in the wrong place and not holding a bouquet of carrots. Sloot took a cautionary step backward.

"Strangely enough, it do-o-oes. It's cursed, though. Reading it will drive you ma-a-ad."

The mighty hand of Sloot's etiquette effortlessly stopped him from asking the circlesmith how he knew that. There wasn't an answer he'd have liked.

"I suppose I'll figure it out," said Sloot. It was as close to a devil-may-care response as he'd ever given.

"Humbug!" shouted Arthur. He pounced from his pile of blankets on the sofa and landed on his feet in a fighting stance, if Sloot were qualified to identify that sort of thing. He wasn't, of course. He wouldn't know a fighting stance from one of Willie's courtly bowing maneuvers, though that might not be a fair comparison. Some of the latter were designed to serve as the former in a pinch.

"What?" Sloot gasped.

"All of it!" Arthur had *that look* in his eyes. Like a rabid weasel who'd been in the schnapps, he was ready to fight anything that moved, or at least berate its flawed notion of metaphilosophical sophistry within an inch of its ego. He also looked like he'd been asleep for over a week, because he had.

"I reject the premise!" the bedraggled philosopher ranted. "There is no existence without observation, sir, and I shall not blink!"

"Vould you look at that?" asked Bartleby, who'd just arrived in a cloud of bats. "Arthur's avake! How'd you sleep?"

"Schnapps," said Arthur, confirming prior similes. "Do I know you, madam?"

"That'll be Bartleby," said Sloot.

Arthur gave her a cursory look up and down. "If you say so. All I see are these blasted stars. Leave some ham within my reach, will you?" And with that, he collapsed on the floor.

"You don't eat for a veek, that's bound to happen. I'll get him back to the couch."

"Er, thanks," said Sloot. "By the way, have you seen Igor? I lost track of him in a less-than-pleasant spot."

"He's buried in the yard."

"What?"

"It's for the best, believe me. The stench vas overpowering."

Sloot had warned Igor not to follow him into Salzstadt Before. As little as he liked having the filthy trickster around, Sloot never meant for him to die beneath a pile of goblins.

A careless thought didn't look where it was going and occurred to Sloot. "How did he get back here?"

Bartleby shrugged. "Valked, I assume."

"Well, that adds up," said Sloot. "The city is full of the walking dead these days, I don't see why Igor should be any different."

"Igor is dead?" boggled Bartleby.

Sloot blinked. There was clearly more at work than he understood, which was reassuring in a backward sort of way. Those in possession of all the facts were called upon to make decisions.

Other people were Sloot's first choice for that sort of responsibility.

Out in the courtyard behind Sloot's apartment, a pile of dirt mumbled.

"What did he say?" asked Sloot.

"It sounded like a svear vord," said Bartleby.

The pile nodded.

"That *is* Igor, isn't it?"

"Yes, it's me," said Igor, sitting up. "This is all you fault, you know? Think about that while I'm resetting my fragrance."

Sloot blinked. Igor sighed.

"You dragged me into danger and abandoned me to the whims of cruel fate," warbled Igor. He was really getting a bard's knack for dramatics. "The things I had to do to survive! Shame on you, Sloot Peril! What sort of person does that to their best friend?"

"You're not … sorry. Why are you in the dirt?"

It's known in Infernal anthropological circles that gremlins are closely related to goblins. So closely related, in fact, that there would be grave concerns about inter-breeding if gremlins were capable of that sort of thing. As luck would have it, gremlins do not participate in parentage. They are spawned of mischief, usually when teenagers write swear words on things that don't belong to them.

Fortunately or unfortunately for Igor, depending on one's perspective, he was spared being torn to shreds by the tower of goblins into which he'd fallen by a dinner party that had happened centuries earlier. A congress of goblins had wandered off in search of something to defile while their pile of meat was rotting in the sun. A gremlin who'd had too much to drink passed out in the pile, lending his particularly pungent musk to its flavor. When the goblins returned to consume the pile and bask in the pursuant flatulence—referred to as the congress being "in session"—they were astounded at the particularly noxious effluvience that resulted. Several goblins near the center of the pile experienced comas, hallucinations, and the urge to tell their friends uncomfortable truths.

"That's why we avoid goblins," Igor groused. "Piles of rotting meat are nice and all, but they're as interesting as, well, piles of rotten meat, if you catch my drift."

"I think I do," said Sloot.

"And who are they to force us into servitude as bouillon, eh? As though we've nothing better to do! Gargoyles' moorings aren't going to loosen themselves, you know."

Sloot gasped.

"I mean, epic songs about … uh … intrepid accountants aren't going to write themselves, you know."

"No," said Sloot, "I suppose they wouldn't." He made a mental note to have the city's gargoyles inspected if he managed to save existence.

"That'll have to do for now," said Igor. His rise from his little pit brought forth the foulest stench Sloot had ever beheld. There was a little demonic part of him that reveled in the pure malevolence of it, but it was shouted down by the rest of him. He lost his balance and dropped to the ground.

"Not qvite," said Bartleby, shoving the gremlin back into the soil with a shiny black boot. "Ve'll check on you tomorrow."

"You want to let him soak up more of that?" Sloot was incredulous.

Bartleby shrugged. "Vhy deal vith today vhat you can put off until tomorrow?"

Sloot was repulsed by the logic but found it hard to resist in the moment.

Karl was gathering up his tools when they got back upstairs. A glittering Transverse Octohedron loomed in his circle's upper segment.

"You'll want to let it cool befo-o-ore you take it for a spin," said Karl.

"Is that vhat I think it is?" asked Bartleby.

"That depe-e-ends. Do you think it's a Transverse Octo-he-e-edron?"

"Yes," said Bartleby, after a pause that was just too long for credibility.

"I'll bi-i-ill you." Karl disappeared in a puff of sulfurous smoke.

It took Sloot a couple of tries, but he managed to achieve the desired effect. With the Transverse Octohedron eclipsing his Portend of Lazy Superstition, he was able to disembody his vision from the rest of himself. It was the only way he could think to get himself into the Cross without Roman and his former self knowing about it. He wouldn't have the use of any of his other senses, but it should be enough to find the Steward.

The sight of himself as a ghost was unnerving. There was a simple explanation *vis-a-vis* coming to grips with one's mortality, but Arthur had put Sloot off philosophy for good. Besides, if Sloot felt the need to come to grips with every worrisome concept that presented itself, he'd never get out of bed.

Sloot's former self plunged through the wall to follow one of the ethereal threads connecting the magical candles in each room of the Cross. He didn't remember looking so timid about it, but memories tell helpful lies. Always looking out for the self-esteem. As long as the results are the same, why be a stickler for details?

Two threads remained. One lead to Mrs. Knife, the other to the Steward. Logic dictated that if he ended up staring into Mrs. Knife's cold, dead eyes, he had only to step back in time and follow the other thread. There was a time when Sloot could trust logic implicitly, but now he knew that was just the sort of pragmatism where unforeseen consequences liked to hide. Disembodied observer, was he? Essentially godlike power within the realm? Ha! This was Sloot Peril they were dealing with. He'd not be lured into a sense of security so easily.

He started with the odds. Fifty-fifty. Well, that was no help. Wait! What had the Coolest called him? "The oddity." He always managed to drag defeat kicking and screaming from the jaws of victory. Impossible odds were destined to come up when Sloot Peril in the game. He could throw a pair of dice and come up with a full house.

He fretted awhile over whether his awareness of his luck—or lack thereof—might play a role in the outcome. He assumed it would, but only if its consideration would work against his favor. That being the case, his only real option was to choose at random.

But how? Sloot knew far too much about statistics and mathematical influences on randomization to ever make a truly random selection, much less get invited to any fun parties. Or, at least, most of him did. In the end, Sloot followed his sense of sight down the path on the left, which appeared more well-lit, insofar as an ethereal thread passing through large spans of solid rock was capable.

It ended in Mrs. Knife, who declined to notice that she was being watched and somehow murder Sloot via his visual senses. He backtracked through time and space, followed the other thread, and found himself staring at a person who process of elimination deemed the Steward. He was a paunchy old man with a wild fringe of white hair standing guard beneath his shiny pate. His brow was furrowed with an intensity that accentuated his bloodshot eyes, which were just a bit too feral to make anyone think "he must be good with children."

Sloot followed him into the streets of his beloved city. Much the way Franka had covered her tracks to Zurogravia, he took a long and circuitous route to a tiny apartment that strangely made Sloot feel right at home.

ON SABOTAGE

"So this is it, eh?"

"It was not long ago," Sloot replied. He knew better than to make guarantees. Anything could have happened between the Steward's walk home from the Cross and the present. In fact, quite a bit had. The Steward had been murdered, for one.

"Best get to it, then." Igor twanged his bit of wire in a dastardly mockery of tuning a proper instrument.

"Well," said Sloot, "I was hoping you could help me out a bit there."

"Don't you worry," replied Igor with a wink. "I've got just the rhyme for 'crippling indecision' worked out. This one's definitely going to make the rounds in the pubs."

"Er, that's fine," Sloot sighed, "but I thought you might, you know, *help me out*."

Igor stared blankly at Sloot.

"Inside the apartment," Sloot added.

Igor's blank stare proceeded with great efficiency into an encore.

"With retrieving the book?"

"Oh, I see! No."

"What? Why not?"

"Because I'm a bard," Igor explained. "We sing ballads about heroic exploits, we don't join in. Wouldn't be proper."

"Of course, but you have other, er, talents, right?"

For his next trick, Igor turned a stunned silence into a smoldering glare.

"You want me to do mischief, don't you?"

"Well, yes," said Sloot. "It's what you do, isn't it?"

"You know very well I've sworn off! How dare you try and lead me into temptation?"

"Sworn off? You're loosening the bolts on that sign as we speak!"

"Oh, that's just—" Igor looked at his hands as though they'd snuck onto his wrists while he wasn't looking.

"Well, it's not mischief," he said.

"Isn't it?"

"Do I go around asking you what's numbers? No. But if I did, I sure wouldn't doubt your answer."

"So that's barding, is it?"

Igor's eyes darted back and forth. "Y-yeah," he stammered.

"Part of the creative process, I presume."

"Sure," said Igor. "I don't suppose you've tried knocking, have you?"

"What good would that do? We know the Steward's dead."

"Taken up a new profession as an undertaker, then? Or have you seen his ashen corpse with your own two eyes?"

"Neither. Franka told me. She knows these things."

"Oh, well, if Franka said! Trust her and ask your loyal bard to toss away his hard-earned recovery! No sense in going to all the effort of knocking on a door when you could simply force a former gremlin back to the life he'd sworn—"

"All right, fine, you've made your point."

Sloot knocked thrice on the door, or would have, had it not fallen in on the first knock.

"I haven't seen you exercising." Igor eyed Sloot with suspicion.

"There's a good reason for that." Sloot examined his fist. He didn't know that it could casually batter a door down. It stood to reason it could do other things he knew nothing about. Best to avoid looking directly at it until the extent of its powers had been assessed. Wouldn't want to make it feel threatened.

The inside of the Steward's apartment resembled the one that Sloot had seen in Salzstadt Before, but it had only been a few months since then. The place looked as though it had stood empty for decades. The curtains had been devoured by moths. The furniture was crumbling. The paint was peeling off of everything.

"He really let this place go," said Igor.

"It wasn't like this at all," said Sloot. "It was lovely, actually. How could it have fallen into disrepair so quickly?"

"Magic."

"What? Who would want to magic an apartment into shambles?"

"It's the other way 'round," said Igor. "Always the same with magical types. They never clean their apartments, just give them the appearance of cleanliness. Illusions, see? Not much bother to maintain illusions, but they have to be maintained. When the Steward's mortal coil got shuffled off..." Igor gestured around the room, giving its dilapidated state the opportunity to speak for itself.

"That makes sense." Sloot breathed a sigh of relief, feeling far less terrified of his own fist. "Come on, help me look for the journal."

"Sorry, no can do."

"What are you talking about?"

"Uncovering what's hid? That's mischief."

"No, it isn't," Sloot protested. "We need it to restore the Skeleton Key Circle. To amend the Narrative!"

"Oh, okay, I'll just trust your amateur opinion on what constitutes mischief. Why wouldn't I? You've only been trying to lead me into temptation since we got here."

Simple arithmetic told Sloot he'd save time by searching on his own, so he did. It gave Igor ample opportunity to craft a ballad for the occasion.

With callous disregard,
Sloot tried to tempt his bard

"Now that's not fair," said Sloot. "I asked you to help, that's all."

"What are you trying to do, sabotage me? Oh, that's ironic!"

"No, I—wait, what do you mean, 'sabotage you?' How does helping open the door count as sabotage?"

"Not that, the song! Not only have you interrupted me in the pursuit of bardliness, you're trying to wipe off all of the poetic license!"

"I was just setting the record straight."

"So you admit it. Straighten your accounting books all you want, but leave my art alone."

"There's a difference between embellishment and lying, you know."

"It's true what they say about artists being unappreciated in their own lifetime. I should really start planning my death. Then I'll get my due-and-propers, I'd imagine."

"Don't count on it," said Sloot. He'd heard religious types talking about how great everything was going to be once you were dead, but he hadn't caught a whiff of any promised glory himself. In his experience death had been more of the same, only he no longer had to get haircuts.

There once was a demon with spindly legs,
He got off on taking his bard down a peg

"Hey," Sloot whined.

Plus his head was too big,

And his nose was all spots,
And the more that he whined,
The worse the song got.

In Sloot's experience, respect was something that happened to other people. He did his best not to listen to Igor's horrid barding while he searched for the Steward's journal.

It didn't take him long to find it, which Sloot found worrisome. He merely asked himself where he'd hide the journal if he didn't want anybody to find it, walked directly over to a loose board in the floor, and pressed on one end with his thumb. The other end of the board lifted, revealing the journal beneath.

All demons have a bit of mischief in them. Sloot must have unconsciously tapped into whatever modicum had been afforded to him. He didn't like the idea of having instincts. Sure, they helped you avoid danger, but who was to say that some recessive trait wasn't waiting to throw him in front of a horse cart if someone sneezed in the rain on a Tuesday?

The journal's cover was leather, though made from the skin of what, he couldn't say and refused to consider further. It was old, that was certain.

"What's in it?" asked Igor.

"Oh, look who's interested in the book now that it's been found."

"Yes," said Igor plainly. "Go on, read us a page or two."

"I wouldn't be able to," said Sloot. "Franka says the Circle keeps their journals encoded." It was a lie, of course. It was encoded, that much was true, but there hadn't been a pattern devised that Sloot Peril couldn't decipher with enough time, a magnifying glass, and someone standing by to take credit for his work.

"Bah," said Igor, "how hard can it be?" The deftness with which he moved was liquid grace. One moment, Sloot was holding the journal firmly in both hands. The next, it had been in Igor's lap the whole time, and he was taking his leisure at leafing through it. Master pickpockets would have loved to take lessons from the gremlin-cum-bard, not that he was offering. You didn't spread skill like that around, lest it come back to haunt your wallet off you.

"Hey, give that back!"

"What are these little squiggles?" Igor squinted.

"It's probably best if you don't—"

Sloot was interrupted and proven right by the same incendiary flash. As sure as it had been a book an eye blink ago, it was now nothing more than a pile of ashes.

"Oh, dear," Sloot groaned.

"That was a neat trick," said Igor.

"A neat trick? You've just destroyed the Steward's journal!"

"Technically, it destroyed itself."

"Because you tampered with it!"

"That's conjecture," said Igor, whose vocabulary apparently had hidden depths. "It's not like I had a chance to spill kerosene on it yet. Besides, tampering is mischief! Exactly what are you accusing me of?"

"I thought I was clear about that," Sloot retorted.

"It's almost like you don't want me to be your bard," Igor lamented, his wounded expression fishing in the pond of Sloot's heart for a trout of sympathy.

"Not almost." Sloot said a swear word which, had he been holding a wooden spoon, would have officially challenged Igor to a duel. "The Skeleton Key Circle can't reform without that book! We need to push Mrs. Knife out of the Serpents of the Earth, and that was our only chance! Hey, did you just cackle?"

"Old habits," Igor shrugged.

"That's a loaded excuse for you."

"Stop impugning my recovery! Besides, how much of a problem is a burnt book to someone who's got the past at his fingertips?"

GOOD OLD DRUDGERY

It wasn't easy, but that was hardly surprising. Nothing was easy these days. If it had been, Sloot would have been right to be suspicious.

"You're sure he's not coming back for a while?" asked Franka.

"Positive," said Sloot. He'd turned up Oxbugger's Crescent on his magic circle to see more of the Steward's timeline and brought Franka into Salzstadt Before on a day when he'd be out for several hours without his journal. Of course, breaking into the place had taken up a few of them. The Steward had been alive at the time, so all of the magical protections he'd placed on the apartment were still in place.

"It's too bad we couldn't have just gone back to when he was already dead," said Sloot.

"We tried that," Franka reminded him. "I don't have the counter-curse that disenchants McGillicuddy's Pyromantic Fizz, which automagically destroys the book if it's opened after the Steward's death."

"Of course," said Sloot. "How much longer to copy it?"

"Ages," growled Franka, "especially if you keep peppering me with questions the whole time."

"Sorry." It was an unusual feeling for Sloot, having nothing to do. One might think he'd appreciate the respite, but the weight of the world did not fall from his shoulders. What's worse, it gave him time to think. Inevitably, his thoughts turned to Myrtle.

Sloot hadn't seen her in months. Years, if you counted the passage of Infernal time. She was counting on Sloot to rescue her, and he couldn't help but wonder how long she'd been upset about it, grousing about what was taking him so long. She'd know, too, if it was taking longer than it should. She was a causation demon before her banishment. She could foresee the results of events as they happened, which was basically like seeing into the future, only the future wasn't as clear as all that. The foresight of causation was as close as one could get.

Except for Sloot, of course. Thanks to Oxbugger's Crescent, he could see very specific futures for people in Salzstadt Before. Well, for the portion of time that his ledgers covered, anyway.

Hang on a second, thought Sloot. The past was already written, but he could affect the future–the proper one beyond Salzstadt Before—by making changes within it. The penniless Hapsgalts squatting in his tiny apartment were evidence of that.

But that was big. It's not every day the global economy dissolves like so much cotton candy in a rainstorm. What about little changes? Small steps, chance encounters? Sloot had heard axioms like hurricanes caused by butterflies flapping their wings on the other side of the world. What if he was making bigger changes than he thought?

Sloot shot up. Franka's eyebrow raised in distracted annoyance.

"I'm going out," said Sloot.

"Just be back before the Steward," she said. "I don't want to have to fight him, especially on his own turf."

Sloot nodded. Moments later, he went dim by upending Sarko's Banality and perched atop the roof of his apartment. He was reminded of the gargoyles that lined every roof in Ulfhaven, though he didn't dare compare himself to one. That was tantamount to striding up to the popular boys' table at lunch and sitting down without an invitation. He might as well pull his own trousers over his head and take a bath in the toilet.

He watched the bustling street below, feeling momentarily envious of his fellow salts as they shuffled through the drudgery of daily life. He missed drudgery. It was familiar, comfortable. Now that he had a quest and demonic powers, there was little time for simple pleasures. What he'd have given for a fleeting moment of ennui! *Alas,* he yearned to sigh, *another in an interminable series of days spent bending my spine over regular ledgers that have nothing to do with time travel!*

"Watch it!"

His reverie was interrupted by the very thing he'd come to see. There she was, the old gran upon whose shoes he'd emptied his stomach the first time he'd visited Salzstadt Before. And there, in front of her, was Sloot.

Well, sort of. He was there, only his presence was muted. To be fair, he'd rarely exuded a strong presence in any room, but this was more literal. He was only a faint shadow, practically a ghost, even though he'd been a demon at the time.

Against all odds, it made perfect sense to Sloot. When an accountant works in a ledger, it's mostly the numbers that do the talking. But the accountant still leaves his own mark, no matter how faint. A sort of signature, in many cases literally that.

When he went into Salzstadt Before, he wasn't there in the same way that everyone else was. He was a visitor, and the fabric of reality treated him just as the wealthy denizens of any city would treat a tourist who'd had more of the local liquor than their system would tolerate. They ignored him and got on with their business.

It could have been far worse. It could have treated him like the working class of said city, hauled him into an alley, and given him the old muddy boots treatment. Thank lazy determinism for small favors.

"S-sorry," said his former self. He faded as he stood, until there was nothing left of him at all. The ghost of his first visit to Salzstadt Before only appeared now insofar as it had changed something, Sloot assumed.

Time to see what he'd come to see. He followed the old gran from above, hopping from rooftop to rooftop. Anyone with a modicum of pragmatism might have wondered why he didn't fly. They might also have wondered why he was equally loathe to try a different haircut. In both cases, Sloot reasoned that he'd reconsider his options when someone wielding scissors gave him a reason.

The gran arrived at home, went around back, sat on an old wooden bench, and started unlacing her boots. Sloot called up his circle and gave Oxbugger's Crescent a nudge, then watched her follow her future along what seemed to be an enviably mundane series of events. No bloody massacres, city-wide fires, or widely accepted breaches of grammatical norms marred the ledger columns of her life.

Perhaps the wings of butterflies weren't strong enough to cause hurricanes after all. Or perhaps it was knowing which butterfly and when. It certainly worked when he exposed the terrible secret about the Hapsgalts' fortune. All he'd done was replace one report with another. Could it be so easy? Could the Axial Ledger tell him, "that one, that butterfly with the red stripe on its wings? Give it a good flap around noon and Bob's your uncle."

He doubted it. Nothing was ever that easy for Sloot. But he had to get on with it, however hard it might turn out to be.

Sloot returned to the Steward's apartment just as Franka was finishing up her transcription.

"You have what you need to take the Steward's oath?"

Franka nodded. "I skipped ahead to that bit. You must promise to bring me back later so I can finish the job."

"Fair enough," said Sloot. "So what do we do next?"

"I'll need the Soul remains in order to soothe the Shades," said Franka, "so I'm headed back to Zurogravia."

"Shall I go with you?"

Franka shook her head. "It's bad enough you've seen it the once. The Steward would have my head if..."

Sloot nodded. Even Sloot had sufficient social graces to know that was a touchy subject.

LITTLE ADO ABOUT THINKING

If there was one thing you could say about the Witchwood, you'd do well to keep it to yourself. The trees themselves seemed to be listening, and who knew what might offend trees?

"No, it isn't," Igor insisted.

"I promise it is," said Sloot. He never imagined he'd have to convince anyone as to the identity of Vlad the Invader, yet there they were. Through strange twists of fate, Sloot both knew her personally and found himself in a situation where there was any doubt.

"She's supposed to have armor on," said Igor. "Everybody knows that."

"You met her once," said Sloot. "We walked into the throne room, you pointed directly at her, and said—and I quote— 'That's Vlad the Invader! That's her, in the flesh, right there!'"

"I remember. *That* was Vlad the Invader. I don't know who this person is. No offense."

"None taken," Vlad replied. That chilled Sloot's blood. Vlad had never weathered insults well, unless a fine mist of blood leaving a freshly cleaved corpse counted as weather.

"Quit yer yammerin'," Agather snapped. "It's bad for the stew."

The wind swept gently through the trees, which may or may not have been paying attention. Their leaves rustled with decorative ambiance. Outside the Witchwood the wind harassed the trees more vigorously. Witches managed no small amount of their magic through intimidation. Agather had likely given the wind a stern lecture about galloping through her parlor without a care. She'd probably even threatened to take the issue up with the wind's mother if it happened again.

"No, I'm sure I'd recognize her," said Igor, who had a particular affinity for ruining stew.

Agather stirred her cauldron and glowered a silent warning.

"What? I'd be able to talk quieter if you'd let me in."

Agather smirked. "That'll be the day. Ye should reconsider the company ye keep, Sloot Peril."

"Yes, Agather." Of course it was the company that kept him, not the other way around. Still, no one ever profited from being smart with a witch.

"The first time I saw her I said, 'That's Vlad the Invader! That's her, in the flesh, right there!' You said so yourself."

"That's true," Sloot admitted, "I said you said so."

"It stands to reason then, I'd recognize her even better the second time around, wouldn't I?" Igor walked in a circle with his finger pointing upward, mocking Arthur's explanatory gait.

In truth, even Sloot had initial doubts about the grey-robed figure sitting on the floor, her legs crossed with her feet atop her knees. That posture struck Sloot as terribly uncomfortable and un-Vlad-ly to boot.

It was a good thing Arthur couldn't hear his thoughts. He'd have plenty to say about what made a person. More than flesh and bones and blood and hair, he'd say. Vlad had laid down her sword, given up her kingdom. What was an invader who never invaded? There was no doubt that this was Vlad, but now that *this* was Vlad, who was she?

Vlad's expression couldn't have been farther from the turmoil of Sloot's inner monologue. She was the unrippled surface of a lake at dawn. Even the wind didn't go near it.

"All's I'm saying is—"

"Look, it's Vlad, all right? Stop taunting her."

"I'm not taunting," Igor gasped, one filthy hand leaping to his sunken chest in shocked offense. "I'm merely acknowledging the stranger in our midst. How do you do, Miss…?"

"Vlad," said Vlad. Not barked, not declared, just said.

"You're really not bothered by this, are you?"

"What cares the sea for the fish that swim within it?"

"So I'm fish now, am I?" Igor snarled.

"I'm warning ye," said Agather.

"Igor, please," said Sloot. He turned to Vlad. "How are you doing that?"

"I'm doing nothing."

"Right, that's what I mean. Hang on a minute! Did you get enlightenment? The abbot said something about that."

"It doesn't work like that."

"That's not what the abbot said." Sloot clamped a hand over his mouth. Had he really just argued with Vlad the Invader? Well, he'd argued with Vlad. More to the point, he'd argued. Vlad wasn't the only one who'd taken leave of her identity.

"That's not what the abbot said *to you*," Vlad replied. "You were only there for a few hours, and most of that was spent removing and reattaching your toes. Don't be surprised that you came away with less than someone who paid the whole nickel for the tour."

"How many people take this tour?" Igor had a twinkle in his eye that you only got when your brain shined with words like "heist" or "caper".

"There are many attainments before enlightenment," Vlad continued, ignoring Igor, which was the only rational choice. "One must attain oneness before that."

"So you've attained oneness?"

Vlad shook her head. "One must attain emptiness before oneness, stillness before emptiness, mindfulness before stillness, and thoughtlessness before that."

Sloot paused. He'd never been good with cadences, and was sure that no good would ever come of jumping out in front of one.

"Quiet your mind," said Vlad, "then open it to the universe. Let it in, let it out, and realize that the universe is you. Simple."

"Yeah, simple," nodded Agather.

"What, you've done it?" said Sloot.

"And whyn't shouldn't I've?" Agather demanded. "Just because I don't have to limber up to sit down, or go around barefoot, prattling about trees falling when nobody's listening? That's rubbish anyway. There's always something listening."

"Sorry," said Sloot, who was. He looked up at the trees, squinting for ears.

"I thought people were supposed to be nicer when they got enlightened," said Igor. Regardless of how true that may have been, Agather was first and foremost a witch. Witches had certain mysterious airs that needed maintaining. One witch breaking ranks could ruin it for the rest. Agather had thus only minored in enlightenment.

"That'll do," said Agather, giving the cauldron one final stir. "Ye'll be wanting yer final dance lesson then, eh Sloot?"

"I suppose. Wait, *final* lesson?"

"Oh, good," Agather smiled. "Ye know how I detest repeating myself."

"Er, yes, it's just that … well, do you think I'm ready?"

Agather laughed hard enough to leave a mark.

"Then how can this be my final lesson?"

"There's no 'how,'" said Agather, "it simply is. Yer overthinking it."

"But what does that mean?" asked Sloot.

Agather sighed. "Ye heard what Vlad said. It starts with quieting the mind. Ye can quiet yer mind, can't ye?"

"Certainly not," said Sloot. There were certain things a worrier simply didn't do. Even knowing himself well enough to answer that question with certainty was too much introspection for comfort. He resolved not to think about it.

"Well, ye should learn. Yer thinking far too hard about it. Ye dance like yer feet are in active rebellion against yer brain."

"Thoughtlessness," said Vlad. Her eyes were closed, her posture both rigid and entirely relaxed. She'd taken in all the tranquility in the Witchwood, starting with Sloot's share.

"But how do I do it?" asked Sloot.

"By doing nothing."

"And how do I do that?"

"You don't."

"I don't think I can."

"You shouldn't."

"But what if I can't?"

"Then you have."

Later on, Sloot would be certain that a dance lesson had happened, but he'd have no idea what went on. He only had the feeling that it had gone exceptionally well, though he wasn't sure why.

MAKING TIME

The apartment felt empty, and largely was. Nan and the Hapsgalts had moved out, which Sloot took as a sign that Franka's oath-taking and bones-soothing had gone well. Willie was both the Eye and Soul of the Serpent, then.

Arthur must have gone with them. Philosophers tended to foist themselves upon benefactors who kept fully stocked kitchens, and demons only ate when it sounded like fun. One demon's fun was Sloot Peril's flagrant excess.

Summoning Bartleby was easy. Place a black candle in a dark room and she'd appear. It hadn't worked the first few times Sloot had tried it, owing to his assumption the candle should be lit. Apparently, that ruined the effect.

When considering which of his friends might know anything the Infernal Ball, Bartleby had been the entire list.

"Vicked," said Bartleby. "And vhere on the first circle is the ledger?"

Sloot shrugged. "Bob believes it's in some sort of vault."

"Not Vinking Bob?"

"I'm probably not supposed to say," Sloot replied, the icy fingers of legal repercussions clawing at his neck.

"Ha! Okay," said Bartleby. She gave Sloot a knowing wink. "Vell, if you don't know vhere it is, then you're going to need time. Oh."

"Oh? Oh, what?"

"That *is* Vlad sitting by the vindow, isn't it?"

Vlad had resumed her feet-in-lap position by the window. She stared off into a distance that didn't exist within Sloot's tiny quarters. She must have brought it with her. She was either concentrating very hard on something, or doing nothing of the sort. Sloot couldn't be sure.

"It is," Sloot nodded.

"Vell, this might be awkvard."

There was a knock at the door. Greta walked in.

"I don't know vhy you vouldn't let me summon you. It's much qvicker."

"It's creepy," Greta replied.

"This from the voman who lived in Castle Ulfhaven."

"That was foreboding, not creepy. There are bats when you do summoning, I've seen it."

"Bats are creepy but a castle full of skulls isn't?"

"No. It's foreboding. Who's your friend?" Greta nodded to Vlad.

"She's my … friend." Sloot was entirely at sea with fiction. His wildest fantasies featured moderately favorable interest rates.

"Right," said Greta. "Hello, *friend*."

Vlad leapt to her feet and bowed low to Greta, then fixed her with a look that wasn't licensed to operate a sauna within the city, but should have been.

"Hello." Vlad's voice was a husky growl, a velvet bathtub full of honey.

Greta blushed. "Okay," she quavered. "Er, what was I saying?"

"Decor," offered Bartleby.

"Later. Why am I here?"

Greta kept glancing at Vlad while Sloot explained that he needed to get to the Axial Ledger on the first circle of the Inferno during the dance contest at the Infernal Ball.

"You really should have told me about this sooner," Greta chided.

"Sorry," said Sloot, predictably.

"It's fine," said Greta, in an upper register associated with sarcasm. Sloot didn't always understand when sarcasm was happening, so he appreciated the cues.

"You vere the first person I summoned," said Bartleby. "I just found out about it myself."

"Look, it's your apartment," said Greta, being perhaps the first person to acknowledge it, "but are you sure that now is a good time to bring strangers into our midst?" She nodded subtly in Vlad's direction.

"I trust her," said Sloot.

"Why? What's her story?"

Sloot pondered the question.

"I can't say."

"Why not?"

"I can't say." Try as he might, the words simply wouldn't move from his head to his mouth. *Vlad is your lost love, and she's here to win you back.* That's it. Simple. They could get on with being happy together if Sloot could simply come forth with the words. He fumed at the inefficiency of it.

"Try," said Greta, her voice tinged with impatience.

"It's not important," said Sloot, who was doing everything in his power to avoid meowing at her.

"Sloot needs time," said Bartleby. "Ve don't know vhere the ledger is exactly, only that it's in a vault on the first circle. Probably. And ve don't know how to open the vault. And Sloot has to dance his vay up from the 99th circle."

"Oh, dear."

Sloot sighed and nodded.

"I'm not sure what you need from me."

"Time," said Bartleby.

"Time?"

"Ve need you to steal it."

"I'm not sure you understand what I do. Are you familiar with clocks? Watches? They measure time, they don't change it."

"They're the same thing," said Bartleby.

"I can assure you, they're not."

Bartleby smiled. Her neck cracked like dry twigs as she rocked her head back and forth. Sloot wasn't sure how sturdy a necromancer-possessed body remained over time. If her head fell off in his apartment, he'd have to move.

It was good that Arthur wasn't there. Bartleby's explanation of time as a metaphysical inconstant sounded philosophical to Sloot, though it probably wasn't. Sloot couldn't say for sure. He could say, with a high degree of certainty, that Arthur would have held the conversation hostage. He didn't have time for that. Nor did he have time for Bartleby's presentational theatrics, but doubted that it would be any faster to ask her to skip them. Bartleby tended to drag her feet when bats and thunder weren't involved.

"So time is a perceptual construct," Greta said, "and the difference between the mortal and Infernal perceptions of time can be manipulated by inversion."

"Vhat?"

"I just said what you said, only I left out the spooky noises."

"Then you didn't say vhat I said." Bartleby harrumphed.

"I got the gist of it. Sloot, how much time will you need?"

"I haven't the slightest idea," said Sloot. "As much as you can give me, I suppose."

"Okay," Greta sighed. She held out her hand. "Let's have your watch."

"I don't have it."

"You're not carrying your watch?" Greta glowered. "What in the Domnitor's name is wrong with you?"

"Long may he reign," said Sloot.

"Long may he—" Greta shook her head.

"Reign," Sloot finished for her.

"Stop it! You've really not been carrying your watch this whole time?"

"I haven't gone back for it," said Sloot. "What's the problem?"

"The problem," Greta spat, "is that you're an imbecile! You expect me to invert transperceptive temporal symmetry across an indeterminate length, and you haven't been charging your watch!"

"I think you mean *winding*," Sloot corrected her, then immediately wished he hadn't.

"I know what I meant! Didn't you hear what Bartleby was saying about biorhythmic object transference over interstitial references?"

"Vhat?"

"Transferring energy into objects," said Greta.

"Vhat?"

"The part where two bats collided with the pile of skulls!"

"Oh, yeah," Bartleby grinned. "That vas the best part."

"People," Greta spat, eyes and teeth clenched against her rage, "have affinities for certain objects. Special ones. For you, I assume it's your watch. If you'd kept it on you, it would be loaded up with energy. From you. But you didn't, so it's not."

"And you need that energy to do a time … thing?"

Greta exhaled. "Close enough. Honestly, did neither of you take theoretical metaphysical mechanics at university?"

Sloot shrugged. Thanks to the large-scale financial fraud the Hapsgalts had committed for over a century, the variety of accounting courses available to Sloot had been staggering.

"My mother gave me that watch when I was a boy," said Sloot. "I carried it with me every day until the Fall of Salzstadt. It's been there ever since."

"Oh," said Greta. "I'm sorry, Sloot, but we're going to need it."

"Oh, dear," said Sloot. "Well, like I said, I carried it all the time when I was alive. Surely, that counts for something."

"Probably a bit," said Bartleby, "but there's not a lot of energy coursing through your average mortal. It vould have been a lot more if you'd carried it as a demon."

"And how much time would that mortal bit be worth?"

"About a second," said Bartleby.

"Oh, dear." Sloot's ability to jump to obvious conclusions didn't fail him.

"That should be more than enough time," said Greta.

"I think you overestimate my athleticism," said Sloot. "Even if I knew exactly where the Axial Ledger was and how to get into it, one second would be just enough time for me to inadvertently let on that I was up to something."

"Have you already forgotten what I said about manipulating the perception of time by inversion?"

"Yes," said Sloot.

"It von't vork," said Bartleby. "Not on the first circle of the Inferno. The time runs nearly at full mortal speed there. That inversion might buy you two seconds more, but that's it."

"Oh, good," groaned Sloot. "We're up to a whole three seconds. At this rate, I may have nearly a minute to find the vault, open it, and compare the Axial Ledger to mine."

Sarcasm was always easy when the chips were down.

"It *will* work," said Greta, defiantly. "Or it'll help, anyway. Did you honestly think tricking the Prime Evils would be easy?"

"No," said Bartleby. "I vas just hoping."

"Myrtle's a causality demon, right? The closer future events come, the more clearly she can see them."

"She was before she got demoted," said Sloot. "Do demons lose their powers when they're demoted?"

Bartleby shrugged. "It depends on who's doing the demoting. I heard Gurblegash the Defiler stripped a demon of everything but its ability to feel pain. Do you know who did the papervork for Myrtle's demotion?"

"Walter the Undying cast the banishment spell," Sloot offered.

"He'll have used an intermediary. They never do more vork than they have to. There's a chance she can still see causality."

"That's good," said Greta. "She can point you on the right path or something, right?"

"Possibly," said Sloot, "but it's still not—"

"If you say 'it's still not enough time for me to pull this off,' I'll feed you your tongue."

Sloot said nothing, a tactic employed better late than never.

"We need that watch, Sloot."

"I know," said Sloot, "but I don't think I can—"

"Good," said Vlad. "Don't think."

"What?"

"Remember what I told you about thoughtlessness."

"You barely told me anything at all."

"I probably said too much."

RIGHT IN THE MORTALITY

Sloot didn't make it into the cathedral on the first try. That would have required the steely resolve of a heroic type, and who knew where they were these days? A bunch of them were in the cathedral, in fact. It had been full of potential heroes at the Fall of Salzstadt. Potential heroes and Sloot.

As he wandered the streets to work up his nerve, Sloot thought about all the salts who died on that fateful day. Most of them had been soldiers loyal to the Domnitor, long may he reign. Then they'd been loyal to Vlad when they broke down the door to the cathedral, and then they'd been loyal to Gregor when he killed Nicoleta and took the blood star. But at one time, they'd all been subjects of the Domnitor, long may he reign.

He made his way back around. They hadn't even fixed the doors, one of which still hung by a single hinge. The other was lying halfway into the darkened narthex beyond. There was an official-looking rope on poles in front of it. Strangers visiting the city might have pointed out that anyone could simply walk past it, and any salt would respond by blowing his whistle until the filthy foreigner was strung up by his thumbs.

This was Salzstadt. You stood in line, you waited your turn, and if you thought of a better way of doing things you kept your mouth shut. Or you spoke your mind and got strung up by your thumbs next to the foreigners. There was always plenty of room.

"Hello?" Sloot felt ridiculous calling into the darkness of an abandoned cathedral, but there was a rope. His voice echoed into the chasm and faded into nothing. A light rain started to fall.

Nice try, Sloot thought. The rain was definitely a test. He'd just step around the rope for a little shelter from the rain, then. Who could fault him for that? Ha! Pull the other one. Sloot Peril was as true a salt as you'd find, allowances granted for former Carpathian spies. He turned up his collar and waited.

"Whad'you want?" asked a shambling shadow after a few minutes.

"Oh, hello, mister…"

"Spackle."

"Hello, Mister Spackle. Well, er, it's hard to explain, actually."

"You look a bright lad," said Spackle. "Have a go."

"Well, I died here, you see, and—"

"And when would that have been, young sir?"

Sloot hesitated. "The … well, I don't know why they call it that. I'm not sure it's entirely polite. Salzstadt is still here, after all, isn't it?"

"You died in the Fall of Salzstadt," Spackle said doubtfully. He leaned toward Sloot with a squint, the pale grey evening casting blessed little light across his gnarled and rotting features.

"Yes," said Sloot, "and I believe my mother's watch is still in there. If I could just—"

"Shove off."

"I beg your pardon?"

"Look here, son," said Spackle, his tone somewhere between

sympathy and threats, "I know times are tough, but these is true salts of Salzstadt what lie within. Loyal subjects of the Domnitor, long may he reign."

"Long may he reign," said Sloot. "I know. I was. I am! I just—"

"And not to judge a book by its cover, but if you really died at the Fall, I imagine I'd find you hard-pressed to explain why your cheeks are still rosy and your legs are still on without splints and garters."

"I'm a demon."

Spackle gave Sloot a squint.

"Then you, my son, are a scientific curiosity. I've never known demonhood to be an optional substitute for death. Granted, I didn't go to university for science or theology, but I do know a bit about what happens post-mortem."

"Oh, it's not a substitute," said Sloot, barely concealing his glee at being able to correct someone on semantics. "I *was* properly dead for quite some time."

"And then what? You got better?"

"Reassigned."

"Re … assigned." Spackle repeated the word as if trying it on for a fit. His sidelong glance asked Sloot if it came in another size.

"Look, I can't really explain," said Sloot. "I was a ghost for a while, and then I got—well, I was given a mission."

"A mission."

"Yes," said Sloot, "and the- and *they* made me a demon so I could fulfill it."

"They? They who?"

Sloot had been waiting his whole life to use this one.

"That's classified," he said. He spent a long moment wondering whether he looked like someone who could pull off a phrase like that. He came to the conclusion that he might have, had he been wearing more expensive shoes.

"Right," smirked Spackle, who'd apparently picked up on the shoes thing. "Sorry, no new watch for you today, son. Off you go."

"Wait," said Sloot, "I can show you! I know about where my body must be, and it's—"

Sloot's eyes darted back and forth in a horrified moment of realization.

"It's what?"

"Oh, what's the use?" moaned Sloot. "Even if I did find my body, my head's not on it! Roman came and took it to—"

"Wait, Roman? Not Roman Bloodfrenzy?"

"The same," said Sloot.

"And that would make you Sloot?"

"That's right," said Sloot after a moment's hesitation. His flight response was giving him a predictable signal.

Spackle closed his eyes.

"Stood right in front of me," said Spackle dutifully. "Held up a freshly severed head and said, 'he'll be back for the rest one of these days.' Looked just like you, come to think of it. Minus the body, of course."

"Of course," said Sloot. "I don't need the rest of me, just the watch. It's important."

Spackle shrugged. "Far be it from me to stand between a man and his … self." He stepped aside. Sloot nodded his thanks and made his way inside.

While Sloot's imagination had prepared him with a modicum of dread, it turned out to be woefully inadequate. The sound of buzzing flies echoed in the vaulted chamber over the carnage. Some of the dead shambled around aimlessly, others played cards or conversed in small groups, but the bulk of them did nothing at all. They lay in their piles, mostly in the very spots where their mortality had expired.

The worst part was the smell, but not for the reason most

people would assume. Sure, it was a revolting mélange of rotting carcasses in the stifling confines of an ill-ventilated room, but what bothered Sloot was that he didn't find it unpleasant. Must the demonic palate differ from the human one so viscerally? By a thin margin, Sloot preferred having his toes reattached to finding this malodor appetizing.

He tried not thinking about it. More important things required his concentration, not that he needed a reason to avoid the strangely tantalizing redolence of months-old piles of corpses.

His remains would be beneath the big pile. Even without another grisly demonic instinct leading him to his own mortal remains, his luck wouldn't have it any other way.

The next several hours surrendered to the blessed fog of immemory. For the rest of his days, Sloot would remember it as a long and fitful nap beset with a nightmare about sorting and cataloging cast-off body parts. Upon waking, he would recall a zombie missing half his face saying, "I don't remember asking you to do that."

He got the watch, though. In the end, that was what mattered. As he left the cathedral, a dark alley to his right made a summoning noise.

"Pssst," said the darkness. Or, more accurately, Walter the Undying. Flavia was with him.

Sloot sighed. He thought about simply walking off into the night and pretending he hadn't heard. Unfortunately for Sloot, pretending was a form of creativity. He walked into the alley.

"Hello, Sloot," sang Flavia. Even if he hadn't been able to see her, he'd have known by the sound of her voice that she was wearing her enormous and nearly genuine smile.

"Flavia," Sloot replied as cordially as he could manage. "Walter."

"It's 'Walter the Undying,'" Walter corrected him.

"Sorry," said Sloot before he was able to stop himself. "Fancy running into the two of you here," he added, knowing he'd fully grasped sarcasm in the moment.

"It's been a while since you've checked in," Flavia gently chided.

"Since the last time I saw you at Dark Corners," Sloot spat, more vehemently than he'd intended. In a flash, some spark of unbidden gumption grabbed the reins and spurred him on. "How did that go, by the way? Did you stand idly by while Mrs. Knife tried to murder my friend, or did you help hold him down?"

"That wouldn't be your friend who tried threatening us, would it?"

The fall from a high horse is particularly painful. Sloot could only point out that horse heights were relative.

"That's the only language you understand, isn't it?" Sloot's eyes went wide with the shock of hearing that sort of bravado come from his own mouth.

"I don't—"

"And before you feign ignorance, please recall that my girlfriend is in the lowest circle of the Inferno because of you, and now you're threatening her with worse. Would you even be talking to me if you didn't want me to deliver the Domnitor to your clutches, long may he reign?"

Flavia's easy, graceful smile fell. Her eyes darkened, her breathing became audibly raspy, and her shoulders hunched in a way that led Sloot to believe she just might be ready to pounce.

"Can we please try it my way now?" Walter the Undying interjected.

Flavia scowled and hissed at him through her nose. "Fine," she said. "I suppose I knew it would come to this eventually."

What was going on with Sloot, exactly? He should have been quivering with dread, worrying over what Walter was about to do. That's not to say that he wasn't worried, but there was a certain strength standing next to his cowardice. A watchful older brother glaring back at the threat. It made him feel like he still might get hurt, but that it would be all right in the end.

Sloot's eyes went dark. His claws came out.

"Be careful, mortal," Sloot warned. He only hoped that Walter was as terrified by the warning as he was.

"I want to bargain with you," Walter replied.

Sloot salivated. The rational part of his brain that wanted nothing to do with these monsters and their ridiculous schemes was given a librarian-strength shushing from elsewhere in his mind.

"What sort of bargain do you have in mind?" Sloot drummed his fingertips together just beneath his nose as his curiosity took over. A bargain! It wasn't the first time he'd been asked; it was getting harder to resist.

"A number two," said Walter. He produced a contract from within the folds of his robes and handed it over. "Souls for earthly power, a standard deal. I'd promise that we haven't changed any of the standard clauses, but you're going to take time to read them anyway."

"Souls?" Sloot was horrified. "Standard deal? They have numbers for these?"

Walter nodded. "A number one is tricking someone into loving you. A number three is revenge, and a number four is revenge against someone who stole your love with a number one. That's mathematically clever."

"Three plus one."

"Nothing gets past you."

Sloot read the disclosures. He had no way of knowing that Walter had not, in fact, modified any of the standard clauses, or even tried to sneak in any nullification options. The arbitration clause stated they'd resolve any differences by staring into the Red Void of Absolute Cacophony until one of them started bleeding from the eyes. He stopped.

"Why?" he asked.

"Why what?"

"Why the change of tactics?"

"Pragmatism," said Walter.

Flavia winced. "We don't often resort to that sort of thing. Coercion is so much more effective. I still think this is a huge mistake, but Walter the Undying thinks you'll be more amenable."

"So your threats against my friends haven't paid off quickly enough?"

"Oh, Sloot," said Flavia, batting her eyelashes. "That's such an ugly way to put it. I mean, yes, but—"

"No," said Sloot.

"No?" Flavia's lower lip quivered.

"No. You can keep your souls." It felt as though a stone had dropped into his gut for turning down such a favorable deal. He'd have a lot of not thinking about those feelings to do later.

Flavia and Walter turned to look at each other.

"I really thought that was going to work," said Walter.

"We'll sweeten the pot," said Flavia. "No more threats against Myrtle, I promise!"

"Still no, thank you." Sloot had an even harder time turning that offer down, but his sense of duty wouldn't have it. The Domnitor, long may he reign, in the clutches of his most brutal and draconian enforcers? Myrtle was already banished to the lowest circle of the Inferno. How much worse could demotion to demon 100th class be?

"What if we got her out?"

It was just as well that Sloot was left speechless at that. His rebuke for their insolence started with "please," had a "pardon me for saying" in the middle and ended with "if you wouldn't mind." The word "anticlimactic" would have claimed new territory.

Get Myrtle out? Now *there* was a compelling offer. How could he reject an opportunity to save his girlfriend from the bowels of the Inferno without considering it? Besides, what was his plan? A dance contest? He may as well hinge her fate on the sun rising in the west or Salzstadt dropping to Second Most Fashionable City in the Old Country Travel Guide.

"How?" asked Sloot.

"You leave that to us," said Walter.

"I would," said Sloot, "naturally. That's how contracts work. But I won't."

"Why not?"

"For starters, I know how Infernal Bureaucracy works. Well, not entirely. Nobody understands it entirely. That's just madness."

"You've got that right," said Walter.

"Anyway, you can't do it. There's no form."

Flavia chuckled. "Oh, Sloot. I thought you said you knew how Infernal Bureaucracy works. We wouldn't fill out forms, we'd do bribes! That's how things get done down below."

"Of course," said Sloot, "everybody knows that."

"Then why—"

"Because *everybody* knows it. Including the Prime Evils and their bureaucrats. Bribery is the fourth largest economy down below! You don't think it's regulated by a committee? There's nothing more sinister than regulatory committees."

"True," said Flavia, "but if you bribe them—"

"Spare me your petty conniving," Sloot snarled, his forked tongue lashing out in barely-controlled demonic fury. "There are forms to track those bribes, and forms to track the bribes to work around those, and so on, into a fiery bureaucratic infinity! If you think for a moment you can—"

"You're upset," Flavia interjected.

"How dare you?" demanded three octaves of Sloot's voice. Horns shot from his forehead and recurved behind his ears. His pointy tail lashed gouges in the cobblestones, and the fire in his eyes cast a malefic glow on the pair of them.

"I'm not wrong," Flavia squeaked.

"Oh," said Sloot, his visage slowly contracting to look more like his proper self.

"Think it over," said Walter. "And be quick. We'll soon have to make good on our ... promises."

"You mean threats."

"If you prefer."

He didn't, of course. Sloot wished he could make the bargain. Beyond the allure of demonic bargain making, he liked being in agreement. With everyone. All the time. He didn't like quibbling over restaurants, much less the fates of nations. But delivering the Domnitor, long may he reign, into the clutches of Mrs. Knife's allies under threats to his loved ones? The social awkwardness of a stern "no, thank you" would simply have to be endured.

Later. He probably had just enough time to strut his stuff at the Infernal Ball, get a look at the Axial Ledger, and save Myrtle himself. With her help, he'd deal with Flavia and Walter the Undying after.

Sartorial Mind Games

"It's about time," said Willie. "You've needed a complete overhaul since I've known you."

"Let's not be too drastic," said Sloot. "Just a little bit of flair, I think."

"You think?" Willie scoffed. "I don't know where to begin!"

"*Vhere*," sang Bartleby in a corrective tone.

Willie sighed and rolled his eyes. "There aren't any other vampires here, Bartleby. I promise I'll pronounce it when—"

"*Vhen* other vampires are around, you'll slip up if you don't practice."

Willie folded his arms and huffed. Sloot was still a bit unnerved that Willie was a vampire now, but at least he was rich again. Not personally, but as both the Eye and Soul of the Serpent, he controlled the society's wealth. Watching him sulk in the opulence of his underground lair was better than watching him sulk in his hammock in Sloot's apartment.

"Maybe just a new tie," said Sloot. "I don't want to go to any fuss. I'm sure that they care more about my dancing than what I'm wearing."

"That's where you're—"

"*Ahem.*"

"That's *vhere* you're wrong," said Willie. He shot a loutish sneer at Bartleby. "What—*vhat* you're *vearing* is the most important thing in your control right now."

"Not my ability to dance?"

"Who cares about dancing? You should be really good at it because of all the lessons you took from your daddy's professional ballet company. The important question—*qvestion*—is vhy didn't he cane your tailor and have him sent to prison for making you vear that awful thing?"

Sloot was sure he would never understand fashion. His ensemble was the height of practicality. He'd seen some of the flimsy numbers that Willie wore, especially his mid-morning singlets that spanned the gap between breakfast tuxedo and pre-lunch gossiping kilt. Should he really to listen to Willie when it came to choosing an outfit? Sloot measured the value of clothing in years. He'd seen Willie throw shirts away before Nan had finished doing up the buttons.

"Look, thanks all the same," said Sloot, "but I think I'm just going to wear this, if you don't mind."

"I mind," Willie declared. "I mind very much! You can't just—"

"Villie," Bartleby interjected, "vouldn't this be a good opportunity to do that thing?"

"What thing? I mean, vhat thing?"

"You know." Bartleby raised an eyebrow and wiggled her fingers. Then she nodded and made a shooing motion vaguely toward Sloot.

"I'm rich again, remember? Rich boys don't have to do innuendoes. I can make you explain it to me."

"Right," said Bartleby. "Vampires can make people do things."

Willie stared at her with the blank look he likely perfected as a child.

"Using hypnosis."

Willie's blank look fortified its position. If it remained there any longer, it would qualify for citizenship on his face.

"Villie, you can hypnotize people to make them do things."

"Oh," said Willie, more out of social obligation than understanding. Then a synapse accidentally fired in his brain. "Oh! I see vhat you mean!"

Willie cracked his knuckles and made a few limbering waggles of his fingers. He cleared his throat.

"There's no need for that," said Sloot, "I'll just—"

"Bartleby," Willie thundered, waggling fingers in the necromancer's direction, "tell me vhat you mean!"

Bartleby sighed. "Villie, use your hypnosis on Sloot to make him vant to use your tailor."

"Oh," said Willie. "That makes sense! You could have just said so."

"Yes, I suppose I should have."

"I'd really prefer if you didn't," said Sloot.

"You'll be fine," Bartleby whispered, leaning in. "Villie needs practice, just humor him."

"Oh, er, yes. Fine. All right."

Willie took his time, making a big production of getting the pose just right. That was just what you did in some circles, namely the ones with so little to do they felt the need to milk everything for all it was worth.

"Sloot," Willie intoned, "Slooooot!"

"Yes?"

"You are under my thrall." He looked at Bartleby. "Thrall?"

Bartleby nodded. "Don't break eye contact! That's important."

"You are under my thrall," Willie repeated, his insane leer falling back upon Sloot. "Aren't you?"

"Er, yes. Sure."

"Good," said Willie, still gesturing expansively. "Just checking. Now, you're getting very sleepy."

"It's not that sort of hypnosis," said Bartleby. "You're using your powers; you don't have to draw him in."

"I know, but the magician at my birthday party did it, and it looked cool."

"Vell, I can't fault that. Go on."

"You're getting sleepy!" Willie shouted loud enough to wake the dead, metaphorically speaking. First-hand experience had taught Sloot that the dead do not, in fact, sleep. Neither did demons, for that matter. Nevertheless, and against all odds, Willie was correct. Sloot felt sleepy.

"How?" He stifled a yawn, or tried to. He was out of practice.

"Villie is a demon 98th class," Bartleby explained. "That's vhere vampires' power derives. Pretty cool, isn't it?"

"I suppose," said Sloot, who didn't care much about vampires, all things considered. He wondered if Willie's hypnotic powers were working, or if he were perhaps subconsciously going along with some sort of demonic hierarchy. He chose to believe the latter, being a huge fan of hierarchies.

"Vhen you avake," said Willie, really getting into the spirit of the thing, "you vill vant my tailor to help you do something about your ridiculous vardrobe."

Sloot nodded.

"Sleepier now," said Willie.

Sloot's eyelids drooped.

"Sleepier…"

Droopier…

"Now *sleep!*"

If everything in the universe played by the same rules, Willie's shouting would have had the opposite effect. However, Sloot had long ago accepted that reality was a nightmarish hellscape designed specifically for his torment. As far as he was concerned, complying with a vampire's orders to take a nap was a battle it simply didn't make sense to fight.

"Now … avaken!"

From somewhere deep in the cold, black bosom of dreamless slumber, Sloot heard the command and obeyed. He assumed he'd been asleep for a minute, perhaps less, but the perception of Infernal time went about as close to infinite as the safety catches would allow. Anyone who cared to do the math would know that Sloot had dreamt for one trillionth of a pico-infinity, or one thousand times the length of the 879th Pre-Colossal Ice Age, or half the length of an elementary school play.

That was the relativity of temporal perception for you.

Sloot gave a very long sigh, the artifact of aeons of dreamless sleep.

"How do you feel?"

"Tired," said Sloot, paradoxically.

"About your outfit," Willie clarified.

"Oh." Sloot looked down at his old wool suit. Practical though it may have been, it didn't inspire any sort of happiness in him. To be fair, Sloot had never been emotional about clothing, but he was now becoming acutely aware of that fact.

"I don't know, I suppose it could use sprucing up."

Willie and Bartleby exchanged smiles that included an obscene quantity of unnaturally white teeth.

"Now," said Willie, resuming his hypnotist pose, "let's make sure you feel strongly enough about proper footwear."

"*Ahem.*"

"Sorry. Footvear."

RIGHT FROM LEFT

"We're doomed."

It was the first time Sloot had ever worn a cape. He was worried he wasn't any good at it. To make matters worse, he was wearing two of them. Worse still, one was longer than the other. Technically, Igor was wearing the longer one.

"We'll be fine," said Igor, who had recently put the final touches on his new patina of filth. That had been a tricky endeavor, to hear him tell it. In Sloot's estimation, worrying about capes was infinitely preferable to exposing his conscious thoughts to the overpowering aroma of Igor sitting on his shoulders.

"It's never going to work," moaned Sloot. "This is a bad plan, I'm telling you."

"Why? What have you heard?" asked Igor.

"Heard? Nothing. Why?"

Igor sighed. "I haven't become famous, then?"

"Not that I'm aware," Sloot replied. In a fit of sympathy he added, "though I've been too busy to pay attention to celebrity gossip of late. Wait, why do you ask?"

"If I was famous, people would know how tall I was."

"That's ridiculous."

"I'm not saying they'd know precisely, but they'd notice an extra five feet or so, wouldn't they?"

"Nearly six," Sloot mumbled.

"Anyway, if they don't know how tall I am, why wouldn't it work?"

For the shadow of a moment Sloot envied Igor, causing him to wonder if sensibility had stepped out for a smoke. Sloot conceived dozens of ways that this could go wrong, but Igor? Igor could use the mankiest sponge of logic to soak up the least of his worries. Sloot, on the other hand, was comparing bids to drain the ocean of his doubts.

"Don't answer that," said Igor. "Consider instead what might be the worst that could happen if it didn't."

"We're trying to sneak into the lowest level of the Inferno," said Sloot. "I'd prefer not to think about the worst thing that could happen in there."

"That's new."

"What?"

"You not wanting to consider worst case scenarios."

"Let's just get on with it."

Sloot walked toward the gate. He concentrated on the capes to keep his mind off Igor's stench, his nerves over seeing Myrtle after so much time had passed, and the degree of personal growth that might or might not have been happening to him against his will.

A gruesome iron gate loomed over the brimstone path in a way that should have been intimidating, but wasn't. Sure, the sign said, "abandon hope all ye who enter here." Naturally, ominous shadows danced across it from the torches that flanked the entry. But it had a flimsy air about it, like the wood-and-plaster castle facades they built for productions at the Salzstadt Community Playhouse. Sloot allowed that the underpaid, underskilled contractors who'd built it had probably done their best, but it was singularly unimpressive. He didn't mind the disappointment, really. It gave him something to keep his mind off the capes.

"Ow!"

"Sorry," said Igor. He'd tugged a bit too hard on Sloot's left ear, though whether it had been accidental, Sloot might never know. Still, he needed to get inside, and this was the only way that sounded remotely capable of working. Igor was technically a demon 99th class, so he could enter freely. Sloot didn't like being driven like this, but had marginally preferred it to a bit and bridle.

All things considered, it was a ridiculous problem to have. Demons' access to the Inferno was based on their class, so why guard the lowest level? Sloot doubted that they considered demons 100th class in the decision, as demons 100th class were rarely considered for any reason at all. He'd have wondered aloud about it, but he foresaw far too many ways in which Igor might realize that he outranked Sloot if he thought about it for long enough.

Igor tugged on both of Sloot's ears. Sloot stopped.

"Hello," said Igor, "my name's—"

"Go ahead," lamented a tortured soul. In the midst of his pity, Sloot wondered whether the position of 99th circle door guard had been invented as a torment by one of the more creative—that is to say, *bored*—judges in the chaos courts. Igor dug his heels into Sloot's flanks. Sloot walked into a wall.

"Silly me," said Igor, "I neglected to push the door open with my left hand. Left hand. *Left.* Oh, that is my left hand, I meant right. Just a little bit higher, that's where I'll move my trusty right hand, and a bit to the right. Sorry, left. There we go! And away we— I— oh, it's a pull, then. And away I … go!"

Igor guided Sloot along a very dark and musty corridor until they came to another door.

"Sidle to the left," whispered Igor. Sloot ran into a wall. "Sorry, the right."

He negotiated their way into a little alcove behind a large urn bearing a bleeding tree that seemed to be weeping. Sloot stopped himself asking if that was natural after Igor hopped down.

"Ready to go?" asked the bard.

"There wasn't a line," said Sloot.

"Correct."

"Why?"

"We went around the back way."

"And why is that?"

Igor blushed, which was particularly unsettling for all of the mites infesting his pores.

"You know what I did before becoming a bard, right?"

"You mean the fact that you're a gremlin?"

"Keep your voice down," Igor hissed. "Yeah, that. Well, it's sort of a cultural aversion, you might say."

"What, standing in line?"

"Front doors," said Igor. "You see, to us—to *them*—it's not really mischief if you use the front door to get in and do it. Welcome guests, that's who comes in the front door."

"You don't want to go where you're welcome?"

Igor shook his head.

"That adds up."

"You're doing math puns now? I have feelings too, you know."

"Sorry."

"It's fine." Igor drew his bit of wire out from his filthy bag and gave it a twang. "All right, let's get in there."

"What, just like that?"

"You want to have a little nap first?"

No, though Sloot, but he couldn't just go traipsing through the door, could he? It had been built up too much! Months or weeks may have gone by in the Narrative since he'd seen Myrtle last, but he'd perceived aeons of Infernal time. Had Myrtle done the same? Did she still feel the same way about him? Was this what she meant by all that talk about dancing the last time he'd seen her, right before—

"Nice suit."

All of Sloot's mental faculties got to work processing the multitude of feelings that welled up at the sound of her voice. As a result, there were no resources available to keep his knees from buckling. He only dreaded the impact in passing because he and the floor were old friends. Not this floor in particular, but all floors had a certain kinship when it came to dealing with nervous people who couldn't keep their feet. Fortunately for Sloot, all of that became moot when he found himself resting gently in the firm embrace of Myrtle Pastry.

"I knew you'd make it," said Myrtle. She was wearing a red dress that made Sloot forget his middle name.

"I'm sorry," said Sloot.

"You don't need to be."

"But it's taken me so long to come and rescue you!"

Myrtle leaned in and gave Sloot the sort of kiss that make poets go sonnet.

"You're right on time," said Myrtle with a wink. She helped Sloot regain his footing.

"Ahem," ahemmed Igor.

"Right, sorry," said Sloot. "This is Igor, he's my … well, he's a—"

"I'm Sloot's best friend," he declared, glowering at Myrtle. "And just so you know, we greet each other even more warmly than that all the time!"

"Neither of those things are true," said Sloot.

Myrtle's face scrunched in an amused grin. Sloot forgot how much he loved seeing her smile. It couldn't light up a room in the literal sense. She'd have to have been a different sort of demon for that. Nevertheless, Sloot couldn't help grinning like a goon in response.

"He's the minstrel," said Myrtle. "That's right, isn't it? I'm sure that I saw a minstrel."

"Bard," Igor corrected her, his arms folded. "Minstrels have to walk from town to town. I ain't got the legs for it."

"My mistake," said Myrtle, her voice creeping up into a keep-the-peace register. "Looking into future causality is hazy at best, and it was a long time ago."

"You've still got your powers then?" asked Sloot.

Myrtle shook her head. "Lost them in the demotion. Saw it coming though, and I get them back after a fashion."

"All right," said Sloot, "what happens next?"

Myrtle's head turned an inch and her brow furrowed. "I just told you I don't have my powers anymore. I've just got the predictions I made before I came down here."

"No, I meant, what do we do now?"

"Oh, sorry."

"Ha!" Igor huffed. "If you knew Sloot half as well as I do, you'd have known what he meant."

"Is he always like this?" Myrtle asked.

"No," said Sloot. "He's usually less oddly possessive and more annoying."

"I'm not sure I understand why you hired him to be your bard."

"I didn't," said Sloot, pointing meaningfully to accentuate the point. He turned to Igor. "I didn't! I want to be very clear on that, I haven't hired any bards!"

"A formality," said Igor. "We'll get the paperwork sorted out in due course."

"It's not a matter of—"

A gong sounded in the next room.

"What was that?"

"The dance," said Myrtle, "it's starting! Here, put these bags on your feet."

TORMENTS POSTPONED

The lowest level of the Inferno was everything that Sloot thought it would be, but only because he'd so deftly avoided thinking about it. He was neither creative nor lucky enough to imagine what it actually was, and he knew it. Hence all the not trying.

"What is that smell?" growled what must have been a sewage demon holding a cup of punch in one of its talons.

Igor smiled. His chest, such as it was, puffed with pride.

"I wasn't going to say anything," said Myrtle, "but it really is awful. And it's a big deal for anyone down here to remark upon it."

"Yes, right," Sloot managed between dry heaves. The drops from his watering eyes evaporated before they hit the floor. He tried not thinking about the confluence of filth through which his boots squelched.

"Not exactly the reunion you'd hoped for," said Myrtle.

"I'd pictured something a touch less pungent."

"We'll have plenty of time in places less fragrant than this," she reassured him.

"Promise?"

Myrtle bit her lip. "I'm pretty sure."

"Pretty sure?"

"Well, I predicted it once, but that was a while ago. The future can change, especially when things step into the path of a major event, or an oddity."

"An oddity. Like me."

"Don't get yourself worked up about it. I like you just the way you are."

Above the mucky floor was a less dense morass of everything that Sloot had ever cared to avoid. It was hot and humid, creating the perfect environment not only for the spontaneous creation of the disturbing unicellular lifeforms that Sloot had no idea he was breathing in, but also innumerable arguments over whether it was the heat or the humidity. That was just the sort of misdirection that kept employees from considering whether the miserable workplace conditions were somehow their boss' fault.

The muck, the heat—*not* the humidity—and the grotesque array of low-level demons milling around in it. There was also the cavernous maw behind the velvet rope, beyond which Sloot saw only darkness and sensed only suffering. There was a sign on one of the velvet rope's posts which read, "Closed for the Ball. Torments Shall Resume Directly After."

"That's the Jaws of Eternal Torment Beyond Which Lieth the Suffering of the Ages," said Myrtle casually.

"That sounds awful," Sloot replied.

"I wouldn't know. They keep bankers' hours and I work nights."

"Dancers, to your marks." The command was gurgled by a pustulent four-armed lower management demon in a loincloth who cracked his whip for emphasis.

"We'll get there when we get there, *Gutsbag*." A one-legged imp scoffed. He lit a cigarette.

"Oh, is that how you want it?" asked Gutsbag. "Fine, have it your way. Your name is going on my list!"

"Oh, dear," the imp replied, though with all of the joviality that one normally didn't apply to the phrase. "How will I ever live with that hanging over my head?"

"Keep talking," warned Gutsbag, "I'm underlining your name now. You see that?"

Sloot knew his type. Lower managers of the mortal variety were no different, extra appendages and literal whip aside. Give them a modicum of power, and they'll do everything within that modicum to annoy you into submission.

"Just don't circle it, will you? I don't think I could live with the shame."

A murmur of half-hearted laughter made its way through the room.

"I'll deal with you later," Gutsbag sneered. "Now, all of you to your marks. They can't get started upstairs until we've sent our winner, and you know how they can be."

Everyone started moving to stand against the walls. That was classic reflected authority. Real leaders knew they had no real power if they had to resort to it, but Gutsbag probably just held a title like "Lead Whatever-Everyone-Else-Was."

"No music again this year," said Gutsbag, "so everybody hum."

"Ahem," said Igor. He gave his wire a pluck.

"Is this really happening?" asked a voice among the crowd.

"Probably some new torment," said another.

"Sounds about right," said yet another.

Igor set to twanging out what might only be referred to as a "tune" if the word were used in quotations. It had no discernible rhythm, and although Sloot was relatively certain that Igor hadn't tried for particular notes, he was playing them flat. That was all to be expected. The surprise came in the form of a stunned, wondrous silence.

"They can't be enjoying this, can they?" Sloot whispered to Myrtle.

"Not legally, no," she replied. "But enjoyment is a relative term. If I had to guess, I'd say that they're tormented by it less than everything else."

Igor was grinning from ear to ear, giving a number of beetles a rare chance to escape his back teeth. By the same measure of relativity, he was enjoying his first standing ovation. They were standing. They were not, however, ovating. Halfway was good enough for Igor.

"No one is dancing," remarked Sloot.

"No one knows how," said Myrtle. "It's your classic grade school dance on this circle."

"Oh," said Sloot, brightening up a bit. He'd hated going to those in his youth, but he'd loved the not dancing.

"Shall we?" Myrtle extended a hand toward him.

"Oh, right. Yes, I suppose." Sloot took her hand and they turned to walk onto the dance floor.

"We have a winner!" announced Gutsbag.

"What? But we didn't—"

"Oh, yes you did! You were definitely about to walk out and do some dancing, we all saw it!"

Most of the wall flowers nodded. Some threw in "yeahs" for emphasis.

"You're the winners, no take-backs!" Gutsbag jammed his thumb into his nose.

"No take-backs!" shouted everyone else, thumbs likewise in their noses. Igor was among them.

Sloot looked at Myrtle. Myrtle grinned.

"That's it," said Gutsbag, "up you go."

They were shooed toward a staircase that dropped from the

brimstone ceiling, splashing fetid muck when it landed on the floor. Sloot looked up into the blackness with double the requisite amount of trepidation. Myrtle, on the other hand, grinned up into it like she'd just won a boat made of cash.

"Get moving," growled Gutsbag. He cracked his whip. "And take your bard with you!"

Groans of disappointment echoed through the crowd.

"What," Gutsbag shouted over his shoulder at them, "you want the bosses coming down here and seeing how good we've got it, our own bard and everything? Yeah, that's what I thought. You too, master musician. Up the stairs."

"Yeah, right," said Igor. "I'll make my own way up, thanks."

"Suit yourself," said Gutsbag. "You two, march!"

They went a couple of steps up and took the bags off of their feet. Then, hand-in-hand, they pushed their way up into the darkness.

The stairwell was tall and dark. Infinitely dark. Sloot's demonic vision couldn't penetrate it. He just put his foot on one step after another, hoping the next step would actually be there. He had a hard time settling into his dread though, thanks to Myrtle's giggling.

"What's so funny?" he asked.

"This." She took her next step at a stomp, sending the sound echoing upward. "No squelching! Do you know how long it's been since I took a step without having to pull my foot out of muck? Because I don't."

The infinite darkness eventually became the regular sort, then faded to hazy grey light, and then they were in the 98th circle of the Inferno. It wasn't that different from the 99th, but there wasn't any muck on the floors. Myrtle giggled at that. There was a black maw behind a velvet rope, only the sign in front of this one also suggested that everyone enjoy their weekends.

"Shall we, then?" asked Igor, wire at the ready.

"How'd you get up here?" asked Sloot.

"Probably better if I don't tell you," said Igor. He thought for the span of a heartbeat and added, "definitely better. Anyway, I know a guy in the kitchens down on the 99th, and he processes sausages for the demons up here. He asked me to rub my backside on the—"

"I thought it was better if you didn't tell me!"

"Right," said Igor. "On an unrelated note, don't eat any sausages."

"We won't be here long enough," said Myrtle. She was right. A second differentiator between the 99th circle and the 98th was the interest in winning. Through some small talk that was more terrifying than scintillating, Sloot learned that the denizens of the 98th really enjoyed punishing anyone who tracked muck up from the 99th. Myrtle's foot bags had robbed them of that entertainment. Sloot wasn't sure whether that helped their popularity or not.

Whatever they'd expected to see on the 98th, it wasn't Myrtle and Sloot. Everyone stared at them in a confused and awkward silence for a moment, which strangely put Sloot at ease. He was at home in awkward silence.

Myrtle, on the other hand, sported a predatory grin. A shark who'd caught the hint of blood in the water.

"Who are you?" demanded a gangrenous demon with a clipboard shoved into its neck. Sloot mused that it was a good thing for Gutsbag he didn't work up here.

"We're the winners from below," said Myrtle.

"But you haven't got … you know … all over you."

"We were careful."

Clipboard Neck blinked slowly, then shrugged.

"Have it your way," he said. "Let's get this over with, we've got a ton of screaming to do. You'd think they'd adjust the quotas for the week of the ball."

"That's upper management for you," Myrtle groused. A mur-

mured chorus of "yeahs" followed.

Everyone shuffled, slithered, or poured themselves into position for the dance to start. Igor twanged out what can politely be referred to as "sound" on his bit of wire, and the dancers started moving.

At least they're making an effort, thought Sloot. It wasn't a good one, but that suited him well enough. He had 97 more levels to go after this one, and he didn't relish the thought of stiff competition this far down. He only hoped that his own dancing was better than the travesty playing out around him. It was performance art at best, an ambulatory tribute to photographs taken in mid-sneeze.

There was a great deal of grumbling as they ascended to the 97th circle, which Sloot could understand. He only stopped apologizing when Myrtle's glare began to singe the back of his neck very literally.

The dancers in the 97th circle were no better. The same could be said of the 96th, the 95th, and so on. It wasn't until they reached the 88th circle that Sloot had to pay attention to what his feet were doing. By the time they reached the 83rd, he had to pay attention to Myrtle's feet as well. At the 81st, he worried he'd reached the extent of his ability.

"You're overthinking it," Myrtle whispered.

"Impossible," Sloot whispered back.

"Just relax and let the music move you."

They actually had music in the 81st circle, much to Igor's chagrin. Despite his best efforts, Sloot felt a twinge of pity for him. Of course, he'd arrived midway through the dance because he refused to take the stairs, and he wasn't a musician in any real sense. Even the unreal senses wanted nothing to do with him, if they even existed, which they didn't.

They held their own, but there was another couple giving them a run for their money. He was a fire sprite who was burning up the dance floor in an all-too-literal sense. She was a rock troll who occasionally moved a limb into a different position, giving her partner a new tableau upon which he might strut his stuff.

"They're an odd pair," Sloot remarked as he twirled Myrtle. "He must have picked the least worst dancer in the place so she wouldn't draw attention away from him."

"Hardly," said Myrtle, doing a little stutter step to adjust for Sloot's clumsy legwork. "That's Grudzrak Shale! She's a legend in Infernal dancing circles."

"Really?"

"Trolls don't dance. They don't understand music. The fact that she's here at all is something of a miracle."

Sloot wondered if he wasn't part troll. It sounded ridiculous, but then so did his Carpathian heritage not so long ago.

"Nicely done," said Myrtle, "keep it up!"

"What?" Sloot nearly tripped. Myrtle managed to get an arm around his waist and dip him instead.

"Sorry," said Myrtle. Her eyebrows creased.

There was a crash, a *fwoom*, and a scream. Grudzrak's fiery partner had been getting noticeably more irritated as the dance went on. He'd obviously not imagined that the contest would take this long, not with his immeasurable talent brought to bear. He got careless. Sloot had seen it before, when too eager a junior accountant had gotten cocky and ended up with half an inkwell across his ledger.

The official forensic report would later show that absolutely nothing had happened, and that the Prime Evils and the endless line of shell corporations holding the Inferno were entirely blameless in said non-existent events. However, in the unredacted version that the middle management demons would occasionally read over for a laugh, the fire sprite missed the cue for Grudzrak's arm sweep and careened into a punchbowl that had been spiked by everyone in attendance. The resulting blaze–which officially never happened–licked at Sloot and Myrtle's heels as they legged it up the stairwell to the 80th circle.

"We need to talk about what happened back there," said Myrtle as they climbed the stairs. She got the sentence all the way out before she realized Sloot had stopped following her. She turned around.

"Sloot?"

He was sitting on the steps and hyperventilating. Demons didn't breathe, but it was the standard physiological response across all species to girlfriends saying, "we need to talk."

She sat next to him and took his hand in hers.

"I wish we had time for this," she said.

Sloot nodded. Myrtle put her arm around him and rested her head on his shoulder. His breathing slowed until it went away entirely, which nearly started him hyperventilating again.

"You're a natural dancer," said Myrtle. "Everyone is, to one degree or another, as long as we don't think about it. You're overthinking it, Sloot. You need to let go."

"Let go? How can I? The fate of *everything* hangs in the balance! The secret to amending the Narrative is in the Axial Ledger, and I've got one chance to sneak a peek at it."

"That's almost right," she said at last, weighing each word with great care.

"What do you mean? Which part? Is all of it partially incorrect, or is there a single part that's—"

She kissed him. Really, properly kissed him. It was a doozy. In the politics of any relationship, certain expressions of affection are used sparingly so as not to diminish their effects when needed most. Sloot blinked, but had nothing to say.

"Remember what Vlad told you about thoughtlessness?"

"I do," said Sloot, "but how do you know about that? You

weren't there, were you? I'm sure that if—"

She risked sending him into a coma by giving him the kiss again. His vision swam.

"Thoughtlessness," Myrtle insisted. "Let the thoughts come, but pay them no mind. Just let me lead."

"Thoughtlessness," said Sloot. He nodded. He wanted to make sense of it, but that was the problem, wasn't it? What made sense anymore? Nothing. Not since the night he'd inherited Carpathian spy duties from his mother. Better not to try, then. Perhaps if he waited for the sense of it all to come to him, it would. If Winking Bob was right, the Axial Ledger contained all the sense he'd need.

"You're almost there," said Myrtle, staring appreciatively into Sloot's blank expression. "It'll do for now. Just follow me and try not to think."

She took his hand and led him upwards. He was dimly aware of the change in temperature when they reached the 80th circle. It was almost cool enough to support human life, which was a refreshing change of pace. There were the chattering skeletons which would have driven any mortal mad. Luckily, they tended to fall apart at the joints when the dancing became moderately vigorous.

Sloot avoided thinking like he owed it money. Most of the 70s were a blur for him. On the way up from the 67th circle, he heard it.

"Move over, would you?" asked the voice.

"I'm not sure what you mean," Sloot responded.

"It's metaphorical."

"What? Who are you?"

"I'm you, Sloot. Well, sort of. I'm properly you."

The next thing of which Sloot was aware was Myrtle's hand over his mouth.

"In your own time, darling."

Sloot realized that he was screaming at the top of his lungs. His only consolation was that he really was doing it, not some inner voice that had seized control of his voice box. He stopped because he wanted to, not because anyone else was doing it for him.

"What was all that about?" Myrtle took her hand away.

"I'm possessed or something!"

"Possessed?" Myrtle fixed Sloot with a look of unbridled terror. "Oh, no! Who's in there? Speak up! If it's one of those entitlement demons from the 72nd circle, I'll have you know that Sloot's got very strong feelings about socialism!"

"What? No, I don't."

Myrtle was silent for a moment, studying the space behind Sloot's eyes. She eventually breathed a sigh of relief.

"Wasn't one of them, then," she said. "You can't keep entitlement demons quiet when they start debating the pitfalls of governmental systems."

"Oh," said Sloot.

"How do you know you're possessed?"

"I heard a voice. It said it was me." Sloot was grateful to be with Myrtle in that moment. She'd been possessed by the ghost of Arthur for years. If anyone knew what to do, it would be Myrtle.

"Oh!" she exclaimed. "It's happening!"

"What? What's happening, and to whom? Is it me? I am possessed, aren't I? What does that mean for my tax liability? Can I claim a dependent?"

Myrtle leaned in, apparently ready to give Sloot another one of *those* kisses, but she stopped herself for a reason that Sloot found disappointing.

"It's only going to get harder from here on, Sloot. Do you remember those plausible deniability demons from the 74th circle?"

"No," said Sloot.

Myrtle's eyes narrowed.

"You're probably telling the truth. Anyway, they were really good, but they're nothing compared to what's up there."

"What are we going to do?" asked Sloot, all-too-familiar panic welling up in his core.

"We're going to dance, and there's no thinking in dancing. How much thinking is there in dancing, Sloot?"

"None," he replied. "Well, not *none,* I mean you've got to—"

"No! You have to concentrate on thoughtlessness! Better yet, don't even do that. Your mind has to be blank, do you understand?"

"I don't know how to do that!"

"You did great through the 70s, and now you have to do better."

"But I didn't do anything!"

"Right," said Myrtle, "and now you have to do less."

It was impossible to convince Sloot not to think at the best of times, not that you could prove it. The best of times avoided Sloot at all costs. Furthermore, asking him not to think right after filling his head with dire consequences was the sort of thing they tried you for in international courts. You'd never be tried for it in chaos courts, of course. They'd probably give you a medal.

Sloot cleared his mind as best he could. Assuming he couldn't get all the way to thoughtlessness in one go, he racked his brain for the most mind-numbing thing he could ponder. Unfortunately, he came up with balance sheet reconciliations. Far too scintillating a topic for a devotee of general ledgers like Sloot.

It worked, to a point. He was still aware that his hips were gyrating. They must have learned some maneuvers while he wasn't looking. He was concerned that his subconscious was showing a worrisome proficiency in running things without him. He'd have said something, but it was *his* subconscious.

Even balance sheet reconciliations could only keep him distracted for so long. Somewhere in the mid-50s, the powerful allure of general ledger accounting lulled a bit, and he accidentally paid attention.

"Don't touch that!"

"You again!"

"Yes," said the voice in his head, "you again."

"But I'm not—"

"You are," the voice insisted, "but keep thinking that way. We're involved in a maneuver at the moment."

That was true. Myrtle was a blur, spinning toward him at an alarming rate. He felt his hands lift her up just as they were about to collide, and then—

"Permanent budget allocations should be delivered in the third quarter."

"That's ridiculous!" Sloot snapped.

"I'll take your word for it," said the voice. "I'm just dipping into your, or possibly my … *Sloot's* professional knowledge to keep you occupied. Someone could get very badly hurt if you decided to take over right now."

Sloot fumed at the suggestion. He clung to his outrage and was dimly aware that it caused his eyes to flare in time with the music that the brass band was playing. He was also dimly aware that Igor was trying to sit in with the band, but they were having none of it. Brass bands are very selective about the instruments they let into their ensembles, and Igor's wire wasn't brass.

It was becoming a tiresome state of affairs. Of all the people who might have been suited to the task of saving the Narrative from annihilation, Sloot's chagrin started with "why did it have to be me," and was presently as far along as "no one said there'd be dancing."

This was the worst part. The waiting. Letting fate happen to him while he … let it.

And while he was bemoaning the state of his affairs, who was this interloper? Myrtle seemed unconcerned. It said it was him, and perhaps it was. That was terrifying. If this other consciousness within his mind was Sloot, then who was *he*?

Sloot didn't know the precise definition for existentialism, but he knew it when he saw it. He was definitely having that sort of crisis.

There was a sudden decompression, a releasing of tightness that he hadn't noticed was there. He wiggled his brain and the room swam into focus. He was sitting next to Myrtle. Both of them were covered in a sheen of sweat. He was completely exhausted, and the threat of having to get up again loomed like a fly buzzing around his ears, looking for a place to start a family.

"What's that look?" asked Myrtle.

"Fly larva hatching in my ear," Sloot replied. No matter how many horrors Myrtle had seen during her time in the Inferno, the face she made proved she hadn't gotten used to it.

"Just worrying about it," he added.

"Oh," said Myrtle. She sighed with relief. "Come on, then. Only 28 more circles to go."

"What? I thought we'd just gotten into the 40s!"

"That would explain why you've been so quiet. I'm curious, have you been talking?"

"To whom?" Sloot knew very well to whom, or at least he had a pretty good idea. He was curious whether Myrtle knew better than he did. That wouldn't have surprised him.

Myrtle said nothing, just gave him a wry little smirk. That was sufficient to keep his mind occupied all the way up to the 13th circle where, to put it mildly, things took a disastrous turn for the worse. Or, to put it in a slightly less ominous but still entirely accurate way, things got interesting.

SEWAGE REVERSAL

Sloot might have been paying attention, had he not been working so hard to avoid it.

Had he heard that his opponent on the 13th circle was Baelgoroth the Destroyer, the name would have sounded familiar.

While Sloot was clerking for Winkus, Ordo, and Mirgazhandinuxulluminixighanduminophizio, he'd seen a case file that had been partially redacted. That, in and of itself, wasn't unusual. The redactions department in the 88th circle was well-funded and overzealous. The unusual bit was the mathematical pattern that had been applied to the redaction. Burzong's Irritating Constant is a not-quite-random number that changes zero or more times per second based on the number of known realities in the universe at the time. Sloot recognized it because every time he thought he'd noticed a proper pattern, it changed.

Burzong's Irritating Constant was designed for confusing livestock and was poorly suited to anything else. As a result of the bad redaction, Sloot learned that Baelgoroth the Destroyer wore lifts in his shoes.

It should have ended there. If Sloot possessed an ounce of luck, it *would* have ended there. Alas.

"Sloot Peril," growled the diminutive figure of Baelgoroth the Destroyer. "Sloot *vile-swear-word-that-sounded-like-the-sudden-death-of-everything-good-in-the-world* Peril is here. *Here!* Within my grasp, having strolled so blithely into his utter destruction!"

"He doesn't seem to like you," Myrtle remarked.

"What?" Sloot was accustomed to being disliked, though it disappointed him enough to shake him from his near-thoughtless reverie.

"Baelgoroth the Destroyer," said Myrtle. She pointed.

"Oh, dear," said Sloot, his brain racing to catch up. When it arrived, he added, "oh, dear!"

"Spare me your weak and pitiful profanity," snarled Baelgoroth, who obviously knew an attempt at swearing when he heard one. "I have suffered at your hands, and lo, you shall suffer at mine!"

"Suffered at Sloot's hands?" Myrtle looked genuinely confused, dashing Sloot's desperate hope that this was part of the plan.

"You have to be twelve inches tall to join the Razing of the Dead. You revealed that I'm eleven-and-a-half!" Baelgoroth's howl was surprisingly loud given his stature. "That half inch is everything! How did you find out, anyway? You didn't even ask for a bribe before you blabbed to the prison guards!"

"I-I'm sorry," Sloot stammered. "I needed to see Roman, and—"

"Spare me your caterwauling," said Baelgoroth. "Save it for the eternity of pain that I have in store for you!"

"Oh, dear!"

"Calm down, Baelgoroth." The admonition etched itself into Sloot's mind. He didn't so much hear it as suddenly remember that it had always been said by an ever-present darkness from which only nightmares could hope to escape.

"There will be no subjugations today," the darkness continued to have always said. "Eternal torments are suspended for the duration of the ball, are we clear?"

"Fine." Baelgoroth glowered at Sloot. "I shall obliterate your pathetic moves upon the dance floor, ascend to victory in the higher circles of the Inferno, and then return to derange you in a series of torments—"

"After the ball," the darkness had always said.

"Oh dear," fretted Sloot.

"Don't think about it," said Myrtle. "You'll need to do thoughtlessness again, and you'll have to mean it this time."

"I meant it before!"

"Not like you're going to have to mean it this time," said Myrtle. "You'll need to—circles of the Inferno, it can't be!"

Sloot followed Myrtle's horrified gaze to the other side of the dance floor, where Baelgoroth stood alone astride a stick horse. Had he been a bit taller, it would have looked slightly less ridiculous. Baelgoroth's stature was such that all of his strength was required to keep the horse's nose from touching the ground.

"I don't get it," said Sloot.

"That's Blagderos." Myrtle's voice quavered.

"Blagderos?"

"Don't say it again!"

"Why not?"

"You really haven't spent any time in the Inferno, have you?"

"A little over sixty thousand years, I think." Sloot straightened his collar and smirked.

"So, no," said Myrtle.

"Dancers," the darkness had ordained in long-forgotten aeons, "to your places, please."

"Your caterwauling shall not spare you," Baelgoroth grunted as he trotted laboriously across the dance floor astride the stick horse. He nearly dropped it twice. His hands didn't quite fully encircle the stick. It might have been easier to walk it across, but there were rules. Even in the Inferno, when one found one's self astride a stick horse, it was understood that one's legs belonged to the horse for the duration.

"You might summon it," Myrtle explained.

"What?"

"If you speak its name a third time. Loads of things get summoned that way down here."

"Why would I want to summon a stick horse? Or, perhaps more importantly, why wouldn't I?"

"Impudent fools," Baelgoroth laughed, "your pleas fall upon the deaf ears of an uncaring malevolence!"

"Hey," the darkness whined from the chasm of history.

"I was talking about the horse."

Sloot sighed. Sixty thousand years in the Inferno wasn't much, but it was enough to know that demons didn't pull your leg, prankster and body-snatcher demons being the notable exceptions.

The music struck up. The dance began. Sloot paid as little attention as possible to his feet. It wasn't hard, because there was Baelgoroth the Destroyer glaring at him from across the dance floor, trotting around on his stick horse.

On Blagderos, Sloot corrected himself. An evil stick horse? It didn't appear to be doing anything but causing Baelgoroth grief. Wait, something was happening. Sloot couldn't say what, and refusing to look directly at Baelgoroth was no help. But avoiding eye contact was just what you did when someone glared at you like a cat whose box hadn't been scooped in eight minutes. You focused on something else and hoped the cat suddenly darted into the other room, having just realized it was late for a nap.

"Uh oh," said Myrtle.

"What?" Panic gripped Sloot's attention. He didn't so much fall as throw himself floorward to see if it would flinch. It didn't.

He scrambled onto his hands and knees, then froze as his eyes met Baelgoroth's. He saw the burning fury of a dying sun made flesh in the tiny demon, who'd turned Blagderos over in his hands to wield it like a sword.

"Why is he doing that?" asked Myrtle, her voice quavering.

"Inevitability," said Sloot. He'd been a boy once. As carefully as he'd avoided having to play outside, he'd been subjected to it enough to know what happens when boys get tired of riding their stick horses around. It never didn't happen, and it never didn't end in tears. There was always a bloody nose, or at least an ear that felt really hot for the rest of the afternoon.

"You shall feel my wrath!"

"Wraths were postponed along with the torments," the darkness had long ago embroidered into the tapestry of time.

Hate and frustration welled up in Baelgoroth, overflowing in a scream. He charged. Sloot ran.

Sloot had never been good at running. He should have managed to acquire some skill during the hours he'd spent evading bullies, murderers, and even Myrtle once or twice. Yet he resembled an avalanche of knees and elbows barreling down a wintry slope, preparing to demolish the sleepy little village of his dignity. It didn't matter. So long as Baelgoroth's swings all missed him, he was safe. Safe, and disappointed.

Disappointed? That was strange. Scared, sure, but disappointed? Where was that coming from? The voice in his head, the one who'd spoken to him before. Whoever—*whatever*—it was, it had some very un-Sloot-like instincts like punching people in the nose, or at least saying, "now you listen here."

"That's enough," read the ancient stones upon which the darkness rendered its edicts. "The challengers shall ascend to the 12th circle."

"No!" shouted Baelgoroth. "My vengeance is at hand!"

"Vengeances shall resume after the ball, along with torments and wraths."

Baelgoroth did not relent. "Hold still!" he shouted. He was still wielding what looked like an ordinary stick horse, but there was a malevolence about it. A vorpal air. Sloot didn't doubt it could sever his head with ease, like so much butter under the hot knife of metaphor.

He kept running. For Sloot, this was open defiance. A demon was chasing him with a flaming sword! No, wait, it wasn't a flaming sword. It was a stick horse, and the wielder was less than a foot tall. Logic told him to stop, but Myrtle had a worried look. That was confirmation it was a real threat, as far as Sloot was concerned. And he was. Deeply.

The stairs descended with agonizing lethargy, showing no remorse for Sloot's endangerment.

"Sloot!" shouted Myrtle. "The stairs!"

Sloot felt Baelgoroth's breath on the back of his neck. He leapt. And missed. He landed on his face just below the descending staircase and rolled, hoping to avoid being crushed by them. It might have been preferable, he thought, as a tiny pair of feet landed in the small of his back with a shrill war cry.

"Your soul is forfeit!" screamed the apoplectic Baelgoroth. Sloot thought he heard Blagderos whicker in anticipation of fresh blood. Then suddenly, the weight lifted from his back. He heard a *whump* and turned to see Baelgoroth sliding to the ground against a wall. The stick horse clattered to the ground beside him.

"We've got to go," said Myrtle, dragging Sloot to his feet. "Now!"

"Hang on a minute," said Sloot. He got to his feet and looked down at the stick horse. "This is ridiculous! I'm running away from a tiny demon brandishing a child's toy."

"There's more to it than that," Myrtle warned.

"Is there? I'm not so sure." Sloot wondered where this cavalier attitude was coming from. Somewhere dark, he imagined, where ruthless villains roamed a desolate wasteland in search of prepositions to end sentences with. He knew he should have fled, but something angry within him wanted to keep going. Needed to keep going.

"What's so fearsome about a stick horse?" Sloot's hands balled into fists. "Nothing! Oh, but give it a name, and suddenly it's—"

"Sloot, don't—"

"—the great and terrible Blagderos, whose hooves—"

Thunder filled the room. Baelgoroth cackled.

Blagderos was massive in his unbound form. His hooves beat sparks on the stone floor and lightning danced between his sharpened teeth. Black flames licked from his powerful flanks, and his red eyes taught Sloot a new meaning of fear.

"I warned you," said Myrtle in a uniquely girlfriendly tone. "Don't say his name again. Was that so hard?"

"I'm sorry," said Sloot.

"You're sorry," Myrtle repeated flatly. "You've brought forth the Death Knell, the Harbinger of Galloping Fright, the Terror of the—"

Sloot imagined the raging beast had more terrifying names than could be easily counted. As the dread steed loomed over him, he wished for a future in which Myrtle could hang each one over his head, reminding him of the time long ago when he angered the Stick Horse of Doom. She'd told him not to, but would he listen?

It was fortunate that Igor showed up when he did. Horses spook easily in the presence of gremlins. One whiff of Igor's aromatic profile sent Blagderos into a panic. There was a puff of yellowish smoke and the smell of sulfur. When the smoke cleared, the stick horse lay on the ground as if a child had carelessly left it there.

"Where did you come from?" Baelgoroth demanded.

"The sewage drains," said Igor. "You know, I figured they'd flow downward from this level. I guess everyone is victim to someone else's sense of humor in the Inferno."

"I will not be mocked by a gremlin!"

"You will with that pompadour. But I'm a bard. Maybe you'll get a different answer if any gremlins find their way up the sewage pipes. Very smooth ride, by the way."

"Thank you," said Myrtle.

"You reversed the sewage?" asked Sloot.

"I had to do something while I waited for you. I've got a work ethic, you know."

Sloot was already in enough hot water over summoning Blagderos, so he didn't bring up Myrtle's burgling of Whitewood *vis-a-vis* her work ethic.

Their competition on the 12th circle was a fractal demon with infinite legs who counted as its own partner. Its legs weren't synchronized though, and it hadn't finished dancing when time ran out, so it was disqualified.

They faced a pair of teenager demons on the 11th circle who had flimsy reasons for why they hadn't practiced and said that dances were lame anyway. Sloot ratted them out for trying to spike the punch on his way up to the 10th circle, where no one had told them that there was a dance contest. Another easy win.

Sloot nearly had a heart attack on his way up to the 9th level, which was the hell for prima ballerinas who couldn't remain humble. The contest master waved them along because the denizens of the circle couldn't agree who among them got to compete.

The 8th circle had special dispensation—following a union negotiation—to continue their regularly scheduled torments in lieu of participating in the Ball. Sloot tried not to look directly at the torment victims, who were being made into sundaes. There were white-hot pokers and rancid cheeses on the toppings bar.

There was no 7th circle of the Inferno because no one would be lucky enough to reside there.

The contestants on the 6th circle had been disqualified for failure to ingest the minimum levels of illegal performance enhancing potions.

"That's surprising," said Myrtle. "The 6th circle is reserved for personal trainers."

The contestants on the 5th circle had been disqualified for failure to sufficiently bribe the contest officials.

The 4th circle mixed up the dates for the Infernal Ball and the annual Chili Cookoff and Murder Jamboree. They'd been at it for hours, so there was no one left standing to grind Sloot and Myrtle into a pot where they might have simmered with peppers, garlic, and onions.

Due to the ethereal nature of the 3rd circle, the dance portion of the Ball was replaced with a trans-substantial debate on the efficacy of guilt as a form of torture. Having been firmly reprimanded for not visiting his mother more often, Sloot followed Myrtle up to the 2nd circle.

"Less festive than most," Myrtle remarked. She was right. There wasn't so much as a balloon or streamer or garland made out of something's guts to indicate that there was a ball underway.

"I have a bad feeling about this," said Sloot.

"As good a place as any to start," said a woman in a suit who looked familiar.

"Ms. Meatsacrifice?" asked Sloot.

"You know her?" asked Myrtle.

"I'm Mr. Peril's attorney," said Minerva Meatsacrifice. "We'll address the dance contest as soon as we've resolved the conundrum."

"Conundrum?" Sloot was confused.

"For your own sake, I urge you not to make me repeat myself. It's incredibly expensive. This way, please."

"You have a demonic attorney?" whispered Myrtle as they followed her briskly down a marble hallway.

"A dozen or so," said Sloot. "It's a long story."

They were led into a room that was only slightly larger than the massive table in its middle. Every seat was occupied by something in a suit. Sloot squinted against the collective glare of gold cufflinks and noted a very expensive smell to the air. An hourglass stood at the center of the table, and nearly all of the black sand within it had drained into the bottom half.

"Next item on the agenda," Ms. Meatsacrifice smirked as she sat at the head of the table. "Collection of the overdue sum of blood that Mr. Peril owes the firm of Nameless, Redacted, and Meatsacrifice. Mr. Peril waives his right to trial on the understanding that it would be far too costly, don't you, Mr. Peril?"

All eyes turned to Sloot.

"You should decide quickly," urged Ms. Meatsacrifice, indicating the hourglass in the center of the table. "You're almost out of time."

"Time for what?"

"The penalty period on your repayment." She smiled like a shark at a Sloot buffet. "In a moment it will be irrevocably past due, and we'll expect payment in full."

"Past due? I never signed anything! I haven't even seen a statement!"

"A statement can be provided for an additional fee," said Ms. Meatsacrifice, "and we don't do signatures in chaos courts. You should know that from your fraudulent work with Winkus, Ordo, and Mirgazhandinuxulluminixighanduminophizio. You could have simply refused representation if you didn't want our help."

"I didn't know that at the time!"

"Ignorance of chaos is no excuse."

"You didn't happen to see this coming, did you?" Sloot whispered to Myrtle.

Myrtle shook her head. "Whatever you're going to do, you'd

better do it fast."

Sloot followed Myrtle's gaze to the hourglass. In seconds he'd learn what fate awaited those who couldn't pay their attorneys' fees on time. In his wildest dreams, there was no scenario that left all of his skin in its proper place.

"I need an attorney!" he shouted. Sloot's heart thundered in his ears. Hands, claws, tentacles, and worse produced cards from within their suits. Sloot fumbled and grasped, his hand closing on a card proffered by a slimy tentacle just as the last grains of sand circled the neck of the hourglass.

"I agree to your retainer!" he screamed.

"I'm afraid your time is up."

"Er, not anymore, if you please, Ms. Meatsacrifice."

A snarl embroiled Ms. Meatsacrifice's face as the hourglass turned itself over.

"What is the meaning of this?" she demanded.

"Client privilege," chirped Sloot's attorney, whose card read "Slanderous Monstrosity, Attorney at Chaos." A noxious goo sputtered from his beak as he continued. "So long as the client is the victim—er, *recipient*—of ongoing representation, he may defer his legal fees until such time as judgments have been rendered."

"How is this possible?" Flames shot from Ms. Meatsacrifice's ears. "And what judgment?"

"My overdue fees," said Sloot. "I never waived my right to trial."

"This is outrageous!"

Slanderous Monstrosity shrugged. "It's hell for attorneys here too, you know."

"What's the most expensive way out of this?" Ms. Meatsacrifice was on the verge of frenzy. Her eyes burned into Sloot, promising to drain gallons of blood from him, stone or not.

"Taking it to trial," said Slanderous Monstrosity. "I recommend dragging it out as long as possible. Far more expensive for my client."

"Is that in my best interest?" asked Sloot.

"It depends on how you look at it," Slanderous Monstrosity whispered to him. "Do you want to pay us several thousand gallons of blood now, or several million gallons at some future date?"

"I don't have any gallons of blood!" said Sloot, selfishly omitting the gallon-and-a-half he had on him.

Slanderous Monstrosity sighed. "So you'll be deferring payment on my retainer as well, then?"

"I can do that?"

"Like I said, it's hell for attorneys, too."

"Then I suppose you're free to go," Ms. Meatsacrifice spat.

"You're not entering the dance contest?"

"It isn't billable. Off you go."

TRY THE CANAPES

Sloot had never seen so much white marble and gold leaf in one place. He and Myrtle were standing on a vast expanse of decorative stonework that put Gildedhearth to shame. Sloot wondered if there were tracts of the place that had yet to be discovered. A gilt-and-marble frontier where wild cherubs roamed the frescoes and danced among the urns.

"It gives people the wrong idea," said a young man in a white tuxedo. His blond hair waved with a luxuriance that made Sloot feel inadequate.

"What people?" Myrtle asked absently as she stared up at the mural on the ceiling. It was positively dripping with cherubs, most of which were presenting urns or apples to buxom naked ladies. Sloot had seen an abundance of bare shoulder on his first upward glance and bade his gaze rise no higher than the wainscoting.

"VIPs, mostly. The ones that the Masters collect personally. It gives them the idea they're in for a very different sort of eternity. Really sets the mood, if you know what I mean."

Sloot reminded himself that he was in the Inferno. In the 1st circle, no less. If his mother could see him now, what would she say? Probably that he should have worn white if he wanted to blend in, and that a good spy would have known that. He'd have had a devil of a time keeping a white suit clean through 99 levels of Inferno, though.

"Can I offer you any refreshments?" asked the young man.

"Nice try," said Myrtle.

"It was?" asked Sloot.

"You'd be surprised how often it works," the young man said with a smirk. "Oh, well. Please call on me if you need anything. My name is Damien."

"What's going on?" Sloot knew there was subtext happening, but he'd be deviled if he could find it. He might be deviled either way, depending on how literal things got.

"Just don't eat or drink anything," said Myrtle.

Sloot nodded. He scanned the room for any clue as to where the Axial Ledger might be hidden. There were three fountains in the room, all ostentatious piles of golden cherubs pouring endless buckets of water over each other. One fountain was slightly larger than the other two, and it looked like there might be a hollow behind the plinth around which a cherub with an urn was chasing two others, one of whom held a basket of apples, the other an ewer that poured out over another plinth bearing an urn.

"Perhaps—"

"It's not in the fountain," said Myrtle.

"I assure you, madam," said Damien, "that there is not a single cherub, urn, apple, or ewer missing from any of the fountains. The Masters make me count them every day, right after my skin has grown back."

"Of course," Myrtle smiled.

"How do you know?" Sloot whispered.

"The contest happens in the ballroom," she replied.

"This isn't the ballroom?"

"No," said Damien, "this is the foyer. Please follow me."

By the time they reached the massive golden doors at the end of the foyer, Sloot had grown tired of counting cherubs. *It must be hell for accountants too,* he thought, considering his fervor for counting.

The ballroom had fewer cherubs than the foyer, but it was still lousy with them. It was smaller than the foyer. Sloot could see all of the walls. What he couldn't see, to his concomitant feelings of dread and relief, was anyone else.

"Where are the, er, well … you know?" asked Sloot.

"The Prime Evils?" Damien basked in reflected glory. "They'll appear in their own time. Can I bring you some drinks while you wait?"

"Still no," said Myrtle.

Damien laughed nervously. "Suit yourself."

Sloot walked arm-in-arm with Myrtle around the ballroom, taking in its splendor and searching for some clue as to where the Axial Ledger might be. It was hard to concentrate, given that this was the first time in ages that he and Myrtle had been together.

"Is any of this familiar?" he asked.

Myrtle shook her head. "Sorry, I have no idea where the Axial Ledger is."

"What?" Panic shot up Sloot's spine. "How could you not know?"

Myrtle stopped walking and dropped Sloot's arm.

"Oh, dear," said Sloot. "Sorry, I didn't mean—"

"Didn't mean?" Myrtle's eyes went steely. Even worse, her hands rose to rest on her hips. No son of the Old Country kept his cool when faced with that level of aggression.

"Do you know how much Infernal time I've spent waiting for you in the 99th circle?"

"No," Sloot admitted, "although there's this rune on my circle, the Subtemporal Exponent, that could help me estimate—"

"It was a rhetorical question!"

"Oh," said Sloot. He didn't have any runes on his circle for rhetoric, and doubted it would help if he did.

"A long time," Myrtle snarled. "I saw the bits that I saw, and that got us this far. You'll have to excuse me for not solving it for you entirely!"

"I'm sorry," said Sloot. He left it at that. He had at his disposal countless reasons, excuses, justifications, and worse. He had defenses. Questions that started with, "oh, yeah? Well what about …?" But he silenced them. They throbbed in the logical centers of his brain, demanding justice, yearning to weigh Sloot's pain against Myrtle's so that a winner could be given a medal or something. But he fought them back. They could threaten class action against him and he would not waver, because following "I'm sorry" with "but" was no apology at all.

Suffering was not a contest. Even if it was, Sloot didn't dare try and out-suffer Myrtle, not after everything she'd sacrificed for him, for his task, for the Narrative. Not after he'd carelessly piled onto her suffering because she hadn't known enough of the future. He needed to apologize, and so he did.

Myrtle's voice shook as she sighed. It was the sound of immeasurable tribulation pent up in her. A single tear welled in her eye, and a smile had just started to break when the smell of sulfur wrinkled Sloot's nostrils.

"That's quite enough of that," said the long, lean devil in the bathtub. His red scales gleamed beneath the pearlescent bubbles. The tub was an opulent gold-and-porcelain affair that Sloot felt certain he would have noticed, had it been there the whole time.

Without thinking, Sloot dove for the floor and prostrated himself before it. "It" being the devil, not the tub. It was a nice tub, but not grovel worthy.

"Woe unto thee, oh Paragon of Vile Malevolence!" Myrtle was

on the floor as well, and they offered up the honorific in unison. Sloot felt certain he'd never said it before but there it was, on the tip of his tongue like he'd said it so often he no longer thought about its meaning.

"Woe also unto thee," sighed the devil, apparently not exempt from honorifics himself. *Hell for the devils too*, Sloot surmised.

"You two had a lovely little strife starting up there," the devil whined. "What happened? I hate to see potential wasted."

"Sorry, oh Wicked Stain," Sloot and Myrtle groveled in unison. That was off-putting, but far less than the fact that Sloot really meant it. He felt a deep self-loathing for having brought penance to what could have been truly bitter bickering. He wanted to atone to the red devil, but how? Chewing on rocks to break his teeth? Not bad for starters, but perhaps he'd also smash his face into the cold marble floor a few dozen times. Nothing got the blood spilling across marble like a broken nose.

"Wait," commanded a yellow-scaled devil who slunk out from a nearby shadow. Her gold lamé dress left little to the imagination. "We're not doing penances tonight, remember?"

"Ugh, stupid Infernal Ball." A quick burst of flame engulfed the tub. When it dissipated, the tub was gone and the devil was wearing a shiny red suit.

"Not bad," said the yellow devil.

"Thanks," Red replied. He straightened his collar. "Heretic skin, just had it made. Shall we get this over with? Damien!"

"Here, your Wretched Monstrosity."

"Who are these vermin who dare challenge us?"

"I'll find out at once, Sire." The whites of Damien's eyes went black. The blues went red. They glowed with the power of Infernal hate as they bored into Sloot, laying his darkest secrets bare for his perusal.

"Oh," said Damien, genuine surprise dripping from his voice.

He bored deeper into Sloot's psyche, breathing deep the scents of his hopes, fears, childhood memories, and other little tidbits that Sloot had hoped to keep to himself.

"Yes, what is it?" demanded Yellow. "Believe it or not, we're waiting for you to speak."

"A thousand apologies, your Hellish Putrescence. It's just that these two are far more lowly than the worms who usually crawl up this far. She is a denizen of the 99th circle, and he … well, he's lowlier still!"

"You don't mean?"

"I do, your Foul Incivility. He's a demon 100th class, and—oh, dear."

"Language," warned Red.

"Sorry," said Damien. He corrected himself with a swear word so vile it made Sloot's eyes water. "It's just—well, he's the oddity."

"The oddity," Red repeated with all the enthusiasm of a wet napkin at the bottom of a garbage can. "Am I supposed to know what—"

"Not the Coolest's oddity?" Yellow fixed Sloot with a lustful stare that made him want to cry.

"Oh! Well, that would explain it," said Red. "I didn't think sewage demons even knew what dancing was, much less had any notion how it was done! They must have ulterior motives for being here, then."

"Several!" Damien suppressed a giggle. He reminded Sloot of a prefect from his school days who delighted in tattling on other students. "Where to begin? Let's see, she wants to escape from the Inferno. No surprise there, I've seen the 99th circle. If the meals you make me eat off the floor are any indication, I'd want to escape from there, too."

"Would you?"

"Only a joke," said Damien. He chuckled nervously.

The Evils looked at each other and burst into fits of laughter. It was terrifying.

"It's hell for comedians too," Yellow confided. "The bad ones, anyway. Continue, Damien."

"Let's see, oh! She's down here of her own free will. Then why does she want to escape? Oh, I see! They're running a long con."

"Do tell," said Red. "It's been ages since anyone dared to steal from us."

"What a refreshing change of pace!" Yellow licked her eyebrows with a forked tongue. "Oh, can we guess what they're trying to steal? Is it the Madness of Emperor Tetrachimon? I think I've got it in an urn somewhere. A cherub is holding it."

"An exquisite guess, your Drowning Vengeance," said Damien. "But alas, no."

"Then it must be the Eternal Sleep of Death," ventured Red. "Everyone in the Inferno seeks it."

"Nearly everyone." Damien made a wistful sigh. "But no, your Scabrous Frightfulness, that's not it."

"What then?"

"The Axial Ledger."

The Evils stared blankly at Damien.

"Are you sure it's not the Blackened Cacophony of Untold Aeons?" asked Yellow.

"Or the Nineteen Seals of Mega Ennui?" suggested Red.

"The Heart of Undying Legions?"

"The Jewel of the Slaughter?"

"The Recipe for Flaming Murder Sours?"

"All excellent guesses," said Damien, "but I'm quite sure it's the Axial Ledger. Isn't that right, Mister Peril?"

"Ooo, *Mister Peril*," said Yellow. "Excellent name for a villain. Good thing you're one of ours."

"It's complicated," Sloot began. "You see—"

"We're not here to steal anything," said Myrtle, having been driven to confession either by pragmatism or to avoid letting Sloot try politics. "Sloot just needs to have a peek at it."

"Why?" asked Yellow, directing the question to Damien rather than Myrtle. Damien's red-and-black eyes bored into Sloot once again.

"He's working for the Coolest ... to mend the Narrative ... oh, this is that business with the goblins!"

"I was wondering when we were going to come to that," said Red. "Oh, but the Axial Ledger? Are you sure? It's just a dusty old book. We've got the Burning Spear of the Completely Insane Dragon around here somewhere, it would be much more interesting if you tried stealing that."

"Er, no, your Ruthless Inefficiency," said Sloot. "Just the Axial Ledger, please and thank you."

"No," said Yellow.

"Oh, er," Sloot began, but then what? Was he going to argue with the Prime Evils? Sloot knew a risk when he calculated one. "Well, I suppose we tried our best. Shall we get on with the dance?"

"Ha!" Red snorted. "Do you think we were spawned of the blackest hate in the deepest primordial space yesterday?"

"I definitely didn't think that," said Sloot.

"You haven't come all the way up through the Inferno to ask politely," said Yellow.

"I haven't?" Sloot looked at Myrtle.

"Don't ask me," she said, throwing up her hands. "I never got any visions of what happens in here."

"Nobody does." Red sighed. "Too much chaotic interference. Believe me, we'd love to have a causality demon on staff up here, saying things like, 'look out, he's got a knife,' or 'look out, *you've* got a knife,' and eventually, 'is there anything I can do to convince you not to use that knife on me?' I'll give you a hint. There isn't."

"Let's dispense with the feigned acquiescence," said Yellow. "I don't have all—well, actually I *do* have all eternity, but I don't want to spend it doing this."

"With respect," said Sloot, "I've never feigned acquiescence in my life."

Yellow sighed. "This is boring. Damien?"

Damien gazed once more into Sloot and came away with a very confused expression.

"He's telling the truth."

"About which bit?"

"All of it."

"All of what," asked Yellow, "all of the subterfuge that he's willing to bore me with until he gets his way?"

"No, your Rancid Pestilence, he's not doing subterfuge. No deceit, no trickery, not even a hint of obfuscation. He really means it! He's accepted your answer and has no intention of bothering you any further about the Axial Ledger."

"Really?" asked Red. Sloot nodded. "Look, I appreciate unequivocal submission to my will as much as the next guy—"

"Ahem."

"Sorry, the next *devil*, but I expected more from the Coolest's oddity! You're sure you haven't got a knife? Damien, does he have a knife?"

"He doesn't, your Pusillanimous Verisimilitude."

"You didn't even look!"

"With respect, Sire, I don't have to. I'm not sure he even has the capacity for guile."

"Thank you," said Sloot.

"Offense intended," Damien replied.

"Oh."

"So you really just want to dance, then?" asked Yellow.

"Well, if the Axial Ledger is out of the question, then what else—"

Red shouted a swear word that made Sloot's teeth hurt.

"How long have you been a demon?" he demanded.

"About sixty thousand years."

"So not long, but long enough to have made a deal. You do know what deals are, don't you?"

"Yes, your Grievous Belligerence."

"Sloot," whispered Myrtle, "don't—"

"Silence!" Damien shrieked, then shrank away from the yellow devil's glare. He ran off to tidy a cherub on the other side of the room that didn't seem to need it.

"We can find another way," said Myrtle. "Making a deal with the Prime Evils won't end well."

Sloot had stopped listening. Not on purpose, of course, but his demonic instincts were screaming across every frequency in his brain. A deal with the Prime Evils! That was the big time. Sure, it would probably mean his ultimate destruction and eternal agony, but what if it didn't? What if he got really, *really* lucky, and—

"No, thank you." Instincts were one thing, but truths were another. Sloot had good reason to question everything that had transpired since the day that he corrected the Pritygud report, but not his luck. Or rather, his lack thereof.

The Evils exchanged a blank look.

"We could command you to deal with us," said Yellow.

"Of course," said Sloot, who knew in his whatever-demons-had-in-lieu-of-a-heart that it was true.

"We could command you to take the least favorable terms," said Red.

"I'd prefer if you didn't."

"Damien!" the Evils shouted in unison.

"Yes, your Pulchritudinous Disgraces?"

"It appears that the oddity is having some trouble understanding how deals with us work," said Yellow. "Educate him, won't you?"

"At once," said Damien with an obsequious bow. He put his arm around Sloot's shoulders and walked with him across the ballroom floor.

"Mister Peril," Damien sang, "have you ever heard the phrase, 'the thrill of the hunt?'"

Sloot nodded. He'd heard it, though he'd never understood it. "The thrill of the itemized deduction," now there was something he could get behind.

"We all enjoy it," Damien continued, "the smell of that first puff of smoke, bellowing at the necromancer, 'why hast thou summoned me, mortal?' It's a real treat, but only for a moment. We have our moment of wondering whether they'll take the deal, and then we get down to business. Do you know what I mean?"

"I'm very fond of getting down to business," Sloot said, picking his words carefully.

"There's a good lad. Mister Peril, I've been in personal servitude to the Prime Evils for aeons. Do you know how many times I've seen them enjoy the 'will they, won't they' of it for more than a minute or so?"

In Sloot's experience, the most pessimistic estimate was generally the most accurate.

"Is it none?"

"Give the lad a cigar! Flirting with them. Woo them. Make them feel like the sorts of senior villains who can still get their hands dirty. 'Can' being the operative word, understand? They lack the patience for the proper nitty-gritty of it. Am I making sense?"

"Of course," said Sloot. He'd worked in the Three Bells Counting House for years and seen countless middle managers working very hard at looking like they knew what they were doing.

"Good. Trust me when I tell you they've hit their limit. Be a good lad and take the deal."

"Oh, I wasn't—"

"What? You weren't what? Holding out to get some leverage? I know. I'm glad to know that you're the oddity, Mister Peril, otherwise I'd probably spend my next thousand or so lava baths wondering what sort of maniac wouldn't want to make a deal with the Prime Evils. I'm sure you're familiar with the concept of inevitability."

"I am." Sloot sighed. He didn't have to be a causality demon to see where this was going.

"I'm glad to hear it. Now, march."

Sloot hung his head and shuffled back toward the Prime Evils. He knew their type. They'd been at the top for so long they no longer considered the possibility they wouldn't get their way in the end. They thought of people as commodities, and considered their feelings with as much compassion as they would the feelings of old shoes.

He was going to make a deal with them whether he liked it or not. The only thing he knew for sure was that he wasn't going to like it.

"We've been getting to know your girlfriend," said Yellow. "Is it true that your head popped off at a wedding?"

"Er, yes," said Sloot. He hoped against hope that she wouldn't have any follow-up questions.

"Do you still have it?"

Sloot shook his head. His new one, he supposed.

"A pity," she said. "It would make an interesting conversation piece. The Head of the Oddity, can you imagine? Oh, well. We'll just have to dance for the Narrative instead."

"Oh, well, that's—what?"

"Do you know how rarely a demon is entrusted with such a large tract of Narrative? If we'd found it in the hands of any other demon, we'd have simply seized it. All demons are our rightful property, except you two. You're the Coolest's pets, so you can defy us. Let's have a test, shall we?"

"I'd rather not."

Yellow glowered at him. "That wasn't the test, but it proves my point. I was going to have you slam your face into that cherub's plinth until your face disintegrated. Would you mind?"

"Er, well, I suppose not."

"Sloot!" shouted Myrtle. "Don't do that, you need your face!"

"Oh, all right," said Sloot. He hoped she'd meant that in a utilitarian way, not that she'd seen the future and he'd need to rely on his looks to make a living. Sloot didn't have the sort of face that people would pay to see. But it *was* his face, and he didn't exactly relish the thought of disintegrating it upon a cherub's plinth.

"Interesting," said Red. "Does she have some sort of—"

"I'm his girlfriend," said Myrtle. "You just asked him politely, and he has a hard time refusing."

"Ah. In that case, would you please accept a trade? A peek at the Axial Ledger in exchange for your swath of the Narrative?"

"Er, I'm sorry," said Sloot, "but I can't. What good would it do to know how to fix it when I no longer can?"

"A valid point," said Red. "I suppose we'll have to go about it another way."

He exchanged a look with Yellow that incorporated far too many knowing sneers for Sloot's taste, not that he'd dream of saying anything to them. It was their look, after all.

"We'll give you your peek at the ledger," said Yellow. "Free of charge."

"Really?"

"Why not? It's nothing to us. After that, we'll finish the dance contest."

"Oh, dear," said Myrtle.

"What's wrong?"

"This isn't a simple *quid pro quo* deal," she said. "They're making it winner-take-all."

"Causality demons!" Red threw up his hands. "The element of surprise means nothing when they're around."

"I was able to draw logical conclusions before I became a demon, you know."

"No matter," said Yellow. "You'll have your peek at the Axial Ledger, and then we'll dance. If you win, you'll go forth from here knowing how to fix your tract of Narrative. But if we win, your souls belong to us."

"The two of us?"

"This is the most irksome part of all of this," said Yellow. "We're supposed to command the souls of all demons, yet here the two of you stand. Standing! Most demons can't rise up from the floor in our presence, yet here the two of you *stand*!"

"What about Damien?" asked Sloot.

"Forced to do it," said Damien with a smile, "against my instincts. Every moment is agony."

"You little rascal," said Red. He patted Damien on the head, then slapped him across the face. A fine mist of blood sprayed across the floor.

"Thank you, your Mercilessness." Damien's smile was full of blood, and his nose was pointing toward his ear.

"It will be good to have you in the fold where you belong," said Yellow. "Now, on with the formalities. Do we have a deal?"

She extended one clawed hand toward Sloot. He hesitated.

"These terms are entirely unfavorable."

"Of course they are," growled Red. "You're lucky to be getting any terms at all. I could simply devour your soul, you know."

"Oh, dear," said Sloot. "But wouldn't the Coolest-"

"Oh, yes, they'd be miffed," Red admitted. "But we're always sore at each other over something. They'd retaliate, we'd get mad and do something else, and the worlds would keep on turning. Your soul would still be devoured, though."

"Then it doesn't seem I have much of a choice."

The Prime Evils looked at each other and sighed.

"Damien!" they barked in unison.

Damien screamed in agony as he wrenched his nose back into its proper position.

"Ah, that's better," he said after an exploratory sniff that left a red tide down the front of his shirt. "There are no means of bypassing free will in making this deal. The Prime Evils cannot force you to enter into it. It must be your own choice."

"But you said—"

"I lied," said Red. He shrugged. "Evil."

"What do I do?" Sloot asked Myrtle.

"I'd tell you not to take the deal, but I know you end up looking at the ledger. It's the reason we've come."

Sloot's first lesson in inevitability had been conducted on the playground, pursuant to a fledgling bully's curiosity about the taste of dirt. He knew certitude when he saw it. He tried gathering his wits about him, but they resisted. He sobbed as he shook Yellow's hand.

"Show Mr. Peril to the library, won't you, Damien?" Red's teeth gleamed in the light of several cherubic chandeliers. "And do offer him a drink while he peruses the ledger."

THE AXIAL LEDGER

Sloot was already sitting in the library when Sloot arrived. That was unusual. He was sure of it.

"I merely do the Prime Evils' bidding," said Damien. "I wouldn't presume to take a side job interpreting manifestations for agents of the Coolest. In fact, I should probably stop talking altogether." And with that, he left.

The library was everything Sloot assumed it would be, from the leather-bound books that had probably never been opened to the enormous window overlooking a lake of fire. It was also several things that he'd not had the foresight to assume, namely that he'd be patiently awaiting his own arrival.

"Come on," Sloot's other self said, "we haven't got all day." So not *patiently* awaiting his own arrival, but there he was. Sloot took a seat at the table across from himself.

"What's going on, please?"

"I'm not sure how to put this in a way that you'll understand," said the other Sloot, "so I'll just put it out there and we'll work our way into it. I'm you."

"Then who am I?"

"You are who you've always been, and that's the problem."

"Then we're both me."

"In a manner of speaking, albeit an incorrect one."

"So, no."

The other Sloot looked thoughtfully upward. "Too much 'yes' for a simple 'no' to suffice. Would you accept that one of us is more Sloot than the other, and that we are very near to determining which?"

"I can try," said Sloot.

"It's a start." The other Sloot drew a copper coin from his pocket. "Do you know what this is?"

"Minimum collateral to open an account at the First Bank of Salzstadt."

"Try again, but simpler."

"A loaf of day-old bread."

"Simpler."

"A likeness of the Domnitor, long may he reign."

"It's a penny!" The other Sloot closed his eyes and let out a long, slow breath. "It's a *penny*, Sloot. But more than that, it's a marker in a cross-section of infinite possibilities."

"How is 'a marker in a cross-section of infinite possibilities' simpler than—"

"It isn't, but I had a presentation all planned out, and now you've—you know what? It isn't important. Just listen."

The other Sloot stood and started pacing.

"The universe is infinite across all axes," he began, "namely possibility. There's another point on the spectrum of universal possibility in which I drew a silver penny from my pocket. In another a pair of dice, another a fish, another nothing at all. Do you understand?"

Sloot nodded. He didn't like where this was going. There was going to be existentialism, he could tell.

"There are further possibilities in which our positions are reversed, or I didn't wear anything with pockets and asked you to pick a number instead. You'd have picked seventeen."

He was right. Seventeen was a strong prime number, Sloot's favorite.

"Some of these possibilities happen all at once. Others take time. Look at us, for example. Had our mother not decided to stay in the Old Country, this grand experiment never would have occurred, and we wouldn't be having this conversation right now."

"Oh," said Sloot. "What would we be talking about?"

"Nothing. You wouldn't exist."

"And you would?"

The other Sloot nodded.

"How do you know—"

"—that I wouldn't be the one who didn't exist? Because I wouldn't be your suppressed ego, I'd just *be* your ego. I mean *my* ego."

They were on firmer ground now. Sloot had heard of egos, though he'd thought they were a curse that afflicted the children of wealthy idiots.

"Everyone has an ego," the other Sloot clarified, anticipating Sloot's next question. "It's your sense of self, your inner voice."

"I'm fairly certain I don't have one."

"Yes, you do," said the other Sloot. "You just never listen! In fact, before this dance contest started, I don't think you ever heard a word I've said!"

"Wait, that was you?"

"Talking to you when you managed to relax your mind, yes. That was me. And now I've got to do anthropomorphic manifestations to hold your attention. Do you know how frustrating that is?"

"I'm having trouble getting past the fact you're here at all."

"I've always been here," said Sloot's ego, "you've just never had the presence of mind to listen. You're going to ask me why, but you're not going to like the answer."

"Oh," said Sloot, scrambling to keep up. "Then I'd—"

"You don't get to not hear it," said Sloot's ego, "or you've come here for no reason at all."

"But I've come here for a reason!"

"Which is?"

"To amend the Narrative," said Sloot. "To repair the damage that Roman's wager has done, to unspill the Dark, to set the world to rights!"

"That's right," said Sloot's ego. "And the only way to do that is to listen to your gut. Metaphorically speaking."

"I don't follow."

"You wouldn't. Look, you're not going to like this, but we're out of time. You don't listen to yourself because you've spent your entire life letting the Domnitor think for you."

"Long may he reign."

"Don't do that again."

"Don't do what again?"

"Recite the honorific after I mention the Domnitor."

"Long may he reign."

"You're not paying attention."

Sloot could no more suppress the reflex than pause his heartbeat. It wasn't a muscle he knew how to stop flexing.

"Sorry," said Sloot, shaking his head in agitation. "What are you doing here, exactly? I thought I was brought here to consult the Axial Ledger."

"That is what you're doing," said Sloot's ego, placing agitated emphasis on every word.

"But I don't see—"

"The forest for the trees! I know! We're an intelligent man, you and I. Why are you having so much trouble with this?"

"Because it's ridiculous! How can you be my ego and the Axial

Ledger?"

"I'm not. Not exactly. You're getting warmer, but you're still not asking the right questions."

"The right questions about what? None of this makes sense!"

"It would, if you'd just let go."

"But *that* doesn't make any sense! Of what should I let go? From the moment I corrected that ridiculous report, everything has gone wrong. My job, my city, my patriotic duty—my very life has gone spinning off into oblivion, and all that's left is me! I'm the only beacon in the darkness, the only thing that hasn't changed, the only person ... clinging..."

The bottom dropped out. Everything went black and spun around him. A pinpoint of light slowly opened into a chasm of stark, unblemished reality. Sloot fell toward it.

"What is this?" Sloot asked aloud.

"This is waking up," said his ego. Sloot looked around but couldn't see it. Him. Himself? It didn't matter. It was bad enough he'd heard such heresy. More terrifying still was the thought that he might want to listen.

Somewhere down there, on the plain of unredacted, full-fat truth, was a better world. One in which Uncle didn't carry jaywalkers off in the middle of the night, never to be seen again. One where swearing was just naughty words you didn't say in front of your gran, and if you did she scowled dutifully until you left and then had a good laugh. There was a world down there where the citizens of the Old Country and Carpathia complained about each other's boorish tourist mannerisms, but didn't go to bed wondering if the other was going to eat their children while they slept. In fairness, the Carpathians never worried about that. They had much more positive propaganda.

It was hard to take it all in a single glance, but Sloot had seen enough to understand one crucial truth.

"My life has been a lie," he said.

Sloot was in the library again. The chair across from him was empty, but he could still hear the voice. *The* voice. And he understood, at last, what it was. He'd been avoiding it his entire life, the voice telling him to stand up. To say no. To make the hard choice.

"Wrong," said the voice. Said *his* voice. No, start again. *Wrong*, Sloot thought.

His life hadn't been a lie. That was an oversimplification. He knew those when he saw them, great comforts to which he'd clung all his life. They kept him from having to look the truth squarely in the face.

Sloot's life hadn't been a lie, but he'd spent it lying to himself. The biggest lie, the one to which he'd clung since he'd first met the Coolest, was the idea that everything could go back to the way that it was.

All that's left is me, he thought. *The only thing that hasn't changed.*

"Looks like someone's had an epiphany!" sang Damien from behind him. "I hope it's brought you some sort of closure or something. You've got a dance contest to lose."

SPIRIT VIOLATIONS

"For the last time," Myrtle sighed, "I don't want any refreshments."

"You'd really be doing me a favor," said Damien, waving a tray of canapes at her. "They might not poison the bed of nails before my bedtime tonight, if only I can—"

"He's really bad at this," laughed Red. "Persistent, though. Ha! We do laugh together, don't we, Damien?"

"We do, your Carnivorous Malfeasance." Damien choked back a tear and shuffled away with his untouched canapes.

"Did you get what you needed?" asked Myrtle.

"I hope so," said Sloot.

"You hope so? We've gone to a lot of trouble, you know."

"I know. Let's just worry about the dance for now, shall we?"

Myrtle merely nodded and gave Sloot a look, reserving the right to say "I told you so" in perpetuity if things went poorly.

"All right, all right," came a false baritone from behind Sloot. "Let's get on with this, shall we?"

"Damien? Why are you wearing a false moustache?"

"Damien?" asked Damien. "I know no Damien! I am Professor Burstingspleen of the Infernal Dance Academy, judge for the final round. Shall we begin?"

"You heard the professor," said Yellow. "Bring out the orchestra, will you?"

Red pulled a velvet cord. A little bell tinkled.

"This is a joke, right?" Myrtle fumed at Damien, or whatever he was calling himself.

"Not a very good one," Red admitted. "We have to follow the rules, but there's no oversight. Going through the motions, that's all. We don't have to be convincing."

"Yes, well, I suppose," Sloot began. He paused. He shook his head. "Wait, no!"

"No?" Red sounded amused.

All that's left is me, Sloot thought. *The only thing that hasn't changed.*

"Rigging a contest is one thing," said Sloot, "but we've got an official demonic bargain on the line! There are other rules, you can't—"

"We *can't?* We can't *what?*" The ground cracked beneath Yellow's cloven hooves. It wasn't a question—it was a warning. And not a very subtle one at that.

"You can't violate the spirit of your own bargain," said Sloot. His heart tried to leap out of his chest, which was far less metaphorical for demons than for mortals, but he was beginning to understand what he'd told himself in the library. He resisted the timid voice in his head that screamed at him to play along and hope for the best. It was time for Sloot Peril to change.

"This will never stand up in the chaos courts," Sloot persisted. "My attorneys will take one look at this and—"

A rapid-fire series of smoky black explosions burst around them. Each one revealed an attorney in an expensive suit. The last was Ms. Meatsacrifice, who directed an imp to circulate a scroll for everyone's signature.

"Conflict of interest," she said simply. "We won't be getting involved. This conversation is billable as a seven-hour minimum consultation. We'll put it on your tab, Mr. Peril."

There was another series of explosions as the attorneys departed.

"That's got to hurt," said Yellow. "They trotted everyone out for that, I think."

"I'd have threatened us with 'my attorney,' if I were you. Singular." Red winked.

"Duly noted," said Sloot. His mind raced. Was this really it? Should he have asked to read the fine print on the bargain he'd made with the Prime Evils? It occurred to him that yes, he probably should have.

"Where is that orchestra?" demanded Red. Everyone turned in the direction that Red was looking. They watched nothing happen for a moment. When that was over, Igor walked into the room.

"Igor!" shouted Sloot.

"Sloot," said Igor.

"What have you done with my orchestra?" demanded Red.

"Nothing, your Desultory Horrificness!" Igor threw himself onto the floor, which wasn't a long trip.

"Then where are they?"

"Boiling in sulfur, I presume."

"And why would that be?"

"They had the canapes." Igor failed to fully repress a giggle.

Red sighed. Yellow laughed.

"What's so funny?" Red snapped.

"Oh, come on," said Yellow. "They ate the canapes! Even these two ninnies knew better!"

"But we can't have a dance contest without music!" Red fumed.

A glimmer of hope! Sloot felt a cool breeze waft across him. If he played the next few moments just right, perhaps he could—

"Perhaps I might be of service, your Voracious Ingratitude." Igor gave his bit of wire a twang.

"Igor! What are you doing?" Sloot hissed.

"Getting you that trophy," Igor whispered. "I've watched you and Myrtle, you're really good! You can take these two, unless they've bribed the judge or something."

"Proceed, wretched subject." Yellow's teeth gleamed with venomous glee.

Sloot sighed. Igor trotted off toward the orchestra pit. Sloot considered hiring Igor as his bard so he could officially fire him.

The Prime Evils were sublime dancers. *They would be,* Sloot groused. It didn't matter that they danced to the tune of an over-twanged bit of wire instead of what must have been a perfectly orchestrated accompaniment for their exquisite choreography. To have called it poetry in motion would have done it no justice. Poets would kill for that comparison.

"Flawless," Professor Burstingspleen gushed. "A sublime performance! Extra points awarded for the unforeseen change of musical accompaniment!"

Myrtle said a swear word. Red winked at her in appreciation.

"How are we supposed to beat that?" whispered Myrtle. "Even if we do, we can't expect *Professor Burstingspleen* to declare us the winner."

She was right. Sloot wanted to give up, to sit down on the floor and settle into a nice wallow. It might be his last one that didn't involve millions of carnivorous insects.

All that's left is me, Sloot thought. *The only thing that hasn't changed.*

"Come on." Sloot took Myrtle by the hand and led her onto the dance floor.

"I hope you've got a plan," said Myrtle, her voice quavering on the edge of despair.

He didn't have a plan. He didn't even have hope. What he did have, in unexpected abundance, was defiance. If this was his last hurrah before spending eternity as a sewage worker's ashtray, he'd choke on bitter embers in the remembrance of dancing with his love. Even if the Prime Evils beat him fair and square, they'd been worried enough to rig the contest anyway. He'd be the ashtray that had stared evil incarnate in the face, and evil had blinked.

"Sloot?" Myrtle gave him a quizzical look.

"Oh," said Sloot, mirroring her confusion. "Why haven't I moved?"

"I don't know, are the Prime Evils playing some sort of trick?"

Sloot waved his arms at his sides. He took an experimental step forward. It worked, though he wasn't sure whether he should be surprised about that or not.

"You're not conceding, are you?" Yellow taunted him.

"No," said Sloot matter-of-factly. "I'm just trying to figure out why my legs won't work, that's all."

"Oh, good," said Red. "I do love it when our victory is embarrassing for our opponents."

"Can you not control your legs?" asked Myrtle. "That would be a problem *vis-a-vis* dancing."

"I can," said Sloot, "but they only work when I think about them!"

Realization colonized Myrtle's face, driving out the indigenous confusion. "You've let go."

"A bit too much, I think."

"The Axial Ledger," said Myrtle, "it sorted you out, right?"

"Sort of. I think it means I have to dance for myself."

Red harrumphed. "Isn't there a penalty for delay of game? Where is the referee, is he blind?"

"Dead," said Professor Burstingspleen, who wasn't fooling anyone. "Has been ever since you went a bit *enthusiastic* in blinding him."

"Hardly an excuse," said Red. "Get on with it!"

"You have to focus," said Myrtle. "Letting go was a mnemonic, a way to distract your timidity long enough for your fearlessness to shine. Now that you know the truth, it's not going to work. You've got to dance for yourself!"

"Hang on," said Igor, the irritation plain in his voice. "All of your shouting has made me lose my place. I'll start over. A-one, and a-two, and..."

Igor launched into a new round of twanging that could only have been considered rhythmic by a skilled mathematician, or possibly a historian. History repeats itself. On a long enough timeframe, everything becomes a rhythm. Even Igor could achieve theoretical fame on a geological timeline.

Sloot suppressed his panic. He'd had some basic lessons, so he wasn't entirely at sea with dancing, but he'd done his finest rug-cutting when he hadn't been paying attention. He'd worked hard at staying out of his own way.

He was just starting to think existentially about his ego when something entirely unexpected happened. His instincts took over.

His whole life, Sloot had been sure he didn't have any. Had he been told he'd taken breathing lessons as an infant, he'd not have doubted it for a second.

He was moving on purpose, but it seemed to be working. Most of the effort was in paying just the right amount of attention. He couldn't give his hips specific directions, but if he let himself feel the rhythm–such as it was–and willed them in a particular direction, they'd fill in the gaps. The most bizarre part was his hands. He knew what to do with them! Before that moment, he'd scarcely known what to do with them while sitting in a chair alone. But now, as long as he wasn't overly specific, his hands moved appropriately along with the dance.

Myrtle was spinning toward him. He risked a glance at her face, and their eyes met mid-turn. That glance held nothing but bliss. He'd have stretched it out for an eternity if he trusted himself not to lose his place when time inevitably caught back up again.

This, thought Sloot. *It was all worth it for this.* He willed himself toward her, and they embraced for a series of steps that would have compelled any children present to leave the room. They glistened with sweat. They no longer needed the music, which was good because technically, they didn't have any. All that mattered was each other, and the certainty that each step was the right one.

They ringed and whirled, dipped and spun, stepped and stepped again until the fiery crescendo, which ended in literal fire. One of Sloot's legs stretched far behind Myrtle, the other pointed straight up in the air. He arched his back like a recurved swan, staring up at the cherubic mural on the ceiling in Myrtle's firm embrace.

The Prime Evils applauded as Myrtle gently drew Sloot back up to his feet.

Professor Burstingspleen said a swear word that singed Sloot's nose hairs.

"I've never seen dancing like that," he added.

"We're standing right here," said Yellow, but she couldn't seem to muster the appropriate degree of menace. She and Red were awestruck.

"Er," said the professor, shaking his head, "rarely have I seen such a close competition! You've earned a commanding second place."

A chuckle fell out of Sloot's mouth. It was followed by another. Was this instincts? He didn't know, but it seemed as plausible as anything else. They'd lost. There would be no appeal, not when the Prime Evils made up the rules on a whim.

"Sloot?" Myrtle's expression was at least one-part concern for his state of mind. It was also several thousand parts panic over having lost her soul to the Prime Evils.

Sloot just laughed harder. What else could he do? The entire tableau was absurd.

"Quiet your tittering, slave," said Yellow.

"And why should I? What are you going to do, torture me *more* for eternity? Or maybe you'll make eternity last longer."

"You've lost," Yellow declared. "The better dancers won, and now—"

Igor hurled a swear word toward the Prime Evils that smelled like rotten fish processed through the guts of rotten cats.

"How dare you?" growled Red.

"Don't get me wrong, your Absolute Tardiness, you two put on a spectacular show. But no one here can honestly say your performance was better."

"They wouldn't dare," Professor Burstingspleen seemed to agree. "Anyone caught using honesty here would be forced to dig their own eyes out with a grapefruit spoon and feed them to the attorneys one circle down."

Myrtle raised an eyebrow.

"So I've been told," the professor muttered.

"I'll tell you what," said Red, "at the end of the ball, it's tradition for everyone to come up and leave through the first circle, so they can all see how much better everyone above them has it. We'll hold off on your first trip to the flaying pits until everyone has had a chance to laugh at your horrible fate."

"Oh," said Igor, "so it's time for that, is it?"

"It is," said Yellow.

Damien removed his false moustache with a flourish, winking at Sloot as though to say, "it was me the whole time!" He took a trumpet from a nearby cherub and blew a long, terrible note. The doors to the foyer opened, and all of the demons they'd seen on the way up began shuffling through.

"Don't think this means we can't find a way to bill you," said Ms. Meatsacrifice. She chuckled mirthlessly. All of the attorneys following her did the same. Sloot couldn't help but be just a little bit impressed by that level of toadying.

Trans-substantial entities, personal trainers, prima ballerinas, and lackadaisical teenage demons all took turns sneering at Sloot and Myrtle as they passed. So did Baelgoroth the Destroyer, who wasn't much good at it, though Sloot shivered as he stared into Blagderos' button eyes.

"This is taking forever," said Myrtle.

"Yeah," said Igor. "It sure does take a lot of time for everyone to come through, doesn't it?"

Sloot nodded absently. He didn't remember dancing against any plague demons, but as a pair of them passed by, their snarls said they remember dancing against him.

"Yep," said Igor, raising his voice. "Pretty soon it will be time to close the doors, and then you'll be out of time. Oh, what a time to be a demon!"

Myrtle squinted at Igor. Sloot was starting to get the impression that the gremlin was trying to tell him something.

"I still don't think it's right that we didn't win," snapped one of the entitlement demons from the 72nd circle, "just because we lost. To whom can I appeal this decision?"

"To us," said Yellow and Red in unison.

"Oh," said the demon. "Well, who has the time?"

"Excellent question!" shouted Igor. "Who *does* have the time? I'd certainly like to know what time it is. Sloot, do you have the time?"

Instinct took over–see, he knew he had them–and he reached for his watch. His watch! He reached up and patted his breast pocket, feeling the comforting hunk of tin. Greta said he'd stored about a second, which she'd turned into three by manipulating the perception of time by inversion. It would never have been enough to find and consult the Axial Ledger, but how much time did he need to escape?

It dawned on him, as he racked his brain for a plan, that everyone was staring at him.

"Er, no," he said, dropping his hand. "Not yet."

Igor sighed in relief.

"You're about to," Red gloated. "You're about to have all eternity."

Sloot suppressed a smile. Not long ago, a very different Sloot Peril would have been near catatonic and whimpering in the fetal position. But now he was the accountant who'd out-danced the devil. They had to cheat to beat him, and now in the face of eternal agony, he had the audacity to hope. Three seconds poised in his pocket, ready to tick, were all that stood between him and a fate worse than oblivion.

Despite all logic, he liked his chances.

"Better you than me," said Grudzrak Shale, the troll from the 81st circle. The fire sprite with whom she'd danced sat on her shoulder. The pair of them paused to take in the splendor of the first circle's ballroom, then sneered at Sloot obediently and departed.

"Far better than you deserve," said Yellow. "Second place is first loser, after all."

"If your opponents don't deserve your respect," said Myrtle, "your victory is worthless."

"Shut up," said Yellow, her face contorting with rage. "I'm going to make you regret that for a very, very long time."

Myrtle said nothing else until the line of demonic faces became familiar. Her coworkers from the 99th circle laughed in delight.

"Thought you were better than us, eh?" Gutsbag snorted.

"We *were* better than you," said Myrtle. "We were better than everyone, all the way up."

"Except the Prime Evils," Gutsbag flounced.

Myrtle grinned at Yellow. Yellow pretended not to notice.

"See you Monday, then?" asked Gutsbag.

"Probably not," said Myrtle.

"There are Mondays in the Inferno?" Sloot mused.

"There are *only* Mondays in the Inferno," Gutsbag corrected him. "Anyway, good luck. Not that it exists."

As they watched the last sewage elementals slouch off through the outer door, Sloot's brain finally found the traction it needed.

"A distraction," he risked whispering to Igor.

Igor nodded.

"Well, that's that," said Red. "Damien, go and close the outer door, will you? My darling and I need to argue about what to shove into Mr. Peril's ear first."

Damien nodded and started walking toward the door.

"How about my instrument?" offered Igor.

"Your … instrument?"

"Yeah," said Igor, "my bit of wire? The instrument of their defeat, as it were. The first instrument of their torture? Poetic, right?"

"Ooo, I do love poetry," said Yellow with a wicked grin.

You would, thought Sloot. He was convinced that poetry had been invented in the Inferno and found its way up to the coffee shops in the Narrative for the expressed purpose of ruining coffee. As if cappuccinos needed any assistance.

"Here it is," Igor said, holding his instrument aloft. "Which one of your Maddening Perturbances gets the first poke?"

"I do," said Yellow, "naturally."

"Naturally?" Red pondered aloud. "Any why is that? We're both spawned of the same wretched blackness, after all."

Yellow laughed. "You don't think it should be *you,* do you?"

Igor winked at Sloot. It was a casual, swaggering wink that acknowledged how easy he'd made it look. He'd earned it, Sloot had to admit. But as Sloot reached for his watch, Igor's wink was forced to make way for wide-eyed panic. Sloot followed his gaze to and saw Damien's hand on the outer door. His time was up!

Almost.

Sloot pressed the button on top of the watch, opening its face.

He didn't know precisely what he expected to see, or whether it would be what he needed, but he needn't have worried about it. After all, it was *his* time, and he had instincts now.

One.

Sloot's first second passed in torpor. He moved through the thickness of it with what passed for speed, given the circumstances.

Yig's Kerfuffle! It was the first thing he'd had installed on his circle, in case he couldn't find his way back to his apartment. His right hand activated it as his left grabbed Myrtle.

Two.

He felt Igor's claws digging into his leg. They slid between the timelines with nausea-inducing speed and banged their elbows on the closing door as the velvet blackness of the void slipped around them.

Three.

THE WAR CHAMBER

"Oh, no," Myrtle groaned, "what circle is this?"

"This is my apartment."

"Oh." Myrtle's eyebrows slithered in discomfort as she looked around the place. It didn't take long.

"It's cozy," she said at last.

"Make yourself at home," said Igor. "Everyone else does."

"Yes," said Sloot, "about that—"

"Then we're really out?" Tears welled in Myrtle's eyes.

Sloot nodded, and had no time to steel himself for the ruthless onslaught of Myrtle's embrace. She hugged him with a punishing fury.

"Are you laughing or crying?" asked Sloot.

"Both, I guess. Oh, Sloot! I knew you'd come!"

"Right. You predicted it."

"You're wasting an opportunity to claim heroic credit."

"Er, thanks, but you did most of the work."

"It's easy to be brave when you call the lowest circle of the Inferno home. There's literally nowhere to go but up. But you walked into the Inferno for me. You had to break in!"

Sloot shrugged. "It's easy to be brave for your true love."

Sloot's face was spared the most brutal kissing of its life by a knock at the door.

"Who could that be?"

"Don't try pretending you're not at home," said Willie. "I can hear you in there, you know."

Sloot opened the door.

"Well, that makes sense," he said. "Vampires have extra keen hearing, don't they? Er, don't *you*?"

"I mean, yeah," said Willie, "but these walls are so thin you can practically see through them."

"Don't you mean *valls*?"

"Bartleby's not here, is she?"

"Wait," said Myrtle, "Willie's a vampire now?"

"Obviously," said Willie, rolling his eyes. "Didn't you get an invitation to my coming out party? Aren't you rich?"

"I'm Carpathian nobility, or at least I was. Sloot, is my house still there?"

"I haven't checked," said Sloot. "We can do it now, if you like."

"I suppose so," said Willie. "Ve have to go to Carpathia anyvay."

"Why?"

"I don't know!" Willie stomped his foot. "It's like a rule or something, but what's wrong with Ws? My name starts with one!"

"No, I meant why do we have to go to Carpathia?"

"Invite me in."

"What?"

Willie's eyes went smoky and bright. His fingers grew joints that shouldn't be there, and his voice seemed to come from within Sloot's own mind.

"Invite me in," Willie whispered into the depths of Sloot's desire, until that was all that he wanted to do.

"Please, come in," said Sloot. He took a step back from the door.

"Thanks!" Willie flashed a guileless smile that would have made a shark cringe. "On second thought, let's go out. Your apartment makes me sad."

Willie turned and left. Sloot and Myrtle exchanged a glance and a shrug, then followed him out into the night.

"Where are we going?" asked Igor.

"Castle Ulfhaven," said Willie.

"It's the middle of the night," Igor whined. "Can't it wait until morning?"

"Oh," said Willie. He stopped dead in his tracks, having been nearly sufficiently intelligent to have grasped the pun. "Yeah, all right."

"Er, you're a vampire, Willie."

"Thanks." Willie struck a pose that was too dressy for casual occasions, but not quite formal enough for white tie.

"I mean, isn't the morning rather inconvenient for you?"

"Good point," said Willie. "I didn't pack a morning tuxedo. They wrinkle."

It would suffice, thought Sloot.

On the walk to the Crags, Willie explained that quite a lot had transpired while Sloot had been away. He also went on at length about the rigidity of the vampire dress code, and Sloot had a devil of a time keeping him on topic.

Gregor was back. If Sloot understood correctly, there was a complication when Franka became the new steward of the Skeleton Key Circle. Ever the forward thinker, Gregor had placed minor enchantments on bits of the Soul remains. A finger here, a toe there. When Franka soothed them, she inadvertently helped Gregor find his way out of the Dark and into the most dangerous place one could make available to an evil necromancer.

"Zurogravia," said Sloot. "All of the Soul remains were in Zurogravia! Oh, dear, there are a lot of dead things there."

"What's Zurogravia?" asked Myrtle.

"An old place," said Sloot. "A graveyard built atop a graveyard."

"And Gregor is there," said Myrtle. "Oh, Sloot, that's bad! What about Franka?"

"Barely made it out alive," said Willie. "Not that it's done her any good."

"What?"

"I mean, she's still wearing mountain climbing gear, or whatever. She's wasting her fashion potential."

Willie knew how to rant about fashion, and his skill had taken a dark turn since his ritual patricide and subsequent ritual murder. His treatises on sleeve lengths had gone from ridiculous to deeply troubling. His eyes were bestial by the time they reached the crags, such that the crazy old demon hunters gave them a wide berth.

"They're calling it 'mass transit,'" Igor explained. Willie already had a full head of steam from his sartorial fulminations, which he ably redirected toward the concept of trains.

"Dangerous idea," he said, shaking his head. "Look, they let poors in here! Maybe they could make them pull the train or something."

"They've got a steam contraption for that."

Willie shook his head. "It'll give people ideas. They'll lose sight of the value of hard work."

"Are you saying that everyone should have to work for what they have?" Myrtle's arms were folded. She longed to be given a reason.

"Not everyone, obviously. Some of us are rich."

"You weren't rich that long ago," Igor pointed out.

"A temporary malaise."

"You were destitute!"

"I got better."

Myrtle rolled her eyes and rested her head on Sloot's shoulder. In spite of the grave danger toward which they undoubtedly sped, he couldn't suppress a smile.

The rest of the journey passed with minimal jostling, overcrowding, and undue turbulence. There wasn't even an excess of panhandling, though the statutory minimums seemed to have been met. They emerged from the cave just before dawn, flying quickly to reach Castle Ulfhaven with Willie intact.

"You could have walked," Sloot told Igor, who'd complained the entire way.

"Fat chance. I'll not be left behind, not when heroics are afoot."

"Well, you'll walk next time if you complain like that."

"You were weaving!"

"There was a flock of ducks!" Sloot was fairly certain there was another name for it, but he didn't want to interrupt the pace of their repartee.

"And you're not curious what happens when duck strikes demon in mid-flight? You're no fun."

"It's different when you're the demon," said Sloot, despite it being obvious. He'd been accused of many things in his day but being fun had yet to count among them.

Upon arriving at the castle, they were escorted by fairy soldiers directly to the war chamber. They paid no heed to Igor's assurances that he knew the way, owing—Sloot assumed—to the chandelier incident that happened to coincide with their last visit.

"Unlucky, that," said Igor.

One of the guards gave a high-pitched harrumph. It was lost in the din of the war chamber, where familiar faces were arguing with each other.

"Captain Hapsgalt has returned," the guard shouted through a little megaphone. "Along with Captain Peril, Captain Pastry, and their *bard*."

"Splendid!" came a tiny voice. It was familiar, but Sloot couldn't quite place it.

"*Captain* Peril?" asked Sloot.

"It was General Dandelion's idea," said Willie. "We're going to war, so we all get to be captains."

"It's only fair," said Dandelion, his chest puffed up as he strode forth to greet them. "Of course, there can only be one general, or else—what is *that* doing here, please?"

Dandelion stared daggers at Igor. Cheese knives might have been more appropriate, given his outer layer of filth.

"Er, that's Igor," said Sloot.

"That'll be *Captain* Igor, will it not?"

"No," said Dandelion, "it will not! Will you explain why you've brought a gremlin into the castle, please?"

"No gremlin here," said Igor. "I'm a bard."

"I know a gremlin when I see one, thank you very much."

"You're welcome. I'm reformed, your generalship."

Dandelion got as close to Igor as his olfactory senses would allow and gave him a good staring down. A military staring down. A sneering maneuver with jaw flexes thrown in, the likes of which would crack casual deceit like an egg and have its yolk of truth sunny side up in seconds. But whether there was no mistruth to crack or Igor was a master trickster, Sloot couldn't tell.

"We wouldn't have escaped the Inferno without him," Myrtle offered.

"That's true," said Sloot. "He's not much of a bard, but he's handy to have around."

"Not *much* of a bard," Igor beamed, "but a bard nonetheless." He batted his eyelashes—or rather the dust motes clinging to his leathery eyelids—at Sloot, who avoided eye contact.

"Very well," said Dandelion. "He's not a captain, though. Provisional Lance Corporal."

"That sounds fancy," said Igor.

"It isn't."

"When do I get some tall boots and a riding crop?"

"You'll be horse-whipped if you're caught with either."

Igor shrugged the shrug of someone pretending to have them anyway.

"Sloot, is that you?"

Sloot turned around and lowered his gaze. He only recognized Nicoleta by the glaring pink-and-orange robes she was wearing.

"Oh, dear," said Myrtle. "What happened to you?"

"It's part of the process," said Bartleby, who was pushing Nicoleta's wheelchair. "She's nearly finished becoming a lich, it von't be long now."

Nicoleta looked to be well over a hundred years old, though Sloot thought she was perhaps thirty last time he'd seen her. That had been a few weeks ago, though a great deal of Infernal time that had passed for him since then.

"A lich?" Myrtle's eyebrows knotted. "I thought you hated necromancy."

"What?"

"I said I thought you hated necromancy!" shouted Myrtle.

"It's not my favorite," Nicoleta wheezed, "but it's inevitable. We'll all be dead again soon. I want to do it on my own terms."

Sloot was suddenly stricken with envy. Not for Nicoleta's decrepit state, but for her spirit. She was the sort of person who could pull off saying things like, "oh, yeah, and who's going to make me?"

"I'm glad you made it back," said Bartleby. "This fight is going to be vicked cool! You vouldn't vant to miss it."

"Indeed," said Sloot, who was as keen on watching a fight as being in one. "Hopefully it'll be over quickly."

"What did he say?" asked Nicoleta.

"He said he hopes the fight vill be over qvickly!"

"Unlikely," Nicoleta growled. "I owe Gregor a death, and I'm going to take my time."

"What, you're going to fight him?" Myrtle balked. "You're in no condition! What if—"

"That's what I'm counting on, dear." Nicoleta placed an arthritic hand on Myrtle's with gentle authority.

"I hope you know what you're doing." Sloot saw Myrtle racking her brain for something less futile to say.

"We almost finished Gregor last time," said Franka, who'd snuck effortlessly up behind Sloot, not that she needed any real skill to pull that off. Sloot squeaked and whirled.

"Your face," he said, his voice filled with concern.

"A scratch," said Franka, tapping her eyepatch with a gloved finger. A scar ran underneath it from her hairline to her jaw. She smiled sardonically. "A convenient gutter for my tears, if I ever take up weeping."

"There are my comrades in arms!" Willie had a remarkable talent for bluster. Sloot wondered if he knew there would be no *hors d'oeuvres* at the battle, or even a cash bar. "Ready to discuss the surrender, are ve? How much vill it cost us to get out of this one?"

Sloot blinked.

"We're not surrendering, you coward!" Franka sneered at Willie in contempt. Sloot was pleased not to be the target of a "you coward" for once.

"And why would we, please?" Dandelion fluttered into the circle of newly minted captains. "Franka knows the battlefield better than anyone, don't you, please?"

Franka nodded once. It conveyed a certainty that a second nod would have ruined with its eagerness.

"Everyone has their orders, I presume."

"I was just coming to that, General," said Franka.

"Very good! Proceed, Major."

"Major?" asked Willie.

"Is there a problem, Captain?"

"It's *Honorary* Captain, thank you, Major."

"Right." Franka sniffed. "How could I have forgotten?"

"So what is the plan?" asked Myrtle.

"I'll need about an hour," said Franka. "Portals to Zurogravia can only be opened from within, part of the magical defenses."

"Speak up, young lady!" demanded Nicoleta.

"There's a chapel between the inner sanctum and the foyer!" Franka yelled. "It's as close as I can get! I'll open the portal there!" And with that, she stalked off.

Familiar panic welled up in Sloot's gastric passages. An hour? And then they'd have to face Gregor? He wasn't prepared for that! He'd just put everything he had into the dance contest! He needed time to plan, to buy a more practical suit, to get some new runes installed on his circle, to make a few investments—was there such a thing as life insurance for demons? He'd already died, but he felt that had been resolved.

It wasn't panic. Sloot knew panic when he felt it. This was different. Like someone had wrapped panic in a blanket, sat on it, and said, "you can get up when you calm down." Behind the roar of panic, there had always been a voice telling him there was a chance it would all work out.

It was different now. He was the voice.

There's a chance it will all work out, thought Sloot. It was remote, but a chance nonetheless. He didn't shout it back across the panic. He didn't have to. He'd heard it this time.

"Sloot?"

"Greta." Sloot blinked away the fog of his reverie. "Yes? Hello! What are you wearing?"

Sloot hadn't expected to see her wearing a suit of gleaming platemail armor. It was well-crafted, not an off-the-rack number.

"Some of us don't have the benefit of demonic powers," said Greta. "Battlefields tend to be dangerous."

"Right," said Sloot, "but why would you—"

"Don't you dare," Greta barked, "don't you *dare* finish that sentence! Do you doubt me because I'm a clock maker, or because I'm a woman?"

"Neither, I just—"

"I've got very little left, Sloot. There was a time when I'd have been content to spend my whole life in the shop with my clocks, but then Willie brought me a mammoth and you tricked me into going to Carpathia." She held up a hand. "Yes, you did. I'm not angry about it. My life changed forever in Carpathia. My time there made me who I am. I learned to fight, though I don't remember doing it, and now my machine and I are going to help the fairies defeat the goblins."

"Your machine?" asked Sloot.

"A goblin organ, based on a book I read while I was Mrs. Knife's captive."

"I didn't know goblins had musical instruments."

"They shouldn't," said Greta, "it sounds awful. But they seem to like it."

"Did someone say 'musical instruments?'" asked Igor, the question loaded to bursting with ammunition.

"No, Igor," said Sloot. "Well, yes, but I didn't mean—"

"You should play it," said Greta.

"What? No! He has no talent!"

"I'm standing right here," mumbled Igor.

"That's perfect," said Greta, suddenly very excited. "It's designed to be played by a goblin, but we don't have any in our ranks. I can't play a proper goblin shanty, even my worst efforts are too melodious. But he's a gremlin!"

"Reformed."

"Close enough. I'll bet your playing can keep them occupied while Sloot deals with Mrs. Knife."

Rotten produce. Rat poison. Carpathian blood brandy. All things upon which Sloot would have preferred choking rather than dealing with Mrs. Knife.

Sloot said a swear word. She was his problem, wasn't she? He didn't have the slightest idea how he was going to deal with her.

"Sloot?" Greta paused, exhaled, and put on a smile. It was an I-want-something-from-you smile, if Sloot had ever seen one. "Listen, I need to ask you some questions that I'm not sure you're going to be able to answer, but that's fine. Don't be nervous."

Don't be nervous. The phrase exists in every language, and it doesn't work in any of them. She may as well have shouted at him to relax this very instant.

"I'll try," said Sloot, who didn't.

"What can you tell me about Vlad?"

Sloot panicked. What if he meowed at her again? Vlad had to win Greta back, and Sloot was mystically forbidden from saying so. That was Bartleby's theory, anyway.

"What do you want to know?" he asked, evading her as deftly as he could.

"Oh, you know. Just the basics, I suppose."

That was a relief. She was being coy! Like most men of the Old Country, Sloot was completely at sea with things like subtlety, hints, and innuendo. He could play dumb, and he'd hardly be playing.

"She's recently come from Blasigtopp," said Sloot, sticking to the safe and boring facts. Hopefully it would end the conversation quickly.

"I knew that," said Greta, "but what else? What's her situation?"

"Er, she's seated." That was true. Vlad's eyes were half-closed, and she sat on the stone floor with her feet on top of her legs. Sloot's knees hurt just looking at it.

"Stop being so literal," said Greta, a scowl probing her facade for cracks. "You know her, don't you?"

"Not well." That was also true. Vlad was well-known by reputation, but the details of her personal life were as public as the inside of a brick.

"Then it shouldn't be hard to tell me what you *do* know."

"She's fierce," said Sloot, digging deep for trivial facts that had a remotely romantic tint. "She won't do what's easy if it isn't what's right. She earns the respect of anyone who meets her and lives to tell about it."

"Lives to tell about it? Isn't she a pacifist?"

"Yes," said Sloot, "but she hasn't always been."

"What was she before?"

Oh, nice one, Peril. He'd over-extended and found himself grasping at straws. His found mystery in his grip. Mystery! He didn't have a talent for that! Oh, well, it was better than "hey, what's that over your shoulder," and running the other way.

"She was what she was," said Sloot mysteriously. "To say more than that would betray her trust. You'd do well to earn it on your own."

Greta's head tipped slightly in thought. Sloot seized the opportunity to nod and walk away.

Mysterious! He'd done it! He resisted the urge to punch the air in celebration.

Vlad was looking at him. Her expression didn't change, but she nodded to him, and for once the subtlety wasn't lost on him. "Well done," said the nod. In all his days, he'd never dreamed to earn a respectful nod from Vlad the Invader. She wasn't "the Invader" anymore, but she was no less Vlad for it. Sloot would carry the memory of that nod with him for the rest of his days, of which he hoped there would be a plurality.

"Sloot!" King Lilacs waved him over to where he was standing with his retinue. "Sorry, *Captain Peril,* isn't it, please? Congratulations on the promotion, though we hadn't considered just how dashing the moniker would be."

"No, we hadn't," said Dandelion. "It doesn't strike you as unfairly dashing, does it, please?"

"It might," said Sloot. It made him sound like someone who wore a cape and stared down from rooftops over the naked city, daring evil-doers to step out of line.

"Oh, dear, that will never do! And with the battle so close at hand, I'm afraid we don't have time to change the paperwork. Whatever shall we do, please? This could be a real blow to morale."

Sloot said nothing. Nothing could have prepared him for being considered obscenely dashing. He stuck out his jaw and stared up toward the ceiling, hoping it came off as what strong, silent types did.

"Your Majesty," said Myrtle. She curtseyed to the king. "Why the dour faces, please?"

"It's Captain Peril," said Lilacs. "Do you think the moniker is too dashing, please?"

Myrtle turned to consider Sloot.

"Well," she said, clearing her throat, "do you remember his performance at the last battle, please? The one with the goblin army at the Old Country border?"

"I do, thank you." Lilacs spared Sloot a sidelong glance. He was too polite to say it, but Sloot had carried himself in a manner as heroic as compost is witty.

"Perhaps," Myrtle continued, "your fine soldiers will think 'Captain Peril' is ironic."

Sloot's heart sank. Bad enough it might be true without his girlfriend saying it.

"Quite possible," Dandelion nodded. "Probable, in fact."

"Well," said Myrtle, "there you have it." She curtseyed and

gave Sloot a kiss on the cheek.

Sloot sighed and nodded. If life had taught him anything, it was that he was ill-suited to occupational heroics.

"May I offer you a piece of advice, please?"

"Of course, your Majesty."

"All of us were what we were," said Lilacs, picking his words as though he were pruning prized chrysanthemums. "And we will be what we will be. There is no reason that the two must agree."

"As poetic as he is wise," said Dandelion.

"I'll be the judge of that, if you don't mind," said a fairy in the king's retinue. He held a book in one hand and a quill in the other.

"My apologies, Mister Poet Laureate," said Dandelion with a bow, "I didn't intend to speak as an expert. Would you like to fill out the Breach of Context form?"

The Poet Laureate smiled. "As long as you were speaking as a layman, I think we can dispense with the formal—"

"I'll be the judge of that, if you don't mind."

"My apologies, Madame Human-Fairy Resources Director," said the Poet Laureate with a bow, "I only thought that we might keep the paperwork to a minimum in the minutes before a major battle."

"A sensible suggestion," said the Human-Fairy Resources Director, "and sensible reductions in overall paperwork are everyone's concern."

"I'll be the judge of that, if you don't mind."

Everyone within earshot apologized to the Underchancellor of Punitive Bureaucracy, Ulfhaven Annex.

"Ah, Miss Urmacher," said King Lilacs, shouting across the room for a distraction. "Would you come over here for a moment, please?"

Greta moved stiffly through the crowd in her armor, doing her best not to clip anyone with the sword at her hip.

"It isn't Captain Urmacher?" Myrtle wondered aloud.

"No, it isn't." Dandelion winked.

"Would you mind kneeling, please?" King Lilacs took a tiny ceremonial sword from someone in his retinue.

Greta looked around, clearly confused. She knelt. Lilacs fluttered his wings and rose until they were face-to-face.

"Greta Urmacher," said Lilacs, "would you defend the realms of the fae from all of her enemies, with—"

Dandelion cleared his throat. Lilacs shot him a look of curt inquiry. Dandelion nodded meaningfully toward the Vice President of Royal Marketing Compliance.

"Right," said Dandelion. "Ahem. Greta Urmacher, would you defend the Incorporated Realms of Carpathia pursuant to the treaties ratified by the United Coalition of Carpathian Monarchies, Incorporated from all of her enemies, within and without, please?"

"Er, that's the plan, yes."

"Splendid! Then by the power vested in me as king of the aforementioned Coalition, I make you a knight of the realm. I grant you the right to bear arms and mete out justice. Arise, Sir Greta."

Greta rose to a round of applause. She couldn't repress a smile, though Sloot was sure she tried.

Using the din of applause as cover, Sloot slipped away from the crowd. He needed to think. "Captain Peril," indeed. He was no soldier. He'd been trampled to death in his first big battle, and did absolutely nothing in the second. Progress, perhaps, but he doubted he was on track for heroics anytime soon.

But perhaps Lilacs was right. There was no reason his future self should approach danger with caution. The future was now! Or it would be any minute.

He looked at Vlad. There she sat on the cold stone floor in her simple grey robe, doing ... what, exactly? Her eyes were open, so she wasn't sleeping. She was just staring into a space that wasn't there.

But that was the point of space, wasn't it? It was there and it wasn't, both at the same time. It was infuriating. It wasn't matter, it wasn't energy, it simply *wasn't*. Why, then, could he consider it at length?

Sloot's eyes went dark. His wings and claws came out. Everyone near him backed away, eyeing him cautiously as he huffed and fumed and pondered. Then he snapped.

"What is the nature of space?" he demanded at the top of his lungs.

"Tell me what you're thinking," said Myrtle, suddenly standing in front of him.

"I have no idea!" Sloot shouted.

"I do," said Vlad. She'd neither moved nor looked up from the space that had so thoroughly infuriated Captain Peril.

"How?" demanded Sloot.

"Come," said Vlad. "Sit. We have much to discuss."

Sloot didn't want to sit. He wanted to *move*. He wanted the portal to open so he could charge through it, scream a swear word, and sink his teeth into the first thing unlucky enough to cross his path. Irony, indeed! They were all about to see what atrocities of war Captain Peril was capable of committing!

"Go talk to her." Myrtle spoke in a low, even voice, the one parents used when acknowledging the injustice of bedtime. "It's important."

"How would you know?" Sloot snapped.

"Because I saw it," said Myrtle, not raising her voice. "This was the last thing that I foresaw. This is your turning point, Sloot. Everything that happens after this hinges on this moment."

But wasn't that always true? Weren't moments just a series of hinges? Sloot shook his head. It made sense, and it didn't. Stupid space! He missed numbers. It had been so long since he'd balanced a simple column of numbers. He longed for black-and-white. He yearned for solid ground, predictability, a warm spray of blood across his—wait, no. What?

"Sloot Gefahr Peril!"

"Yes?" his demonic visage withdrew at the sound of his middle name.

"You go and sit with Vlad this instant!" Myrtle's hands were on her hips. Sloot knew that look. Every child, or adult who had been one, knew that look. It was a challenge. It was the fury of the storm, the unblinking resolve of a mother prepared to count to three. There would be no two-and-a-half.

"Yes, ma'am." Sloot and his hangdog look did as they were told. His silent defiance was foregoing the feet-bent-atop-the-legs position that he'd never have been able to pull off anyway.

"Right, then," said Sloot, doing his best to veil his impatience. This was Vlad the Invader, after all. "What's this all about?"

Vlad smiled, possibly for the first time. It was unsettling. "If I could tell you that, there would be an entire monastery looking for work."

"Then what's the topic of discussion?"

"You. And the natural order of things. How did the dance contest go?"

"We won," said Sloot. "Or we should have. The Prime Evils picked the judge."

"But they let you go," said Vlad. "That's a victory."

"Not exactly."

"Oh." Vlad sounded genuinely surprised. Another first. "Perhaps 'Captain Peril' is better deserved than everyone assumes."

Sloot couldn't suppress a smile of his own.

"Nevertheless, you need to be careful."

"I shouldn't need any help managing that," said Sloot, with a snarl of self-recrimination.

"Remember," said Vlad, "thoughtlessness is but the first step on the path to enlightenment. You've the look of a man who's run right past mindfulness and stillness and gone to war with emptiness."

"I blame space," said Sloot. "How can it just sit there, taunting me like that? Or not. I can't tell."

"Because you've not embraced mindfulness or stillness. Thoughtlessness brought you through the Inferno, but emptiness can madden the untrained mind."

Sloot nodded thoughtfully.

"Pretending to understand won't help."

"Oh, fine," said Sloot. "That doesn't make any sense! How aren't thoughtlessness and emptiness the same thing?"

"Just as you aren't the same, neither are they."

"That's nonsense mathematically! And mathematics are empirical, so you owe me an apology!"

Vlad's eyebrow raised just enough to let Sloot know where he was in relation to the line. His toe was firmly upon it.

"Sorry," said Sloot.

They sat in silence, both staring at the space where the portal might open at any moment. Sloot contemplated the war zone that would lie beyond. Take *that*, space.

"What will you do?" asked Vlad.

"When?"

"When we go through the portal."

"You're coming as well?"

"I wouldn't be in the war chamber otherwise."

"Good point." Sloot realized then that he had no plan. Why was he there? He knew he couldn't *not* be, but as Vlad pointed out, he hadn't done stillness yet. He needed something to do.

"I don't know," he admitted. "But if I'm going to amend the Narrative, I need to be here. There. You know, when it starts."

Vlad nodded. "Mindfulness follows thoughtlessness. Step through the portal and be mindful. But don't be still—you're not ready for that."

Sloot nodded, understanding without the assistance of metaphor. He decided Captain Peril wasn't the sort of person who stood and waited for danger to plow through him.

"What about you?" asked Sloot. "What will you do?"

"My path is clear," Vlad answered.

"Greta?"

Vlad nodded.

"Good luck."

"You don't need luck when your fate is your own."

Sloot filed that one away in the back of his mind and promised himself he'd return to it when he had a month to contemplate it. He presently had minutes at best, and hoped mindfulness worked quickly. He walked back over to Myrtle, where she was talking to Greta.

"Hopefully it won't come to that," Myrtle was saying, "but I took down a fair number of goblins at Nicoleta's tower. We'll defend the organ."

"For as long as we can," said Greta. They nodded to each other. "Come on," Greta said to Igor. "Let's get you strapped in. Just don't start playing until we're through the portal, understand?"

"I understand," said Igor with an enormous grin.

"Er," said Sloot, raising a finger.

"Don't worry," Greta confided, "the baffles aren't attached. I'll do that at the last minute."

"She really does think of everything," said Myrtle after Greta and Igor had wandered off.

"Do you have to go?"

Myrtle looked truly taken aback.

"Why wouldn't I go? Did you ask Vlad the same? She's a woman too, you know."

"What? No, it's just—you just got out of the Inferno, and now—"

"And now I'm going to find out why I went there in the first place. This is as much my story as it is yours, Sloot. Don't forget that."

He *had* forgotten that. Everyone in the war chamber lived in the Narrative he was working to amend. Sloot stole a glance at Dandelion politely giving orders to his legion of fairy soldiers. He thought of Franka and wondered what cruelty she was enduring at that very moment for the preservation of all they held dear.

Of *course*, Myrtle was going. How could she not?

"You're right," said Sloot. "Sorry."

"It's all right," said Myrtle. "And while you're making well-deserved apologies, don't ever make me use your middle name like that again. If our relationship starts to resemble too closely the one you have with your mother, the Narrative might be better off obliterated."

"Agreed."

Myrtle's arms enveloped Sloot in their warmth. His arms responded in kind. He closed his eyes and had just enough time to wonder why Myrtle's hair always smelled of lavender when the portal crackled to life.

And just like that, they were rushing after fate like it had stolen their wallets.

CAPTAIN PERIL

Myrtle and Greta went through first, pushing the goblin organ on its cart. Sloot shoved his fingers in his ears as Igor began to play. It was less "musical performance" and more "felony in progress." The absence of discernible rhythm sent Sloot's deep understanding of mathematics clutching at its pearls.

"Move!" Franka shouted. She was covered in blood and grime, arms held aloft, grimacing under the effort of keeping the portal open. Sloot stumbled through it and into the chapel. To his right, he heard the cacophony of far more goblins than he'd ever feared existed. To his left, beyond a closed door, some singing abruptly stopped. That made sense, insofar as anything did. Trying to carry a tune in the presence of a blaring goblin organ was as manageable as carrying a gallon of water with only a fork.

Mindfulness, thought Sloot. That was what Vlad had told him. Be mindful, and his path would become clear. It wasn't working! As the seconds slipped away, icy fingers of doom gripped his heart. He needed to *do* something, but what?

The fairies poured in through the portal and lined up behind the goblin organ. They took a cue from Sloot and plugged their ears as well. They didn't want to be impolite, but it wouldn't be fair if only Sloot got to do it.

Vlad emerged from the portal with no more urgency than sunrise on a spring day.

"We'll hold them here," she said. If Dandelion had offered her any rank, she'd refused it. "Just remember, we make our own fate. If that isn't true, there is no need to fight."

Fatalistic predestination it is! shouted an ever-receding voice in the back of Sloot's mind. He briefly considered the ease of calmly awaiting oblivion. He had a hunch it would only hurt for a moment.

"Vicked cool," said Bartleby and Willie in unison. They burst into laughter.

"What's so funny?" shouted Nicoleta.

"Vampire joke," shouted Sloot.

"Oh." Nicoleta rolled her eyes. "Let's just get on with it."

"Are you sure you want to be here?"

Nicoleta shrugged. "Destiny catches up to all of us eventually."

Nicoleta was probably being poetic. Sloot didn't really understand poetry, especially when it didn't rhyme. That was just regular sentences that had gotten into the liquor cabinet.

"I'm coming with you," said Sloot. Said *Captain Peril.*

"I'll think about it," said Willie.

"What?"

"He can come," Bartleby interjected. "Ve could use a demon on our side in there. The more, the merrier."

Willie shrugged. "More like 'the more, the less exclusive,' if you ask me. Vhich you didn't."

Sloot felt a hand take his. Myrtle pulled him behind a cracked and crumbling pillar held up by the strange white vines wrapping around it. They challenged everything he knew about photosynthesis, not that he put up much of a fight. As sciences went, biology had too many exceptions for Sloot's taste.

"This is it," said Myrtle, her eyes locked on Sloot's.

"Yes," said Sloot, who wasted no time regretting it. If ever there was a time for Captain Peril to say something dashing, that had been his opportunity.

Luckily, Captain Pastry had bravado to spare. She took Sloot firmly in an embrace specifically reserved for covers of trashy romantic novels, stared arduously into his eyes, and said, "take me dancing again soon?"

Sloot's knees went weak. For one blessed moment, he couldn't think of anything but lying in a spring meadow. Myrtle's hair, warmed by the sun, lying across his chest. The whisper of her breath on his neck as they watched the sun sink purply below the horizon.

She kissed him hard. The world fell away.

"I'll take that as a yes," Myrtle grinned. She relaxed her embrace and Captain Peril's boots found purchase beneath him.

"We'll hold them off," said Myrtle, straightening up.

"I'll try not to take too long."

"See that you don't." Myrtle winked. She kissed him again and went to stand with Greta. Sloot thought he saw her skip.

"Ahem," said Bartleby. "Shall ve?"

"Let's," said Captain Peril, with far more certainty than he knew was in him. He strode to the door, put all of his weight into a kick, and threw himself backward upon the floor.

"Ow," he said.

"It's got a knocker," said Willie. "My valet usually operates those. Vhere is Roman?"

"Prison," said Sloot. He got to his feet.

"Oh, dear," said Willie. "The result of some elaborate prank, I assume?"

"More like a bet."

"What do you want?" The question came from a pair of eyes

peering through a slot in the door. "And can you cut out that racket? The soul of the people is trying to cry out for justice in here!"

"Sorry," said Sloot, "we'll—wait, no. No, we won't! It's Captain Peril to see Mrs. Knife, please!"

"Captain Peril? I don't think I ought to open the door for that. Sounds Carpathian."

"I get that a lot," said Sloot.

"Has Sloot kicked the door in yet?" asked Nicoleta.

"It's a vork in progress," Bartleby shouted.

"It's got a knocker," said Nicoleta, "why don't you—"

"Yes, ve've done that, and there's a man—"

"You there," boomed Willie, "talking door. Do you know who my father is? I insist that you open up for us at once!"

"I'm not a—"

"I'm not interested! If you don't vant your next dinner party to be the laughingstock of the opera season, you'll open up this instant!"

"Hang on," said the voice on the other side of the door after a long pause.

Sloot turned around at the sound of a scuffle. He saw Vlad evade a goblin so vigorously that it slammed head-first into a wall and vanished in a puff of shadow.

"What's taking so long?" asked Nicoleta. "I've got a mortal coil to shuffle off!"

Another goblin leapt past the organ to be taken down by Myrtle's claws. Most of the congress mingled around the organ, taking no interest in advancing into the chapel.

"This isn't going to last long," said Greta. "You need to get in there, now!"

"Out of the way," said Nicoleta. She didn't wait for a response. Sloot dove for cover as a rainbow of flame and sparks disintegrated the door.

"I was saving that," she grumbled.

Beyond the doorway, Sloot saw a barricade made mostly of inexpensive furniture. Flags sprouted from it like weeds. Heads wearing bandanas peeked out from the gaps between dinette sets. The insistence of a snare drum gave the entire affair a certain spirited lift.

"Viva the Old Country!" arose a shout from beyond the barricade. Sloot's fist nearly shot up in accord, but stopped short when he saw the sky above. Beyond the fact that there should be no sky inside a mausoleum, this one was all wrong.

It wasn't a sky at all, but a rupture in the gossamer curtain between realms. The Dark was leaking through. Not a raging torrent like the one that had spilled into the Narrative when Willie exploded. This was more like looking up into the shadowy, undulating roots of an impossibly black tree.

That was bad enough, but in Sloot's experience, "bad enough" never was. The whorls of dust in the infinite blackness reminded him far too much of something he'd seen before.

"It looks like the Well of the Void," he said.

"Vicked," said Bartleby. "I'm going to have a closer look." She exploded into a colony of bats and fluttered upward.

"Are you a tyrant?" demanded a voice from beyond the barricade.

"No," said Sloot.

"Prove it!"

"What?"

"Prove you're not a tyrant! We're not suffering them anymore."

Several hisses and boos floated from the piles of furniture. Sloot thought he might have heard one of them shout an epithet in a dead language.

"Hang on a minute," said Sloot, "that's Arthur's revolution!"

"No we aren't," insisted a ringleader-ish voice. "We're the people's revolution, and we refuse to bow to the yoke of oppression again!"

"Yeah!" thronged the revolution, and other sentiments to that effect.

"I don't know how to prove I'm not a tyrant," said Sloot.

"Have you ever oppressed anybody?"

Sloot thought about it. He was pretty sure he hadn't.

"You have to answer honestly," shouted the ringleader, "it's the law!"

The revolution shouted their agreement again.

"I don't recall ever having done."

"What's he saying?" asked Nicoleta.

"He's asking if I've ever oppressed anyone."

Nicoleta rolled her eyes. "Revolutionaries?"

Sloot nodded.

"We don't have time for this," she said.

"I can take care of it," said Willie. Everyone balked. "Vhat? I have a note."

Sloot didn't know which part was most baffling, but he was out of ideas.

"Very well, then."

Willie *did* have a note. He may have been many things, but a liar wasn't one of them. One has to understand the truth to lie properly, and Willie understood very little about not much.

"To the formerly glorious revolutionaries of C.R.A.P.," Willie read from the wrinkled paper, "from its founder, Arthur."

"Not Arthur Widdershins?" The ringleader's head peeked up over the top of the barricade.

"That's right," said Sloot. He didn't trust Willie to know the surname of anyone who didn't own a vineyard.

"He's *persona non grata* around here."

"Why and what is that?"

"It means he's not welcome," said Sloot.

"Yeah," said the ringleader, "because the boss chucked him out!"

"The boss?"

"Mrs. Knife."

"Right," said Willie. "Vell, this concerns her, too. Is she back there vith you?"

"Sort of," said the ringleader. "I mean, she's got better things to do than hang around at the barricade, right?"

"She's back there with the bones," said another voice, "her and Mr. Gregor."

"The Soul remains!" It suddenly added up. They were having another go at the Serpent of the Sky! If they were able to lift the cloak that Nicoleta had cast over it, the goblins would be able to find Svartalfheim and go to war with the dwarves.

"Fine," said Willie, "I'll just read it to you. *Ahem.* You bunch of vacuous ninnies," he began, "vhat has gotten into your tiny little minds? I'd expect this from the artists, but you know how it is vith them. Vhen a sculpture about birds experiencing regret doesn't solve their problems, they ask their parents for money so they can go home. But the rest of you are supposed to be philosophers. Honestly, vhat vere you thinking? I'll bet you're standing around right now, *standing*, holding a sword or a pike or something. You probably told yourself it's ceremonial, but you've got to know that isn't true. By the time my friend Villie—aww, isn't that sveet—has finished reading this note, it vill probably be too late.

"You're dealing vith the implementation of bloodshed. Not the results, not their ethical implications, the actual vhatnot that soldier types get on vith. Do yourselves a favor and go home. Philosophers, I'll be at the Bespectacled Skeptic on University Row if you vant to argue about moral turpitudes. Artists, go see if the poets and musicians vill have you. You're not invited to my next revolution! Sincerely, Doctor Arthur Viddershins."

A thick silence ensued, diluted only by the faint, irritating tones of the goblin organ far behind them.

Klang, went what sounded like a sword. Or possibly a pike.

"Arthur's right," said a yet unheard voice from behind the barricade. "We've gotten things in motion, haven't we? Time for the proletariat to get on with the doing."

Klang, went another weapon. And another. And another, and a dozen more. An armoire shifted from beneath a pair of load-bearing chaise lounges, and revolutionaries began streaming out.

"What's the address here?" asked a young man with a ponytail and a paint-spattered smock. "I need to have my dad send me some money."

Sloot advised the former revolutionaries to stay away from the chapel until they'd dealt with the goblins, and that a portal back to Salzstadt would be made available shortly. Several of the artists resolved to ask their parents for money anyway.

A colony of bats coalesced into Bartleby. She did her best to shake off the layer of dust she'd accumulated.

"Vell, it's not the Vell of the Void," she said as she shook out her hair, "but I think that's vhat Gregor vas going for. Fortunately, he's an idiot."

"Who's an idiot?" asked Nicoleta.

"Gregor," Bartleby shouted. "He probably tried to raise the dead that vere down here, but they ran out of vitality centuries ago. Now the Dark is full of the ashes of the dead."

"Idiot. Let's go kill him!"

"It's not going to be that easy," shouted Bartleby. "He's got back up!"

"What? Who?"

"The Serpents of the Earth. Some of their best vizards are in there. They must not have heard that Mrs. Knife isn't in charge anymore."

All eyes turned to Willie, who was making strange circular motions with his hands. He stopped when he saw that everyone was staring.

"What?"

Bartleby glared.

"*Vhat?*"

"Was that supposed to be a spell or something?"

"Oh," said Willie with a dismissive wave, "no, just some science I've been meaning to do."

"Nobody ask him," said Sloot.

"What science?" asked Nicoleta.

"My hands," said Willie, "they can touch anything but themselves! I thought I'd—"

"Good idea," said Sloot. "Listen, Willie, can you prove that you're the Eye and Soul of the Serpent?"

"That's not necessary," said Willie with a chuckle. "Everybody knows it's me. That's how it works—*vorks*—vhen you're fancy and rich."

"Usually, yes," said Sloot. "But supposing you came across someone who didn't know. How would you prove it to them?"

Willie stared at Sloot. He blinked a few times, then looked up at the dust clouds floating around in the Dark.

"Let me get back to you," he said eventually. He resumed his scientific experiment.

Sloot said a swear word. A goblin popped into their midst and barely had a chance to cackle before Bartleby sent it exploding into shadow with a purple zot from her wand.

"We'll have to risk it," said Nicoleta. "I don't have much time."

"Myrtle said they'd hold the goblins off," shouted Sloot, "she said—"

"*I* don't have much time," Nicoleta snapped. "Let's go!"

Without another word, Bartleby steered her wheelchair past the barricade and into the darkness beyond. They didn't have to go far before a circle of chanting wizards came into view.

"Friends of yours?" Sloot asked Willie.

"My friends dress a lot better than that."

"Fools!" boomed a familiar voice which seemed to echo from all directions at once. "You dare enter my domain?"

"Gregor!" Bartleby shouted. "Ve both know you're not this cool! Does Mrs. Knife know about your bed vetting?"

"Silence! I will suffer your churlish taunts no longer, Bartleby! Throw yourself at my mercy, and I may murder you quickly."

"Ha!" shouted Bartleby. "Your threats don't scare me. You're as scary as you are handsome, you rancid sack of manure!"

"That's far enough," said Nicoleta. Her breathing sounded labored and phlegmatic. Standing from the wheelchair sapped what little vitality she had remaining.

"Go," she said. "Deal with the wizards. I'll handle Gregor. *Go,* Sloot. I don't have time for questions. I'll see you on the other side."

"But—"

"She'll be fine," said Bartleby. "Vell, part of her vill. In a manner of speaking. Come on, Villie, time to talk to your vizards."

"What—vhat—do you say to w-vizards? I don't think I've ever met one."

"I'm a vizard," said Bartleby. "So is Nicoleta. Half your friends are vizards."

"I've seen no evidence of that."

"Just ask if they know who your father is," said Bartleby. "Always a good opener."

Sloot didn't like the idea of leaving Nicoleta alone, but Bartleby didn't seem worried. So he strode boldly toward a dangerous enemy and disliked that instead. He started to turn around when a rumbling sound started up behind them, but Bartleby put her hands on his shoulders and marched him forward.

"Hey!"

"You don't vant to look," she said. "Trust me."

"What's happening?"

"You'll see soon enough."

The rumbling was joined by a light breeze, a sizzling sound, and intermittent flashes of light. Pink light. Then a low, metallic *wub-wub-wub* that get faster as the wind increased.

"Ve should valk a little faster."

"Hey!" Willie objected. "Push Sloot if you must, but I'm a very important-"

"There may be a mild explosion," warned Bartleby. "Vouldn't vant to ruin your cape!"

Sloot had seen Willie run once before. He hadn't practiced since then. Not that Sloot's form was any better, as he ably demonstrated.

There was, in fact, a mild explosion. Their long silhouettes spread before them on a field of pink light. A wave of purple smoke roiled over them. *Whump, whump* went the warm air above. Sloot looked up in time to see a sparkly pink dragon roar. It flapped its way up into the darkness, pink lightning cascading between its wings.

"Vicked!" shouted Bartleby.

"Is that Nicoleta?" asked Sloot.

Willie laughed.

"What's so funny?"

"She made you push her all this vay vhen she could have flown," said Willie. "That's aristocracy! Half of amassing a fortune is convincing people who don't have one to do things for you for free."

"Oh, dear," said Sloot, pointing beyond Nicoleta. "What's that?"

In the foggy distance, another pair of wings flapped. A massive shriek reverberated in the open maw of the Dark. A gout of green flame shot over Nicoleta, giving momentary illumination to another dragon, its bones showing through rotten gaps in its putrid flesh.

"Ugh, probably Gregor," said Bartleby. "He's alvays doing

things like this. It's like one-downsmanship. Honestly, he's an embarrassment to necromancers everyvhere."

Hold yourself together, Captain Peril told the gutless craven within him, reasoning that no dragon would worry itself with a tiny accounting demon while there was another dragon around. The craven panicked anyway, because that's what cravens do.

Nicoleta banked and dodged a yellow fireball from the ground.

"That vould be your vizards," said Bartleby.

Willie nodded. "They are good, aren't they? Oh, right."

Willie and Bartleby exploded into colonies of bats and flew toward the wizards. Sloot ran after them but was barely within earshot when half the bats became Willie again.

"You three, stop—hey!"

A bolt of red light sizzled past Willie from one of the wizard's wands.

"That's Lord Hapsgalt's boy," said a second wizard, his hand pushing the first's wand aside.

"It's his own fault," said the third wizard, who was so tall the sleeves of his black robe failed to make the journey all the way down to his wrists. "He shouldn't go coalescing in front of wizards who've got wands out."

"A fair point," said Bartleby. "Hey!"

"Simon!" shouted the second wizard, with a headmaster's indignation that was always looking for a reason to lecture someone.

"Don't 'Simon' me, Gravus. I'd *just* finished saying—"

"No harm done," said Bartleby. "There's a demon vith us too, please go easy on him."

"Thanks," said Sloot, breathless upon arrival.

"Right," said Gravus. "Look, I don't know what you're up to, but we've got a dragon to take down."

"It's about that," said Bartleby. "Tell them, Villie. Villie?"

Willie was staring off into space. He blinked himself furiously back into the present.

"What? I mean, *vhat?*"

"Tell them vhat you vant them to do."

"We're a little busy at the moment," said the third wizard. "Look, out of respect for your father, we'll forget this little incident. Now, if you don't mind?"

"Not at all," said Willie. "Pardon us."

"Villie!"

"Vhat?"

"Lord Hapsgalt—this one—is now the Eye and Soul of the Serpent," said Sloot, "and he orders you to aid him in apprehending Mrs. Knife and the wizard Gregor!"

The three wizards exchanged bewildered glances. Then they burst into laughter.

"Fitting he made his little friend do it for him," said Simon, wiping away a tear. "I've heard Little Willie Hapsgalt can't even order his own brunch!"

"Hey," said Willie, "I'm a big boy!"

The storm of laughter thundered in the sky of their amusement. In the ashen darkness above, the dragons had at each other with flame, tooth, and claw.

"Villie can prove he's Eye and Soul," said Bartleby. "Go on, Villie. Show these fools you're their master!"

"Oh, we know," said Gravus.

"You know?"

Gravus nodded. "We just don't care. Now, if you please, it's not often we get to kill dragons."

"Hang on," said Sloot, "it was ordained by the Convocation of Shades! Mrs. Knife is excommunicated! Willie, tell them!"

"If you say so," said Willie. "Sloot's really good at this business stuff. He doesn't look as good in a cape as me, though."

"We don't *care,*" Gravus repeated. "Why should we listen to a bunch of decrepit old ghosts? All they do is lurk in the Hereafter and demand blood."

"Listen to Willie, then," said Sloot. "At least he'll walk right up to you and demand blood."

"I am a bit peckish," said Willie.

"You don't get it," said Simon. "Things are good under Mrs. Knife. We're getting some proper villainy done! With the Hapsgalts, it was all money and extravagance. It was *boring.* People are afraid to walk the streets at night again! We're the terror that snatches you up in the darkness now, not just boring old darkness that's probably just as afraid of you as you are of it, so leave it alone and it won't bother you. Where's the fun in that?"

"Look, you just can't!" said Bartleby. "The Book of Black Law clearly states that—"

The retort that came out of Gravus was profanity gymnastics. He swore it at the top of his lungs. Some of the words he used were so repugnant that the dragons above stopped fighting long enough to cast shocked looks in his direction.

"That's what you can do with your precious Book of Black Law!" he spat.

"I don't think I could," said Willie. "Not after the handle broke off, and I had to buy a new one."

"He vas being metaphorical," said Bartleby.

"This is getting ridiculous," said the third wizard. He aimed his wand at Willie. "I'm about out of respect for your daddy. Run away, the three of you, or we'll do this the easy way!"

Simon and Gravus raised their wands, pointing them at Sloot and Bartleby respectively.

Bartleby giggled in a disturbingly high pitch and pointed her wand back at Gravus. Willie bared his fangs and hissed in classical vampire form. Sloot's eyes went black, and he bared fangs of his own. Captain Peril, it seemed, had found the dangerous end of his demonhood.

Tsk, tsk, tsk, came a spiteful clucking from behind Sloot. The hairs on his neck stood up. Coupled with his demonic aspect, it made for an impressive mohawk.

"I don't like these odds," said Mrs. Knife. Sloot could hear her grinning.

"They seem fair to me," said Bartleby.

"That's the problem. Mind if I cut in?"

"That's Mrs. Knife, isn't it?" Willie went pale, which was impressive for a hungry vampire.

"It is," said Sloot.

"In that case," said Willie. If there was an end to that sentence, his colony of bats had trouble pronouncing it. They scattered in all directions.

It had been a long time since Sloot had heard Mrs. Knife's laugh. It had always filled him with dread. It still did, but now there was also rage. He turned to face Mrs. Knife, and for the first time, she regarded him with something other than gleeful malice. It wasn't fear, Sloot wasn't sure she was capable of that. More like impressed discomfort.

"I didn't think you had it in you, Peril," she sneered, the gleeful malice sliding back in. Her knife flashed and spun from hand to hand. "These odds seem a lot more fun to me, what do you think?"

"Not quite to my taste," growled Sloot. "Bartleby, get out of here."

"Vhat?"

"Bartleby," said Mrs. Knife, tilting her head toward the necromancer. "I thought we killed you. Clever little minx!"

"Get out of here," Sloot repeated.

"I'm not abandoning you now," she refused.

"You told me to run, and I ran," said Sloot. "Do the same for me now. Now!"

"But Sloot—"

"Do you see any new hosts around here? Sure you can dominate a wizard if you're cut down? Go, now!"

Bartleby stood there for a moment, her mouth hanging open as her mind scrambled.

"I alvays liked you," she said at last, before exploding into a cloud of bats.

Mrs. Knife chuckled. She and the three wizards started walking slowly in a circle around him, wands and knife trained on him.

"Whatever else I might say about you," cackled Mrs. Knife, "you're certainly unpredictable. I never thought you the self-sacrificing type."

"It's not myself I intend to sacrifice," said Captain Peril, his eyes smoldering with yellow-hot fire.

"Then allow me. Any last words?"

"Only one," said Sloot with a grin. "Blagderos."

"What?"

"Blagderos."

"No!"

"Blagderos!"

The thunderclap was deafening. It wasn't actually a thunderclap, but that's how Sloot's mind interpreted it. When witnessing something as incomprehensible as a rift opening between two unconnected dimensions, a demon's mind leaps like a cheetah for the nearest gazelle of familiarity.

"Fool!" shouted Baelgoroth the Destroyer from the back of his flaming steed. "You have inadvertently summoned your destructor!"

"Not inadvertently," said Sloot. *Foolishly,* he thought to himself, *but that's different.* He clumsily flapped his wings and took to the air, barely avoiding a stabbing from Mrs. Knife.

"You thought these wizards would defeat me, then? Ha! Witness as they writhe in their insanity! The mortal mind cannot comprehend the Death Knell, the Harbinger of Galloping Fright!"

And writhe they did. Once three of the most powerful wizards in the Serpents of the Earth, they were now qualified for little more than attending boulderchuck matches with their faces painted. Sloot had counted on that. He'd clerked the Humanity v. Shambling Monstrosity case, which ended when the mortals who'd shown up to court could do nothing but scream in terror when Shambling Monstrosity–whose proper name was redacted to avoid further madness–entered the room. Sloot reasoned that the appearance of Blagderos would do the same.

"Do you simply long for death?"

"Guess again."

"I'll not play your games! Baelgoroth the Destroyer dances for no one's amusement!"

"I called you here to apologize."

Baelgoroth laughed. "Your pleas fall upon deaf ears! What makes you think—"

"This," said Sloot. He wrenched a clawed hand in a circular motion. He hadn't been able to reach his magic circle from here because of Zurogravia's enchantments, but an interdimensional rift changed things. He reached through it, across the Inferno, along the ley lines that crisscrossed the mortal realm, found his apartment, and gave Ixbal's Prudent Indemnifier a nudge.

"Yes?" said the imp who'd appeared in a puff of black smoke. He was carrying a book and looked bored.

"I have no patience for this," bellowed Baelgoroth. "Prepare to—"

"I, Captain Sloot Gefahr Peril, do hereby apologize for falsely claiming that Baelgoroth the Destroyer is less than twelve inches tall."

"Too late! I—"

"Sign here, please," said the imp. Having so few opportunities to show off, Sloot reached across the cosmos again and tapped

Egregious Cursive. His signature appeared in flaming golden loops in the imp's book.

"So recorded," said the imp. He vanished in a puff of black smoke.

"And what was that meant to accomplish?" Baelgoroth chuckled.

"You are now officially not less than twelve inches tall," said Sloot, "according to my official declaration. That makes you eligible to take part in the Razing of the Dead."

Baelgoroth gaped at Sloot. "Is it true?"

"Go and see for yourself."

"But how? You can't lie to a notary!"

"Did I? I've never measured you. Logic dictates that if I lied about you being less than twelve inches—"

"Then I must be over!"

"Just stay away from yardsticks, will you?"

It was a gamble, but Sloot wasn't betting on his own luck. He was betting on Baelgoroth's greed.

"Don't think this makes us even!" shouted Baelgoroth, as he rode Blagderos back through the rift. It closed behind them with a *pop*.

Sloot barely had time to notice that Mrs. Knife had vanished before he was struck from above. He barreled toward the ground beneath the weight of two dragons. If there was any space for optimism, he might have found the experience exhilarating. Alas, there was not.

Sloot managed to roll from beneath Nicoleta's scaly flank just before the impact. He landed hard atop a broken tombstone. For nearly a minute thereafter, the air was full of dirt, debris, and smoke.

Smoke cleared, dust settled, and Sloot got to his feet. A sound rose from the rotting skeletal dragon that offended both bloodthirsty screaming and maniacal laughter by artlessly combining the two. The pink dragon lay still at its feet.

Sloot gasped. "Nicoleta!"

The pink dragon shrank and shriveled into the broken, lifeless form of Nicoleta.

Gregor's rotten dragon form reduced to that of a rotten goblin. He stood over her, his shrieks and cackles offending the very air around him.

"Vicked," said Bartleby, who'd floated up beside Sloot in a cloud of purple smoke.

"I can't believe it," Sloot replied softly.

"Vhat?"

"Nicoleta. She's dead!"

"Again, yes."

"What do we do now? How can we defeat Gregor without her?"

"Cower before me," Gregor boomed, his blood star cast a murky red glow around his clawed left hand. "Victory is at hand! There shall be mercy for none!"

"Thanks for handling that mess vith the vizards," said Bartleby. "To be honest, I vasn't sure how ve vere going to get out of it."

"You're welcome," said Sloot, "but I'm afraid we've got bigger problems now."

"Just vait." Bartleby grinned and gave Sloot a wink.

A tiny movement drew his attention back into the crater. A tiny wisp of light drifted upward from Nicoleta's broken corpse and popped in the air. Then there was another. Two more. Five more. Seconds later, the air was effervescent with magic. Sloot had to shield his eyes as pink-hot flames engulfed her and exploded. When he could see again, it looked like someone had tied a firecracker rainbow to a joke shop skeleton, and it was erupting in slow motion. If that weren't sufficiently terrifying, it had razor-sharp wings of steel as well.

"That's better," said Nicoleta. "Now, where were we?"

"She's done it," cried Bartleby. "She's a lich!"

Nicoleta and Gregor flew toward each other, wands thrusting and parrying in a lightning fight that Sloot had trouble believing, despite the evidence of his eyes. He backed away, not because Captain Peril was fearful, but because he'd tactically decided against approaching bravery from a position of stupidity.

"Vicked cool, eh?" said Bartleby, backing away as well. "A vizard has to have a big death to complete the Rite of Lichery. A dragon fight against a necromancer vas just the thing."

"Mrs. Knife!" In all the excitement, Sloot had forgotten about her. "She's not here, where has she gone?"

"Vhere could she do the most damage?"

Sloot's eyes went wide with horror. "What happens to a wizard's enchantments when she dies?"

"They die as vell," said Bartleby. "Vhy?"

"The Serpent of the Sky! Nicoleta's enchantment was hiding it! If it's out in the open—"

"Mrs. Knife can use it to lead the goblins anyvhere she vants. Oh, that's bad news!"

"She's got to be headed for her goblins. You have to warn the others!"

"Vhat vill you do?"

Sloot looked at Gregor and Nicoleta. The fury of their duel hadn't abated in the slightest.

"I'm going to take out Gregor," Sloot declared.

Bartleby raised an eyebrow.

"Sorry I'll have to miss that," she said. "Good luck!" She exploded into a colony of bats and flew off.

It seemed like ages since Sloot first visited Castle Ulfhaven. He remembered Nicoleta explaining the curse that Gregor had placed on Vlad's grandfather. He never thought it would come in handy, yet there they were.

Nicoleta sent a bolt through Gregor's defenses that pinned

him to the ground. A howl of triumph went up from the dazzling pink lich as she descended on him, wand swinging overhead to deliver a killing blow.

"Stop!" shouted Sloot.

Nicoleta froze in midair, inches from the necromancer's prone and bleeding form. Gregor smiled up at her, baring rows of needle-sharp teeth in defiance.

"Ignore the coward," the necromancer laughed, the sound cutting off in a gurgling cough. "Finish me, if you can!"

The sparkling lich turned her gaze to Sloot.

"My vengeance is at hand!" she shrieked. "Give me one good reason not to—"

Forks of red lightning stabbed into Nicoleta, severing one of her arms and sending her crashing through a nearby obelisk. Gregor got to his feet, the blood star crackling with crimson energy. The necromancer laughed and turned his attention to Sloot.

"Almost enough to earn you a quick death," he said. "Almost." His palm twitched. The blood star rose upward and floated toward Sloot, lightning arcing from it.

"Amnesty!" shouted Sloot.

"That's it," Gregor chuckled, "beg me for—"

"For you," said Sloot.

"For me? Why would I possibly need amnesty? I have the upper hand!"

"From reality."

Gregor's smile fell, much to Sloot's relief. His dental neglect was truly off-putting. The blood star stopped moving.

"You were Ashkar once," said Sloot, "isn't that right? You made a deal with Vlad the Invader centuries ago. Exemption from reality, remember?"

Gregor nodded. "I was betrayed."

"By another Vlad the Invader," said Sloot. "You laid a curse on

Carpathia. No one would join the army while Vlad's lineage wore the crown. Guess what? You won."

"Won?"

"Vlad has stepped down. The fairies rule Carpathia now."

"I won!" Gregor cackled again. "I should celebrate. I know, I'll hang up some garlands! Your guts should suffice."

"I don't doubt that you could arrange that," said Sloot. "Or you could let me grant you that exemption properly."

Gregor licked his lips. Sloot sincerely wished he'd had the opportunity to tear his eyes out first.

"The Invader could only do it politically," Sloot continued. "By the power vested in me by the Coolest, I can do it properly."

"Why should I trust you? I've been betrayed before."

"I'm supposed to fix the Narrative, right? Why would I want a venomous old necromancer roaming around in it, cursing nations and settling old vendettas?"

"You give me your word, Peril? You'll write me out of reality, once and for all?"

Sloot produced the ledger from his jacket. "The Twilight realm. It lies on the edge of Immemory, between here and the Dark. Do you know it?"

"I've heard of it. I thought it was a myth. They say that it's where all things lost may be found again, things forgotten are revealed."

"It's no myth," said Sloot. "I clerked for a chaos firm who sent someone there as a prank. I can tell you the way. Sign here promising never to return, help me end this conflict, and I'll write you out of the Narrative."

Gregor grinned. "Done." He signed the ledger with a series of primitive runes. His true name, Sloot was sure of it.

A sparkly beam of energy sliced through Gregor without touching him.

"Nicoleta!" said Sloot.

"What?" Nicoleta looked as innocent as a one-armed, steel-winged, sparkly skeleton could while aiming a wand. "Wasn't that the plan? Lure him into a false sense of security, and—"

"No," said Sloot, "We have an official agreement, so don't try to kill him again. It won't work."

Gregor cackled with malice and drew his wand.

"You either," Sloot snapped. "That'll be breach of contract, and the deal's off. Is that what you want?"

"No," Gregor sulked. "What happens now?"

A peal of thunder ripped through the mausoleum. The Dark churned above them.

"The Serpent of the Sky," said Nicoleta. "We're too late."

GOBLIN MEATS

They hurried from the mausoleum, Nicoleta and Gregor muttering curses at each other. Not the turn-you-into-something-nasty type, just very hurtful words. They weren't contract-breaching offenses, so Sloot left it alone.

The gruesome squawking of the goblin organ drifted in at the edge of Sloot's hearing. It meant his friends were still alive, which was good, but he couldn't help wishing the awful noise would stop just the same.

There was a crash, and the organ went silent. Of all the times for Sloot's wishes to come true!

Unfortunately for Captain Peril, he still ran like Sloot. An impromptu arrangement of knees and elbows that was late for something.

There were goblins everywhere. Sloot caught a glimpse of Mrs. Knife disappearing among them, their eyes meeting just long enough for it to be weird.

The fairies held the line at the door, though the sheer weight of the goblins was pushing them back. The toothy devils cackled as they poured into the chapel past the fairy defense. Myrtle, Greta, and Franka managed to put down most of the stragglers.

Vlad ably dodged attacks from a few goblins in such a way that they ended up hurting themselves or their comrades, proving the best offense was good self-defense.

"My music," Igor moaned. He fiddled in vain with a ruptured pipe on the ruined organ. "Oh, what's the use? I can't fix it! My talents couldn't lie farther from 'fixing!'"

Gregor and Nicoleta rushed into the room, more concerned with which of them arrived first than jumping into the fight.

"What's happening here?" shouted Nicoleta.

"—pening here?" echoed Gregor, not wanting to be outdone.

"The goblins," said Sloot, "and Mrs. Knife is here somewhere. We've got to do something!"

"Vell, if it isn't little Kitten Bear!" Bartleby taunted.

"Restrain yourself," Gregor sneered.

"Sloot, did I ever tell you vhy ve called him Kitten Bear?"

"It's not the time!" snapped Sloot. "Gregor, you're a goblin, can you—"

"My *host* is a goblin."

"Fine. Can you speak to them?"

"And say what?"

"Anything," said Sloot, "just stall them long enough for me to think!"

Gregor flicked his wand in the goblins' direction. The ones in front stopped fighting, bent over at the waist, and broke wind in unison. If the stench was anything like the volume, Sloot was sure there would be casualties.

"Hold, please!" shouted Dandelion from among his troops.

One of the goblins chattered something. The rest grunted in response.

"What was that?" asked Sloot.

"The congress has been called to order," Igor translated.

Goblin anthropologists have often remarked on the truly disgusting nature of congressional practices. Every last goblin in a congress is a deeply disgusting creature of darkness who has a higher regard for his or her own flatulence than anything important.

"It will only take a moment for them to realize that there's no pile of rotten meat for them to devour," said Gregor. "Whatever you're going to do, do it fast."

"There are too many of them to fight," said Greta, sweat streaming down her face, grime smearing her dented armor.

"Not that we won't go down swinging," said Franka. She pulled a strip of fabric from her cape and tied it around a wound on her forearm.

"Tell them we'll pay their debt," said Sloot.

"What debt?"

"They had an alliance with humans ages ago," said Sloot. "They—*we*—were greedy. We got rich while they got cast into the Dark."

"That's not fair," said Lilacs. He hovered over Sloot's shoulder, eyeing Gregor suspiciously.

"Big deal," said Bartleby. "Vars have vinners and losers. I've seen loads of them in my day."

"True," said Sloot, "but the winners are supposed to make a place for the losers. They get to live in peace under a new flag. Nobody offered that to the goblins."

"They're *goblins*," said Nicoleta. "They're vile abominations! They don't have souls, they don't deserve mercy!"

"It's a good thing I know you're not a despot," said Sloot, "because you're doing a remarkable impression."

They all stood in silence for a moment. Well, not silence, but what passed for it considering the agitated growling of an angry congress with no pile of rotting meat.

"Gregor," said Sloot, "tell them they can come with you into the Twilight."

"What? That wasn't part of the deal! I don't want to live with them!"

"The Twilight is vast, you'll never see them. Besides, there's enough forgotten stuff in there to keep them occupied for ages. They won't even care that you're there."

"Perhaps," moaned Gregor, "but—"

"But nothing," declared Captain Peril, "this is the deal! You agreed to help end this conflict, and this is how we do it."

Gregor sneered. Everyone else took up defensive positions, but not Sloot. He looked Gregor straight in the eyes. Captain Peril did not flinch.

Gregor turned to the congress and barked something that sounded like a bear with a cold clearing its throat.

"What's he saying?" Sloot whispered to Igor.

"He said, 'hear me make mouth talk at you face.'"

The goblins turned their heads to Gregor, regarding him with what seemed to Sloot like bewilderment.

"Is his goblish bad, or is yours?"

"We both speak perfect goblish, don't be judgy."

"Sorry."

Igor went on to translate Gregor saying, "for what bad men do you, that man sad." Gregor pointed at Sloot. "Him want give meat. Meat in dark place, not Dark. Me take you. Come now."

Amusement, malice, and lunacy collaborated on a laugh that represented them all equally. Behind it, Mrs. Knife descended from the shadows, landing atop Vlad and pinning her to the ground with a knife through the shoulder. She pointed another knife at Gregor and turned it in a slow circle.

"You'll do no such thing," she said. She gave her knife a twist in Vlad's shoulder.

"Don't," said Sloot, his palm extended in Greta's direction.

"She knows you're behind her, she'll kill Vlad."

"Let her go," Greta spat from between clenched teeth. Mrs. Knife's response was another twist of the knife. Vlad's face was a mask of serenity, the sort parents keep handy for when toddlers reveal embarrassing truths at volume.

"Gregor," sang Mrs. Knife, "be a dear and end the lives of all these interlopers, will you? Hey!"

A burst of pink sparks knocked the knife from her hand. A second obliterated the knife altogether.

"An enchanted knife," said Nicoleta. "How long has she been commanding you with that?"

"Far too long," said Gregor. He cackled and raised his wand.

"No," said Sloot. "Nobody else dies today!"

Mrs. Knife howled with laughter. "Promise them the moon, too! This one dies as soon as I will it. And then I'll get revenge against the dwarves!"

Mrs. Knife gnashed her teeth and grumbled at the goblins.

"Eat that flesh," Igor translated, "eat all up! Then eat dwarves too, with me! Am queen of you!"

Sloot turned to Nicoleta. "Can you open a portal?"

"To where?"

"Halfway between the Slumbering Horizon and the Cave Where All Whispers Are True. That's the entrance to the Twilight."

"Ha! Right under my nose this whole time." She waved her wand in a pattern like three bunnies planning a robbery. A shimmering portal came into view. Beyond it was a sunset that started with amber and passed through purple on its way to indigo.

The goblins regarded it in stunned silence. Nobody moved.

Sloot thought a swear word. *It isn't working! We've failed!*

Igor shouted something in goblish and pointed at Sloot. Several of the goblins looked at each other, shrugged, and started leaping into the portal.

"No!" shouted Mrs. Knife. She shouted something in goblish which elicited a few cackles from the goblins as they rushed passed her. A few of them chittered something at her in passing.

"What did you say to them?" asked Sloot.

"'You go nice place or him give meat at dwarves.' They still want revenge, and they get it by denying their enemy meat. A little bit of justice the easy way. Goblins aren't big on hard work."

Mrs. Knife screamed. She twisted the knife in Vlad's shoulder again. Vlad didn't move.

"You have to let me kill her," said Greta.

"No one else dies today," Sloot insisted.

"What about Vlad? She's dying right now!"

"Excellent idea," said Mrs. Knife, who seemed thinner and paler than she had a moment ago. "I'm an inch from her heart, I just need to—"

Vlad dodged. It defied all logic, but she was suddenly standing several feet away from Mrs. Knife.

"How?" said at least four people in the room, one of whom was Mrs. Knife, though none of whom were Myrtle or Greta. They were too busy hurtling toward Mrs. Knife with claw and sword ready.

Vlad dodged again. Several times, in fact, between Mrs. Knife and her assailants. It was a complicated yet gentle maneuver that left Myrtle and Greta sprawled on opposite sides of the chapel, and Mrs. Knife unarmed.

"No one else dies today," said Vlad. She nodded at Sloot.

"You're a fool," Mrs. Knife mocked. "As long as I still have strength, your lives are temporary inconveniences!"

"Your strength is leaving you," said Vlad. She motioned toward the line of goblins leaping into the portal. "When they've all left, you'll be no queen. You will die."

"So be it," glowered Mrs. Knife. She was having a hard time keeping herself upright. "I have no regrets. I am what the world has made me."

"But you can die in peace," said Vlad. "Let me take you to Blasigtopp. The monks will give you comfort in your final days. Who knows? You may even find peace."

"You can't be serious," said Greta. She pointed her sword at Mrs. Knife. "She nearly killed you!"

"No," said Vlad. "I let her believe she could, and it kept her from harming anyone else."

"That's brilliant," said Myrtle. "Other than your mangled shoulder, of course."

"Wounds heal," said Vlad.

"No," said Greta through unchecked tears. "She wanted to kill you. I can't lose you. You can't—"

Greta charged Mrs. Knife at a full sprint. She brought her sword down toward the frail old ghoul and missed. Vlad asserted herself between them in a remarkably polite yet firm way that suggested to Greta that she might be more comfortable sprawled out on the ground again.

The end of the line of goblins came into view. They were nearly all gone.

"Don't—" said Vlad. She had more to say but couldn't with the river of blood pouring from her mouth.

Greta screamed. Mrs. Knife cackled, wiggling a knife between Vlad's ribs. Sloot didn't see where she'd had it hidden. He watched helplessly as Vlad collapsed into a pool of her own blood and did not rise.

The last of the goblins leapt through the portal. Only Gregor remained.

"You monster!" shouted Greta. She tried to lunge forward, but Myrtle held her back.

"It's over," she said, pointing at Mrs. Knife. She looked like she'd been dead for ages, her skin a dry, ashen casing for her brittle bones. Her face clung to the rictus of mania.

"A lunatic to her bitter end," said Bartleby.

No one else said anything. Greta wept and wailed. Everyone else simply stood in mute sadness for their fallen comrade.

"Well, I should go," said Gregor. "Remember our deal, Peril."

Sloot nodded. Gregor stepped through the portal and Nicoleta closed it behind him.

"This is a disaster!"

"Gwen?" Sloot looked puzzled. "When did you get here?"

"Just now," said the love demon. "How could this have happened? I was so sure that they'd reunite in the end, and now Vlad is dead!"

"No!" Greta wailed. She threw down her sword, crawled to Vlad, and cradled her head in her lap. Her sobbing echoed in her soul, an empty cavern of loss and despair.

"My love," she said, her tears splashing unhindered down over Vlad's unblinking gaze into empty space. "My love."

"I'm ruined," said Gwen. "Ruined! That's two major productions that have utterly failed! No one's going to hire me now. My career is in tatters!"

"Well, there's a bit of good news there," said Donovan. He and Lucia and Marco were standing on a filthy pile of rubble in impossibly clean white linen suits.

"The Coolest!" Gwen threw herself onto her knees in front of them.

"Cooler than everybody," said Dandelion, "*and* they get to wear white without getting dirty? That's hardly fair, if you please."

"Hardly," Lilacs agreed.

"Always a pleasure to greet the fairies," Donovan smiled. He turned to Sloot and rolled his eyes.

"I can't start here," said Marco.

"Why not?" asked Lucia. "It's centrally located, it's the nexus of the events leading to the end—"

"There's no style," said Marco, flicking a cigarette carelessly off into the shadows. "Razing should start in the center of a city, where there are people who matter. Barely anyone will see these people's faces melting off."

"That's the whole point," said Donovan, "no one will ever know that any of this existed. This one isn't going in your file, big guy. It's *pro bono*."

"What?" Sloot shrieked. "You can't be serious!"

"I'm afraid so," said Donovan, his brows huddled around a fragment of actual regret. "You've done the best you could, kid, but you had to know that it would come to this sooner or later."

"I most certainly did not," said Sloot. He'd have remembered if Donovan had said death was inevitable, and all of this was just a last laugh on the way to oblivion.

"It was a tough decision," said Lucia. "It's just easier to make the rest of the Narrative work without this bit."

"Don't take it too hard, kid," said Donovan. "This was a doozy of a paradox."

Sloot remembered Roman's paradox. His wager with Gwen over whether love was the greatest evil in the universe spelled doom whether he won or lost.

"Roman never should have been able to make that wager," said Donovan, "and now the universe unravelling. When we say that those secrets are Unknowable, we're not messing around."

"We are messing around," said Marco, "right now. In this dusty hole. I could be raining sulfur in Salzstadt right now."

"Easy," said Lucia, "don't look too eager to get on with the slaughter of..." she pointed around the room at all in attendance.

"Subtle," said Donovan. "Anyway, we've done all we can, but it's going to collapse any time now. Nice try, but—"

"Hang on a minute," said Sloot. "I'm not finished yet."

"You beg to differ," said Marco.

"No, *you* beg to differ," Lucia corrected him.

"I don't beg. He'll have to do it."

Fortunately for Sloot, he knew a thing or two about tricky reconciliations. He looked at Greta, still cradling Vlad's lifeless form, the pair of them covered in blood.

"What about them?" he asked.

"What *about* them?"

"You see her face? That's love."

"No," said Marco, "that's just a dead lady's face."

"The other one," Sloot clarified. "Gwen said she failed to make Greta fall in love with Vlad again, but how can that be true? That's clearly love!"

Donovan consulted his watch. "Vlad was already dead when she realized it. That's a shame, so close!"

"Here's the thing," said Sloot. "According to the bargain, Gwen can't spare Greta from death. When she dies, she and Vlad can be together in the Hereafter. Alive or not, they're in love."

"Good news for Gwen's career," said Donovan, "not that she'll be around to benefit from it."

"Uh oh," said Lucia. "We've got another problem!"

"We have?"

"You have," said Sloot. "You see, Gwen's production officially failed, yet Greta and Vlad will live happily—I mean, *be in love* happily ever after. That's another paradox."

"One that stretches into the Hereafter," moaned Donovan. "We can't raze the Hereafter! The Auditors will notice!"

"There's a way," said Sloot. "Hear me out. King Lilacs, may I meet with your lawyers, please?"

Time didn't seem to pass in the underdark of Zurogravia, though a lot of it certainly did. The fairies worked in shifts to keep the coffee on while Sloot, King Lilacs' legal staff, and a massive throng of imps summoned on the Coolest's authority processed a slew of paperwork. When they'd finished, Roman's Unknowable secret was placed in a double-blind trust. The fairies would manage the trust on the condition that absolutely no one got to know it, for reasons of fairness. The ghost of Vlad, having attained emptiness in life, would be given custodianship of the secret. She could look directly at it and not learn it, because technically, no one was there.

"It's a good start," said Donovan, "but it hardly nullifies the paradox."

"With respect," said Sloot, "it does. Gwen convinced Vlad to lay down her sword, which led her to emptiness. She did that for love. That means love isn't the greatest evil in the universe, because it was the answer to keeping Roman's Unknowable Secret ... secret."

"So all of my productions have been successful!" Gwen squealed.

"On a long enough timeline," said Sloot.

"But what about the Dark?" said Donovan. "It's still spilling into the Narrative. It's leaking into the mausoleum right now!"

"That's no paradox, just some maintenance. I'm sure you've got people who can handle that."

"He's right," said Lucia.

"I don't know," said Donovan. "Probably still easier to raze it."

"That's my vote," said Marco. "Two against one."

"Do the Auditors review your financial statements?" asked Sloot.

"They review *everything*," said Donovan. "It's grueling."

"And you're aware that I'm in a tremendous amount of debt to the chaos firm of Nameless, Redacted, and Meatsacrifice?"

"Hey," said Lucia, "those are our attorneys. Did we send them for Sloot?"

"At his own expense," Donovan clarified. No favoritism, I was clear about that."

"Right," said Sloot, "but you did send them. When I'm dead—or rather, when I will have never existed—that debt will still be on their records."

"They'll just have to write it off."

"Ha! They're a chaos firm! They'd never walk away from that much equity. They'll go after whoever hired them in the first place."

"They wouldn't try to sue us," said Donovan.

"Oh, yes they would," said Lucia. "I know Minerva Meatsacrifice. She once lost a nickel in a drain and sued the inventors of public sanitation."

"I'm not worried about the money."

"What about the paper trail?"

Donovan flexed his jaw. It looked like snakes limbering up for a dance-off against a rival gang.

"You've really thought this through." Donovan couldn't help smiling at Sloot.

He hadn't, though. He'd love to have considered every option, then double- and triple-checked his figures. But Captain Peril had time to act, not think.

He smiled back. "What sort of fool would I be if I hadn't?"

REVOLUTION TAX

Sloot was running late. He was always running late these days. It didn't bother him as much as it once would have, but he still didn't like it.

"Trust me," said Myrtle.

"I can't imagine what they all must be thinking." Sloot fidgeted. "They know we can teleport. We've got no excuse."

"So we won't make one. You're a full-fledged equity demon now! Besides, it'll be best if we walk in exactly two minutes and ten seconds from now."

Myrtle had her powers back, which was nice but occasionally irksome. Arguing with demons who knew the future was futile, and arguing with girlfriends was just dumb.

"One minute, fifty-six seconds," said Myrtle. Sloot's hand slunk guiltily away from his watch.

"I'm just nervous to meet—"

"The Domnitor, I know."

"Long may he reign."

"That's up to you, isn't it?" Myrtle rolled her eyes. "Hands out of your pockets, you haven't carried a whistle in ages! Do you really want Uncle to carry me away?"

"Of course not."

They stood in silence. Sloot coughed.

"How—"

"One minute, twelve seconds!"

"No," said Sloot, "I was going to ask how I should walk in."

"Oh."

"Should I smile? No, they don't smile in diplomacy, do they?"

"Only to each other's faces," said Myrtle. "Don't overthink it, just walk in. Everybody in there knows you."

Thirty-four seconds later, the sound of splintering wood on the other side of the door coincided with Myrtle pointing at it. The remains of a chair clattered across the floor as Sloot walked into the room.

There was now a massive table in the war chamber of Castle Ulfhaven. Vlad wouldn't have been pleased, but then this wasn't her father's Carpathia.

All eyes were on him, and no one looked happy.

"So things are going about as well as I expected," said Myrtle.

"Very funny," Lilacs harrumphed. He shook his head. "To be fair, we're all a little on edge. But everyone is here, working together. It's a start."

"Is anyone ever *actually* being fair?" asked Willie.

"Rhetoric!" shouted Arthur. "For the last time, rhetoric isn't philosophy. Stop doing it wrong!"

"But is it possible to *actually* do things wrong?"

If Arthur was trying to exhale through his ears, it was going poorly. If he was trying to make his face redder than usual, it was going extremely well.

Sloot turned to whisper to Myrtle. "Can you remind me how Arthur is still alive?"

Myrtle shrugged. As best she could tell, the Coolest had brought everyone in Sloot's orbit back to life after the Spilling of the Dark, then reimplemented the deaths of those who'd died since the Pritygud report. Arthur died before that, so he must have been an oversight.

"What I can't figure out," said Domnitor Olaf von Donnerhonig, Defender of the Old Country and Hero of the People, long may he reign, "is why the people decided to do revolution in the first place. Don't they like being the unwashed masses?"

"The proletariat!" shouted Arthur, flecks of spittle accentuating the retort.

"Good idea," said Olaf, "that sounds fancier. They're less likely to revolution again if they feel fancy."

"That's a good point," said Willie, who knew quite a lot about feeling fancy.

"The proletariat have always controlled the means of revolution!" Arthur fumed.

"Have they?" Olaf looked confused. "I feel like that's the sort of thing we should control on their behalf. Oh! We could tax them for it. A revolution tax!"

"Good idea, Sire," said Flavia. She was sitting next to Olaf. "Would you like to use the standard enforcement procedures for that?"

"Hang on a second," said Sloot, "you can't—"

"Sloot is right for once!" shouted Arthur. "The right of revolution vested in the proletariat shall not be infringed by—"

"Can anyone ever *actually* have rights?" asked Willie, apparently of the ceiling.

"For the last time, that's not philosophy! Don't make me throw another chair!"

Torches flickered. The table shook. Sloot's heart pounded in his ears.

"Don't threaten Willie again," the walls echoed.

"It's all right, Nan," said Willie. "After all, does anybody *actually* know vhat's philosophy?"

Arthur launched into a recursive argument about arguments and was quarrelling with himself in seconds.

"It's been like this all evening," Winking Bob confided in Sloot. "I've got no love for philosophers, and even less for meetings with people who don't owe me money, but it's impressive watching him work."

"That's philosophers for you," said Sloot. "They'll shout for a week to avoid an hour's work. How's business?"

"Ugh, don't ask." Bob rolled her eyes. "I didn't realize the extent of the Three Bells' debt when I asked you to give it to me."

"I took you for a shrewd businesswoman," said Sloot. "Didn't you know what you were getting into?"

"I had wizards, and con men, and worse. I had *lawyers*. But none of them were a match for the bookkeepers at the Three Bells! I'm still finding debts I didn't know about. It's positively ruining my—*ahem*—less well-documented operations."

"But your books say you're in the black," said Sloot.

"That's for the stockholders," said Bob, "and just for the operations that *have* books. Oh, don't give me that look."

It was a new era. One in which no one told Captain Peril how to look.

"Ugh, fine! I'll start keeping books for the rest of them. Eventually."

"References to future events coming to pass on non-specific timeframes, e.g., 'eventually,' shall be understood by all parties to be inconsistent with enforceable commitments."

"Thank you, Edmund." Bob smiled. "Now, Sloot, would your girlfriend happen to know anything about upcoming moves on the open market? I've got two major enterprises that could use a boost."

"Verbal solicitations for financial insights shall be understood as casual conversation free of intent to capitalize on illicit sales. Any responses to said solicitations failing to return less than seven hundred percent interest within one month shall be punishable by—"

"Let's stick to the disclaimers, Edmund. No need to bore Mister Peril with the fine print."

Edmund shrugged the way one did when one wanted to appear aloof, which meant he was telling Bob off in his head.

Somebody ought to, thought Sloot, who then realized he was somebody.

"It sounds like this might be too much for you," said Sloot. "Perhaps I should have someone else run the Three Bells? Let you take your chances with your old enterprises?"

Bluffing! Sloot Peril was bluffing! He wanted to bounce on the balls of his feet and clap his hands like a wind-up monkey with cymbals on.

"You're bluffing," said Bob. "Besides, my 'old enterprises' are the only game in town capable of settling all of the Three Bells' debts. I'll manage. I always have. It may just be a decade or two before I turn a profit."

"That sounds fair," said Sloot.

"Is anything *actually* fair?" asked Sloot.

"Oh," said Lilacs, "that's a fair question, actually."

Arthur fumed. He launched into another lecture about the proper way to do philosophy, all the while assuring them they'd never get it right.

It must be exhausting, Sloot thought, *spending all that time moving goalposts around.*

"It depends on your definition of fair," said Myrtle.

A collective gasp went up from King Lilacs and his retinue. It was the sound of thousands of years of fairy existence colliding with simple truth. An oversight.

"*Your* definition of fair," said Lilacs, rolling the idea around on his ethical palate.

"We can all use mine," said Olaf.

"Very generous, Sire," said Flavia.

Sloot glared at Flavia. Myrtle put her hand atop his.

"Just let it happen," she whispered.

But that was how things had gotten so badly offset in the first place! Let it happen? Why hand matches to children who'd already burned down a house?

Sloot sighed. He knew he couldn't turn the place into a utopia overnight. Well, he *could,* thanks to his ledger. Every soul in Carpathia and the Old Country was in it, many of whom could run the show with humility, grace, and kindness toward their fellow citizens. And he didn't get to let any of them do it.

That was the second worst part. The worst part was that he understood why. The only way to appease the auditors was to make as few changes as possible. That meant not simply chucking out adolescent despots and notorious criminal overlords for good and reasons.

Kindness toward their fellow citizens. Weren't Flavia, Winking Bob, and the Domnitor–long may he reign–his fellow citizens? They were what the world had made them. Mrs. Knife had said that of herself, and she'd been right. Long, long ago, in a history that had since fermented into legend, Mrs. Knife had been a young woman. She'd been the daughter of a king, married off to a goblin prince to seal an alliance. She hadn't chosen that, and Sloot couldn't imagine anyone would choose to become Mrs. Knife when she grew up.

We are what the world makes us, thought Sloot. *And we in turn make the world.*

"Ha!" barked Arthur. "The definitions of learned men shall determine what is fair, what is right, and who is stupid!"

Olaf glowered at him. "I said I'd listen to you, but don't forget who you're talking to. I'm the Domnitor, after all."

"Long may he reign," echoed several people in the room, Sloot included.

"Would you like to have him conversationed, Sire?" asked Flavia, radiant with cheer.

Olaf pursed his lips and stamped his foot three times. It was considered and deliberate, the way one would teach math to horses.

"I'm not supposed to conversation people anymore," he said.

"You let me decide what's *supposed* to happen," said Arthur. "If you ask me—which you should, since I'm your intellectual superior—the only problem with Uncle's methods is that they've been using them on the wrong people!"

"Oh?" Flavia seemed genuinely curious.

"Oh, dear," said Sloot.

"Just wait," said Myrtle. She winked.

"Uncle only conversationed enemies of the state," said Olaf.

"Enemies of the state? That was the proletariat getting dragged out of their homes in the middle of the night! Shop keepers, lamp lighters, and … I don't know, what else does the common man do? Elocutionists? Anyway, we need to go after the bourgeoisie! The city council, the mucky-mucks! They've been oppressing the common man for far too long!"

"You can't conversation them," said Olaf. "I know those people! They come from good families!"

"Every family is good," said Sloot, "until the world makes them otherwise."

"To be clear," said Flavia, "Uncle is willing and able to have a conversation with anybody."

Olaf turned and looked at Flavia with a gravitas that one rarely sees in an eleven-year-old, despotic or otherwise.

"Can anyone really *be* good?" asked Willie.

Sloot and Myrtle slipped out while Arthur was yelling, yet again, about what philosophy was and who was licensed for it.

BEYOND THE NARRATIVES

"We should have stayed," said Sloot, as they climbed the steps to Nicoleta's tower.

"You said what needed saying," said Myrtle. "Didn't you see the Domnitor's face?"

"Long may he reign," said Sloot. When had he started saying that? He thought of it as cultural, if he thought about it at all. But it was insidious, wasn't it? *Long may he reign.* With everyone saying it, there was no room to say, "maybe we should give someone else a go at it."

"Olaf's a good kid," said Myrtle. "It's the world that's made him otherwise, but he's starting to see. It won't be long before he sees Flavia for the sycophant she is."

"And Arthur?"

"He can barely manage power over himself, much less anyone else."

"I suppose Flavia and Arthur are what the world has made them, too."

"People can change, Sloot. Look at us. We're not even people anymore."

Somewhere deep in Sloot's soul, a tiny voice fretted in existential panic. He resolved to think about it later. Or perhaps not.

"Oh, look," said the door at the top of the stairs. "It's a couple of—"

The door shattered. Myrtle rubbed her knuckles.

"Hey!" shouted Nicoleta. "That was my door!"

"Vicked!" Bartleby clapped.

"I'll buy you a new one," said Myrtle.

"Hang on," said Sloot, shaking his head. "Did you just commit murder?"

"No," said Nicoleta. "The door wasn't alive, it had just absorbed enough latent magic over the years to master sarcasm. Still, it was a nice door."

"I said I'd buy you a new one."

"A nice *oak* door."

"If you insist."

"With recessed steel fittings."

"They were brass!"

"Does your house have a door on it?" Nicoleta's skeletal hands rested on her sparkly hips. "It would be a shame if someone were to punch it."

"Steel it is," said Myrtle. "How are you getting on?"

"I'd like to have had more time to prepare," said Nicoleta, errant sparks jumping from her skeletal form like tiny fireworks. "It's fine, though. Liches are usually dark and tormented. I added glitter to the incantations."

"Still the Carpathian court wizard?"

"Ve vere just talking about that," said Bartleby.

"The fairies aren't terribly pleased that I've cheated death," said Nicoleta. "I'm sure you can guess why. They're also too nervous to say anything, which I'm taking as a compliment. Still, I'll probably have to move on sooner or later. Necromancy comes to me more easily than anything else these days, and that's not the sort of magic people expect at court."

"Not in Carpathia, anyvay," Bartleby added. "There are other realms vhere people have fewer qualms beyond the Narrative."

"That's too bad," said Myrtle. "We'll miss you. You'll haunt us when you get the chance, won't you?"

"Of course."

"Speaking of necromancers beyond the Narrative," said Sloot, "any word on Gregor?"

Nicoleta and Bartleby exchanged a look.

"Oh, dear," said Sloot.

"I vouldn't vorry," said Bartleby, "he's just taken the whole 'exempt from reality' thing farther than I'd expected."

"How far?"

"He's not corporeal anymore," said Nicoleta.

"Oh, dear," said Myrtle.

"Oh, no!" said Sloot, in response to Myrtle's *oh, dear.*

"Yeah," said Myrtle, "that's going to become a problem."

"When?"

"We've got time," she said, "but the sooner we start reasoning with him, the fewer trees he'll have planted in the Forest of Madness."

This was why Sloot had insisted that Myrtle needed her powers back. Reality had a lot of moving parts, and knowing which ones needed attention before it was too late was a big part of managing it. He'd reminded the Coolest of the Hapsgalt family fortune to make his point.

"Tomorrow, perhaps," said Sloot.

"Tomorrow will be fine."

"Oh, that's handy," said Nicoleta. "Can you tell me where I'll go when I leave Carpathia? It would make it so much easier to pack."

"Sorry," said Myrtle, "you're far too whimsical for an obvious trajectory, and too powerful to be bound by the usual constraints. I'm afraid you're an outlier."

"Oh," said Nicoleta, but in a perky, self-satisfied way. She smiled, not that skeletons did otherwise.

"Ve should go to the Necropolis," said Bartleby. "Everything's been dead for a really long time! It's vicked cool."

"Sounds fun," said Nicoleta. "Do tell Vlad and Greta we said hello, if you see them."

"They're haunting us right now," said Myrtle. "We'll see them as soon as we get home."

SMELLS OF HOME

The sun was setting over Salzstadt. Sloot and Myrtle watched the bustling queues moving freely through the main gate, which hadn't closed in over a week. That didn't sit well with the traditionalists, who were working around the clock to find a loyalist way to disagree with the Domnitor's decision on the matter.

"Long may he reign," said Sloot.

"He will," said Myrtle, "but you don't have to keep saying that."

"It's tradition."

Myrtle smirked.

"It'll have to go eventually," Sloot conceded, "but we can't do it all at once. There would be panic."

"You're telling me the future now?"

"It's not the future yet."

Sloot had far more influence than he'd ever wanted to wield. Even Captain Peril wasn't entirely comfortable with it, but he preferred it to the Coolest razing the Old Country from the Narrative.

Clouds drifted lazily across the pink and purple sky, which

had only just run blue and amber out, and would shortly be told by indigo that it didn't have to go home, but it couldn't stay here. Lights shone in the windows as Sloot and Myrtle walked home arm-in-arm.

"I've still got my place in Carpathia," Myrtle mentioned for at least the hundredth time, all pretense of subtlety having long since fallen away. "I know you love Salzstadt, but your apartment is depressing, and we can teleport."

"I know," said Sloot. He knew they'd end up there eventually, but for the first time since being trampled to death in the cathedral, Salzstadt felt like home. It would never be what it once was, but it was familiar. Even with everything he'd changed to save it, the Old Country was the Old Country. It was home.

"You shouldn't let Roman stay there," Myrtle said. "He'll turn the place into a betting parlor the minute your back is turned."

"He can't," said Sloot. "The Coolest adjusted him when they wiped his memory. He shouldn't have been able to make that wager in the first place, and they're sure they've fixed him this time."

"Igor will be there, too. He spends hot afternoons walking behind the horses that pull the fish carts. He positively reeks!"

"That's cultural," said Sloot, "You can't be mad at him."

"I'm not mad at *him*," she grumbled as subtly as a faceful of hammers.

"Maybe he and Roman will have gone out for a pint?"

"Did you think I was guessing when I said Igor will be there?"

"You might've."

"If the window is closed, I'm not staying."

"You don't know if the window will be open?"

"I didn't say I didn't."

Sloot still didn't have a knack for bluffing, or for telling when someone else was. It didn't matter. Myrtle never fought for the upper hand in their relationship, she just always had it.

"Hello, boys," said Myrtle with the enthusiasm of a mother whose sons had never once tidied up after themselves.

"Myrtle!" Roman was suddenly on the far side of the room from Sloot's magic circle, attempting to look far more innocent than he actually managed. "You're looking lovely as ever."

"Shh!" said Igor, his ear pressed against the closed window. "I think I hear them coming!"

"Some lookout you are," sneered Roman.

"What were you doing over there?" asked Sloot.

"Just taking in the length and breadth of the room," said Roman. He lunged his right foot forward with his hands on his hips in a mockery of modern calisthenics. "It's nearly as big as the cell I recently escaped."

"It's bigger than your cell," said Sloot, "and you didn't escape. I got you released on the promise of your best behavior."

It wasn't easy for Roman to look innocent, which was why he failed. Even Sloot could have seen Roman bluffing from space.

"I can't imagine what I've done to warrant such suspicion," he said, hand over his heart. "Besides, they did a real number on my memory. I can barely remember my own name sometimes."

"That's probably for the best," said Sloot.

"We're not staying here," said Myrtle. "Igor's been trying to cook."

"How dare you?" demanded Igor.

"It's true, isn't it?"

"Certainly not! You can't go accusing people of cooking just because they've set fire to things."

Myrtle sighed. "I was trying to give you the benefit of the doubt."

"Where are my curtains?" asked Sloot.

"Let's not get wrapped up in who was burning what, or which curtains belonged to whom," said Igor, feigning annoyance.

Myrtle took Sloot by the hand and pulled him aside. It was only half a step, but the significance was lost on no one.

"I know you love the Old Country," she said, "and I do too. But there's a lot to love in Carpathia, namely my house that's got intact curtains and no active fires."

"I know," said Sloot. He looked around the apartment, substituting wistfulness where any sane person would have gone with revulsion. To Sloot, this was home. Sure, it was too small, it smelled like burning, it was in a horrible part of town, Roman had no intention of leaving anytime soon, and Mrs. Knife had stabbed him here…

"My mother's apartment," said Sloot. "She has no intention of coming back from Kadaverstraag, perhaps she'd sell it to me."

Myrtle shrugged. "Perhaps. I'd consider spending the night in Salzstadt every now and again if we had a proper place."

"Oh, we could got out of this hovel!" said Roman.

Myrtle clenched her jaw. Smoke rose from her ears.

"Roman," Sloot hastened to intervene, "perhaps we could maintain the lease on this place for you? Give you some autonomy?"

Roman nodded and sighed. "I can work with that. If you'll just unlock the circle so I can—"

"The circle stays locked," said Sloot. "Now, if you'll excuse us, we were just leaving for Ulfhaven."

"Oh, right," Roman winked. "We'll talk about the circle later," he whispered.

"No, we won't," Sloot whispered back. Then he linked arms with Myrtle, and the pair of them were suddenly elsewhere.

"About time they left," said Igor. "I like Sloot, but Myrtle is cramping our style."

"Gremlins have style?"

"Careful, that's culturally insensitive. Besides, gremlins have loads of style."

"News to me," said Roman. "None of the gremlins I've met had any."

"Hey," said Igor, wounded to his filthy core.

"Present company provisionally excluded! To be fair, none of them had given up gremlining to become bards."

Igor straightened up and gave looking smug a try. "I'll bet I've got more style than any other bard you know."

Roman's pupils dilated. He breathed in sharply and licked his lips. Igor was no better at recognizing a bluff than Sloot, which was just as well. Roman was out of practice. He leaned back on the sofa, perhaps too casually for credulity, and asked, "care to make it interesting?"

ACKNOWLEDGMENTS

When I first started writing, I thought my ridiculous characters would be the most important voices in my work. As it turns out, there are a multitude of ridiculous people in the real world whose support and influence have made me the writer that I am. I'd like to acknowledge them here in lieu of financial compensation.

First and foremost are my wife, Shelly, and my son, Jack. They are my reasons for getting up in the morning, and I forgive them for that. (But seriously, you are the light and joy in my life. I love you and I like you.)

To Dee Dee, my mother-in-law, for being Jack's best friend (and overnight babysitter so Mommy and Daddy can have a date night every so often).

To Trinity, for teaching Jack several of the best non-swear words he knows.

To Stephen Homestead, tireless champion of the arts in Orange County.

To Buzzy, for teaching me over the course of a lifetime that life *is* art. You've just got to pay attention.

And last but not least, to Lindy Ryan and the amazing team at Black Spot Books. You're the best publisher a fella could have. Long may you reign.

ABOUT THE AUTHOR

SAM is definitely not a horrible monster who crawls from the sea by the darkness of the new moon, dons a meat suit, and writes strange novels in a windy cave full of spiders. He lives in Orange County, California.